The Luckiest Fool on Earth:

The Twisted Yarn of America's Greatest Flagpole Sitter, Alvin "Shipwreck" Kelly.

By Phillip S. Roberts

Zazel Publishing LLC

P.O. Box 17172

Fountain Hills, AZ 85269

https://zazelpublishing.com/

PUBLISHED BY:

ZAZEL PUBLISHING LLC
ZAZEL PUBLISHING LOGO BY TIKI TONY

P.O. BOX 17172
FOUNTAIN HILLS, AZ 85269

ZAZELPUBLISHING.COM

ISBN-13: 979-8-9985042-1-1

FIRST EDITION, 2025

PRINTED IN U.S.A.

COVER DESIGN: BOOK COVER BY THE BOOK COVER WHISPERER: OPENBOOKDESIGN.BIZ

TYPESETTING: ZAZEL PUBLISHING

LIBRARY OF CONGRESS CONTROL NUMBER: 2025907534

ALVIN SHIPWRECK KELLY - HISTORY - 20TH CENTURY - FADS - NOVELTY - JAZZ. FLAGPOLE SITTING - STUNTMEN - DAREDEVIL - CIRCUS - AVIATOR - ADVENTURER. POPULAR CULTURE - UNITED STATES - NEW YORK - HISTORY - ROARING 20S. CONFIDENCE SCHEME - GRIFTER - CRIME, CON MEN - SCANDAL - STEEPLEJACK. JOURNALISM - SCANDAL SHEETS - MOVIE STAR - POP CULTURE -EXPLORER. ATLANTIC CITY - WORLD RECORD - REPORTER - MARATHON DANCE - FLAPPER. TITANIC DISASTER - HOLLYWOOD - HINDENBURGH - WORLD WAR 1 AND 2. DEPRESSION ERA - 1920 - 1930 - ART DECO - -SKYSCRAPER - GANGSTER - FREAKS BARNUM - MAE WEST - AL JOLSON - GATSBY ERA - OOFTY GOOFTY - EMPEROR NORTON - POLAIRE - BROADWAY - VAUDEVILLE - ZAZEL - DIAVOLO

For Marcella, who had to suffer as a writer's widow many nights during this book's creation, and Sophia who may one day read this and wonder.

Great thanks to Karyl Garland for her consultations and editing.

When I was researching my first book, Waikiki Tiki: Art, History, and Photographs, I became curious about a nautical bar located not far from Kalakaua Avenue. I had found a postcard of the restaurant built out like a Spanish Galleon and then a Tiki mug. In the 1970s, a nautical restaurant chain started showing up near a few airports, trying to capitalize on the "Polynesian" craze. The "Shipwreck Kelly" brand failed to become popular and faded out without fanfare. The Honolulu location did not seem related to this mainland franchise.

The internet was in its infancy in the early 1990s, and as I looked up the restaurant where "Billy K and the Seamen" played, the name of a flagpole sitter kept popping up in the results. Honestly, not many results. I kept running into Alvin Kelly. I became fascinated about his life, and further could not understand why there was not a book about him in the Border's Book and Music store at Ward Center or the library. I started writing, but my focus was on the other book.

I kept making notes. I looked up his name on old newspaper archives. I researched, but had a problem. How to write a book about a guy who made his living atop a great height, but basically doing nothing but attract attention. It seemed a daunting problem. Finally I realized, it's not about what happened on the pole, but underneath, around, before and after. I had a first draft, and then a second. His past started to come together. He had a manager, a wife, and eventually a son. He had friends and family, but also imitators, as well as enemies.

By 2020, I had a huge folder of news clippings and tons of bookmarks. I'd bought a few photographs and artifacts on E-bay. Then came the pandemic. I thought deeply about isolation, and tried to tap into those feelings. As I continued to re-write and revise, I felt closer to this person who seemed to be haunting me to get this story told. I hope you enjoy it.

Phillip S. Roberts

Chapter 1 –
The Luckiest Fool on Earth

"The fool doth think he is wise, but the wise man knows himself to be a fool."
— William Shakespeare, As You Like It

The "Forepaugh and Sells Brothers Circus" marches their parade through the Dewey Arch in Madison Square with all the pomp and circumstance befitting a major occurrence on April 22, 1898. Those ticketed for the matinee follow a plethora of attractions; colossal elephants, grease-painted clowns, ornately costumed bareback riders, lithe acrobats, and more proceed toward the Big Top erected in the park and then to the mini-compound built to accommodate them during their run in New York City.

Once the attendees are in place, the brass band whips into a frenzy with an unrestrained crescendo until the director's baton signals an abrupt stop. Throughout the troupe's performance, there is barely an instant without an ooh or aah from the enjoyment starved audience. Each presentation had been stupefying, arranged in such a whirlwind pace that the viewers hardly have a chance to gasp. The floor lights are extinguished before the closing act.

"Ladieeeees and Genteel-men! I direct your attention to the center ring."

A single spotlight appears. It illuminates the ringmaster in the vibrant felt regalia of his craft. He holds court like a barrister in a powdered peruke with a cardboard cone that he points at a microphone.

"Quiet, please. The breathtaking spectacle you are going to observe requires undiluted concentration. It is the most dangerous undertaking tonight and thus a perfect culmination of the evening."

The figure in the shining beam is the focus of 8,000 transfixed ticket holders; not even one dares munch popcorn from the bag resting on their laps lest the crunching disturb the artist.

"Absolute silence, please. Diavolo's life depends on noiselessness. Centrifugal force is so hazardous, an ambulance is near by just in case. He risks his essence for his family and also for YOUR entertainment."

The conductor motions for the drum roll on the snare. A second beam of light now hits the middle ring; the totality of brightness focused 80 feet in the air on a platform. On it, John Carter Baker poses in a blood-red devil costume with a flowing cape. A horned hood covers a helmet, his cardinal-colored gloves heroically on his hips.

Mirrored goggles reflect the sliver of luminescence and to the gallery he looks like a personification of Lucifer posing next to a glistering silver-plated bicycle. A looping of metal and highly polished wooden slats is revealed as he motions to the onlookers below. Inspecting the track, he knows approximately 20 feet exist until the drop into a steep incline. Everything looks satisfactory. He grabs the handlebars and runs furiously, gaining momentum. With a practiced, deliberate motion, he swings a leg and mounts before hitting the slope.

Zooming at a breakneck tempo, he pedals on the groaning slats and then reaching a sufficient velocity, launches. He has completed countless revolutions but it still raises the goosebumps when he loops-the-loop, completing a full spin and defying gravity.

This application of scientific method never feels run-of-the-mill, he thinks. He has been exhibiting daily, Wednesday to Sunday, for two years. Risking the upside-down circle maneuver, nets him a princely sum—$1,000 a week. Today tragically, a weld buttressing the front wheel gives causing Diavolo to careen chaotically.

He flies and despite the heavily-padded scarlet suit feels the brunt of the impetus as he hits unforgiving ground. Knocked out, the crack of a vial containing ammonia wakes him. Helped to his feet, he acknowledges the anxious onlookers while clasping his injured side. A tiny amount of blood stains the corner of his mouth.

The gathering is informed he will continue his death-defying. The truth is somewhat divergent. His understudy continues to ride while Baker heals from three broken ribs, and a concussion. The earliest individual to be popularized as a "daredevil" retires quietly and without announcement. Others take his mantle and continue secretly in his stead as the original.

daredevil 1 of 2
dare-dev-il adjective
: recklessly and often ostentatiously daring
dare-dev-il noun
: a recklessly bold person

"Woman survives Niagara!" Paper-sellers in midtown Manhattan all bellow a variant spiel to draw customers to their stack. "Widow braves rapids."

In the late afternoon of October 24, 1901, Annie Edson Taylor cascades into Niagara Falls. The sexagenarian schoolteacher (and her cat,) is unstoppable as she is towed in a customized, padded Kentucky oak whiskey barrel near Port Day. The rope is cleaved, and she thunders pulled by the rushing currents. Like Mercury bearing Psyche up Mount Olympus, she becomes immortal as the first to survive the pitch. She bobs in the water near the Canadian shore after 17 minutes and the rescue boat corrals the wooden cask after the 188 foot plunge at the bottom of Whirlpool Rapids. With a crowbar, her saviors pry open the lid. They ascertain she is alive, and discern the woman has suffered a minor scrape on her forehead plus a few bruises.

The "Queen of the Mist" has a confab with several newsmen on the riverbank an hour after her harrowing slump. She poses for photos, with her tabby, who has also lived through the exploit. Reporter Joseph Emmerling poses a question.

"Mrs. Taylor? Would you risk the excursion again? I mean, now that you know what you know?"

"If it was with my dying breath, I would caution anyone to not attempt the feat, young sir," replies Taylor. "I would sooner walk up to the mouth of a cannon, knowing it was going to blow me to pieces than take another trip down Horseshoe Falls."

After that well publicized proceeding, two other incidents transpire to make the world smaller. In May of 1903, Horatio Nelson Jackson and his mechanic Sewell Crocker begin peripatetically moving on America's unmaintained roads. Their goal is to be the first to complete a transcontinental automobile journey. Cranking the motor of the two cylinder, 20-horsepower, Winton touring car he names 'The Vermont,' the drivers traverse the bumpy paths visiting rural settlements and big cities alike. Negotiating dried riverbeds and railroad tracks, the duo drives far off their planned route eastward.

Filing stories about their travel experiences to the *Oakland Tribune*, they enthrall untold devotees as other newspapers reprint their daily wanderings. Mud, mechanical complications, and rickety bridges hinder their route, but the motorists persevere along their path. In Boise, a bulldog is purchased from a farmer for $15. They fit their new mascot with goggles, and name him "Bud." The triad are treated as celebrities while refilling petrol, waiting for parts to be delivered by train, or taking a rest-break. After 63 days, 12 hours, and 30 minutes, as July 1903 comes to an end, Jackson wins a $50 wager as the vehicle trundles across New York state lines. Greeting the men at City Hall Park, Mayor Seth Low reads a proclamation comparing the trailblazers favorably to Lewis and Clark. Jackson's achievement nurtures America's romance with the roadster.

The second occasion that changes the world happens on December 17, 1903, south of Kitty Hawk, North Carolina. The Wright brothers, soar 852 feet at the Kill Devil Hills. Advances in aviation's pioneer era come swiftly in response to Orville and Wilbur's fulfillment of man's dream to fly like an osprey.

Chapter 2 –
Twine Twists Like the Destiny of Men

"Not all things end up tied with a perfect bow. Sometimes the ribbon frays. Sometimes you get a knot. A very messy one."

— *Anonymous*

In 1904, 11-year-old Alvin Kelly is beckoned to the stateroom of his Captain, Thomas Arnold Jacobi. The sailing master is fifty, born on Christmas Day of 1853. His tar-tinged mop is streaked with grey, wrinkles stream from the corners of his eyes like spray shooting aft a rapidly-fleeing duck, and he flourishes a well-trimmed beard.

Jacobi's maritime logbook includes his commission as a cabin boy with David Glasgow Farragut of the Union Navy. From that day on, he has hoisted sail almost 30,000 leagues in his circumnavigations. His current position of authority is commander of a 95-foot freighter, re-christened in the name of his beloved matriarch, Helene.

The lock on the heavy portal is bolted and a cloth obstructs the porthole to prevent prying. The inner sanctum is decorated with an oil likeness of his mother during her youth, unclad and in a scandalous pose. Captain Jacobi has a tattoo of the risqué painting inked on his inner left forearm. He sits at a desk with charts strewn across it. A compass and a sextant are on a shelf with a finically curated library of calf-hide-bound classics. The four-striper signals Alvin to sit on the low pouffe. Jacobi opens his giant palm to display a golden coin to his charge.

"From the first day I liberated you from that dingy 'Home for Destitute Children,' you have learned well and become my trusted mate. I see myself in you. Pledge to undertake a chore, and this token will be yours."

The British coin is an asymmetrical shaving of resplendent metal—a six-shilling florin bearing the profile of the Duke of Aquitaine, Edward III gleams as a side catches a reflection from a hanging lamp swinging in rhythm like a pendulum with the welter of the waves. Jacobi begins a homily on the antiquity of the object so the boy will appreciate its uniqueness.

"Struck in 1343, by the order of Richard II, the bulk of this specific coinage was melted to make into other currency. This collector's item comes from Blackbeard's own hoard on the *Queen Anne's Revenge*. In 1718, the gold was bestowed upon a midshipman who had taken a lead musket ball propelled at the privateer. Relayed from senior to apprentice since, the bit has a reputation for conferring providence on the bearer. It shall without exception prise its owner to his port of origin."

He hands the boy the coin. The metal feels marvelously warm.

"Thus, you clench upon the rarest memento. Many would murder to have it. I was handed this relic by Rear Admiral Farragut himself before the Battle of Mobile Bay."

Alvin craves this item. His inner dialog races. *I've had a rough start and thankfully my Captain had the foresight to snatch me off of Hell's Kitchen's crowded, dirty streets. Of all the waifs he could have chosen, it's a miracle he picked me. The open sea is a much better place to live in than that malodorous city. Jacobi is like the father I never had. I trust his counsel, and I'll do anything he asks of me without question. I could happily sail on the ocean blue until the end of my days. It is a wonderful feeling—being free. I am lucky indeed.*

"Flash the coin not to mates, who will likely betray you. If moneyless, know wealth can always be obtained. Sell it if you must, only in the most dire emergency. Pawn it not, as brokers will not honor its true value. Play not with it when idle, for if lost, it is doubtful to come back to you. Despite temptation by the fairer gender, even if she be Amphitrite herself, refuse to cede it. Should you approach my age and have gracious means, find a virtuous cadet to guide into manhood. If you retire or are truly without orientation, you can rely on its security as your prime season moves into Winter."

Jacobi pours apricot brandy and takes a gulp. He hands over the mug. Alvin slurps a mouthful, and feels warm inside.

"Should I die on the bombora, impart my final demise to my dear mumsy in Queens. If she is alive, tell her my final words were that 'I loved her as no son ever has.' If she has gone to the Great Beyond, place a white rose on her gravesite and you will be released from your sincere oath."

Jacobi hands Alvin a small pouch to keep the coin in.

"I swear to complete the errand you have tasked. Let Poseidon's angry wrath send violent storms to scuttle any ship I bunk on to Davy Jones's Locker should I fail."

Other episodes that mold the American landscape occur while Alvin sails on the *Helene* past the Tropic of Cancer and the Equator to

Porto de Santos. While on shore leave, he has a small crucifix tattooed on his left shoulder as a reminder of his faith.

In Pittsburgh, 5,000 miles absolute bearing, north from Brazil, 250 bodies pack the inaugural Nickelodeon's opening on June 19, 1905. Among the flickers are The Great Train Robbery. As a bandit on-screen turns to draw his gun, a viewer unholsters his firearm. He unloads a volley and holes appear in the white sheet being used as a screen. Patrons stampede out and the resulting tumult puts the enterprise on the front page of *The Pennsylvania Gazette-Times*. The mention helps the concessionaires, Harry Davis and John P. Harris quadruple their traffic on the second day, bewitching the 1,500 queuing to see the 15 minute repeating cycle of films. Soon a slew of cinemas modeled upon their success are opening in almost every constituency.

Among those at a heavily promoted event in Morningside Heights on July 3, 1905, is Joseph Emmerling. He is currently stringing for *The Brooklyn Eagle*. Harry H. Gardiner causes a crowd-puller by scaling the 159-foot dome of Grant's Tomb, using handholds and nothing else. Approximately 500 observers applaud as he conquers the mausoleum. After the 35-year-old trods on terra-firma, Joseph asks a few questions for his write-up of the curiosity.

"I have never seen a perilous endeavor like that Mr. Gardiner. Did you know that President Cleveland stopped by? When asked to comment, he joked that you must be 'a human fly.' Harry, would you care to provide a statement for *Press Internationalé* readers?"

"Say, that's pretty catchy nickname. I like that. Tell kids not to try this. They'll hurt themselves. I am a virtuoso. I will keep surveying taller buildings to gain the thrills I seek."

"Thrill-seeker. That is snappy. I can use that. Thanks for the scoop."

thrill-seeker 1 of 1
thrill-seek-er noun.
: a person who enjoys taking part in extreme sports and other activities involving physical risk.

In 1906, Alvin is 5 feet 6 inches, and the 13-year-old's sunburnt skin represents the internship he has spent on the seas. He has become a respectable middy under Jacobi's tutelage. The verdant thicket glistens in the distance as the *Helene* hugs the Panamanian coast. The vessel is tied by a cleat hitch to the pier at a modest fishing village. The crew jettisons supplies as Jacobi and Alvin wander ashore.

The pair stride deliberately toward a little café. The server brings carimañolas and cerveza. The town Alcalde, informed Captain Jacobi is in town, comes by to propose a rich conveyance. Repatriating Vivian Frances Steele to San Francisco will reap a lucrative meed.

The Steele family had headed by ship and rail to meet her grandparents in Manhattan 20 months ago. The lone daughter of a well-off clan, the nine-year-old has had all the pampered benefits of her fortunate upbringing. Private tutors, equestrian lessons, and fine silk dresses do not prepare her for the rigors that she sees during a visit to a poor village in Panama. Three months later, on the way back across the Central America isthmus by train, she is abducted by bandits. Before the lawbreakers responsible can be brought a ransom, Federales riddle them with bullets. The preteen is not found among the dead. Her rich relatives spend 17 months and a trove on sherlocks searching for her, but efforts are unfruitful—eventually departing to California to grieve their lost child.

Now, almost 11, Vivian slinks into the settlement caked in dried blood. She hops onto a crate to rip a reward poster bearing her image from a wall. The girl produces a knife and lets no male approach her. The sheriff is summoned. He fetches his wife to clean her up while he rides half a day by horseback to a more sizable town to transmit a cablegram.

A terse, skeptical acknowledgement comes from the Steele compound—"If the lost enfant trouvé is her, they will gladly pay the reward upon receipt but nothing in advance."

Alvin runs a Bill of Lading to the first mate that the ship will be taking on supplies bound for San Francisco. That means gambling on the unpredictable Cape Horn. Jacobi is apprehensive about rounding Chile, yet the incentive for the carriage is worth undertaking the five week voyage. The windjammers aboard the *Helene* mutter with apprehension as she boards. The crew considers her as if she is a mouse out to nick their last morsel of cheese. Escorted to the skipper's quarters, she is locked in. The key is placed in Alvin's hand, and he is given the duty of attending to her needs. He has some questions to ask of his Captain.

"Why are the men afraid?"

"The hands fear her because of superstition. Despite living in an enlightened era, fallacy is problematic to squelch. The ship's camaraderie has not had much schooling, and thus unsubstantiated rumors trade amongst each other. The uninformed do not easily shake their belief." Jacobi packs a pipe with tobacco while he considers how to explain the quandary. "An 'old-wives tale,' postulates that conveying bananas or preachers is risky and prone to bring jeopardy to a ship. I will not fill my hold with either. I don't consider the myth to be true, but that other subordinates in my command might and I need their devotion. Sprinkling salt on a net is imagined to attract more fish. Is the billow not brackish enough already?"

"I'm not sure. I . . . ."

"During the Middle Ages, seafarers interpreted Friday as ill-fated. Many refuse to launch a voyage on the Sabbath, as by legend that is the eve of the week that our lord Jesus was betrayed. A baker's dozen join the Last Supper, so when that number is commingled with Friday, the convergence is regarded as blighted. On Friday, October 13, 1307, historians wrote that the French King Phillip 'The Fair,' imprisoned the Templar, tortured their leaders, and seized their riches. That was a woeful day but are all Friday the thirteenth's ill-starred? I think not."

"The nuns told me when I was born on a Friday the thirteenth, my mother died. Am I doomed?"

"No," Jacobi realizes he's spoken too allegorically. "Good or bad, we live what we choose for ourselves. Luck is happenstance interpreted incorrectly. Real miracles are rare. I've never seen one."

Alvin is still puzzled what unfounded beliefs are associated with the maiden.

"So, the ships's company believes having an 11-year-old girl aboard will bring us misfortune?"

"Possibly. Many mariners will not transport an unescorted female; as trouble can arise amongst the lonely men. We must safeguard her until the journey's end. She has suffered some trauma that we can never comprehend."

Vivian glares at Alvin when he brings her meal. A week into the sail, she hasn't uttered a syllable. Her thoughts are confused and jumbled like the pitch of the ocean. *I am not sure of what is going on. Who are these men? Are they like those in the jungle? What is this ship? Is it taking me toward safety or more troubles? How did my situation change for the worse so quickly? Why does this uncertainty excite me? I know I hate the feeling of not being in control.* Abruptly, like a branch splitting from the weight of snow, she gushes words while brandishing a blade.

"I slit their throats for what they did. Are you also bad? I don't like bad men." Vivian rages loudly, her voice echoing in the cramped quarters. "Where are you taking me?"

Alvin backtracks in haste, closes the door, and whispers to her.

"To San Francisco . . . Home, to your family."

"They will bleed too. For leaving me behind . . . ."

Alvin can hear glassware smashing against the wooden barrier. He recollects when he was an orphan who had to scramble to survive, so he sympathizes with her callousness. Emerging from the bowels of the ship, he discloses the dramatic event to Jacobi who is scanning the seascape from the foredeck.

"Maybe she's healing, but she now begins another tumultuous period," came Jacobi's assessment. "Only the strongest mind can survive such an ordeal and it alters a soul. She may never be normal."

In a month, Jacobi allows the girl to stretch her legs on deck in full sight of the sailors who avert their direct gaze. She and Alvin have become attached as he is the sole contact she has had on the ship. Enwrapped in an infatuation, he accompanies her as she stares at the cerise sunset from the bow. The breeze whistles a bubbly tune through the rigging and in the encroaching shadows, she kisses him on the cheek. He is exhilarating in the moment as her lips brush him like the gauzy touch of a butterfly's wing. She grasps his hand. He approaches his Captain at the steering wheel as the west coast looms in the yonder. The boy dares to voice an intimate request.

"Will you marry us?" asks Alvin. "That is part of your rank's most joyful oceangoing duties, correct?"

"You are too naive to realize the gravity of your petition. I could, but a ceremony would not be legal due to your ages. Her parents would be incredibly displeased, assuming that I brought her home with a husband. I will not compromise our bounty."

The following few days are unperturbed and that no mishap has befallen the *Helene* soothes the ship's complement. Dropping anchor at The Embarcadero in March of 1906, Jacobi, Alvin, and Vivian ride a streetcar to the Palace Hotel near Nob Hill. Mrs. Steele weeps uncontrollably engulfing her daughter with a tight embrace as her husband hands a valise of freshly minted bills to Jacobi. The girl begs her mother and father to force Alvin to remain. When he declines, she pleads for rescue. Her elders drag her away, screaming. The Captain apologizes for the disturbance to the hotel manager.

In the span of a few minutes, Jacobi sends a cablegram to his grand old lady, deposits the funds in the hotel's repository, and orders port wine be sent to the room. After the tense exchange, he feels the need to decompress. Later, after the bellhop uncorks the fermented grape, he relaxes in an armchair as Alvin sits on the rug near the crackling fireplace.

"I would like to see her again," ventures Alvin. "I hope that might be possible one day. Do you think that I can be so lucky?"

"Miracles can happen. They are not just verses in the bible," smiles his captain. "She has a path to find away from the ocean as you are in possession of a life upon the swells. As we chart our own course between jagged shoals, she will have to navigate different waters. I have found a multifarious number of women and a profusion of routes that can be taken to happiness. You can even choose to reinvent yourself wholly. Once, I knew a scamp. 'His eminence, Joshua A. Norton, Emperor of America.' His legend is a rigmarole that you cannot purchase from any bookstore. I once had the distinct pleasure of shaking his monarchical mitt."

The 13-year-old is wide awake and attentive. He truly enjoys the sporadic conversations when his Captain discloses wisdom to him. Jacobi can really spin a yarn like tying a "Monkey's Fist" knot out of hemp. He pours Alvin a soupçon of port from his jug. The boy sips the sweet tasting fortified berry and likes the woozy feeling it brings.

"Arriving in San Francisco from South Africa, the rumor mill implies that Norton is Napoleon's illegitimate son who fled La République to avoid the guillotine. He invests in real estate ultimately owning much of North Beach. Overhearing the canard speculate on how a famine in China will result in a temporary cessation of rice exports, the gluttonous landlord mortgages his properties to purchase a cargo hold of Argentinian grown grain. The staple that feeds the coolies completing the Transcontinental Railroad skyrockets in price from 4¢ to 36¢ a pound. He counts on multiplying his grubstake into a mint, but Chinese junks stuffed to the gunwales with rice, cast anchor in the harbor before his ship and the value subsides. The speculator begs a court to void his transaction but is denied. He goes on his knees, lamenting that he is bankrupt, but his creditors refuse to take pity on him. Norton's prime lots are auctioned off to the highest bidders for pennies on the dollar."

Kelly wonders *what it must feel like to be rich and then lose all. He hopes he never finds out.* Captain Jacobi continues weaving the intricate details; embellishing the legend of the scallawag.

"He sprints in celerity from the Barbary Coast. A decade slips by and he rematerializes in the city as a daft unusualness. Norton is grand and altruistic in all respects. He dons a battered beaver-skin hat, embellished with an ostrich plume. Adorned in proud regimentals with epaulettes, his chest is sparkling with a swath of tarnished medals. A vermillion sash fastens a cavalry saber to his ponderous waist. On a soap box in Golden Gate Park, he proclaims himself imperator as well as the protector of Mexico. He orders Congress to disband. Gladdened by his outrageous manner, a majority of San Franciscans decide he is utterly nutty."

The Captain takes a draw from his briar pipe and adds a modicum of liquid to Alvin's glass. He smiles broadly, enjoying the retelling the saga as it was told to him and adding his own trivialities.

"Mark Twain based a character on him in Huckleberry Finn. Regular readers of San Francisco's dailies the *Chronicle* and the *Examiner* become devoted to his capers. Their outlandish articles are reprinted statewide in *The Pacific Appeal* and *The Sacramento Daily Union.* The dynast issues wholly farcical proclamations that are ahead of their time."

"What kind of ideas?" Alvin asked. He is curious and invested in the narrative.

"Dissolving the Congress. Annexing Mexico. Zany notions such as a bridge should be built to connect San Francisco to Oakland, or that anyone who refers to the 'City by the Bay' as 'Frisco,' shall be fined $25. He never works and rarely is in possession of funds to finance his lifestyle. Occasionally he prints and sells 'imperial bonds,' promising 5% interest. The rascal has carte blanche at the finest restaurants whose chefs create memorable cuisine. Restauranteurs even install bronze plaques in their vestibules to boast of Norton's patronage. Theatrical producers keep a reserved box vacant in case the blue-blood should demand an evening of distraction."

Jacobi rises to stretch his legs. From the window of the upper floor suite, he can see the soupy fog steeping into the city like tea from a fresh bag does into hot water. Another dram of liquid passes the dry lips, and Jacobi turns toward his captive audience. He retakes his seat to continue his recounting of the facts as he knows them.

"After Norton halts a race riot in Chinatown, the mayor confers him a shiny medal with a ribbon. When his garb begins to look ratty, the board of supervisors authorize funds so the finest tailor in town can fit him for a fine uniform. Witnesses report that the "Emperor" whimpers as he is presented his effervescent livery, au courant with the knowledge that his citizens truly love him. Their mock ruler continued his benevolent reign unabated, delighting in the rank and file's adoration.

As all must, Emperor Norton I dies in 1880, and more than 300,000 line the procession route to watch his "wooden overcoat" be wheeled by on the way to the cemetery. Barroom gossip conjectured that he was immensely affluent but played the pauper because he was so stingy that he could not bear to part with a farthing. At his low-cost room, every floorboard is ripped up by looters hunting for his objet de vertu. All the treasure hunters locate is $8, a quartz-topped, gnarled blackthorn wood cane, and a battered ceremonial saber."

As Jacobi had drained his flagon, he finishes the tale.

"Residents hallowed his inane buffoonery; his actions eased them into a carefree frame of mind and relieved the pressures of every day problems. The way of the world has innumerable swerves—that are not foreseeable or avoidable like earthquakes, fire, and drought. Norton provided the disadvantaged a chance to giggle, during their distress and nonsensical predicaments. We must all wallow in whimsy to give us relief from our complex realities. You would be wise to bear in mind that no future is set in stone."

The *Helene* steers southwest to Tahiti with the soft trades. The ship moors in Papeete harbor. Before shoving off, Jacobi poses a classic philosophical question to the seamen for contemplation during the succeeding leg of the voyage.

"If a vessel was replaced by one timber daily, would it be the same boat upon completion of the restoration? Our valued mate has jumped the rail and thus will be left behind. You will assume his duties and his share divided. Meditate on that until we moor at Easter Island."

Subsequently, the navel of the universe is a such uncustomary anchorage that Jacobi and Alvin saunter around Hangaroa, marveling at the hulking fallen monoliths while provisions for the sheep ranch are unpacked. In the morning, the vessel heads east across the Pacific to Chile and then around South America to the Atlantic.

In 1909, Jacobi accepts a consignment of explosives bound for the Panama Canal construction camp up the Rio Chagres. The delicate payload is fraught with danger and thus incredibly profitable for such an alacritous cruise. Approaching the mouth of the watercourse, waves and weather batter the deck. The Captain shouts commands as lightning brightens the horizon. A strike hits the mast. It splinters and pelts Jacobi dead. The *Helene* writhes. A coal boiler explosion detonates the nitroglycerin. The boat tears asunder with a stomach-churning crackle that sounds like a walnut crushing under a size 14 shoe. Fiery fragments of the boat set the jungle ablaze on both sides of the river. The 16-year-old is spared from the disarray as he is cast from the bulkhead into the drink, while the others suffer the abyss.

Alvin clings to a rectangular section of wood. The current draws the exhausted teen out to open sea. He prays for divine intervention from Manannán mac Lir, the Gaelic god of the sea, Tangaroa the Cook Islands atua of fishermen, Jesus (who walked on water,) and any other deities he can think of. He feels for the pouch around his neck that holds his lucky charm. He wants to execute his guarantee to his Captain. Two days elapse before a boat chances upon his feverish, dehydrated shell. He reeks worse than the smelt the fishermen keep as bait. The mariners warily drag the torpid boy aboard and knock their catch out with a belaying pin.

Everything goes dark.

Alvin strives during the next four years of conscription to circumvent his servitude, return to "The Modern Gomorrah," and satisfy his covenant. Yet as an Arab proverb of yore states, "The wind does not blow as the ship desires." During that interval of his compulsory enlistment, scads of "attention-getters" capture infamy by the implementation of offbeat feats. In 1911, Englishman Bobby Leach becomes the second swashbuckler to survive Niagara in a barrel. The eight-foot, metal enclosure in which he rides demands a heavy physical toll. Pulled from the inlet, he heals for six months from two broken knee caps and a fractured jaw.

Meanwhile, an intrepid gentleman is touring the midwest with a crackpot talent. Acrobat Bud Launtz "walks" inverted, his feet catching nooses strung on a ladder suspended 25 feet above the sawdust. He does not employ a net, defying gravity. Billed as "The Bat," his legerdemain has looker-ons holding their gulp of air until they must exhale. They cannot avert their collective gaze, lest the upended gait misses a coil. One day he does, breaking his neck.

Even the era's most distinguished prestidigitator, Harry Houdini, is not above pandering to the bizarre. The Lieutenant Governor of Massachusetts dares the escapist to "emulate Jonah" and tempt eternal damnation inside a "monster" stomach. A rotting dollop that resembles a whale crossed with a squid washed onto a beach near Boston and was preserved in an ice warehouse.

On September 11, 1911, the manacled mage forces himself through a slit in the preserved specimen's blubber while his accomplices sew the gash and wrap the lump in chains. It takes 15 minutes for him to emerge from the putrid flesh. Joseph Emmerling, watching the initiative for the *New York Evening Journal*, is on hand to question Houdini. He takes photographs to accompany his article. This is not the first meeting the newspaperman and performer have had.

"Harry, how uncomfortable did you feel? Contained in the flesh of the gullet? I cannot imagine being surrounded by those revolting, slimy innards. Disgusting."

"I concede it was the most abstruse test I ever attempted, Joseph. I nearly succumbed from the smell of the arsenic fluid used to preserve the blob, but I am devoid of its paunch."

"Will you ever participate in another trial like that?"

"No comment."

It takes a while to accomplish but in early 1912, Alvin Kelly secures a hammock that will take him across the Atlantic. He will finally be able to bring to fruition his troth. While he traverses the salty remoteness as an engineer's helper, the American population is demanding unrestrained diversion to inject some excitement into their mundane lives.

Parachutist F. Rodman Law springs from the Statue of Liberty's torch on February 3, 1912. Frederick free-falls 40 feet before yanking his ripcord. In 305 feet, he rolls on Bedloe's Island's turf. The *Pathé Movie Company,* for filming his historic vault, remunerates him with $1,500. Joseph Emmerling is situated at the colossuses base.

"Rodman, that was quite a hurdle. Would you care to say a few words for *The Lexington Dispatch* and the other associated compendiums of *Press Internationalé's* syndicate?"

"I have planned many mad tricks for the cameras. I took a leap of faith, and it was a rush. I would like to thank the good lord. That was an amazing stunt, man."

"Stunt-man. Thanks, Mr. Law. I will spread that word."

The reporter originates the phrase, and Law becomes the earliest to be recognized as a "movie stuntman"—a storied tradition.

Movie stuntman 1 of 1
Mo-vie stunt-man noun.
: a man who performs stunts
especially : one who doubles for an actor during the filming of stunts and dangerous scenes

As Emmerling is filing his report, 3,625 miles away in Paris, Austrian tailor Franz Reichelt gambols from the Eiffel Tower in a parachute of his own design. His alteration fails to unfold, and he zips 187 feet from the observation deck, perishing on French soil.

Alvin returns to Queens on April 10, 1912, and goes to Widow Jacobi's address in the Forest Hills neighborhood. The residence has been replaced, and no one he asks knows where her final resting place is. He lays a rose on the steps of the building constructed on that lot as a single thought goes through his membrane. *I hope I am not damned in perpetuity for failing the mission given to me by my captain.* The sea dog boards his ship as it is heading back to Fiume. Days later, in the Atlantic, the all-hands-on-deck siren whines. His divine decree is going to be recast.

Chapter 3 –
The Enigma that is Joseph

"*To produce a mighty book, you must choose a mighty theme.*"

— Herman Melville

Joseph T. Emmerling's personal telegraph clacks out an urgent communiqué on April 15, 1912. His heart flutters like a Yellowhammer woodpecker tapping out a bright beat as he deciphers the dots and dashes by ear.

TITANIC HITS ICEBERG. SHIP LOST.

He rushes to gather information on the worst cataclysm of his times. Perhaps in the horrific details, he will dowse a worthy theme to capitalize on. He requires a stirring narrative.

Early reports about the *Titanic* puts in motion a hierarchy within news bullpens worldwide. Editors order a "reset" to put out an "extra" edition. Casualty lists dominate the desks of the division chiefs who mobilize their minions to scrutinize any iota of information. Pencil pushers browbeat sources for details of the unfortunate who have embarked upon the traversal. Art departments hastily assemble illustrations. Reams twist between the ear-splitting printing presses— copies with scarcely dry ink are rushed out to the stalls and paperboys on street corners. The herd lays out their coins to ingest details like a hatched chick hungry for a worm.

As the proprietor of the *Press Internationalé* wire service, this sad affair portends a stack of greenbacks. Emmerling's syndicate provides for a need . . . one that fills space and his wallet. His epigrams remit a quarter-penny per inch. Quantity is his livelihood, not quality. He churns out the fodder that supplements regional periodicals for whom the resources to hire staff is unavailable. His discounted vacillating write-ups run far below the fold and deeper in the pages than the farm futures. His peers consider him a "hack." He has a file cabinet with oodles of scrawl; cross referenced by category. The tittle-tattle creations are formulated with pawky, temerity, and unsubstantiated innuendo.

This calamitous mishanter of the *Titanic* will sell bazillions of 2¢ sheets . . . as many as can run through their clamorous printing machines. Readers will gravitate to the largest font available. The broadsheet that squawks calamity the loudest will stain a sizable amount of hands in "The Five Points" and beyond.

Phillip S. Roberts

The gravity of the plight demands he send out a "bulldog edition" for far-flung presses like the Honolulu's *Hawaiian Gazette,* Fargo's *Bottineau Courant,* and 67 others. Emmerling fills his billfold with his trade's favored tools—crisp ten dollar bills.

He is an imposing figure with a cleft jawbone. The Falstaffian consults his pocket watch from the waistcoat that contains his girth wrapped in a double-breasted suit. He does not want to strike someone as rushed and full of hubris. His blond curls are tucked under a straw boater as he saunters closer to the moorage. A few try to engage him in polite conversation. He expeditiously chats but is fixated on rushing to the waterfront. At 32, the muckraker is storied enough to be nostalgic —he thinks back to when equine miasma permeated the thoroughfare. He almost prefers that whiff to the exhaust from the gas-powered vehicles that rumble on the hectic streets.

Born in 1880, Joseph's widowed mother re-marries after the mourning period. Her second husband, Abe Emmerling is a Jewish immigrant from Austria. His stepfather operates the Postal Telegraph in the hamlet of Berwyn, Illinois, nine and a half miles from Chicago. The toddler is raised with his name and is inundated with Morse Code. The clicks and clacks develop into a covert communication between the child and parent. After the days lessons at Mt. Airy School, the brainy little nipper earns tips by distributing messages for his dad. He does not neglect fishing and other puerile pursuits. When he is seven, he breaks his leg jumping from a tree. During his convalescence, P. T. Barnum's autobiography becomes his favorite thing to read. He admires the compère's hucksterism and self-aggrandizement.

In June of 1888, the Barnum & Bailey Circus plays a week in the "Windy City." Joseph implores his family to take him. Among the 19,000 watching, he signals his approval by clapping so briskly that his hands hurt. He is keenly entertained by the trained dog act and the sword waving Bedouin Arab caravan astride camels. The tot observes exotic animals—zebras, leopards, and giraffes—for the first time. There are wagon loads of grease-painted pantaloons, a human cannonball act, and the Lawrence Sisters performing their double-trapeze "Winged Mercurys" routine.

Meandering the midway booths, Abe wins him a teddybear despite the fact that the carnival operator has bent the sights on the popgun. Entering the "Ten-in-One Freak" tent, the youngster shakes the paw of "Major Atom," the two-foot, two-inch dwarf and his polar opposite, the seven-foot, seven-inch Austrian giant, "Captain Urick."

After taking in the articulated skeleton of the gargantuan African elephant "Jumbo," Joseph recalls when the train crashed into the mountainous mammal, crunching its bones, and killing it. He takes a trip down memory lane back to when *he fell from that branch and how much he hurt when he broke his own femur.* The boy winces as he feeds a peanut to the fallen attraction's widow, "Alice."

A photographer captures a shimmering tear on his cheek as Barnum himself appears to pat the adolescent on the head as if to comfort him. The picture runs in *The Chicago Times.* The child tacks the clipping on his bedroom wall. He is blessed to have met his idol.

Joseph consumes the topic of what living is like under the main tent. He saves 60¢ to mail away for the showman's treatise on "How to Create Wealth." The maxim he feels most inspirational about is "The noblest art is that of making others happy." He copies the phrase out in flowing cursive and pins the writing next to his grey-tone portrait with the showman.

For his 10th birthday in 1890, he is given a "Fulton Printing Outfit #1" with a grapheme alphabet. He duplicates a page of kiddie gossip and peddles his *Berwyn Snitch* to his classmates with the slogan, "Cuz You Wanna Know." Rising early on Saturdays, he bikes the neighborhood, distributing *Barton's Free Press,* to his 36 house route.

Barnum departs this mortal coil after four score on April 7, 1891. The 11-year-old authors and prints a page celebrating the impresario. He slips it into his next Saturday's route. The gazette's owner, Zachariah Barton gets wind of the unauthorized addition and has his editor pull the budding wordsmith in for a stern lecture.

"It was wrong to insert your opinion without permission. Your writing skills lack the grammar and excellence that we strive for."

The boy tells Barton he plans to "run a newspaper like him," and pledges to study his lessons intently. He becomes a star pupil during the next two years. After school, he helps out at the paper's bullpen, soaking in knowledge from the older employees. Thanks to a growth spurt at 13, he towers above his schoolmates. His teachers encourage him to play basketball, but he rebuffs them explaining that he wants to "join a metropolitan paper" and needs to focus on study. He has a schoolboy dose of puppy love, but the girl spurns the lanky bookworm's charms. Joseph finishes 8th grade at the head of his class both figuratively and literally.

In 1893, his editor elevates the teenager to "cub reporter" and assigns Emmerling to pay a visit to the "Columbian Exposition." Celebrating 400 years after the navigator claimed territories for Spain, the gathering is the most grandiose spectacular ever put on in the United States. The high schooler lusts to encounter as much as he can in 72 hours. Joseph is bug-eyed at the cornucopia of astounding exhibitions he beholds.

Even though officially not part of the festivities, "Buffalo Bill Cody's Wild West Show and Congress of Rough Riders" camps near the Expo entrance and sells tickets for daily re-enactments of General Custer's final battle at Little Bighorn. Joseph walks the deck of the replica of Columbus's carrack *The Santa Maria*. He also boards a copy of the 9th century *Gokstad* viking longship from Norway. From the deck, he sights contemporary Navy cruisers moored in Lake Michigan.

The parkland becomes incredibly ornate after nightfall encroaches. Fountains are lit in tinctures of blue, green, and red. The glow beguiles those who come like a bloat of hippopotamuses to bask in the sunshine of progress. The World's Fair flairs like a nearby sun as alternating current powers a million incandescent bulbs. Emmerling finds himself seated at a table, face-to-face with inventor Nikola Tesla at a press luncheon. He cannot believe his luck.

"Can you comment about the power system that electrifies this fair? What fantastic strides can humanity enjoy soon?"

"This is what lies ahead. I look forward to free air transmission of sound and energy to be feasible. America will be a utopia," the Croatian-born engineer states straightforwardly as Emmerling uses shorthand to scribble his words. "It is coming like Chronos the Titan's rule . . . he is . . . that is . . . what is . . . on the way."

The inventor's eyes shine as he thinks of the future.

"A true Golden Age where men mingle with gods . . . the World of Tomorrow."

"Thomas Edison says . . . ."

"Let me ask you a question, sprout. How many Edisons does it take to screw in a lightbulb? No clue? Edison does not screw a bulb. He screws you, sir. He stole that idea and does not deserve his own joke."

Joseph moseys away with quotable words for his article. He is dumbfounded as he sightsees in the stretch of temporary plaster establishments dubbed the "White City." Every few steps, pitchmen spout hurly-burly. The divertissement in the Midway Plaisance ranges from games of chance to technical demonstrations. Spending a few pennies, he takes in "Camera Obscura," views of the fair and peeks at the whirring animation of a horse galloping at the "Anschuetz Electric-Photographic Tachyscope" booth. A few feet further, he tarries to watch a demonstration. Two divers, immersed in bulky suits, perform activities like sawing wood planks underwater and recouping objects for the audience from a large glass tank.

Emmerling tries many products being introduced—Wrigley's Juicy Fruit, Cream of Wheat, and Pabst Blue Ribbon. He is saddened that the 264-foot Ferris Wheel is not operational, but he finds many other things that intrigue him. His "informational packet" contains a souvenir—an "elongated" copper penny from the sundry "squasher" machines that create exonumia throughout the park.

Touring the international bazaar for three days is an enlightening experience. The fledgling has a nip of scotch as he climbs a half-size reproduction of Ireland's Donegal Castle to kiss a facsimile of the Blarney Stone. Merchants from Chicago's Italian neighborhood dish up spaghetti bolognese while stereopticon images project Pompei's destruction.

A souk is imported from Cairo—fully stocked with camels and snake-charmers, it enraptures the turnout. Anthony Comstock, chairman of the "New York Society for the Suppression of Vice" lodges a formal complaint concerning "indecent undulations and swiveling hips of 'Little Egypt' and her belly dancing attraction."

He demands the revue be shuttered. Chicago mayor, Carter Harrison replies with a one word telegram—"No."

France's contribution to the fair includes a "Folies-Bergère" show. Joseph is propositioned by a brunette burlesque dancer. For $1, she guarantees to teach the him the practicality of Parisian intimacy. Behind a curtain, the hand job lasts a few seconds. He does not enjoy the experience and comes to doubt she was even French.

Emmerling channels Jules Verne for his critique "Around the Fair in 80 Hours." It is so well received that Barton arranges to have his article reprinted in journals with a greater influence. The opinion is that the "wet behind the ears" reporter will have a bright progression in the fourth estate. He frames the critique and adds a copy to his bulging sample folder. The 13-year-old is proud of his initial byline.

In 1898, 17-year-old Joseph embeds with U.S.S. *Charleston* as a "Spanish-American War Correspondent" for the Hearst newspapers group. When the destroyer arrives on the scene in Agaña Bay Guam, Spain's ranking envoy surrenders the garrison without a shot due to the fact that the armory holds no gunpowder.

Joseph interviews the Spanish Commandant of the fort who drunkenly tells him, "La guerra es un infierno. War is Hell. We were ready to die, but it is God's miracle."

Emmerling files his lackluster report from the radio cabin. His boss demands a more potent narrative, cabling him for a "re-write full of blood, guts, and glory." He misrepresents the truth and the item runs without a credit. The budding writer learns a valuable lesson—*I prefer it that way . . . anonymous. Without a by-line, news is but a fiction based on fact.*

Back in Illinois, Joseph finds his parents have passed away in a train derailment. The son has conflicted feelings. *They were good. Why would a just god allow something like that to happen? Why does he not smite evil-doers instead? On the other hand, if the allotted span is so haphazard, then it must be better to live life to its fullest. Everything could be concluded in a snap.* He decides not to worry about the "Grim Reaper" nor be constrained by any religion.

He liquidates the family assets and uses the funds to purchase a building in the upper west side of Manhattan near Central Park. He settles in the four story, five-room unit at 13 West 89th Street. A telegraph wire is installed as well as a telephone line and a safe. He leases out the bottom units.

Emmerling registers the *Press Internationalé* name and commences to establish his place in the industry. He holds the optimism is that his nascent enterprise will one day be able to fund his high-brow inclinations. He is accepted to Princeton's ivy-walled surroundings and its hallowed halls of learning.

Majoring in English, Joseph's sesquipedalian vocabulary is noticed by his teachers. With his journalism experience, his professors recruit him for *The Daily Princetonian*. He is never without his state-of-the-art favorite tool—a Kodak Brownie camera. He soon becomes bored churning out banal dribble relevant to the 1889 "Tigers" football squad. At the team's ten year reunion, the freshman profiles the former halfback, second cousin (twice removed) of Edgar Allan Poe. He has an epigrammatic, discreet dalliance with Samuel Poe and comes to the decision that he prefers his own gender.

In 1902, the senior is seething when the college will not allow an expansive expose to be printed and he resigns from the school paper. Dean Samuel Ross Winans tells him, "The racy subject you broach regarding Princeton fraternities contesting (amongst themselves,) to see which house can take advantage of the most sorority sisters at nearby Evelyn College" is not acceptable as it violates the code of conduct, and he expels him from the institution. Emmerling is infuriated at not graduating after investing almost four years in pursuit of a degree. He rails against the patriarchy and privilege. He vows to get his story in print as revenge.

The budding freelancer hawks the investigative piece to *The Newark Evening News*. The publisher wants to get the article in front of their large readership. Joseph does the unexpected by assigning the rights to the article for free. He asks for a byline for only the second time in his career. The editors counter that he join their ranks as a reporter. He declines, explaining his plans for a wire service and that he would rather enlist the news organization to distribute his content. They become his earliest patron on a purely speculative basis, paying a (low) flat fee annually.

The 21-year-old parlays his disquisition into a meeting with higher-ups at the *New York Herald* offices at West 35th Street and 6th Avenue. He rejects their suggestion of him occupying a desk at the bureau and pitches the newspaper into joining his growing fold of subscribers. They hand him a freelance assignment to cover a harum-scarum daredevil stunt at Niagara Falls.

Disposable articles become his stock in trade. He excels at succinct compositions of prompt, dross writing interspersed with 14¢ words. His droll style is exquisite for the scandal sheets. He finds he can conjure a hundred lines of fluff easier than researching facts.

As the idle rich's scandalous conduct boosts circulation, hearsay informs Emmerling's preoccupation as he stays in the "Seat of the Empire," utilizing his skills with morse code to file his salacious stories far and wide by telegraph. Joseph conscripts a network of snitches to beat the bushes for the elite's excesses. Coat-check girls, mixologists, pharmacists, as well as the parking valets feed him details of the bad behavior of society cads and daffy dames. He is so tied-in to goings-on that even city detectives request his help in reducing crime.

Publishing firms, searching for the next literary prodigy have no approbation for those who work in the newspaper industry. He will prove the "big-money-men" wrong by having an opus of the highest quality reside beside the classics of the literati. Working on themes for a fictional piece obsesses him and takes the rare spare time he has. He wishes to validate his command of language with an attestation that he is a brilliant writer by creating a best-selling page-turner. When famous, he speculates *they will pay through the nose for his next effort.*

His inceptive manuscript is sent for review to the major printing companies in 1902. "The Three Rings," sets forth "the suspenseful machinations of an ignoble Hungarian carnival hornswoggler who uses legerdemain and fakery to usurp the throne." He considers his tale tensely written like Sir Arthur Conan Doyle's finest Sherlock Holmes whodunit, but the work is cast aside as "lukewarm horror."

He buys a Ford Model-A and moseys along the eastern coast in search of odd stories. He uses the eight-horsepower vehicle to chase any carnival he can find. Composing Homeric prose on these unrestrained characters, he spends most nights clacking away on his portable typewriter. He mails his articles to his typist, who parcels them out.

In 1904, a second spine-chilling manuscript is sent out. "Anger Under the Canvas Tent," is a chronology of incidents that happen during the hunt for a murderer hiding in plain sight with the aberrations in a sideshow. The narrative is not released. Next, the 25-year-old writer finishes a pastiche featuring a Navajo gumshoe named Hawke-shaw in 1906. "The Elegant Savage of the Heart Mountain Range" does not garner any interest, nor are his other ideas considered. His work is rebuffed as trite, despite that he is undeterred, believing his labors will be noticed by a publisher of fine literature.

Outlets that rely on *Press Internationalé* material number 62 by 1911. After years traversing the seaboard states, Joseph decides to focus on writing about "The Melting Pot" that is New York City.

Emmerling grinds away, bringing in legal tender from a number of revenue streams. Besides writing, he dabbles in stocks and is a co-owner in a horse racing tip-sheet. He writes press releases and skits for Broadway revues. A Tin Pan Alley pianist has him penning lyrics, hoping for a hit. By escorting ravishing actresses and singers around town, the rumormongers do not envisage him as a loner.

At the 5th Avenue Public Library, he skims the latest releases for a spark of creativity. A work of fiction he bases on his wanderings is panned as "nostalgic tripe" by reviewers. The continued lack of recognition and rejection stings him like a hornet from a disturbed nest, but he keeps adding to his stack of unpublished projects.

Joseph is 31 in 1912. His contractees have been bolting to rival wire services *The Associated Press* and a newly emergent syndicate, *The United Press*. Subscribing to their content is far less expensive than his. He is forced to take forays further from his base to gather his information. Emmerling realizes having exclusives will keep him relevant.

Park Row outlets headquartered in New York City; *The Times, The World, the Tribune, The American,* (along with a plenitude of other nearby papers like *The Syracuse Herald,*) are rushing resources and staff to investigate the *Titanic* disaster. Worldwide agencies are doing the same. A provocative coup would be a feather in his cap . . . perhaps providing another gem of writing to frame and affix to his office wall of fame.

Optimistic and joyful, Joseph Emmerling is convinced that divine providence will gift him the spade to dig up an angle no one else has found. He needs an eyewitness report to be pertinent in his chosen industry.

Chapter 4 –
The Floating Demarcation

"Women and Children First."
— Lieutenant-Colonel Seaton

Phillip S. Roberts

At 2:23 am on April 15, 1912, the pride of the White Star Line, R.M.S. *Titanic* ceases to be buoyant—victim of a deck-jarring collision with an ice floe. A gash exists, ripped in its iron hull, and no ship is close enough to render aid. Their "C.Q.D." signal is faintly heard by sister ship, R.M.S. *Olympic*, 200 nautical miles away. Altering direction to assist, the ship's radio room relays the "S.O.S." across the North Atlantic. Decks awash, the rowboats are laden with the elite first-class cabin's inhabitants praying for deliverance. Except for the gentle lapping aqua on the tenders, the scene is eerily silent. Sucked into the frigid depths are 1,500 passengers and crew.

R.M.S. *Carpathia* is first to rendezvous at the "unsinkable" liner's coordinates after fully evanescing beneath the brine. The boat's massive screw propeller turns at quarter-speed as the liner navigates the ice field, keeping a fair distance from hazards before the captain orders full stop upon sighting castaways. Alvin Kelly is among the able-bodied sent with a gaff to secure the collapsible Engelhardt boats. Manhandled to the deck during the next desperate hours are 710 voyagers—mostly shivering women and children. The sheer perplexity is stupefying—frozen corpses will bob inaudibly in the freezing water until other boats come. Those who are alive assemble below the vessel's deck.

TITANIC SUNK. SURVIVOR LIST FOLLOWS.

Telegraphic messages relayed from the flotilla are decoded by employees manning the experimental Marconi station at the Wanamaker Department Store at East 9th Street and Broadway. Staff displays the survivor's list in the front window. The "dying to know" assembly gasp when John J. Astor's wife's name is posted but his, the richest magnate in the world does not. Days later, nearing the east coast, a féth fiada enshrouds the liner limiting visibility and speed as the Royal Mail Ship brings *Titanic's* living cargo to safety at Pier 54.

On April 18, 1912, thousands of New Yorkers are loitering in the mizzle at West 13th Street near 12th Avenue, anxious for details of their loved ones. As the ship bearing the glum survivors inches past the Battery at Manhattan's southern tip, the assemblage's hosanna rises, cheering. Under grey skies, the keel rasps against the wharf while sliding into anchorage.

The landing is buzzing with activity. Press corps are lobbing questions at dignitaries dockside. Answers are few and far between. Emmerling takes some snapshots with the newest model "Vest Pocket" Kodak. Cordons of security struggle to constrain well-wishers who let loose a tumultuous crescendo as the traumatized de-board. Euphoric to be safe, a few voyagers weep and kneel in devout prayer—thankful to be on solid earth.

Joseph, on the outskirts of the covey is taking in the full scene, jotting details. He can almost smell the relief survivors convey at being on land. He hopes to glean a licentious tidbit while trying to obfuscate his reason for hanging around. After a few hours, the preponderance of scriveners have left. The purlieus has become a serene environment, lacking the fizz of the quizzical.

Disembarking at this time is Alvin Kelly, lugging his sea bag. The 19-year-old is 5 feet 6 inches, and his black hair spills out from a cap. His skin is leathery from years on the breakers. He is not thick, but his muscles are rippling from unrelenting duties in the engine room. The metropolis has undergone a significant transmogrification from when he was an orphan. He scans the majestic skyline and surmises, *somewhere in the interior of this town, I will be able to find a place to lay my noodle.*

With less than 15¢ in his pocket, he's open to possibilities. His golden heirloom is around his neck, but mindful of Jacobi's counsel, rules out selling. *Times are not so bad. I am fit. Perhaps a different sailing outfit will value my experience. But right now, I need a little time away from the foam,* muses the sailor. Spying a penny on the ground, he crouches to pocket the copper; it is an auspicious augury.

"Sir? Okay if I take your photograph?"

The man asking wears a straw boater with his press card in the hatband. Joseph Emmerling has been dawdling by the gangplank for an eyewitness to tie his quasi-fictional narration to. *This bloke might fit the bill. He can play the part, and he looks a bit broke,* calculates the reporter. The seaman assesses him as the bulb flashes. Kelly's incipient impression is that the city slicker is well fed and well dressed. He has a certain obsequious charisma, and Alvin is wary as he sniffs the slightly too-sweet cologne emanating from the fellow.

"You were on *Titanic?*" Emmerling asks at full tilt. He takes a beat and modifies his tone to a velvet sheen. He is smooth as a greased turbine and pivots right to the point.

"What a catastrophe. I can spend dollars for information. You will not have to say distasteful things. Just tell me your part in their emancipation. What is your name please, sir?"

"I, um . . . Alvin Kelly, sir." He murmurs. "I saw . . . I will never forget . . . ."

The reporter's finger moves to his lips, cautioning him.

"I am Joseph Emmerling, checking into this egregious desolation for the *Press Internationalé* syndicate." He hands him a calling card bearing the Latin phrase, 'Credo Quia Absurdum.' Alvin quizzically scans the words. "It means, 'I believe it, for it is absurd.' I specialize in documenting the strange, and unusual."

Scanning the ship's roster, Joseph is cognizant that a few prominent Kelly's are on the passenger list, but the juddering sea rat before him is not one of them. He has already generated the disaster's substantial details. He just needs a name to tie to his account, so it hardly is of consequence which sailor he can convince to talk.

"The globe keeps turning, but ravenousness doesn't wane for examples of bravery."

Emmerling points at the "Landmark Tavern" at 11th Avenue and 46th Street. He plops a shiny silver dollar in Alvin's hand.

"I will join you in a jiff. Don't converse with anyone but me."

Kelly is apprehensive going in the bar. That is how he lost his liberty in Central America. However, he is thirsty, and soon the bartender is describing the specter of a Civil War tarpaulin who haunts the saloon. Joseph enters, orders a scotch, and gestures Alvin to sit at a table. He flips open his pad.

"You are courageous. It was dicey, risking all to save them. I will weave the narrative around your eyewitness details. I will ask questions when I need explication."

"I was on watch when the klaxon sounded. Topside, I shined my torch on those praying in the dark. I manned a spar to salvage those I could from their tribulation. Even after we supplied broth, blankets, and whiskey, they were shivering. Not because of the cold, or fear; the cause was an intense sadness. The bloating, buoyed bodies emitted a stench and the blood aroused predators. I tried to pull a fellow out, but as I did a monster emerged from the depths. Cobalt globes blink at me before ripping into him. The shark's colorless orbs are full with bloodlust as razor sharp incisors are slashing through the flesh and bones. The body is shrieking as I am left holding half a man."

Kelly howls and other pub patrons turn to stare—silenced. The seaman is reliving the shock.

"The sound and the smell of slaughter. If I could unsee . . ."

"That is, um, a vibrant witness statement . . . ."

His observations are perhaps too graphic to print. Emmerling plans a hasty escape; he frees a sawbuck from his roll and is ready to pay, but the words are spewing forth like a trip of thirsty goats smelling a brook nearby. The maunder is fascinating, and the journalist hesitates.

"I've been sailing since I was six . . . I must be the most hapless man to ever be carried on the ocean. I was lost on a remote island near the African coast; sieged from bloodthirsty cannibals, ferocious jaguars, and venomous reptiles. Saved from five wrecks during my nautical career . . . ."

Kelly cannot discontinue his cry from the heart. His narrative is flowing like the waters of the Nile in rainy season, overpowering a levee, and flooding the delta. He is embellishing stories told to him by Jacobi and others he has served with.

"I am rowing contrary to the undertow with a single oar. Can you please toss me a life-preserver?" Alvin Kelly is on the verge of weeping. "I petition to your better angels, sir . . . I am a foundling in the place of my birth."

"Praise the lord. Mana hath been brought forth whilst wayfaring in an arid wasteland."

This is exactly what Joseph has been hunting for—an opulence of anecdotes. He can transform this chance meeting into an astonishing portrayal. This lion heart possesses knowledge that is as yet uncommitted to print. Emmerling will leverage that information to forge fierce language. His contemplation is interrupted by a din.

The bartender has placed bread, and salty meats out. Hungry men gravitate to the free buffet. A slight bump, a hotheaded shove, and a brutal sockdologer kickstarts a melee. Kelly is hit on the button, shrugs, and lands a rapid combination on the aggressor. Joseph pulls him away from the fray, and they duck outside as the boys in blue flood in to quell the disturbance.

"You are handy with those fists," pants Emmerling as he whistles to hail a taxi.

Joseph's rooms are fastidious, dominated by his office jammed with books, teletype, stock ticker, telephone, and a spacious writing desk. The walls are full of framed compositions that Emmerling is bumptious to have created—a tribute to his writing. The faded photo with Barnum is under glass as well as a copies of his two articles with bylines. A certificate from the *Foreign Press Association* notes the quality of his 1910 commentary, "Houdini Aloft in Australia."

"Let us fill in some details." Ice clinks into glasses as Joseph pours out two fingers of bourbon. "What is your age? Any family I should know about?"

"I am all alone in the world. The nuns at the orphanage told me I was born in 1893, so, if that is right, I'm 19. The penguins also told me that my pa died in an oil derrick explosion before I was born, and my ma did not live after my birth."

"Stick with me, and you will always have a friend."

Joseph taps the keys on his Oliver Standard typewriter. He keeps revising, adding zip and examining words with more care than his usual three-paragraph task. This writing has to sound idyllic for the scheme he is hatching. The ashtray is choked with butts; crumpled sheets of drafts muss the floor. But, after a while, he considers his work is acceptable.

"I will put this in the morning editions while humankind cares," he says withdrawing from his now snoring guest. The sailor rouses to the earthy smell wafting from a percolator. Joseph grins and hands him a mug.

"You are going to be paradigmatic."

The Luckiest Fool on Earth

Alvin is unsure of what the word means. Nevertheless, Emmerling is brimming with glib conviction. He will resort to a bohemian arsenal contained in his metaphorical tool box to hype this seafarer. He counts the days until he can reap boundless opulence from generating a star.

"The bevy will know your name. I am proposing an alliance. In trade for the rights to your story, I will take care of all financials while I compose. You will not want—neither clothes nor food. But this is not a handout. You will not laze around—I shall have you toiling at tasks that suit your unique skillset. As *Press Internationalé's* president, I disseminate developments. During my jaunts, you will wend your way as my aide. A nest egg will provide for you after we part. If you wish to desert our propinquity, and owe more than your share, you'll settle accounts with me. Sound satisfactory?"

"All I have to do is tell you about my past? Really? And this is all above board? It sounds unbelievable."

Emmerling catches a glint in the gray iris as Kelly grows enamored with the chance to be unimpeded by the constraints of normalcy.

"How can I be as well-known as say, Roald Amundsen, Mary Pickford or Houdini?"

"I believe I can influence the press to make you renowned by using my intellect and command of the English language. My plan is to create a bestseller. I will title the work something like, 'The Rollicking Times of Alvin Kelly; the World's Most Inauspicious Sailor.' I will need you to confide with me all the secrets and the ways of the sea."

"Do you think this 'writing' would take much time? I want to ride on the waves ultimately. The sirens sing sweetly, calling and tempting me like Ulysses. I cannot be lashed to the mast forever."

Joseph is impressed the gob knows (and understands,) Homer's Odyssey. The poem had been one of Jacobi's favorites on the *Helene,* and he read the epic to Alvin frequently. Unschooled as the seafaring man is, Emmerling finds the fellow worldly and well-read.

"I am not sure. Quality takes time to create. Melville took more than a year to finish the initial work on 'Moby Dick?' Have you read that book?"

Alvin has indeed. Of the many volumes his Captain had owned, a dog-eared copy of the nautical tale was a best-loved of his. *I've often considered Ishmael as a kindred spirit,* he reasoned, *since we were both orphans and the only surviving crew from our respective vessels.* Jacobi and his cabin boy often discussed the plots he'd read deep into the wee hours of the morning. Kelly still likes reading, although his tastes have matured toward detective and jungle-adventure genres.

"I am weary of being poor. Once the populace knows about me, I'll become rich?"

"Moolah? Sure. So much. But, we first have to elevate your reputation to John Q. Public. As your status rises, the population will grow to crave you."

He glides a contract and a pen on the table toward his guest.

"Stay the course and we will be in the lettuce, chum. Soon, we will be dining with the ritzy 5th Avenue denizens under their crystal chandeliers. Put your squiggle here and we will embark upon a grand campaign . . . to generate a master stroke that will still be relevant in 100 years. If not, you can second-guess for all of your days what might have been."

Maybe it is smart to modify my life, cogitates Alvin. His sailing izzat as a Jonah is circulating through the merchant armada, and it might be arduous to convince a boat owner to give him a berth. To ride once more on the white horses, he might have to purchase a ship and steer to other latitudes. This business venture gives him a chance to raise enough to do that. He barely skims the pact before signing.

"As the Admiral said, Damn the Torpedoes! Full speed ahead!" Alvin clasps Joseph's hand as he flashes a toothy grin. "I promise I will not fail you."

"I call the plays from now on. You shall be my vavasour. You sleep in the spare bedroom. Let me know if you need anything."

The transaction ensures he will become quintessential and well-heeled as a result.

"I have engineered to put an item in the local journals. I've established a backstory that will allow you to upgrade your station."

Joseph reads the first paragraph aloud.

NEW YORK AMERICAN — APRIL 16, 1912

TITANIC LUMINARY TO BOX. AS THE DOWNCAST VOYAGERS OF THE ILL-FATED SHIP LANDED IN CHELSEA, ALSO DID ALVIN KELLY. BORN ON A FRIDAY THE 13TH, HE REFUTES THE MYTH THAT THE DAY IS CURSED. HE HAS BUILT HIS MUSCLES BY SHOVELING COAL INTO BOILERS AND SPORTS AN UNBEATABLE RIGHT. HIS AMATEUR TALLY IS 3 WINS AND 0 LOSSES. THE HELL'S KITCHEN WELTER-WEIGHT WILL SPAR LEADING UP TO HIS PROFESSIONAL DEBUT. AFTER RESCUING SEVERAL MOROSE PASSENGERS FROM R.M.S. TITANIC, HE'S WITNESSED TOO MUCH EXTIRPATION AND WILL UNVEIL HIS FLAIR IN THE RING. "IT'S THE GAIETY OF COMBAT I SEEK," SAID THE FORMER SHELLBACK. "I AM NOT AFRAID TO TAKE ON ANY-COMER."

The following sentences chronicle his reversals of serendipity. Alvin neither corrects the mistakes nor elaborations of his swaggering persona.

"Boxing?"

"Yes. You do not have to start great, but you do have to start to be great."

He hands Alvin two packages. One contains two unused sets of naval rigs, and the other holds a scrapbook incised with "The Luckiest Fool on Earth" on the cover.

"We will keep your many notices within the leafs. To play up your nautical brand, you will always wear a uniform when you enter the ring. You will train before we draw attention to your pugilistic dexterity. You are in possession of good basics, but I know a trainer who'll work on your strength and skills. I want you hearty, so let's tack some girth on your frame. How do you feel about a steak and a baked potato?"

As they dine, Alvin's gut tells him he is choosing correctly, but he wonders how Joseph can entice anyone to care about him as he fills his stomach with the Blue Plate Special.

Chapter 5 –
A Ringside View of the Ceiling Lights

"When you're at the end of your rope, tie a knot and hold on."

— Theodore Roosevelt

\

In 1912, more than 1,000,000 residents live in America's megalopolis. The 57-story Woolworth Building is nearly finalized. Untrammeled beguilement spawns in the theater district; vaudeville revues at Ziegfeld's Criterion and Loew's State Theater are considered its crown jewels.

Midtown is congested with blinking, animated neon—flogging products like "Maxwell House," "White Rock Ginger Ale," and "Kellogg's Corn Flakes." Impatient motorists honk incessantly to keep traffic jams moving and pedestrians scurrying. A bottleneck pounds on the thoroughfares, the steps sounding like mini jackhammers while rushing to their destination. The unabating bustle gives Alvin the agitated feeling of being a landlubber. His heels tread in Emmerling's wake to a chamber that caters to marginally less urbane personages. Boxing matches are illegal in state, but a loophole in the law allows "amateur sporting contests" to be held in athletic clubs. Many saloons have become fly-by-night "gyms" to skirt the law and draw patrons.

The unruly pack in to Starkey's, on Columbus Avenue near West 67th Street. The regulars gaping at the action in the ring have not come to analyze the noble science of the ninth marquess of Queensberry. The cheap price of an admission has them blowing off steam—slinging epitaphs at the bums who heave last-ditch haymakers. A long-in-the-tooth adversary is handpicked for Alvin's debut. The squaddie is full of bravado as he steps onto the apron to salute the arena. The ruffians guffaw as the laced-on gauntlets are too large to fit through his cuffs and he spares no effort to remove his jumper. Kelly blushes as a razor-blade is fetched to slit the sleeves.

The ring attendant clangs the bell. Alvin steps in to face his foe and flicks a few jabs that don't connect. His opponent uncorks a solid left to the mid-section that deposits him into a heap on the mat. Kelly whines as the referee finishes the ten-count and signals the knock-out. The hooligans boo as Joseph escorts his lightheaded fighter to the locker room.

"I have usually fought when I was stewed . . . or on a humming and hawing ship. I guess I'm not used to a ring that doesn't rock back and forth."

In his next fight two weeks later, Ed "E.Z. Street" Cole scores a technical knock out by clouting Alvin like he is pounding mallets on a marimba. In a subsequent collision of titans, he fails to win the day as Anthony "The Shantytown Brawler" Longette goes the knuckle on an uppercut that brings Kelly's stats to 0–3.

In his fourth match, a developing scrapper's right cross connects with Alvin's chin. He is punctually sent to a state of torpor. Troublemakers pelt the ring with garbage. The loser's share is a $3 gain in their finances. The funds barely cover the cost of the locker at the gym run by a former middleweight who trains Alvin a few days a week between matches.

"All your strenuous sparring wouldn't have helped you dodge that wallop. However, I see a silver lining Alvin. You were not far from lasting into the second round."

A break from the fight game allows a visit to Indiana for the second running of "Indianapolis 500." On the brickyard track, 198 laps in, mere car lengths separate the leaders. Ralph DePalma's Mercedes dislodges a piston. *The National Motor Vehicle Company* car, driven by Joe Dawson, hurtles past the smoking hulk to take the checkered flag in his blue and white, 4-cylinder racer.

Emmerling phones in his description of the nail-biting finish. After he concludes, the editor informs him that Wilbur Wright has flown this plane of existence to meet the Lord. He contemporaneously dictates an impassioned remembrance, lionizing the initiator of aeronautics. The newsman recounts the innovator's spirit as the "embodiment of mankind's goal to soar into the uncharted." The article is syndicated to five local papers in New York.

Subsequently, Alvin portrays a punching bag. A battle-scarred palooka sends the 135-pound lightweight floundering like a rag doll in a hurricane. An errant slobber-knocker caps off his fifth loss. His manager doesn't want to admit to himself that *Kelly will probably always be a ham and egger.*

The audience grumbles their disapproval. Stirring, the groggy boxer hears a refrain echoing throughout the hall.

"The sailor's been shipwrecked again."

Phillip S. Roberts

It's humiliating hearing them chant while I am lying here on my back, blinking at the ceiling lightbulbs. I have a sneaking suspicion that Joseph doesn't know much about this fight business.

His cornerman has another slant on the cantillation. "They gifted you a catchy sobriquet. 'Shipwreck' has a nice ring to it. I shall order you a robe with that nickname embroidered on the back."

In the four months after the chance meeting, Alvin and Joseph have become inseparable—late night conversations about the sea, trips to see the freaks at Dreamland Park on Surf Avenue and visits to take in various nightspots of Gotham City. Between scrimmages and pumping out words for his clientele, Emmerling is abstracting and fleshing out chapters for what he hopes will be a commercial success. Alvin trusts his friend will not steer him wrong.

In July, Joseph and his companion hotfoot northeast to watch the events of the "Third Annual Boston Aviation Meet." Emmerling's former colleague from *Leslie's Illustrated Weekly*, Harriett Quimby is to be a featured airwoman. She is the first lady in America to procure her pilot's license. The pathfinder wins notoriety as she dares to soar across the English Channel solo. Regrettably, on the April day she triumphs by landing at Dover, her accomplishment is not noticed— overshadowed by the *Titanic* disaster.

She voyages back stateside, unheralded. Nicknamed "China Doll," the diminutive damsel becomes revered by air enthusiasts. Quimby endorses an agreement with the "Vin Fiz Grape Soda" company. The beverage firm provides all purple fashions for her to wear: a diaphanous, lavender, satin blouse, and violet flight glasses. An aubergine scarf wraps between her neck and the flight jacket for warmth in the cold air of the skies. She smiles when she shakes Alvin's hand.

She is demonstrating her prowess in a 70-horsepower Blériot XI two-seater monoplane. Without notice the craft lurches and wobbles in turbulence at 1,000 feet. Her co-pilot, the gathering's organizer William Willard is ejected as the plane flips. Quimby cannot regain control from the spin and is also disembogued into the muddy bank of the Neponset river. Emmerling sends a periwinkle sympathy wreath to the Woodlawn Cemetery in the Bronx.

When the duo comes back from Beantown, hundreds are watching on the East River's shore near Pier 6. Handcuffed Harry Houdini, encased in heavy galvanized steel chains, is nailed in a packing crate and lowered into the aqueous. Emmerling pushes Kelly into the liquid.

"Save Houdini."

Unprepared, Alvin splashes into the estuary, jolted from the curglaff. He coughs as he swallows and treads saltwater. In 57 seconds, Houdini is loose of his bonds, surfaces to an ovation and notices the roiling water near him. He extends a hand to Alvin, pulling the wet sailor and himself aboard the wherry *Catherine Moran*. Joseph documents the happening with his camera.

THE NEW YORK TRIBUNE — JULY 8, 1912

AN ESTEEMED CREWMAN FROM THE 'TITANIC' DISASTER WAS SO VERKLEMPT WITH EMOTION, HE TRIED TO AID THE MAGICIAN BY SWIMMING INTO THE RAGING EAST RIVER. HOUDINI APPRECIATES HIS CONCERN, BUT IT WAS MISPLACED. THE ESCAPIST JEOPARDIZES HIS VITAL SPARK DAILY, AND TODAY HE WAS HONORED TO SAVE THE LIFE OF A HERO. SOGGY BOXER 'SHIPWRECK' KELLY, HAS BEEN GIFTED SEATS TO TONIGHT'S PERFORMANCE AT HAMMERSTEIN'S THEATER ONCE HE DRIES OUT.

The rectangular print is saved in his treasury. Perhaps it is the pause, or the emerald robe embroidered with the new epithet, but, in his next bout, he is skirmishing with conviction. A euphoric feeling rises in him. He charges in like a bull, only to be swatted harder than a Tris Speaker double. The ringster knocks him senseless with a surfeit of clouts. Kelly wakes to the now familiar chorus.

"The sailor's been shipwrecked again . . . ."

A few days later, Emmerling is profiling Katherine Stinson, the fourth woman to become licensed to operate a plane in North America. The brunette takes in a considerable wage working air rallies. Joseph dubs the demure, 21-year-old, "The Flying Schoolgirl" in a paragraph for the *Camden Post-Telegram*. The nickname catches on with both other reporters in competition for stories on the same beat and the general public. Even the pilot herself likes the moniker and paints the phrase on her fuselage.

Meanwhile, Kelly has accomplished a flawless professional tally in reverse. Beaten from pillar to post in the span of the last few months, his boxing wins and losses stand at 0–11.

Perhaps prizefighting is not the right sphere for his protégé, thinks Emmerling. A local syndicate has propped up a doughy, hapless, patsy from Staten Island for his next ring test. Mobsters have bet heavily on the boxer's first win, telling "Battling" Jack McGee to sink to the mat after the initial salvo. The jobber targets a first poke to his opponent's snout—a nosebleed starts. At the sight of his own blood, Alvin thumps to the canvas as the referee ends the rumpus while the rowdies jeer.

"The sailor's been shipwrecked again . . . ."

As Alvin Kelly falls short of distinction, Jim Thorpe wins both the pentathlon and decathlon at the 1912 Summer Games. Swedish King Gustaf V, as he decorates the athletes with the gold medals for track and field, rhapsodizes over the Native-American competitor from Oklahoma.

"You, sir, are the greatest athlete in the world."

When Thorpe, Kahanamoku, and the other Olympians disembark the ship from Europe, Mayor Gaynor arranges for an effervescent celebration. Ticker-tape spills to earth from windows that line the route from Battery Park to City Hall. The rejoicing echoes through the "Canyon of Heroes" in reverence for the august sportsmen.

Alvin is not full of beans when faced with the prospect of stepping in the ring again, but Joseph insists. He has already promised the bout to a fight booker he knows. Body odor and stale ale permeates the club. The goon across from him is snarling. Joseph is giving advice and mopping his brow with a sponge. As the bell rings, Kelly sniffs something sticky and treacly. He stands weak at the knees. The first ferocious swat slams him unconscious. Attendants lift him to the locker room on a plank. Smelling salts waved under his nose jolt him awake like Little Nemo in his bed after an adventure in Slumberland.

Meanwhile, Emmerling visits the owner of the venue to settle accounts. He knocks meekly and is beckoned to sit. The windowless workroom's walls are layered with portraits of bare-knuckle ringster's like John L. Sullivan, Pittsburgh's Frank Klaus, and "Chrysanthemum Joe" Choynski.

"I told you he had to stick it out one round," rebukes the squat booking agent behind the desk.

"Gangsters planned for that brute to massacre him. In those few minutes . . . dead . . . in that ring. I persuaded that kid to try this rigged game. I don't think that I could live with his death on my hands."

The former heavyweight contender, "Sailor" Tom Sharkey motions at a handbill.

"Dat is me sparrin' wit da great champ "Gentleman" James Corbett. He was da man dat beat de man. Your fighter ain't him. I di'nt trust your scrapper could get over in tiddlywinks, so dat is how I bet." Smoke trails from the white-hot cherry as he ashes his cigar. "Lousy canvas-back ain't got no stayin' power. I manipulated dis racket for years, and I know what you did. An amateur move like that wasn't smart. I took in a pile, but a mobster did not. If I were to air my suspicions . . . your companion . . . he would be separated from . . . Well, he shouldn't oughta' reserve a table for dinner. At the minimum, both your thumbs gotta be broken. But, you have always been square with me . . . so gonna' break just one."

"Anything that could be done right now, to . . . ya know, to look the other way?" Emmerling has nervously pulled out his money clip.

"If I held, say maybe $500 of their money for them. . . dey might not be so unhappy . . . I might be able to . . . anyway my advice is to scram town for a while. Word takes some time to filter out. Some gunsel might not hear . . . ."

Throughout the 15 minute taxicab drive from Lincoln Square to his upper west side brownstone, Joseph apprehensively squints into the dark cross streets of Amsterdam avenue, but nothing has the air of being awry. He could desert the sap; however, he delights in their heart-to-heart conversations about life and the sea. Joseph finds he enjoys having a platonic relationship he can rely on. *The opposite coast is a smart move*, he surmises. He taps out some urgent communications on his telegraph ticker then turns to Alvin who has been holding some ice wrapped in a cloth on his sore chin.

"That pugilism game is saturated with graft and hooey. You are done taking a pounding for the light end. Fill a suitcase. We are going to California. Listen, I know 'a guy who knows a guy' there who might be able to find us some nice, easy work in the moving pictures."

Chapter 6 –
Orange Groves and Celluloid

"If you can't bedazzle them with brilliance, baffle them with bullshit."

— W.C. Fields

The Southern Pacific steward uncorks champagne while crossing the California State line on November 28, 1912. Most of the 350,000 who live in the sprawling "Town of Our Lady the Queen of the Angels," do not notice two additions to their ranks.

Joseph registers at the opulent Alexandria Hotel in Los Angeles. So many projects are sold to producers in the Egyptian-designed lobby that the Persian carpet under their feet has become known as the "Million Dollar Rug." Here, Emmerling reasons he will meet the influential movers and shakers of the moving picture business. It is as if all the establishment's employees are involved with a project; the bellhops practice pratfall comedy, the desk clerks are screenwriters, and the shopgirls tap dance as well as act. Everyone sings; chirping like a charm of Darwin's finches in the Galápagos.

I will submit my great ideas and tout my compatriot for the movies simultaneously. A little flash and panache can move us forward in this town, reasons Joseph. *I'll spread a little dosh around to build my status around these high rollers.*

Portraits are taken of Alvin, and he purchases a quarter page in the *Los Angeles Times* extolling the virtues of the nautical man as if he was Sinbad the Sailor reincarnated. He buys a notice in *Variety* magazine heralding that the brave hero from the *Titanic* fiasco, "Shipwreck Kelly," will try his hand at acting.

E. W. Scripps, owner of *The United Press*, covets Joseph's client list and concocts a generous proposal. Emmerling reaps a hefty sum from the sale, and the amalgamate is renamed *United Press International*. As a bonus, he negotiates a retainer and the caveat to have his future articles, distributed to his original client's newsrooms free of charge.

Emmerling is invited to an advance viewing at the "Woodley Theatre" in September of 1913. After the western "Arizona" screens, the movie's distributor holds a press reception and wrap party. Joseph approaches a group standing around an elderly gentleman wearing a Stetson. He recognizes the lanky cowboy in the middle of a scrum as the celebrated former-lawman.

"Wyatt Earp? From Tombstone? I'm Joseph Emmerling from *United Press International*. Can we chat about the movie?"

The former marshal nods and flaunts his brass "Peacemaker" badge bestowed to him by the "Grateful People of Dodge City—April 1878." Lately, he has been working as a consultant for directors. Joseph notes that his long coat shows a bulge like it might contain a sidearm, and he is wearing rattlesnake-skin boots. He asks for java, no cream or sugar, from the staffer carrying the martini tray.

"Liquor is a devilish bandicoot," he sermonizes with a Kansas twang. "I reckon' to keep my memory straight and prone to state fact. Fer instance, I was overseeing the dude ranch when that playwright fella had the concept for this flicker. How they put it on screen was lousy. That gunfighter was not like that at all."

He taps his noggin under his hat with his trigger finger. Alvin is impressed by the legendary hero's gravitas. The server comes back with a cup.

"Movie boys will treat my tale better," continues the shootist as he taps his duster's pocket. "If not, I will spook 'em. Or worse."

"I could unquestionably make sure your story is written right," insinuates Emmerling.

"I ain't a simpleton. There is a saying on the range—If ponies come back to the trough, they know it must hold sweet-water." Film people are invariably trying to convince me there ain't no merit in my assistance, but I know better since they keep asking for help. The unvarnished truth will cost you $2,000 for the primary consultation. I know that might sound to be an unobtainable number, but my insight is indispensable.

He shakes hands with Joseph and Alvin. Earp produces a calling card with his contact information and excuses himself to trek to the copper mine he owns in the parched Mojave.

"Most folk know his name. How will I become more recognized than him?" Kelly asks. "I'm not feeling more famous now than when we first met."

Alvin requires a little encouragement to remain dedicated even though their goal is currently stymied. Joseph obliges with words that buoy his desire to be famous.

"We must keep our nose to the grindstone, my Jack-Tar. As we tread a circuitous path, we will trod the road as a duo. The publishers will pay us with piles of simoleons when we offer them your biography."

In March of 1914, stuntman F. Rodman Law is filming for a serial at Atlantic City. His plan is to ascend 1,000 feet and then engage the parachute. He shins into a container shaped like a missile and waves he is ready. Almost 600 watchers are on edge as his sister, Ruth Law lights the powder fuse. The string sputters—800 pounds of dynamite detonate with a whomp, and the canister travels through air and shatters into smithereens. He slams in a forceful collision with the unforgiving slats of the boardwalk. About 25 feet from the ignition point, his sibling directs underlings to smother the flames. Assistants toss buckets of water to drench Law, who regains his senses and stands unsteadily. His padded suit has saved him from lethal injury, but the heat of the explosion has singed him bald.

"Darn it. The test run had a favorable outcome."

He limps down the boardwalk unassisted, cursing and promising to try as soon as a replacement projectile can be built.

The same day in Los Angeles, 17-year-old Georgia "Tiny" Broadwick is attempting to be the first woman to parachute from an airplane. She has been leaping out of hot air Montgolfier balloons from the age of 12. Today, billed as the "Doll Girl," the flyweight bounds out the open hatch and opens her silk canopy. The chute allows her to end safe on a field in Griffith Park. Joseph is watching for *United Press International,* and the uncredited item runs nationwide.

HEIR TO AUSTRIAN THRONE ASSASSINATED.

The headline on Joseph's daily copy of *The Los Angeles Times* on June 29, 1914, reports Archduke Franz Ferdinand and his wife are killed after escaping a bomb attack hours earlier in Sarajevo. Within weeks, Austria-Hungary declares war on Serbia. Europe is plunged into hostilities. Alvin is eager to take the King's shilling and sail again, but Joseph counsels restraint.

"America is not even involved. Perhaps cooler heads will prevail and this regional conflict will be settled quickly."

A few days later at Cole's, Emmerling tells his pal of a consequential development while waiting for French dip sandwiches.

"I have arranged for you to take part in a moving picture."

The vacancy turns out to be a stuntman job for a "Keystone Pictures" production. Celluloid is a prized resource, so director Hal Roach demands shooting scenes in a single take. Alvin is filmed being tossed the length of a bar and ducking as a knife-throwing actress pins his ten-gallon hat to the wall. The cameraman cranks at half-speed during a chase as he and a tramp are pursued by an Indian war-party. Kelly accumulates a meager payday for his lumps.

After the shoot wraps, actor Charles Chaplin, clad in hobo rags, converges on Alvin with a lady on each arm and introduces the brunette who had been performing the dagger gimmick.

"She says you have met before."

"I am upset that you did not come back for me Alvin Kelly," chastises Vivian Steele as she wags a disapproving finger. "Was I just a fair-weather love, or one of the many harem girls you maintain in every port?"

He becomes conscious that the woman "is" his passing fancy from the *Helene* and is gobsmacked. Her Stygian curls hang in bangs. *I like the dimples that appear when she smiles. Her blue eyes shine brightly in the afternoon light. She has a nice figure and a cute button nose.* She plants a brief peck on his cheek. It reminds him of the lightest flutter of a hummingbird wing. She jokes with him.

"I've missed your pug face."

Their meeting was not synchronicity but an engineered miracle. Her underhanded friends have been watching Emmerling spread gelt around since he stepped on the train platform in New York. Shadowing him all the way west as a candidate for one of their flim-flams, they consider him "a plump ram to be fleeced." While baiting the trap, (a fake movie studio switcheroo,) she realizes that Kelly is the boy from her past.

This will be easy pickings, she schemes. *He hasn't anybody. I can fill that void.* Alvin tells her an abbreviated version of his path. She catches him up on her route to this instant.

"So much has taken place . . . that horrific jungle lingers in my . . . I . . . ."

Vivian's thoughts go astray. *It was almost ten years ago when the incidents happened, but I am still haunted by those moments I cannot block out. I still wake in a cold sweat, tortured with nightmares that must be culled from my repressed memories.* Lost in a mental tangle, she strives to regain her composure. She is wordless for what seems a lengthy time. Alvin squirms awkwardly until she continues speaking.

"After you left me in San Francisco, I could not sleep as creaks and squeaks bring me the terrors. My parents committed me to a facility that ministered to my oscillating gloominess and brusk wit with mild electric shocks. I was blessed, though. While locked away in that awful clinic, an earthquake causes a gas leak, a spark lights a vapor, and boom—No family. The executor relocates me to Los Angeles; a relative becomes my legal guardian. She squanders my inheritance. Now, I take great pains to keep body and spirit intertwined. Anyhow, I am better. Okay?"

Beaming broadly, she winks, and gives him another kiss on his cheek. He is smitten. She omits plenty of particulars, like how she became adept at sleight-of-hand, purloining shiny jewelry. At 13, her petty thievery cultivates from dipping to lush moil, liberating the contents of suit coat pockets from the blottoed on the Pacific Electric Trolley with a razor. Pinched, in the act by a transit security guard, a court remands her to a reformatory. Released to her aunt after a year, the 14-year-old acquires a rudimentary knowledge of the confidence trade from the slickest swindlers and riffraff. Vivian ropes in older quarry who like dominating youth, intoxicating the marks and palliating their savings. Her head is on a swivel, scanning for both schlubs and the bunko division of the police department.

The 18-year-old Vivian Steele refuses to be separated when he says his goodbyes—following him home. The two talk in hushed tones, deep into the morning. She takes a swig from a rum bottle and kisses him on the lips. He stutters that "he is a virgin." She tells him it will be okay. The coitus is clumsy and quick. He watches her doze in the moonlight as he puffs on a cigarette.

Unbelievable. She is so beautiful. Not in my fondest dreams did I expect I would ever see her again, nor that this magical coupling would ever come to pass. It is another miracle!

She exits the abode early in the morning and returns toting her suitcases. The woman hangs her dresses in his closet and unpacks.

"I thought my first romance was with the sea, but I was wrong," he fills in Joseph when he introduces Vivian to him. "I love her. Is there some provision for this in our agreement?"

The consociation grows to a triad. Vivian is advised that she will have to contribute some for expenses. Emmerling's impression is that she is as cloying as apple pie; coy and full of sangfroid. The woman has a strange personality, he assesses. *I don't trust her. Her appearance now is too much of a coincidence.*

A few days after she moves in, an epistle addressed to "Joseph Emmerling" appears in the mail slot. He opens the envelope—out pops a dollar and a handwritten note.

This sacred text was copied originally by Zorin Barrachilli in Italy and has traveled the world. Whoever breaks this chain will suffer greatly. Obey these instructions, and good will result. Create 20 copies, and enclose a "lucky buck" with each, if you wish to prosper. Send them to the first participants on the list, and add your name to the bottom. The mail carrier will remit responses to an address on file.

The following exists as definite evidence of this letter's power in creating wealth: Cardiff's Lucy Field won £5,000 in the Irish Sweepstakes. Omaha's Eunice Ambrose was hired on at a salary of $100 a week. Atlanta's Simon Melvin ignored this warning and his house burned, losing all.

Trust in the lord. He who suffered, gives thought to us. You will gain great prosperity in nine days, if you act in accordance with these instructions.

Joseph is irked that he is on the list but will not (just in case,) defy tradition. He requires as much good fortune as he can acquire, even if he does not believe in destiny. Alvin copies the script, and bills are inserted in the envelopes. Vivian indicates she is going out and will take him with her to buy stamps. Outside, she whistles for a cab, and, once in the backseat, opens the envelopes with a blade and shucks the contents like she is looking for a pearl.

"Spend a buck to multiply it twenty-fold. I am famished from the wearying work."

"But . . ." he stutters. "Breaking the chain brings . . . ."

"Wise up. Were you born yesterday? There is no such thing as luck, good or bad. Who do you think arranged for the letter to show up? Greedy men can be convinced of anything, easily."

A few minutes later, she hooks her fella by the arm and steers him into a diner on East 6th Street. She glides into a booth, hugs him and purrs in his ear.

"We could liberate his bankroll, and he would have no recourse. It is demeaning how he treats you—as if you were his servant. He is 'a bad man.' Unless you love him. Do you?"

"That is not the . . . We are, um . . ." He is unsure on how to define his situation. "Accomplices . . . partners, in business. He handles the finances. Having a bona fide confidante has helped; making being away from the ocean bearable. He is writing my history."

"Sounds like a grift to me."

Afterward, she checks her mail drop and extracts a few envelopes. "Buy four stamps. A sheet is 24 so you'd have that many left in case he asks."

Kelly feels uncomfortable as if he is a hide being stretched taut across tenterhooks. Vivian blows a kiss to him as if to remind him that he is hers.

"I'm not so sure that he has the magic to put you on the cusp," she says on the way home. Marveling at his naïvety, she adds, "But I will lend a hand as best I can."

"Hey, tightwad," she says to Emmerling while handing him two $20 Federal Reserve bills. "I had to buy the stamps. He didn't even have a nickel. So, when that good fortune comes calling, remember I deserve a cut of that prosperity too. Miracles don't happen every day, you know. Can't you part with some dough for him regularly?"

"I should know the score financially," admits Alvin. Vivian excuses herself. Emmerling has been expecting to talk about money since she joined them. The woman has been whispering more than sweet nothings into his ally's ear.

"Are you displeased with our arrangement? I can assure you our finances are in the red. I can open the ledgers, if you'd like. I have been more than generous."

Joseph chews on bidding farewell to the pair, but Alvin is honoring his side of their contract. *He has a girlfriend now. A physical relationship changes everything. I have long stopped trying to comprehend the feminine mind. This may yet work out. If I concentrate on having the damsel who loves the hapless salt to bare her heart, maybe I can include her tale in his memoir. Or if she won't tell her story, I can simply base a character on her. This story needs a love interest. For now, I'll play nice. Maybe she won't stay around long.*

"I was embarrassed when she paid the check."

"Do you feel uncomfortable when I pay for things? How much do you want?" Emmerling asks solemnly but does not expect a response. Alvin is quiet. He does not pay attention to what items cost. "We are not breaking even, but you should have a few bucks a week for expenses. Most Americans are happy to have a job that pays a dime an hour. Let's say a dollar a day?"

"Joseph, I know you are boosting my influence. Vivian was 11 when I first met her. It is an astonishing reunification. I am with you and this project for the duration. It would be nice if I had love too."

Emmerling continues sending out treatments. Vivian is pertinaciously gabbing apoplectically, proposing gambits for potential riches. He declines her nimiety of petty malfeasance as too impetuous.

"She's trouble," he forewarns to Alvin. "These glorious set-ups she foists as easy money making opportunities, risk a residency in the iron bar calaboose."

In March of 1915, Joseph is commissioned to cover the Panama-Pacific Exposition in Alameda. The three sashay north to San Francisco and ride the California Street line. Vivian starts sobbing as the sound of the brakeman grabbing the cable brings back a flood of memories and sobbing, she jumps to the street as her mind wanders.

Even though I have complicated feelings about my parents, and their abandonment of me, I recall happier days. This city has rebuilt after the destruction of 1906, but I still see ghosts in every doorway I pass.

She walks to Chinatown to seek out an opium den, but Yee-Mee who runs the Siberia Gambling Club in Ross Alley tells her it is too dangerous and sends her away with a small whiskey bottle.

"She is more capricious and irrational than usual," remarks Joseph cruelly while checking in. He dislikes her rapid influence on his shadow. Emmerling feels a pang of jealousy, like a child seeing a larger lollipop being licked by a schoolmate.

"Vivian has not had an easy upbringing. She survived some horror in the Panamanian jungle she won't tell me anything about. Her whole family perished in the quake and fire just after she returned to San Francisco. Being back in this town must dredge up some awful memories for her."

She walks into the hotel room a few hours later, and shuts herself away in one of the bedrooms.

By the time they breakfast and set foot on the Harbor View area, it is ten a.m. Touring the "Phantom City," seems to have tamed Vivian's melancholy. She is rapturous in the susurration of the fair. Joseph tells where to meet him later, hands Alvin a few bucks, and leaves the pair to their own devices—in the shadow of the Jeweled Tower.

Emmerling cannot resist boarding a basket on the Ferris Wheel and when the ride stops briefly at the apex takes a snapshot of the extensive grounds. *I am giddy,* he notes. *I feel like a wet-behind-the-ears cub reporter again. I hope I can do this grand affair justice.* Passing the international villages, the talkers, and the many attractions he does not have time to visit, he feels ecstatic. He stops to gander at the "World's Smartest" horse, "Captain Sigsbee" counting and answering questions by stomping his hoofs.

He takes his meeting with the headliner, Lincoln Beachey at a beer-garden in the "Joy Zone." The hometown luminary is the world's most recognizable pilot, referred to as "The Man Who Owns the Sky." He has chiseled features and an aquiline nose. The 28-year-old enlightens Emmerling on his derring-do in the clouds.

"This is a special day for me. My mother is watching. Four years ago, I got my first taste of glory, diving my plane into the Niagara gorge. Fighting gravity all the way; 20 feet above the swirling rapids, I swooped through Honeymoon Bridge. When skeptics say it can't be done, I say I can. Night-flights in Los Angeles? I did it first. Just beat a race-car and a locomotive at the Chicago International Aviation Meet. Maybe I was wack-a-doo for letting my wheels bounce on trundling boxcars, but what do I care? Ya only spin around once on this crazy planet, dig me?"

As the aviator displays a shiny medal he was presented by the nation's leader, Joseph preserves the image with his camera.

"In February, I buzzed the Capitol, scaring the Secret Service. When I landed in front of 1600 Pennsylvania Avenue, I told the President, 'If I carried a bomb, your White House would be microscopic shards.' Congress's lack of foresight in funding the Air Force is reprehensible. Wilson proposed to appoint me the military branch's director, but I refused the battlefield promotion."

Beachey uses his fountain pen to doodle an elaborate autograph for a female admirer and adds a phone number. He invites her to take a "special" ride, and lustfully watches her fade into the crowd before continuing. He whistles lecherously.

"I have never made love to so many women. Females must smell the danger on me. It makes their hearts race. I don't want to sit at no desk. Life's for living—in the open air. That's why I practice what I preach. I'm a barnstormer, earning my daily bread as a stunt pilot."

"That is a unique way to refer to your fervor," Emmerling states while notating the phrase in his pad. "I have not heard anyone utter that word combination before. Mind if I borrow that?"

Stunt pilot 1 of 1
stun-t-pi-lot noun
: a flier who travels around the country giving exhibits of
stunt flying and parachuting

"Sure. I made an awe-inspiring plan for today's performance," he says while making a tracing in the air of a woman's figure. "And got a date with a good-looking blonde after."

"That does found fun. Tell me about your show?"

"Can you keep this strictly confidential until after? I built a wooden three-quarter-size dreadnought shaped like the U.S.S. *Oregon* and painted it gray. The president is doing me a favor, ordering the actual battleship to cruise by. To reveal my array of aviation skills, I, the Demon of the Sky will perform insane figure eights and loops. I let loose a smoke bomb and when the air clears, the replica battleship is unveiled. I will sweep upon the fake like an eclipse of moths flitting at a flame and set it afire. We have rigged black-powder charges for when I wing by. As it burns on the bay, spectators think I sunk the real cruiser. I will push my monoplane to its mechanical limit, transitioning into my showstopper—the Dip-of-Death. I will rise to 5,000 feet, and then I, the Master Birdman, will cut the gas to the engine. Arms outstretched, I will dive until the very final second, defying gravity and power the ignition on, cheating the dark angel of a soul."

Just before 4 p.m., his routine is going to plan. Then like a locust swarm assailing a wheat field, engine booming, he is airborne, looping near the 50,000 heads in the bleachers. He zooms to an altitude so distant that those watching for free from the nearby hills can barely see him. Approximately 200,000 are hanging on his negotiations. He dares to hold back until it is almost too late and flips the prop on. The motor fails to function. He tries to activate the engine a second time but is too low to pull out. Hitting the bay at a tremendous velocity, the plane's pinions disjoin. A groan rises as the grandstand knows surviving such an atrocious bone crunching and sinew twisting contact is impossible.

Emmerling gives an account of Beachey's final seconds to *The Evening World* by telephone.

"Here's the slug. "Barnstorming Stunt Pilot dies in Frisco Bay."

He reads his transcription of the airman's last words so the paper can run the interview as a sidebar. The muckraker draws a nice bonus. Joseph asks for a byline. It is the third credit in his career.

"My bosses respect the exemplarily way you handle yourself," says the sub-editor on the other side of the continent. "If you would consider a position, we have one available that comes with a title, a girl Friday, and a corner desk. How soon can you be back?"

Emmerling informs Alvin that he is going east.

"A newspaper has offered me a flabbergasting amount to return to 'The City that Never Sleeps.' My social position will move us toward our sought-after result. You can come too, but I can fathom there are reasons you might prefer to stay in California."

"I will talk to her about your suggestion," replies the former deckhand. "Perhaps Vivian would benefit from different scenery."

The trio stops briefly in Los Angeles to grab their few belongings and head to the train station. After six days, they step from the Pullman car onto the platform, walk under the astrological mural at the Grand Central Terminal, grab a taxicab to Emmerling's vacant flat and move back in.

Chapter 7 –
Kelly Joins the War

"We fight not to destroy a nation, but a nest of evil ideas . . . ."

— H.G. Wells

European military action is mired in the muck. Neither side is gaining any tangible land, and the brutality is unparalleled. As Americans argue which path would be better to pursue, the quandary is reflected in the three dwellers of the brownstone apartment. Alvin thinks the nation needs join the Allies. Vivian is staunchly isolationist and denounces any bloodshed. Emmerling continues his neutral stance so he can take (and write about,) both sides.

However, on May 7, 1915, the devastation of war cannot be ignored when R.M.S. *Lusitania* is swamped by a German torpedo. Among the 1,200 drowned on the English ship are 128 U.S. passport holders, but President Woodrow Wilson barely amends his stance. Joseph's hunt-and-pecker is spitting out opinions; concocting sugary words to tug at reader's heartstrings. To avoid the debate, many divert their heedfulness to other action-packed barnstormers.

At Cicero field, Katherine Stinson completes a loop in her Curtiss JN-4D biplane. She becomes the first female flyer to add the touch-and-go feat to her repertoire. She adds barrel-rolls to her gripping routine. Increased star power has her headlining air shows, gracing the cover of magazines, and out-grossing the male flying aces who perform same maneuvers.

Houdini promotes his tenure at Hendersons's Music Emporium on Coney Island with his packing case escape. Encumbered in leg-irons, he is secured in a box. Hefted by a sheerleg, he is cast into the turbid salt chuck at "Ward's Bath." Emmerling's early boosterism of the wringing wet thaumaturge grants him a confidential question and answer session as he dries.

"Joseph, I am grateful that you believed in me before I clinched veneration."

"You have some plans for your next astonishing feat, Harry?"

"I am most interested in what might come at the end. Does something exist after this world? Could I converse with my sainted mother one more time? I have been pondering the notion with Arthur Conan Doyle. His wife is a spiritualist. As the world's sons die in battle, fakers and frauds are victimizing those who are grieving. I would ease their heartache. Exposing the tricksters fraudulent methods and hypocrisy is a noble role I am uniquely qualified for."

The triumvirate enjoy Houdini's sold out afternoon of sleight of hand and escapes. Invited backstage after the final bow, his wife Bess brews tea for Vivian while the men converse. The ladies befriend each other right away.

"Your husband is certainly the catch," innocently babbles Vivian. "And not hard on the eyes. How did you meet?"

"At Coney Island. I was working in the mermaid concession . . . ."

"Really? I do tarot and psychic readings there, now . . . . Gee, what a small world."

Due to the European war, shipping companies need to hire experienced sailors, and Kelly is interested. Drawn by a bonus, hundreds apply to be in the merchant flotilla. Supplying the Allies with armament is akin having a license to print currency. Alvin embellishes his sailing history.

"I was due to ship out on the *Lusitania*, but I missed weighing anchor. Before that I was running corn mash and ammunition, but you won't find any manifest showing that." Alvin sweats heavily, wondering if the recruiter will believe his lie. "I am a very competent sailor."

His falsehoods are not challenged, as the company is desperate for sea dogs to staff their convoy. The hiring agent hands an agreement to Alvin who is so eager to be back on the ocean, he instantly endorses it.

"I pray you will not repose in a pine box. But in any case, I will play your heroics to the hilt," Emmerling says when being informed of his decision. "If you can, write me of your escapades, ya know, for the book—the one I'm working on about you . . . ."

Vivian does not take the pronouncement as stoically, pounding Alvin's chest and is screeching like she is an 11-year-old again; being pulled away from him by her parents. She sobs inconsolably, demanding he reconsider.

"You promised me your love, and now you want to hurl our romance aside like a bucket of fish heads being tossed astern from a trawler? You insensitive brute. I trusted you. Am I so broken that you need to get away from me so badly? I need you, because you calm the voices of my past. You want to jettison me, just so you can board a ship? During a war. You imbecile. What if you are killed or worse, wounded? What if you cannot . . . I'll return to Los Angeles. I don't have any friends or anything to keep me in New York. I'm not staying here . . . with him."

She pitches a porcelain vase at Alvin's head like a Grover Cleveland Alexander beanball; high and hard. Ducking just in time, the pottery misses him and disintegrates against the wall. Vivian flees the scene. Three days later, she comes back, resigned to the fact that he is deserting her. She won't say anything about where she was or what she was doing. Alvin can smell the gin on her clothes. Before he reports for duty, she is determined that any time they have left together will be memorable.

The next night, Joseph takes the couple to the Ziegfeld Follies. The production's staging is nationalistic. Kelly chortles at W.C. Fields's comedy juggling. Singer Bernard Granville pauses his schmaltzy ballad to have the spotlight highlight the "brave mucker" in the box, ready to oppose the Huns. After the final curtain, chorus girl Marion Davies joins the social function. The foursome heads to "Sherrys on 5th Avenue" for a light, late-night snack. Comedian Ed Wynn and Palace Theater headliner Sophie Tucker are seated at a nearby table. Emmerling sends them a bottle of 1912 Dom Perignon Brut. Busboys push the piano to her table and Tucker, the uncrowned "Queen of Broadway" serenades the diners with a song called, "I'm Glad Daddy's in Uniform."

"To Shipwreck Kelly. Off to beat the Kaiser," interposes Joseph. The ad-hoc party lifts their champagne flutes. "Raise a toast to our valiant companion!"

A few days later, Alvin ships out to join a Dutch freighter. Watching the rippling whitecaps break from his perspective on the deck has him feeling deliriously rapturous to be sailing again. The transport attempts to run a blockade to convey much needed supplies to the British. The stratagem does not go auspiciously. As the ship is set afire by a U-boat's deck guns, Kelly escapes into a lifeboat. That craft is violently bowled skew-whiff by the surfacing submarine—with all sailors ejected into the drink.

Phillip S. Roberts

The windblown jack treads water until a British cruiser rescues him. He's lucky to be saved. Once aboard, he is cloaked in wool, handed a Cadbury chocolate tin, and poured a hot tea. He unships and is escorted to the Harwich Infirmary. An administrator orders bed-rest. Alvin pens a mawkishly sentimental love letter to Vivian and sends it to New York. Emmerling forwards the envelope to Los Angeles where Alvin's sweetheart has returned to her other passion, crime.

When doctors think Kelly well enough, he is re-assigned to a British battleship. He spends ten months afloat on different vessels as superiors keep transferring the sailor considered a 'Jonah.' During the Battle of Jutland on May 31, 1916, Alvin is on a ferry taking a brigade across the English Channel to Calais. A bombardment brightens the aether.

"Those damn Marmaladinger sure construct a hell of a juggernaut," he raises his voice to alert a second lieutenant as a shell broadsides the ship and the deck catches fire. He wonders, *if he is a jinx, or he is cursed for not consummating his oath so many years ago,* while aiding in the evacuation. He abandons the ironclad before his berth goes to Neptune's realm. Rescued from the choppy water, he is transferred to a different command again.

A German Unterseeboot sinks the U.S.S. *Housatonic* on February 3, 1917. America withdraws its diplomats from Berlin. In April, as Woodrow Wilson finally asks congress for a war declaration, Alvin is riding the waves with a French-flagged vessel. Americans are buying war bonds and raising funds for those sent to Europe.

Stateside, Jack "The Amazing One," Williams escalades the six-story Cadillac Square Hotel on December 19, 1917, to benefit *The Detroit Times* "Tobacco Fund." More than 7,000 watch the fly tackle the building by hand. After passing the hat for donations, his helper counts almost $700. The climber takes 30%, and the remainder purchases cigarette cartons for American doughboys fighting overseas.

Just after baby-new-year-1918 is birthed, Harry Houdini holds a black tie benefit at The Hippodrome Theater. Unprecedented prestidigitation is assured. For the finish, the audience is astounded as handlers lead "Jenny," a 6,000 pound African elephant on stage and with a wave of the wand, the mage achieves her vanishment. After the show, the press-boys surround the magician, Joseph is chosen to ask the initial question.

"Mr. Houdini, has any practitioner of chicanery ever dematerialized such a colossal animal?"

"No. Not until now. And this evening of illusion raised $2,000 for widows."

Alvin is sent to join the U.S.S. *Edgar F. Luckenbach* on March 14, 1918. His fourth bob-fly flaps from the mast, and he is conferred the rank of ensign; thrilled to be serving in the U.S. Navy. He pens another gooey love letter to Vivian, and posts it to Emmerling. The recipient sends it to her most recent address in Los Angeles. She is a devil in the "City of the Angels," working for a "bucket shop," selling fake stocks, oil well futures, and commodities.

A month later, an "Alvin Kelly" is listed as a casualty. Joseph engages the operator and does his utmost to console Vivian. She slams the handset on the cradle, hoping that the bad news is a mistake. *I did love him*, she concludes while wiping a few tears away. *I was hoping he'd come back whole so we could continue our affair of the heart. I was wrong to let him go to war. I should have stopped him somehow. I could have told him I was with child, or faked an illness, or made up some other lie.*

Emmerling is among the hundreds who have gathered to raise money for charity in chilly midtown across from the Wilson Building on September 19, 1918. High-diver Tom Quincey leaps from a five-story ladder into a large tank of water in Harvard Square. Teeth chattering, "The Man without Fear" vends Liberty Bonds and gives away autographed postcards. Joseph asks the circus performer for a quote for an item he's submitting to the *Five Mile Beach Weekly*.

"Sales look to be booming as briskly as shares of oil in the stock market. Despite the nippy climate, you drew quite an animated crowd. Maybe 1,500? What is next for you?"

"I'm going to soak in a bathtub. We sold $400 worth of war bonds to support our exemplary American lads fighting in Europe."

A week later, sideshow attraction Jerry "The Kid" Scheyer pedals his tiny bicycle on a ramp and whirls through the wintry air. The dwarf flips several times and lands in a net strung across

Columbus Circle. Watchers donate their loose pennies to a St. Vincent de Paul charity fund. Joseph is scrutinizing the activity for *The New Haven Sunday Register.*

"That was a pretty killer-diller jump, Kid," comments Joseph. "I have not seen a bicycle stunt so meshuggeneh since Diavolo."

"Thanks. We raised $300 for orphans. Want a ticket to see my full act with the Hagenbeck-Wallace Circus this weekend? Could you mention our show in your article?"

Germany signs the Armistice after a hurried negotiation on November 11, 1918. "The War to End All Wars" price has been immoderate—40 million military and civilian casualties. Alvin credits his survival to the lucky gold coin around his neck. He hopes the token will pull him back to New York soon as Captain Jacobi had once foreseen. Kelly tries to join the jocund armistice celebrations in Trafalgar Square, but the exuberant burgesses is too much for his enochlophobia. Later, lying in his bunk, he falls to sleep. Hypnos, the greek goddess of dreams releases him from the rigors of war and blesses him with happy thoughts—sailing with Vivian on the *Helene*, traveling through America with Joseph, and being famous with plenty of money to buy whatever he sets his heart on.

Prior to the 1919 season, the New York Yankees squad works out during spring training in the Grapefruit League. Club manager Miller Huggins pulls outfielder Ping Boidy aside. He jokes with the player "he can earn the final spot on the roster," if he beats an ostrich named Percy in a spaghetti eating contest. "Fence-Buster," who stands five foot eight inches and weighs 190 pounds accepts the challenge— slurping more noodles than the fowl from the Jacksonville Zoo. The beast is neck and neck with the ballplayer, both devouring bowl ten. During the next serving, the bird has eaten enough and wanders away. As his besotted teammates urge him on, Ping devours plate number 11. He seals the victory, his teammates lift him on their shoulders like his hit has won the World Series. Boidy is (unofficially) declared Earth's Most Prodigious Eater on April 3. Despite hitting .259, his team finishes third in the standings.

Another inordinate diner, slapstick comedian Roscoe "Fatty" Arbuckle handcuffs "Sailor" Tony Pizzo to the handlebars on his

"Crown" bicycle on May 21, 1919. The navy recruiter reads a statement to the reporters and shutterbugs at Venice Beach before he pedals east.

"I will embark on a cross-country trek," says Pizzo. "Once I set foot at my destination, I'll be freed with this key I am entrusting to the U.S. Postal Authority. My plan is to coast into the 'Greatest City in the World' before November 1st and rake in $3,500 in pledges for the Navy Charity Fund. May god bless our boys in the military."

F. Rodman Law crosses into the ultimate frontier on October 14, 1919, in the Greenville Municipal Hospital. His sister, Ruth Law, clasps his hand as the 34-year-old dies from pulmonary tuberculosis. She commits to keeping Frederick's work prevalent. Emmerling lauds that he "will live forever on celluloid" and adapts a line from Shakespeare's *The Tempest* for his obituary. He refers to the innovative stunts as "the stuff that dreams are made of." The tribute runs in a few US newspapers.

On Halloween, after six months, "Sailor" Pizzo wheels the bike into the lobby of the McAlpin Hotel. The night clerk opens the fetters from the handlebars. Joseph hands the cross-country cyclist a folder holding his winnings while noting the scene for the Los Angeles paper, the *Evening Express*.

"Well done Tony," says Emmerling. "How was pedaling across the nation?"

"Some days brought unforeseen confrontations during the journey. My escort was hit by a car outside of Louisville and had to be put in a doctor's care. I had to plot the route by myself from then on, but it takes a certain kind of resiliency to be in the Navy. I'd recommend joining the service for any young lad who wants a brighter future."

Kelly is honorably discharged. He returns stateside on January 10, 1920, and temporarily bunks at the "Armed Forces Club." The gob applies for work at the Brooklyn Navy Yard, but is not hired as the seams are bursting with a surplus of men back from the warfare.

A week later, Joseph is surprised to see Alvin is reclining on his stoop. He hugs him briskly. *It's like he's risen from the dead like Jesus. It's a miracle. His war-stories will be a welcome addition to my unfinished manuscript.* The switchboard operator is engaged to ring the west coast, but Vivian does not pick up, so he uses his telegraph key to tap out a message to her most likely Los Angeles address, c/o General Delivery.

"The wolf is probably out . . . wearing sheep's clothing," says Emmerling as Alvin scowls. "You were reported lost . . . at sea? What happened?"

"I lived through a most horrendous incident. I credit ruggedness and motivation for my salvation. Hjalmar the Swede and I were ordered to ride on a scow that was being towed across the channel. Just after dark, a torpedo came straight for the tugboat's bow, off the starboard side. We were carrying ammunition and gun-powder, so I grabbed an axe and severed the towline. Through dense fog in the Atlantic, we drifted from the main shipping lanes. The sub's commander went seeking larger prizes. We bobbed in the drink on a 256 foot steel whaleback barge. Three days, became a fortnight, and we sighted no others. Day 20, I woke, and my shipmate was gone, over the side . . . I observed shark fins . . . ."

"Skip that part, please . . ."

"The pontoon floated unmolested, and after a month, I went a little nutty. I collected rainwater and ate the raw fish I caught. On day 85, a trawler came upon me, dehydrated but alive. As soon I was free of the barge, I lit that ciggy I'd been saving for almost 3 months. That stale tobacco was the most satisfying smoke I ever had. I could have blown myself to kingdom come anytime, but I have self control and determination—Endurance, that's my game. An admiral awarded me a medal for saving the munitions.

"Let me photograph you wearing your uniform and decoration. It will be a good addition to your story. Your 'whale of a tale' reminds me of a passage from Coleridge's 'The Rime of the Ancient Mariner.'"

Emmerling pulls a volume from his library shelves, and recites.

>Day after day, day after day,
>We stuck, nor breath nor motion;
>As idle as a painted ship
>Upon a painted ocean.

The Luckiest Fool on Earth

Water, water, every where,
And all the boards did shrink;
Water, water, every where,
Nor any drop to drink.

"I got plenty of . . . um . . ." Alvin says uncomfortably. "Stuff to talk about, ya know . . . um . . . the very bad things I saw, that I could tell . . . ."

"Are you saying . . . you want to continue our arrangement as before? Look, the spare bedroom is empty. See if you can fall asleep and we'll discuss it tomorrow."

A month into the modern decade, on January 29, 1920, a spotlight array is riveted on "The Wild-Man," George Polley as he takes on the gothic Woolworth Building. Heading toward the 792-foot green top of the world's tallest man-made structure, he fails to achieve his aim. As he springs into an open aperture on the thirtieth floor, he is apprehended by a state trooper.

"I only had 27 stories left," the climber complains as he is schlepped to jail for trespassing. "I'd have gotten to the uppermost needle—a world record for scaling buildings by hand. Even Harry Gardiner hasn't attained that statistic."

His imprudence is rewarded with ten days in the crowbar inn and a $100 fine. Emmerling pays him $50 for an exclusive chat from the slammer, freelancing for *The Providence Rhode Island Journal.*

Almost a month later, Rear Admiral Robert Peary dies from anemia after 35 blood transfusions. Joseph's eulogy about the Arctic explorer wins praise from the *New Amsterdam Writers Association.* He frames the quadrilateral newsprint and selects a place on his wall to nail his award.

The next evening, the telephone rings in Emmerling's apartment, and Vivian Steele is on the line, calling from California. The connection is scratchy, and difficult to hear her every word clearly.

"I am doing well . . . in the movie business . . . my boss read some of your treatments . . . wants you to come to Hollywood . . . I wired train tickets for you both to visit . . . ."

Joseph hands the phone to his running mate after agreeing to come west. While Alvin gets an earful, Emmerling ponders if she is being on the level or if she is trying to play him for a chump. After a few minutes, Kelly cradles the receiver.

"I hope it was not a party-line," Alvin is a bit flushed. "When she's flirty, she talks very dirty. Joseph, do you understand women?"

"No. I'm not sure any man's gray matter can come to a logical conclusion about that subject. Do you know who Albert Einstein is? He is a mighty thinker nominated for a Nobel Prize. But the scientist is not near to solving the conundrum that is the female. He had a wife, divorced her and then wed his cousin. I have had casual relationships with both men and women, but, to tell you the truth, I do not care for either. Sex. It's just too messy . . . ."

Emmerling wonders if he is sharing too many intimate details. Alvin has never cared about his proclivity. He has never known Joseph to be in the throes of passion. The acknowledgment of homosexuality doesn't rankle him.

"I prefer celibacy. My main love, is language. Other than my bosom buddy, Mae West, I find few women that I am fervid on fencing with . . . verbally or otherwise."

When the duo arrives in Los Angeles, Kelly has a sweet reconciliation with Vivian. Circling in her orbit, he is unwilling to waste a nanosecond. *I'm so happy to see him again. It must be kismet. We are destined to be bound,* she thinks. *I guess I was wrong. Miracles can happen.* Their lovemaking is sublime and loud. Joseph is grateful for the radio set he uses to drown out their amorous activity.

The next morning Vivian reveals she is running a casting business out of a bungalow in the Beverly Hills Hotel. She lures aspiring actors and actresses to her, selling promotional headshots at a reduced rate.

"I recommend a complementary photography session with a shutterbug. He convinces them to disrobe. Shocked, I warn the gullible that their naked portrait may be printed in an 'adult' magazine like 'Fine Arts Quarterly.' I pressingly burble it is imperative that the negatives are retrieved. I advise I am available to assist . . . for a price."

"Do you ever feel guilty squashing someone's dreams?"

"Some find leading roles. Hollywood brings an inexhaustible influx, all trying to become thespians."

"It's mean and cruel."

"Everybody can't be stars. We need soda-jerks and cigarette-girls, too."

The pair traipse to "The Pacific Dining Car" at 7th and Westlake. Patrons keep visiting their booth to say hello during the meal. Some pass on gossip, and others pause crisply, awaiting instructions. She introduces her better known comrades while she fiddles with the switchblade in her coat pocket.

"This is 'Shuffles' McKay. He is a cardsharp—an expert at dealing seconds and bottoms. Meet 'Yuk-Yuk' Malone. She is the alibi queen. For an eensy-weensy fee, you were with her. Shake hands with 'Soapy' Jones. He is a world class ventriloquist who sold a talking poodle . . . The dog's valedictory message to the sucker was, 'I am so angry with you. I'll never speak again.' Pretty swell, huh?"

"You know a lot of charming folks. Are they in your gang?"

"We are a loose confederation, aligned with common interests. We are a source for each other to draw upon when a specific dexterity is necessary. I am working on a tidy payday, but it takes intricate planning and a smidgin of menace."

"Is that why you carry a knife? For protection? Is someone trying to hurt you?"

"No," She holds a vacant, faraway gaze. Her thoughts drift back to the dangers of the trackless jungle—*I never know when I might need to splice a rope, gut a fish, or slice a throat.* "I have some other reasons."

"Do you have an alias too?"

"No."

She lies. Her cadre know her as "The Steele Rake" for her finesse in accumulating the insatiable like a gardener gathers brown leaves on a lawn in Autumn. Vivian leans in to Alvin and broaches Joseph's unconventional mentorship.

"He consumes all the 'spinach' leaving you to scramble for discarded coins. Let me take what you are owed and we'll go live like royalty in South America."

He declines.

She's frustrated by Emmerling's grip on her admirer. Back at the rented abode, Joseph reveals important information he has to share.

"Jack Dempsey is in town in a few days to film 'Daredevil Jack.' His representative, 'Doc' Kearns owes me a favor, so I was able to arrange you a role on set, doubling for the villain. I also mentioned you are available to spar as he prepares for his bout with Billy Miske."

The movie stunts had gone well, with Kelly doubling for actor Lon Chaney. The next afternoon, Vivian waits at home while the boys attend a private showcase for sportswriters at the "Spring Street Newsboys' Gym" on the edge of Los Angeles's skid row. Kelly steps through the ropes of the ring. *Perhaps this is my chance for grandeur,* ponders Alvin while limbering up. *I know he won't hurt me in this exhibition—the champion just needs to sling a few combinations for the photographers. He's about half a foot taller and outweighs me by at least 50 pounds.*

Alvin circles the mountainous boxer and smacks a left toward the chin that does not connect. "The Manassa Mauler" levels a weak right cross at Kelly who faints like it was 1912. Emmerling expresses regret to Dempsey's manager while waking the unconscious human sprawled on the mat.

"Sorry. I got scared, I guess. I never realized what a big fellow he is." Joseph is reflective during the taxi ride back to their quarters.

When the duo returns to the duplex that Vivian rents, the faint aroma of ironed currency hangs in the air. The mountebank has borrowed the phony money from the best forgery expert she knows, Victor "The Count" Lustig. Printed bands encircle each stack that she arranges in a valise. Genuine currency is placed on the carefully curated piles so she can grab the bundle with ease.

"Resembles $25,000, huh?" She beams at her artistry. "It is such good work, the bills can pass as real money if no-one looks too closely."

She is dressed to the nines in a pink ensemble and a fashionable hat. Normally, she attires to be unremarkable, like any other gingham-clad shopgirl. Not today. She is playing a glamorous role.

"My date is with a rich oil tycoon."

"What if he wants to counts it?"

"Unlikely. At that point, my art will overtake the narrative. We show the real dough once but then make a switch—from then on, he holds worthless paper. We bought every possible combination in the third and fourth races to let me handle the winners. I will show him small winnings. By the fifth race, he will be pulling at the bridle to place a sizable bet. We guide him to a $5,000 bet on a 5–1, 'Let it Ride' by telling him we have interchanged a slow nag for her faster identical twin. If the horse wins, we bring out the fake proceeds. Then while celebrating, we toast to the steed, and we engineer a sweet brush-off—it's a distraction that is so simple. If the horse loses, we leave. We keep the five large either way."

Some hours later, Vivian enters the domicile in a panic.

"It went badly. I had to stab his bodyguard to escape. They were going to kill me. People got shot. We should vamoose right now, or we will be very dead. I procured a ride for us that is safe. Their clique does not ask any questions."

Alvin, Joseph, and Vivian jump into a passing streetcar, missing by the narrowest of margins the minacious hoods who would have murdered them. Meeting a convoy trucking north, along the coast, they slide in a truck-bed at the rear of the procession. The imperilment has cooled slightly a week later when the motorcade crosses the Canadian border, but gunsels are still combing the continent for the camouflaged trio.

Chapter 8 –
The Hazards of Chicanery

"No thief, however skillful, can rob one of knowledge, and that is why knowledge is the best and safest treasure to acquire."

— L. Frank Baum

The conveyance Vivian has hired to tiptoe away from trouble is "Earl's European Shows." The 28 Romani in the caravan accept the strangers without any interrogation. These roamers play the remotest of settlements, contravening the tedium with their uncommon pleasures. The group traverse from British Columbia toward Quebec playing lumberjack barracks, mining camps, and other provincial settlements with no room to swing a cat that have few stores to spend their paychecks. The plan is to tour the provinces until late fall and then burn rubber to Florida before the winter temperatures in North America turn nasty.

An adult entry to their impermanent wonderland is 10¢. A soundtrack provided by a calliope augments vendors hawking penny lemonade, salt-water taffy, and kettle corn. Others amusements like the ring-toss, a mechanical shooting gallery, and a high-striker rig are all modified to give the concessionaire an edge. Flamboyant banners accentuate the hullabaloo that stokes interest with the audience.

Emmerling is animated—he wants this insight. He is not going to squander his chance to mine the valuable information of the goings-on and inner workings of the carney. He plans to tailor these experiences to base a novel on. Vivian explains the road warrior's credo.

"It is us gypsies against everybody else, especially the locals," she says. "The constabulary will be sniffing around but just until their payola is tendered. Those church-going hayseeds will look with disgust upon us as if we were beggars. However, the temptation is too much to avoid our snare. We will cull the yokel's bones cleaner than a ferret in a coop and they will thank us for the excitement. This flock of dodos will never accept a "stolen egg" like us into their nest until we chip in. I will be dancing the hoochi-koochi. This ride ain't gratis, so figure out a way to fit in."

"We are paying? To escape from your mistake?"

"I am coughing up . . . for all the gasoline," she continued. "We will hide in plain sight. We are fortuitous to not be dead. A sizable bounty is on my head, if someone were to let our location be known. You two, right or wrong, are regarded as my partners, so it is prudent to follow my lead and shut your mouth."

After a time, the newcomers become accustomed to the grind. Alvin is sweating it out as a roustabout. Joseph possesses an adeptness for puffery that entices patrons into the tent. Gabbing for their consideration, his words gush extemporaneously.

"The grotesque miracles you'll see—as never before. It is 100% guaranteed, these whatsits will ensnare . . . snake-charmers, sorcerers, a nucleus of midgets, and a unique crowd-pleaser. Ten productions—just one silver dime."

He never lets his discharge become rote, honing his verbosity in his recitation to perfection, adding more quavering and ostentatious descriptions to his banter.

"See Maximus! How many tons can he lift with his pinkie? Know the future! Digest the evinces from Zahdra, the Prophetess from the 23rd Century. Grander in disbelief at nature's most unaccountable oddities—The Loretta Sisters; conjoined contortionists. Meet Ajax the Blockhead. Watch in disbelief as he hammers steel nails up his nasal cavity. I know how spartan your lives are, so put those dimes back in your pocket. Folks, I'm empowered to cut the price in half. Yes, a buffalo nickel shows you acts bound toward . . . ."

His articulation lowers, and the townies lean in to hear better. The vacuous are gannet-like lapping up his discounted entries like cherry ice cream on a humid summer day.

"Coney Island. The park for the languorous metropolitans. Glamour. Ugliness. Titillation. All within the confines of the tent. You will leave with fond memories. However beware, some stuff inside might become part of your most nauseating nightmares."

Vivian's act is used as "the blow." She is imitating a peepshow by wearing a skin-tight nylon leotard that skirts the "blue" regulations. The nubile's striptease is an hit. The farmer's ankle-biters drool at the unclothed sexpot in her prime. Once the hooting and whistles abate, she lip-syncs a saucy, blues melody scratchily playing from the music box and propels a garter. She proffers naughty images for two bits and then ducks from sight.

As soon as the portière draws to its logical conclusion, the bumpkins are told that, for a "trifling pittance," a bonus can be added —a glimpse at her sinful boudoir. Joseph gathers the nickels and draws the drape to lay bare a four-poster bed below a naked oil painting of Vivian. The vixen is nowhere to be seen. The ignorati murmur with dismay, shepherded out past a plaque reading, "This way to see the egress."

Once past the tent flap, townies mill around the wagon housing Dr. Irwin Davis's Oddity Museum. Next to a rack of curative salve, patrons consider an ancient mummy, the "Really Real Frog Band," and a gaff depicting a "Devil Spawn." The province's natives know they are being cheated but do not care; visitations are so rare to their out-of-the-way tracts. Some leave with a curio—a cane with a porcelain head shaped like a dog, a chalk-ware hula girl figurine, or a kewpie doll.

Occasional scrapes with the law and irate lumberjacks occur. A few acts ebb and flow as the convoy inches toward civilization. As the seasons turn, the carnival dashes from Toronto to Florida. Vivian has skimmed a heap from the suckers, enough to buy a second-hand Model-T. The triad joins their companions at the encampment.

It is a combustible backdrop when the itinerant converge in the "The Sunshine State." A decadent, three-month sabbatical is excessive —stimulated with moonshine, marijuana, and other diversions. The winter months are normally the time for carneys to trade dodges, have cabinet card photos printed, and commission banner artwork. The unskilled laborers play poker into the wee hours and doze during the day. Riggers and musclemen arm wrestle for bragging rights. Concessionaires skim the catalogs restocking cheap prizes such as water-pistols, pencil toppers, and jawbreakers.

Joseph registers at the motel while Alvin and Vivian take a jaunt as the sun is setting. Aroused by the throbbing engine, she accelerates the car. Alvin is a little perturbed at her devil-may-care attitude as she steers onto a country road and pulls into a deserted mango orchard.

"Oh, our gas tank is empty," she says in a kittenish tone, as she lays out a blanket. "My goodness. I worry that gators shall come upon us and feast. You will protect me, right?"

After a moonlit, al-fresco frisk, she puts her frock on and drives back at a less-fraught pace. When car pulls into the motel, a bonfire has been lit in the empty lot across the street. Alvin and Vivian join cast members from disparate concerns around the circle. Joseph, his eyes shining brightly, is excited to be accepted by the carneys. His nose drips from bumps of cocaine. As the mason jars containing amber liquid are being shared, shop-talk swirls around in the air like a murmuration of starlings taking flight.

"Those townies were upset. I warped the lips on my milk cans. If you threw the ball just perfect, it would drop in, but a win was uncommon . . . ."

"That hamlet is full of simpletons; almost as smart as a bag of hair. I banked stacks . . . ."

Another jug rounds the circle.

"This affectionate vintage reminds me of my former fiancée, Juliana the Mexican ape-girl who works for the Miller Brothers," a manikin interjected after a sip. "She envelops you in those fuzzy limbs, as if you were a baby being swaddled."

The fire-eater whose painted banners proclaim him as "The Inflammable Wang" stokes the embers and lights a cigarette with a coal he's grabbed from the hot pile of wood. The peculiar attraction hails from Des Moines, not Shanghai as billed. Perplexing misshapen silhouettes oscillate on those sitting in the circle. The comments turned to what municipalities were trouble, where the law was lax and other notes gleaned from the tour.

"That sheriff is a cantankerous weasel who confiscated a whole shelf of prizes 'cause his brat nephew cried about bent sights . . . ."

"But, if you are unlucky enough to be nicked, that is the place. His wife cooks a spicy fried chicken," interjects a woman named Octavia who is a snake-charmer by trade. She uses an obscene hand signal. "Can't really tell you if I preferred the thigh or the breast . . . ."

"Have you heard of 'The Magnificent Zazel—the Human Cannonball?' Her path to fame is a unique one."

The assembled odd bunch whisper "Zazel" as her name is spoken by an aged juggler as he twirls bottles while relating her contribution to circus traditions.

"Her real name was Rossa Matilda Richter and as Zazel, originated our credo. She first uttered 'The show must go on.' In 1877, the 12-year-old girl transforms into a bona-fide box-office hit. Shot from an artillery gun at The Westminster Royal Aquarium Playhouse, Zazel blasts 18 feet into a net. The gambit had never been attempted before, and Victorian theatergoers provide raucous acclamation for her unflinching bravado. The ingenue became the chatter of London-town. The diminutive female assumes headlining cachet in a short while."

Joseph is all ears, as the historical anecdote is one he has not encountered before. The story conjures a memory—*the performer he saw in Chicago as a child must have been Zazel.*

"In filled to capacity theaters, the pint-sized funambulist saunters to the lip of the barrel. She disappears into the muzzle. A fuse is lit by the device's inventor. The tension grows as the yarn infused with potassium nitrate and sugar burns ploddingly, sparking the gunpowder. The subsequent ignition is deafening enhanced by tumultuous strikes on tympani drums."

The elder retelling the legend, passes the carafes he's been twirling to the thirsty watching the bonfire. Each bottle of hooch goes a different route; passed through the winter camp fire-circle, individuals quaffing the shine as he continues his re-telling."

"The chance of being hurt during the gimmick is low, as the cannon is not a functional ordnance. The falconet, created by an Italian illusionist named Guillermo Farini, conceals a spring loaded tension plate that sends her airborne when released. The precariousness is in the landing. Zazel's renown grows, and she doodles her name on a lavish covenant with P. T. Barnum to conquer America."

More rotgut jugs are uncorked and sent around the circle. Some are drunk already.

"After an unfaltering run of decades, a recent hire miscalculates the angle and she misses the net. A nauseating whump is heard as she lands on sawdust. Harlequins bear her twisted physique away. Her courageous concluding words inspire us. Facing the Angel of Death unflinchingly inspires us to live while we can, for three-score years, and ten is a short time. We commemorate her sacrifice and honor her by presenting the Cannonball act today. Let us toast to the magnificent Zazel."

The camaraderie guzzles and then chants in unison.

"One of us . . . The show must go on . . . One of us. Zazel . . . Zazel . . . Zazel . . . ."

On Alvin's left is Edward Leedskalnin. He owns a modest lot near the encampment in Florida City and mostly keeps to himself. The wanderers engage him during the winter to restore their mechanical rides and gewgaws. He has an erudition for engineering and cobbling together parts in a Goldbergian way. Kelly hands him the fifth containing 80 proof tommyrot.

"No. T-Tank you." The thin character with a heavy levantine accent passes the bottle to his left. "I am Edvvard."

"Alvin. From where do you hail?

"I vvaz born in Reega in 1887."

He tells of heartbreak. His family was poor. With no formal education, he taught himself to read. At 26, he is betrothed to Agnes Scuffs, a girl ten years less his age. His "Sweet Sixteen" cancels the matrimony an hour before the ceremony. Grief-stricken, he immigrated and devoted himself to process lumber at camps in the Pacific Northwest. Clinicians confirm he has tuberculosis and prescribed sunshine to cure the "Consumption." His disability indemnity is parlayed into a few acres in Florida. He built a shack to live out his days. His malady went into remission.

Leedskalnin plans to contrive an homage to his infatuation. He lacks the nuance of the English language to portray his feelings in elegant poetic form; thus, he efforts to express his love in stone. A sculpture garden comprised from the pure oolite he mines from his land will validate his love and declare his undying devotion. As he quarries granite, the raw material compulsory for his marvelous feat, he thinks of cosmic construction, and creating a modern megalithic monument.

If anyone was outside after midnight, a sharp ear might have detected the clank as pick-axe hits stone. Hidden in his compound, he is whittling the boulders into unorthodox shapes. Spectacular beauty is being hefted from the poundage as he plans a grand and symbolic ambit for his creations. He yearns for the day his former fiancée will again be at his side.

"Have a good time. I am going to bed," Vivian says while handing over a pint. Edward takes a cursory glance when she stoops to kiss Alvin's cheek.

"You haff a big heart, habibi. Zis is so vvonderful," Ed takes a dinky nip from the bottle and grins. "Try not to lose zis feeling, yalla, ok?"

The Latvian, haltingly and then rapidly grows enraptured, nattering on transcendent mysteries—Atlantis, the Pyramids, and Rapa Nui.

"Easter Island? I went ashore on that isle while on the *Helene*. I am at a loss to tell you how the natives put those monstrous statues into place."

"I vveel tell you vvhat I know, wallah . . . ."

Chapter 9 –
Stretching the Boundaries

"Just like jazz, life is better when you improvise."
— George Gershwin

86

In 1921, Emmerling is the weekly supplement editor for *The Sunday World*. The position comes with an expense account. He is still endeavoring to help 26-year-old Kelly become more notable, but the right fit is elusive. He asks a colleague for a favor; insert an innocuous profile when he feels Alvin has not been in the glare of the media's eye recently.

EVENING CALL — APRIL 8, 1921

LAST NIGHT TITANIC'S "SHIPWRECK" KELLY SAVED A CAT FROM A TOWERING OAK TREE. NOT CONTENT TO BE A HERO TO JUST HUMANS, HE HAS EXTENDED HIS RESOURCEFULNESS TO FELINES IN NEED.

Alvin dutifully cuts out and pastes the notice on a page in his memory compendium. Joseph has him functioning as a hardhat on the Cunard Building. Vivian is snooping in Emmerling's writing room when the boys are globetrotting. She has found a safe but cannot solve the combination. She tries a different permutation on the tumbler whenever she is unchaperoned.

"We can take the car upstate and catch Al Wilson's Cloud Riders. His finale is a night flight through a fusillade of pyrotechnics," hints Emmerling. "He is a pal. I am sure I can ask him to take you wind borne."

"That sounds socko. I would certainly . . . ."

"I forbid you to fly," lambastes Vivian as the expression on her face becomes sour. "I regret letting you go to war. Those contraptions are deathtraps. Swear to me you won't. Ever."

Alvin promises he will not, mostly to placate her. She is correct; the skies are clogged with notorious aces. A glut of planes has made the supply inexpensive, even though, the machines are exceedingly precarious. A week rarely goes by when a manifestation of god's will or an unusual stroke of fate crops up, the code tapping out erratically across Emmerling's teletype.

Laura Bromwell sets the mark for the fastest air speed flown by a woman, averaging 135 m.p.h. She is well on her way to becoming famous. The former N.Y.P.D. dispatcher twists her aircraft into 99 consecutive loops working for "Ruth Law's Barnstormers." When Emmerling's profile of her is printed on June 5, 1921, she is unrecognizable—a charred body resulting from a fiery crash a day earlier.

Bess Coleman becomes the first African-American woman to own her plane in the United States on September 3, 1921. In France, she becomes a knowledgeable master in aviation intricacies. She is a tour de force. After performing hell-raising dives at Curtiss Field, Joseph interrogates her for *The Harlem Beacon.*

"Miss Coleman, tell me how this career commenced for you?"

"Three years ago, I said, 'What the hell.' I had enough for a ticket, so I took a boat to France, bought an airplane and shipped my property back. You would be amazed at how many flyers there were eager to give me lessons, and school me in their frenchie ways." She winks. He understands her inference. "There ain't no racism in Paris. I am 'Queen of the Sky.' No one is going to keep me from being airborne. You wanna come, handsome? I can give you a good ride, sugar. Like I said, they showed me some things."

He ignores her invitation. "Why risk your time on earth? Doing this dangerous profession?"

"Cuz 'up' is the only place without prejudice, honey. The wind does not care what color my skin is. I am as close to freedom in the clouds as a woman can be in this world. If I die, at least I will be doing what I love."

In California, Roscoe "Fatty" Arbuckle is celebrating signing a million dollar multi-film commitment with Paramount Pictures on September 7, 1921. He garners an unheard of salary, well deserved for the roly-poly actor who popularized the pie-in-the-face gimmick. He drives to San Francisco's Saint Frances Hotel with a cellaret in the trunk that conceals 20 quarts of contraband booze. A raucous, three-day bacchanal materializes, and, as a result, a partygoer, Virginia Rappe dies from a ruptured bladder.

The supposition does not dwindle away that the 300-pounder raped the aspiring actress. Demands for an arrest mount as legal eagles argue that a nefarious element is attempting to extort the defendant. A

Grand Jury indicts him, alleging he forced himself upon the unwilling 25-year-old.

Hearst's *San Francisco Examiner* prints reams—mean tittle-tattle that their readers pounce upon like an alligator chancing on a dozing flamingo. Rumormongers publish that the actor "splattered her with his enormous girth." Other scandal sheets dig deeper, some even giving the impression with unbridled glee that the actor "uses a beverage container to stash evidence of the encounter." On the other coast, Joseph is complaining to his boss.

"You did not print my editorial? What about the concept of 'innocent until proven guilty?' Or 'no one is above the law,' and other things we hold dear." Emmerling demands an explanation from the editor. "Sure, Arbuckle is in a predicament, but our stance should be to advocate for him. Free speech. Freedom of the press. My sources say he is being squeezed like a lemon in a juice press."

"This is the most commodious incident since the *Titanic* floundered. This is going to drive our circulation for years. Formulate the rumors, if you have to. You know the ignorati in California; ones who will debase themselves to say mighty untruths to earn a buck. That is why you have an expense account, and why you are paid so well. Dig us some real scandalous dirt. Fetch us something even the most disreputable rag won't run."

"I will not steamroll a man's good reputation to pocket a buck. Find another toady. I quit."

Once home, Joseph recommends packing clothes for a month of paid vacation. All three decamp while he considers his next career move. The troika checks into a Florida motel. He sows the seeds he has nurtured from the carnies to sketch out a narrative on his portable typewriter. Headway toward getting Alvin noticed is again in limbo, and that does not sit well with his wife. In intimate settings, she continues to tarnish his partner.

"He is writing stories, except yours. He keeps you busy so you won't notice."

"I rarely spend for anything, and he keeps my name in the public's mind."

"One day, those scraps of type he produces will not buy you a Scotch."

"He plucked me out from obscurity. I am meant to be someone, but I hear you. If he does not some gain ground soon, we will rotate to another tack."

"How much time do you want to wait? You are not growing any younger."

Alvin is reticent to jettison the security that his compact provides. Vivian makes some mental calculations. *I see an opening and I am going to force that chasm further apart. Playing the slow game is a good idea. He gets upset when I push too vigorously.*

They return to the city after a month in the panhandle and things get back to normal.

Joseph heads with Kelly in tow, to Pinehurst, North Carolina. There, the world's preeminent sharpshooter is entered in a skeet shooting competition. Upon visiting the gun-range on April 16, 1922, Annie Oakley uses her Winchester rifle to break 100 clay targets apart in a row. The 62-year-old poses for Emmerling's camera to accompany his profile for the *New York Morning Telegraph*. Alvin, on train ride back, does talk about his anxiety.

"I appreciate your help. Are we are still on track to lift me to be a someone? Like that lady shootist?"

"Yes. You must be patient, my Crackerjack. Stay close to me like Bingo the dog does to Sailor Jack and soon we'll grasp the prize at the bottom of the box."

Vivian belittles him later, when she hears the results of the confabulation.

"He is a jackass. We could melt into the heartland," she encourages. "I have squirreled away a little. We could buy a farm and raise a family."

Alvin hesitates, and she tactically retreats.

At Long Island's Mitchel airfield, Hubert Julian unclips his harness and parachutes from a plane piloted by Bess Coleman as she turns in a spin. He loves the stimulating liberation that the silk canopy brings as he floats to earth. Weeks later on September 3, 1922, "The Black Eagle" bounds from a hatch while wearing a crimson jumpsuit and snatches at the ripcord. Tooting on a golden alto-saxophone, Julian gently lands at St. Nicholas Park. He is beset by Harlem's youth like a colony of ants swarming over a discarded bread slice. Beseeching him for attention, children are thrilled to be near their knight in shining armor—a hero whose skin matches theirs.

Amelia Earhart achieves an altitude record for women on October 22, 1922. Emmerling formulates a laconic poem that runs with her grinning portrait in *The Concord Daily Tribune.*

> *She flew high, not afraid to die.*
> *14,000 feet is a height that is neat.*
> *Amelia, celebutante to girls,*
> *that is a feat you should oft repeat.*

Joseph gifts Vivian and Alvin tickets to the premiere of "The Sheik," starring Rudolph Valentino. The Italian actor has had a meteoric rise to become exalted—an on-screen Adonis. His angular kisser graces numerous movie magazines. The Rivoli Auditorium is stuffy, and like a prickle of pigs at a trough during dinnertime, is bustling with patrons. The "Latin Lover's" visage fills the screen. A matron faints into the aisle, and staff remove her.

"You think that women will faint when you glance their way?" Vivian laughs. "You are blessed to have one who cares."

The three head south to fritter away another December in Florida. Ed unfolds the blueprints for his striking sculpture: twisted chairs, heart-shaped sundials, and remarkable alien symbolism to be chipped out from solid stone. Alvin does not understand how he will move it.

"I am sure you vvill not understand, but I tell, " the artiste winks. "A complex calculation suspends gravity. Tapping into zee planet's magnetism, polarity iss transposed. When zee circumference iss at zee exact phase of horizon, vvhile compensating for zee drift oof continents, I heft zee limestone as if beach balls by changing dere gravity."

"What?"

Chapter 10 –
The Unshrinking Victors

"*Actually, we're just glorified flagpole sitters.*"
—Warren G. Harding

The "Charleston" is the frenzy that is sweeping the social clubs in 1923. A 16-year-old Bee Jackson, a chorus girl from the "Ziegfeld Follies" popularizes the tousled gambol. It seems as if all the flappers and debutants across the nation are reproducing her unbridled steps.

The "Scuffed Floor Loving Cup" is won by Alma Cummings; waltzing for 27 hours at the Audubon Ballroom at West 165th Street in Chi-town. Dance marathons blossom as the ultramodern activity to bring in observers like a gaze of raccoons dining at an open trashcan. Hoofers gyrate endlessly until slumping exhausted to the floor—eliminated from contention.

The craze catches on. Vera Sheppard twirls 69 straight hours, pirouetting on the ash slats. The "American Organization of Terpsichore" files a legal case asking to criminalize these meets by avouching the skirmishes are perpetrating an "irresponsible obsession with disgraceful gyrations." Their rationalization fails to convince the magistrate and no injunction is enjoined. Emmerling takes Alvin and Vivian to the "cut a rug" revelry in case the infatuation has appeal.

"What do you think, Viv?"

"Too many stepped on toes. We do not need a toaster or some other cheap consolation. There's only one cash prize, and winnowing out all the chaff is fickle. I wish I'd thought of this scam."

"I hold more gumption and staunchness in my pinkie than those twice my size. I figure we can beat a bunch of amateurs."

"That is it!" In the twinkling of an eye, Joseph has finally gained clarity. "Endurance. You outlast all. A modicum of sophistry will seduce the aggregation. You have got the pedigree and the smartest promoter since Barnum."

Vivian cannot repress her odium. She loathes his self-aggrandizement and rolls her eyes.

"Spectators pay to watch these skirmishes and witness the sorties," stresses Emmerling. "When a horrendous smashup is imminent, the natural thing for people is not to avert their gaze. The fear of missing out on an atrocious donnybrook would be lamentable. Keep 'em sticking around, and we can harvest plenty of coin. The problem is quarrying a vein that will distinguish us from the common larks. We need a trademark."

To proselytize his upcoming film release "Safety Last," comedian Harold Lloyd has paid Harry F. Young to escalade the Hotel Martinique facing Broadway at West 33rd Street. On March 5, 1923, at least 20,000 watch in Greeley Square Park as the man weaves up the side. He loses his grip trying to wrest himself onto a ledge. Shoehorned in close quarters, the assemblage recoils in unison as gravity seizes hold. Newsreels film the 10-story mischance and the horrific aftermath. His hysterical widow is strapped to a gurney and rushed to the nearest hospital by ambulance.

The deceased was "The Bad Risk" club's founding member. The society is comprised of practitioners with unsafe vocations, to whom surety companies will not sell certain insurance policies. The membership pools a portion their pay to underwrite themselves. Their governing council awards his wife a settlement, establishes a college fund for his two sons and arranges for his eternal resting place.

At 71st and Broadway in the Alamac Hotel's "Congo Room," Joseph raises a toast. Even though prohibition is in full swing, "The Capital of the World" is lax in the statute's enforcement with an estimated 10,000 unsanctioned establishments.

The hotspot is a chaotic, expressive jungle milieu. Flamboyantly tinted murals exhibit expatriate artist Winold Reiss's uninhibited design. Diners swing to Paul Specht and his Hotel Orchestra in a tropical fantasyland. The dining hut walls are adorned with war clubs, ritual carvings, and tribal lamp fixtures. Reposing in figural chairs, which Alvin recognizes as being based upon Tahitian tattoo symbols, the party orders dinner.

"This state will enact an ordinance," postulates Vivian after a sip of the grape. "Soon it will be unlawful to negotiate skyscrapers by hand as these 'fly' do."

"It is not an original trifle, but the throng was transfixed, watching. We want to find a niche for you Alvin," assesses Joseph. "As a boy, I read that when P. T. Barnum opened his American Museum in 1864, he was the best attention-getter in the world. Downtown, where the financial district is today, near Broadway, Park Row and Ann Street, you could see a real fee-jee mermaid, 'Grizzly' Adams's California Bear Menagerie, Chang and Eng—the Siamese

Twins, and Colonel Fremont's nondescript Little Woolly horse among other singular exhibits. Three days prior to the opening, Barnum hires a lad to perform a Herculean task.

Every 15 minutes, the young man transports a painted gold brick to the opposite corner. He is unresponsive to anyone who asks questions. After another quarter-hour, he moves the brick to the next corner. Crowds stop to watch the ritual. Newspapers cover the happening. This activity continues 72 hours, even by torch light to the same schedule. Finally, he walks up the steps to the facility with the gleaming rectangle, and knocks on the door. Phineas opens the portal, and invites him in to see the exhibits for free. He then orates to the convened crowd what is to be seen at 10¢ a head. See, once he had their attention, he began the bally, then came the real money . . . I met Barnum, you know, in 1888. He was famous when I was a kid . . . He wrote pen-pal letters to those who shaped the opinions of our world—Queen Victoria, Abraham Lincoln, Cornelius Vanderbilt, Thomas Edison, and Mark Twain all called him friend."

"If you want to keep eyes watching, you need to have a gimmick that is dangerous," points out Vivian. "You have to avoid harming those who stroll below, so you aren't arrested."

"We figure out some activity that looks very risky; more than the act really is," contributes Alvin. "As dicey as painting a flagpole."

"Tons of those in the city," interposes Emmerling. "We could open a painting concern and then just twiddle your thumbs at the pinnacle . . . maybe even for days . . . until you attract attention . . . We say the paint has to fully dry before leaving." They chortle at the absurdity of the thesis.

"Let the courts weigh in. I love it. I think that a cliffhanger would gather in eyeballs," admits Vivian. "Freeloaders might hang around. But who is going to pay you? Donations are unreliable."

Emmerling is flummoxed by her concession. Their suppositions have never brought her positive comments. *Perhaps she wants me to fail so she can insist she is able to do better, and take Alvin away from me,* he calculates. *Maybe she's just been sipping too much wine, which has loosened her tongue. I will have to pay closer attention to her actions.*

Phillip S. Roberts

"I will arrange guaranteed compensation from the merchants. We will print handbills and purchase advertisements to draw a considerable number. The premise will be pricey. We need equipment and inculcation."

Vivian's soothsaying becomes de jure. Worried that copycats will multiply, the local aldermen approve an ordinance forbidding such extravaganzas without obtaining expensive insurance policies and permits. Ascending structures by hand is now prohibited. It is a far too excessive tariff for most to have the wherewithal to exhibit in the city limits, but Emmerling foresees it will not dissuade the most avaricious opportunist. The punishment for scofflaws is heavy—$500, ten days in jail, or both.

Joseph establishes a license for the *Specialty Painting Company*. Alvin is designated as chief steeplejack. If threatened with incarceration, the plan is to produce a work order.

"You might want to practice? Before you embarrass yourself in public?"

Joseph is in a rare place, agreeing 100% with Vivian.

"If a sparrow collides, you will be a grease spot to be cleaned by the sanitation unit," she continues. "Can we somehow take the hazard out of this equation?"

"Edward Leedskalnin can fabricate us a safe dingus," puts forth Alvin. "He knows science stuff."

The trilogy pile into the car and, after two days, are greeted by the isolated artist in Florida. He considers their quandary and assesses Alvin as a couturier might for a gaberdine suit. *How much did the man weigh? Could the spire bend, and still be thick enough to bear his weight?*

"Et is possible. I vvill haff to calculate ze parameters."

Promptly, Leedskalnin sends word he is done calculating. His recommendations are for several apparatus. For stationary poles, he suggests a molded rubber English-riding-saddle-type of construct with stirrups that can be strapped on a round finial. He notes this one is not the safest option and only good for a fugacious sit.

Second, when the staff that can be wrested horizontal, Ed thinks amalgamating a tire drum on the tip and attaching a heavy wood platform to the rim before pushing it upright is best. In theory, he thinks this option is much more stable.

Third, he is convinced fashioning a temporary stave measuring 12 feet and forged from three iron tubes that secure with butterfly bolts is the best solution. Affixed to the metal section, a locking platform with a padded cushion. A tripod base bolsters stability. On the bottom section, a spring tension peg locks the spear securely in place when the legs are deployed. Sandbags add stoutness to the design. The rig can fit in a car trunk. He adds an arm with a block and tackle.

To allay her consternation, Leedskalnin recommends Alvin to prop himself up with a rigid batten. The rebar will add sturdiness in heavy gusts. Joseph hands the artist a partial payment. Ed projects six weeks to construct the foundation and accessories. Vivian is alarmed that the men are agog with the dizzy dodge. She feels that she could state a zillion excuses to not continue.

"Can he rig you a harness? You will never be able to live normally if you forge ahead with this folly."

"I want to be celebrated. We need their focus on me. A safety device would be counter-productive."

"We will have to tote that heavy ore over all of creation."

There is consideration of the pros and cons as well as other logistical problems, but while quixotic, the process cannot be halted now. The equipment is in the boot. Joseph is in an affable mood. He sketches out a tale as the automobile scurries back north.

"To continue where buffoons dare to tread is a divine mission," relates Emmerling. "Whims arise in an instant. In 1910, I was consulting Willie Hammerstein. He went into hock to import a rail-thin Algerian chanteuse. Emilie Marie Bouchard goes by 'Polaire' and uses a cobalt eye shadow with a jaundiced foundation that enhances her emaciated, ghostly image when the lights shine from behind. The femme-fetale has a silver nose ring. She favors bedizened taut lace and corsets that give her a wasp-like waist. When the stage-lights turn on, she resembles a skeleton."

Kelly imagines what the attenuated figure looks like.

"Her saucy Parisian warbling did not translate well into English. Sophisticates do not come to hear her throaty vocalizations.

The would-be impresario is shedding shekels like a longhair cat in summer. I submit we tailor her portrayal. She goes from being billed as "Paris's Most Treasured Singer" to the "Ugliest Woman in the World." We don't tell her, and she doesn't know, for she is not fluent in english. Placards are pasted on outdated posters, and the simple herd comes in droves. Admirers purchase her elaborate flower bouquets begging for her considerations. The Palace Theater sells out 12-weeks straight. Hunger for extrovert's act blooms, and she demands additional emoluments. He says no and she threatens to sue. I was present as Hammerstein rebuffs her, packs her suitcases, and drops her at the pier to board a boat bound for Europe. She cries as he hands her tickets. Spitefully, we hire a repugnant female impersonator to portray the mademoiselle for the ensuing two months of the engagement to rabid spectators. After receipts tank, we paper the light posts with playbills announcing a culminating month. All the drag performances sell out, patrons petitioning to gain standing room admission. The climax is much more expensive than any ticket ever sold before on Broadway, and every one is snapped up as soon as they become available."

"Why don't you focus on that stuff? It's far more captivating than your usual bullshit."

"The story holds several nonconformist views that the ordinary will not fancy. Readers prefer straightforward allegory in black and white, not shades of gray. The public wants alacritous gratification. I just finished a profile on racer Michael Matthews. The 'Madman' spent 48 hours circling the track in his Essex Super-Six Cylinder until plowing into the hay bales piled on the perimeter."

"Is he okay?"

"His car flipped and caught fire. He is burnt to a crisp, but surgeons give him a 30% chance to live. I hailed him as a lion-heart; pushing the boundaries of persistence."

Kelly brings forth an opposing opinion.

"I think two days will pass in the blink," says Alvin, full of braggadocio. "In my youth, I spent many tedious stretches on a yardarm, keeping a weather eye out. I dare say I could settle for a week."

"Maybe when you were a boy," retorts Vivian with incertitude. "Half the time would be in the pitch black. Are you ready for that?"

"My mental resoluteness will conquer the world," replies the ex-sailor. "The inner essence can tap inexhaustible willpower when a human is endangered."

She scoffs at his insanity. *Yet, if he becomes famous, he can buy me any house I want,* she schemes. *Let's just see how this goes.*

"Do you know who 'Oofty-Goofty' was?" asks Emmerling. The riders in the backseat say nothing, so he continues. "This is exactly how I heard his story. Leonard Borchardt was born in 1852 in Frankfurt. The family wished to immigrate to America but possessed barely enough Deutschmarks for two fares so their youngest is smuggled aboard, packed in a steamer trunk. A purser catches the stowaway and the *S.S. Fresia's* boss has him shovel coal as part of the ship's black gang as payment for his crossing. The demanding drudgery turns his skin inky."

Alvin understands the derogatory reference about stokers. He has done spadework in sooty boiler rooms.

"Once on dry land, he joins the Cavalry. His commander, who considers him a 'darkie,' details him to clean the stables rather than teaching him how to fight Indians. Chagrined, he goes A.W.O.L. and joins a nomadic circus of sideshow attractions. He tends to the carthorses that move their wagons. One piercing night, he recedes from camp, sneaking away with a mare. While foraging for their dapple, the freaks come upon a disquieting, gruesome scene. Clothing is strewn around the terrain, and multiple teeth bites scar the half-devoured animal carcass."

Vivian is intrigued. *Where the parable is leading?* She wonders *—How does Joseph know this tall tale? Is he making it up?*

"This is what I read in the *San Francisco Vindicator* archives— In 1884, mischievous rogues raise a brightly tinted tent in Golden Gate Park. Handbills are tacked on anything that does not move. Rotating orators hoarsely repeat their selling speech, even by lantern-light. 'A must-see,' these carpetbaggers vocalize to their herd. The blither is captivating, and innumerable dwellers spend their pennies on an entry. Once in the interior, a saga emotes from another intermediary. His apologue lays out a claim that an undomesticated hellion was captured in the snarl of the Borneo jungle. This fierce behemoth dreads no animal. During the patter, bars rattle, and loud yowls are audible from behind a cloth barrier."

Alvin is rapt with attention. He imagines the screams of the imprisoned peculiarity.

"Apprehended at an exorbitant cost, entrants will be able to inspect the ferocious jungle cannibal in captivity. The cloth is lifted from the cage sheltering an untamed bogeyman. A complex muddle of tresses obscure his nakedness, and the monstrosity is uncloaked. Ladies in the front row lose consciousness as he howls in his preternatural tongue. Rancid scraps of raw horse flesh are thrust between the bars that hold the wretch under lock and key. He shrieks while ingesting the meal. Without notice, the door of his skookum house clangs open. Blood curdling howls continue as the ogre jumps from the elevated prison, causing onlookers to run to the tent's vent. The ticket selling takes place from dawn until dusk. The gate receipts pour in; his handlers dine like potentates as he devours fetid meat. Inhumane treatment allegations tickle the ear of the judiciary who orders the rancorous performance shut. When the law appears, the co-conspirators have skipped town, leaving the tormented, broken creature to take the fall."

Joseph's description of the modified geek show has Alvin feeling sick to his stomach.

"The bodach is stretchered to the County Hospital, fully coated in sticky tar and horsehair. His cries can be heard for blocks when doctors use scalpels to cut the mane from his skin. He yawps as they attempt to loosen the caked on ooze by laying him in the sun. Nurses turn him, dousing his skin with lukewarm sponges. The patient is mishegas and wails endlessly. *The San Francisco Chronicle* sends a reporter to his bedside to hear his woeful tale. The misfit now refers to himself in the third person. 'Oofty-Goofty did this. Oofty-Goofty did that.' He carries the printed square of newsprint in his pocket until his last day."

Vivian is hanging on every word, knowing that the rejection must be imminent.

"A local watering hole in San Francisco hires him as a bouncer. He tries to curtail a skirmish, but his intervention ends in abject failure. Projected into the thoroughfare by the ruffians, he is surprised the incident causes him no setback and he seems immune from harm. He feels impervious and takes to announcing himself as the "King of Pain," the "Prince of Poke," and the "Jester of Hurt." He allows anyone the chance to whack him for a fee. Oofty-Goofty even prints a menu advertising the blunt objects he carries around in a bag. He entertains any speculation to earn easy scratch including having himself nailed in a crate and mailed to Sacramento to win a $20 bet. Attempting to bully a wheelbarrow from California to Oregon, he reaches as far as Pinole before quitting. To win $100, the buffoon leapfrogs from a cliff near the San Francisco presidio. Military police arrest him and hold him on a charge of desertion. He avoids Leavenworth when a tribunal deems him infirm."

Joseph smirks as he retells the confrontation. His smile reminds Alvin of when Captain Jacobi told him tall tales about Emperor Norton and other larger than life personalities.

"He emerges at the 'Bella Union Burlesque Hall' in a Shakespearean lampoon entitled 'Borneo and Juliet.' When he tries to kiss his co-star, 375 pound 'Big Bertha' Heyman, she knocks him senseless with an iron frying pan to end the skit."

"Most cheaters worth their salt have heard of her," interjects Vivian. "She is the 'Queen of the Swindlers' who combined the 'Lonely Hearts' dodge with the 'Spanish Prisoner' con. With a bullseye on propertied Jewish mensch, she represents to be affluent but cannot access her accounts in Prussia. She demands suitors prove their seriousness to court by investing in her real estate gamble. As security, she opens a valise crammed with jewelry, which is traded out for paste replicas during an Rabelaisian tryst. She misappropriates the loot but is not arrested as her victims are too embarrassed to admit that they fell for her diddle. By and by, one exploitable does press charges. She is arrested and convicted. The villain is ordered to lease a storefront 'South of the Slot' and confess her sins in public until her fine is paid. She tells of her numerous heinous misdeeds in gaudy detail once an hour to collect pennies. To end her busking, she warbles a lascivious aria before the drapes are pulled. Have you heard the phrase, 'It is not over until the fat lady sings?' That is the origin. She ruined numerous families and squandered several estates. One day, the wicked harpy goes away startlingly. She is never to be heard from again. Was her evanescence foul play or of her own volition? No one knows for sure."

Joseph is itching to draw an inference but holds his tongue. He had not heard that part of the tale before and continues his narrative.

"One night, a 'Brahms and Liszt,' Oofty-Goofty, bumps into pugilist John L. Sullivan and spills his pint of beer. He refuses to apologize. 'The Boston Strongman' raps a pool cue's heavy end on his skull. Not phased by the impact, he dares the mick to swing for the fences and hands him his hickory baseball bat. Sullivan accepts the wood club. The jarring, crushing thump ruptures four vertebrae and the formerly indestructible one walks with a limp during his residual days. Drifting with a number of oddities, his demands grow. The camarilla strands him 60 miles outside Amarillo. Crawling in blistering torridity to town, he begs the Texas oilmen to whack him with their tools for a drink of tequila. He goes from being on the cusp to inconsequential."

"I have a sneaky feeling that is the end of the story," asserts Alvin. Joseph is indeed ready to conclude.

"Oofty withered without fanfare; penniless, and hopeless. The loss of laurels—you do not want any part of that. My responsibility is to make sure you will not suffer the same end."

Joseph arranges an open air test at a theater in Bayridge. He trades for an advertisement in the local newspaper that runs a week prior to the sport's establishment.

BROOKLYN EAGLE — AUGUST 30, 1923

THE WORLD HAS ACQUIRED A MANIA. A FELLOW WILL SIT TOMORROW AT THE ELECTRA THEATER ON 3RD AVENUE FOR A FULL DAY AND NIGHT. WHY? TO DISPROVE THE COMPREHENSIVELY HELD CONVICTION THAT FRIDAY THE THIRTEENTH IS ROTTEN. THIS INTREPID GALLIVANTER WILL SEQUESTER. ALVIN "SHIPWRECK" KELLY IS DECLARED AS A DIGNITARY. THIS "KING OF THE SKY" WILL SURPASS ANY PERIOD OF DOGGEDNESS. BEAR WITNESS AND EXPERIENCE HIS STAUNCH BRAVERY DURING 1,440 MINUTES ABOVE THE MARQUEE. REFRESHMENTS WILL BE FREE FRIDAY.

Perhaps it is the lure of the free soft pretzel, or boredom, but 16 of the 5,000,000 city's taxpayers gather to watch Kelly on a perpendicular staff. Emmerling's invited newspaper colleagues fail to attend. He is noticeably tense as he inches toward the vertical. This is to be his introductory shindig, spent unassisted in the night. Alvin feels as if he is on lookout in the crow's nest on one of Alfred Bullhop Stormalong's ship masts, hewn from timbers so large that they have hinges to avoid scraping the moon. He considers his current task equal to the folklore sailor's epic battle with the giant deep-sea Kraken.

"You are gonna break yer neck, you nincompoop," razzes a heckler. "I think you will be gone before nighttime."

Joseph requests a sidebar with the doubter from the scrum and hands him a food voucher. From his abutment, Alvin holds onto the sides of the wooden square. He's memorized a speech that Emmerling has written to commemorate this auspicious juncture in time.

"I must tell you that strength is in the mind, not the heart," advocates Alvin to his sparse congregation. "I aspire to be the earth's most accomplished athlete—a paragon of today's most modern gladiators. Have no trepidation for me. I have survived many blood-curdling moments. You are watching the genesis of a modernist sport. If you return tomorrow, you shall see that I remain."

Sprinkles of clapping come from beneath. A few consumers focus awkwardly at him before venturing through the lobby to catch the film. As the day progresses, less notice him in brumation. Blackness encroaches and celestial bodies shimmer on the anchorite. His aerated musings keep him company as the uncomfortable accommodation props up its charge. Joseph persists being insomnolent by having a nearby cafeteria constantly refill his cup of Folgers.

When the late movie lets out, the neighborhood groans, energetic with sounds he has seldom noticed so intelligibly. Shoe leather scuffles on pavement. An ambulance siren tails in the distance. A traffic signal clicks as taxicabs rattle by. A infant bawls. A brightly lit sign pulses. Clothes rustle on a fire escape. A dog howls and others respond to its call of the wild. Faint strains from an aria from Puccini's "La Bohème" scratchily plays on a Victrola in a nearby apartment.

Alvin wills his limbs into submission, stemming extraneous movement and latching his digits onto the rim. His brow and clothing are drenched with perspiration. Just 26 feet from the unforgiving concrete, he has peace and quiet as his intellect wrestles on questions.

Is my life better since I abandoned the sea? If Jacobi had lived, would I be skippering my own ship's helm, and plotting my own course? What if I had lingered before debarking Carpathia? Would I have still met Joseph? Was it chance or divine intervention that my boxing losses led to a reunification with Vivian? How serendipitous was it that fleeing California had introduced me to Edward Leedskalnin? Am I on the right trajectory? He doesn't come to a conclusion, but hopes he's chosen correctly.

He touches the tiny bag around his neck that conceals his coin —its presence reassures him. Kelly is sure neither roommate knows its hiding place when he is not wearing it. Collywobbles wash inside his mind. He regains his composure and does not jiggle nor fret.

Transcending intervals is Alvin's ceaseless task. He recites verses from the bible to keep mentally agile and prays to let god know he is penitent for his sins. He counts cars and then stars. Stumblebums bumble on the avenues without taking notice and he meditates upon if he is invisible or not. He has to urinate and stalls until he squirms. With an immodest smirk, he unzips, and relieves himself in the air. Time is ticking by too ploddingly, so he removes his wristwatch. He belts out a dirty whaling shanty for his own pleasure.

Alvin Kelly went away to sea,
Girls a many he loved, I tell ye'
He took his pole and put it in the hole,
She were his downfall, I tell ye'
For now he got a wife and nine bay-bee . . .

He hopes to fascinate the early morning rush, but the straphangers are too self-involved to chat. He is purposive, although his teeth chatter in the chill. He has survived the opaquest hours of his profession. Now, he takes aching muscles to a soft mattress at the

The Luckiest Fool on Earth

apartment for an equal time as he was in air. When he arises, his feats are immortalized in *The Brooklyn Eagle*. The print is snipped out of the newspaper for posterity and he adds it to his book of clippings.

"Once another tries what we have perfected, we'll harvest fistfuls of green," prognosticates Emmerling. "It is a spot in time to anticipate with pleasure."

Alvin jots a "thank you" to let Leedskalnin know that the steel construct had managed well, and he plans to take in the grandeur the mystic is coaxing from the stones on his next visit. Kelly is convinced that the following is true. *The Latvian must know some ancient prowess to coerce the boulders into the air. Could he be persuaded to share his technique of creating a miracle with me? If so, the skill would ensure my impregnability and take all the chance out of my new passion.* In the next weeks, they sit in the five towns of Long Island—Cedarhurst, Hewlett, Inwood, Lawrence, and Woodmere. He and Emmerling scout locations outside the Big Apple, bringing their ministry of stoutness to other counties in the state.

Kelly finishes a full day on a stake near the "Old Hudson River Line" on September 25, 1923. While he has been immobile above Albany, Henry Sullivan breaststrokes the English Channel in 27 hours and 25 minutes. That record becomes well-known about, while his own attainment is barely noticed. He is woebegone, yet a few have come to gawk at his absurd finial. Erudite in his opinions, he warns those walking below from his angular slant.

"Be careful while crossing against the signal as some automobiles hastily brake. I saw a ghastly collision from here but, fortunately, no serious injuries."

The next evening Emmerling announces he is going to Atlantic City for the preview of the F. Scott Fitzgerald play "The Vegetable."

"His inner circle is heading to see the play before the Broadway debut. Mae West and I have tickets," gushes Joseph gleefully. "Please don't wait for me. I shall be out late tonight."

Left to their own devices, Alvin and Vivian quarrel regarding the finances and the direction their lives are going.

"We need to have a place for ourselves," states Vivian. "Far away from his influence."

"I know we do not have the extra funds to buy you a house yet. Joseph has slogged endlessly for me, but I don't think we are making much money yet."

"I have consulted my Ouija set and the apparitions foretell what lays ahead," proclaims Vivian. "You slave away, and he ends up 'rolling in it.' You deserve what you are due."

"When was the last time you bought anything with your own funds? He takes care of all our needs. Did you ever do anything nice for him? You are here as part of my covenant. I told him I love you."

"Maybe we could try to have a baby. I'm certainly of the age when those things happen."

"I would certainly like a boy, but . . . "

Vivian is frothing and the squabble escalates to ululating and scratching. She grabs a kitchen knife, and he disarms her. After she slaps him, he struggles her into a clenching embrace to stop her from hitting him and they kiss. The danger has added flavor the way spice does to a savory stew. Feelings erupt into a mélange of perception; every nerve in their bodies burn. The gentlest touch is an exceptional spur of the moment to be savored for the intertwined couple.

I've never felt more in love, he meditates. Kelly goes to the kitchen as she showers, and pours himself a glass of water. He makes a resolution. *I'll watch our finances with more diligence. I've saved $75 so far and feel prosperous. My golden treasure is well hidden. It is certainly not a good plan to unveil it. She'd harangue me until I cashed it in to put a payment on a house. Then, my good luck charm will be gone forever.*

Joseph is home. He crosses the threshold, lightly-sauced, humming the hit tune, "Yes. We Have No Bananas."

"The play was a horrible bunfight. A postman ends up residing in The White House to non-hilarity. F. Scott was crestfallen and Zelda was mullered by the intermission. I was chatting with *The New Yorker* magazine's theater critic. Alexander Woollcott invited us to a social function. Dorothy Parker and other members of the 'Algonquin Round Table' might come to his soirée."

Emmerling yearns to be a satellite, gravitating in the planetary orbit of the informal writing society but lacks the reputation or cleverness to be in their midst. He addresses Vivian.

"Promise you will not embarrass me by boozing too much. This is important."

"Despite Alvin working all the time, I got absolutely nothing fashionable to wear," pouts Vivian ignoring his plea. "I want a turquoise chiffon dress, a calot-style hat, and matching shoes. If I wake early tomorrow, I can have my hair and nails done, too."

Kelly looks pleading at Joseph who unenthusiastically peels bills from a stack. She takes the cash and leads Alvin by the hand back to the bedroom.

The next night, the upperclass eat canapés from silver trays while insider tips are traded of which commodities to buy and sell. Among the intellectual gathering are Harpo Marx, actress Tallulah Bankhead, and fashion designer Hattie Carnegie. Joseph is feeling uncomfortable until his crony, Mae West joins the gathering to contribute to the small talk. Another round of Southside Fizzes is poured. Vivian is already on her third drink. She is tipsy—feeling no pain, and waves at a passing guest asking to dance. Alvin tugs at her arm, and she woozily slurs something he cannot discern.

"I want to play golf in Egypt," gleefully purrs a tipsy Vivian. Her pantomime golf swing verges on toppling a server's tray of hors d'oeuvres. "Wheeee."

"You know that kingdom is one sprawling sand bunker, dearie." Mae condescendingly snipes before turning to Alvin. "Your wife is squiffy, honey."

"You saying I am dumb?" stammers a blottoed Vivian. She looks crosseyed at Mae. "I ain't no bluestocking."

"We're not married," responds Alvin.

"Take my advice. Don't."

Vivian spins wildly, turning toward Mae with a raised fist, but trips, and falls flat on the floor. She cusses loudly. Their chaste host, upset due to the imbroglio, asks the group to say their farewells. An inundation of drunken insults ensue while dragging her out. Alvin and Emmerling push her in the back seat of the taxi and sit on either side.

Mae hops in the front with the driver and the cab speeds toward Joseph's residence.

"Imbecile. His fancy words have you bewitched. He IS a bad man. You want glory. Why? I tell you, it is far better to be unknown. No one pesters you."

Vivian passes out. The cabbie idles the car as Kelly escorts the muddled lady upstairs.

"She is in the land of Nod. I doubt she will be sure of much when she wakes. She has never been able to handle the potent stuff," apologizes Alvin as he hops in the front seat. "I will just tell her she had a terrific time and was the élan vital of the whole shebang."

"Say, I could ingest a highball," directs West. "Driver, take us to the '300 Club' at West 54th."

Upon arrival, John Barrymore, the Shakespearean actor is leaning on the bar and chatting to "The It Girl," Clara Bow. Mae's compadre, "Texas," the proprietress of the shady nightspot buys a round of gin cocktails.

"Have you ever met George C. Parker?" inquires West. Joseph has heard of him, but Alvin has not. The actress continues her boozy monologue.

"He is the artiste who sells the "Brooklyn Bridge" to the trustful. In fact, you can see he is heating his branding iron right now. The con-man will show land grants and sales receipts that pretend to be the real stuff as he weaves his web of lies. He has been defrauding the unsuspecting since 1886."

The hoodwinker unfurls charters from his valise and shows them to the unsuspecting victim. Splosh flows between hands, and the flim-flammer drifts away, scouting for other squabs to displume. Joseph takes a mental reminder to base a character on him in a novel.

"Vivian would be dazzled," adds Emmerling as he spins a silver dollar on the bar. "She would be bending his ear. He sells the lie that the unimaginable is millimeters from their grasp. If I tell you this token is rare, you will be imprinted to be convinced it is."

Alvin wonders, *Does Joseph know about my lucky charm? Should I find a better hiding place? Was Captain Jacobi being truthful with me?* Finishing their brandy sour Sidecars, they clear out just as the fuzz raids the joint. When the sun rises, Vivian's memories are a hazy blank. She does not clearly recall anything that happened after arriving at the festivities.

Joseph requires Kelly's likenesses on the tallest heights to accompany articles, so he befriends crane operators to facilitate the lifting as he takes photos. He frequents a tavern where the third estate knock-em-back. He meets a foreman who finagles his man a few day's wages as a riveter's aide.

Emmerling questions the "Playboy of the Sky," Carter Buton so he can include him in a retrospective he is writing on pilots. The blond-haired, blue-eyed flyer has a dashing profile. He is a capacious draw at air meets with the fairer sex. After their palaver, they lift a glass in Hackensack. Buton wants to equip a biplane with a strut for Alvin to ride. Shipwreck is hung-ho.

"I think it would be a grand eccentricity. A stunt that no one could ever beat."

"An ascendancy unlike any other, for sure. Complete with pictures at 5,000-feet. I will charge you just $500. That price is quite a staggering bargain."

"I will mull over your offer." Emmerling calculates the variations. "Can I let you know?"

June 13, 1924, is a Friday, and Kelly is in Pittsburgh. Watchers are spellbound as he takes in the sights of the "Paris of the Appalachians" from 98 feet above the street. It is a sweltering day, and he is attempting to cool off. He leaves his seat after extending his mark by 24 hours.

Possibly the whole of Harlem is watching on the embankment at East 139th Street. Entering the cockpit on July 4, 1924, "The Black Eagle" is ready to take the first step in his pilgrimage to Africa. Emmerling is lingering until the takeoff for the *Amsterdam News*.

"I re-named her 'Ethiopia,' and have refitted the seaplane for an expedition to Liberia's capital, Monrovia," the pilot booms into the microphone. "I am confident that the transatlantic . . . ."

He is interrupted mid-sentence by the entrepreneurs who sold the plane to him. The reprobates insist he still owes $1,400 in gasoline and storage fees. A hat is passed. The former owners take what is raised and leave.

Hubert Julian lifts from the ripples like a Kingfisher after a dive to loud cheers. Half a minute into the holy crusade however, one pontoon loses a bolt. The unbalanced machine staggers into Flushing Bay. After backstroking to safety, the soaking aviator gives a cocky statement to reporters.

"I will obtain another plane . . . . I will fly to the promised land yet, god willing."

A few months later, George Oakley is clawing onto a ledge. The daredevil attempts to jerk himself to the 5th floor by hooking the rounded part of a cane on a bicycle inner tube being held by his wife. She loses her grip and he takes a header to meet solid Philadelphia concrete. With her husband dead, she leaps, the day's second fatality.

That same day, Joseph is waiting for the qualifying heats to finish at the Syracuse Speedway so he can bang out an interview with Indianapolis 500 winner Jimmy Murphy. The racer skids sideways. The collision disintegrates the wooden rail that runs around the oval. A oaken shard pierces the windshield and enters his heart. Aficionados monitoring the race are appalled at the accident's aftermath. Emmerling's jocular feature turns to a mournful swan-song.

"I was going to ask him if he would have you wave the starter's flag at this year's race. It is a shame that won't happen now, but I still have plans to improve your notoriety."

"I know you will try to keep your word."

Emmerling has gotten a supporting role for his folderol at the Virginia State Fair. "Mable Cody's Cavalcade of Pilots" is the main draw. Her maniac aeronautic display includes a multi-phase move called the "Breakaway." The 30-foot leap from a racing plane to a racing automobile is combined with wing-walking, acrobatics, and suspenseful dives.

Alvin dialogues on physical fitness to watchers from 13 feet above the grass field. Vivian peddles a "Revitalization Tonic" below. The medicine is 90% intoxicants. She has refined her sales speech.

"This cordial invigorates the heart muscles, animates the liver, and regulates the kidneys. The potion restores health and vitality while curbing fever. The mixture heals diseases to internal organs in two shakes of a lamb's tail. An absolute cure-all healing blotches of the skin and pox of rare kinds. The consumptive's rejuvenator fortifies the system. This cure-all easily is worth $1 a dose. However, I sell my concoction to you just a few pennies more than the production price— a whole tube costs 25¢."

Alvin devotes a night shift at the American Theater on December 3, 1924. He is higglering for the Erich Von Strohiem film "Greed" starring Zazu Pitts. Intermittently he dangles what looks to be a $5 bill on a string near commuters and giggles as gluttonous beings partake in a mad scramble. A few swear upon realizing the paper is a worthless advertisement and shake a fist at the prankster far from where the steam flows through manholes and street grates. Emmerling has brokered a flat fee of $250 to put their finances in the positive for the first time. Kelly is anticipating a hot chocolate and a visit to the Southern peninsula for a promised December vacation.

A week later, Leedskalnin informs them he has some improvements to their equipment. He adds a cushion, a four-foot augmentation and a pulley system durable enough to lift an onlooker for a brusque consultation. Joseph pays Ed. After three weeks in Florida, the trinity roves the coast northward by the light of a Full "Cold" moon.

Chapter 11 –
The Explorers Club

"It's no use going back to yesterday, because I was a different person then."

— *Lewis Carroll*

"Save your peepers," cry the many peddlers hawking useless smoked-glass. "With these you can safely watch the eclipse."

The Woolworth Building opens their observation deck at dawn on January 24, 1925. The moon is due to meander on a path blotting out the sun. The crème de la crème draw opera glasses to gaze at the corona despite scientific warnings not to. West of 96th Street is shrouded at 9:11 a.m. Swathed in an eerie light of gloaming during the totality, Joseph reminds Alvin he is preparing for the day when he will beguile as well. Later, the writer pours milk into his bowl of Washburn's Gold Medal Wheat Flakes and starts to relate a story.

"In the early 1800s, a rag called *The Sun* was well read in Manhattan. While reputable editions sell cheaply, this creation is expensive. Crammed like sardines in a tin, the words are laden with unsubstantiated insinuation. Subscribers read the preposterous output and chortle. The four pager outsells the other publications, and the proprietors are living on easy street from advertising revenue. One day, the front page is dominated by heavy uppercase type."

ASTRONOMICAL REVELATIONS BY SIR JOHN HERSCHEL.

"Observed by a very big telescope in Argentina, the dynamic magnification reveals the moon is teeming with inconceivable sentience. Unable to be seen with the naked eye and credited to an English astronomer, the description of the lunar veneer is improbable. Viewed by the polished convex lens, dense growth forests with surreal flora and wide lakes filled with tangerine-hued serpents come to light. Scientists observe bat-winged celestials worship their incongruous deities in sacred temples. Gigantic unicorns and beavers battle across the wastelands."

Alvin butters a piece of toast while the enchanting fable unspools before him.

"The next day's imprint spotlights the abnormal disquisition and details more strangeness on our nearest satellite. Lavish verse explaining the scientist's theory behind the ancient culture thriving on our planetary neighbor are put into print. Owners expand the page count and bump the cost double while being unable to procure enough raw pulp to satisfy demand. Every edition sells out. Competitors print that the investigation is without honesty and deviant fiction at best, but the serialization is read by men, women, and children. Five weeks after the initial installment, sales dip. The author ends the chronicle by reporting that the exaggerated spyglass was moved to research a nearby celestial body. The ferociously magnified heat of the star burns the observatory and thus the chance to learn more about the alien cultures is finished. Sir John, the ascribed astronomer, exhausted from all the looney questions, sues for slander and wins his case. *The Sun* refuses to print a retraction and pays the damages quietly. The hoax spawned a division of followers who understood the report was fake but hankered after the thrills anyway. Readers preferred harmless recreation from the real horror that abounds in our world. What does 'truth' mean anyway?"

Vivian cannot answer that question.

Joseph's current job is helming the leisure section of *The New York Telegram*. He churns out reams, rehashing the boisterous notices that stuff his file cabinet. He eschews a by-line in favor of his independence.

Emmerling schedules a day aloft in the Elmhurst area on February 13, 1925. The four-story construction holds the "Benevolent and Protective Order of Elks–Lodge Number 878." The group is raising funds to build their National Memorial and hope his originality will bring in prospective members. Alvin will mimic "Simeon the Stylite" on the building. Vivian suggests a ruse to add to the gig.

"I will bring a date. When he makes a pass, you assist me," she plans. He nods. "I'll be dispatched to give you a kiss. You announce, 'we want to be married.' You do, don'tcha?"

The Fraternal order is escorting prospective members on jaunts of their headquarters and end on the uppermost floor. Alvin is reaping the benefits from a modest inquisitiveness in his unstirring locus and shifts into a standing position. Vivian shows with a redheaded abetter.

"He's a stunning beast," she beams. "What a tiger, huh, Jimmy? You got any of that in Brooklyn?"

"He's boring," her co-conspirator says in his Irish brogue. "You know what is terrific?"

Her confederate is squeezing her behind too tightly and a bit too lasciviously. She yawps as Kelly rappels halfway down and boots at the fellow who retreats.

"Come and face me if you have the nerve," pleads Alvin while her hired hand takes a hasty withdrawal. "Send her up so I can thank her for letting me defend her chastity."

Lifted and duly motivated by the gawkers, she plants a smooch on her saviors cheek. Smattered clapping comes from the brotherhood.

"It's the real McCoy. True love. Please, someone send for a preacher," jokes Alvin. A collared man steps out from those watching.

"You are a beautiful twosome," he drawls. "Did I hear you wanna git hitched?"

Alvin nods in assent. She has hired a minister as part of her deception.

"Then, I declare you're married. You may kiss the bride."

A lensman frames the lovers suspended and canoodling. Back on the ground, Vivian arranges for the photograph to be mailed to her and settles with the clergy who hands her a marriage certificate. Alvin announces that he is ending his obligation early to consummate the conjugal bond.

"Congratulations," fumes Emmerling as he stomps out. "You two numbskulls deserve each other."

"It did add oomph," Vivian points out later. She lies, telling Joseph the marriage is not legitimate. Still, his feelings are hurt that he was not apprised beforehand.

"I would prefer if you let me handle the planning," Emmerling says acidly. "Phew. That was wasted effort. I would have arranged more press and more hoopla."

"You set the rules," she admits while crossing her fingers behind her back. Vivian is hiding her effervesce, recognizing Joseph's possession of her husband will now be tenuous. "We can re-enact the sham if you want. It was a fun contrivance."

"Jacobi should have conducted the ceremony on the ship," Alvin complains later when they are alone. "I love you. We should tie the knot for real."

She assures him that eventuality will happen soon.

Their nuptial night enfolds in a profusion of pleasure. Days later, Harry Gardiner escalades the seven-story Princess Martha Hotel in St. Petersburg. The 55-year-old basks in the noise vocalized by the 8,000 who have come to see "The Original Fly" waving from as high as a peregrine falcon can soar before a dive.

Alvin is going to grace the outcropping at Rialto Theater on 7th Avenue on May 12, 1925, for 13 hours. After setting the equipment, he and Joseph chat with the owner in the projection room. A flabbergasting sequence is flickering on the silver screen. Gladys Roy and Ivan Unger are volleying a tennis ball on the wings, while Ruth Law pilots the biplane, zipping through the welkin.

In June, Alvin and Joseph are packing their equipment in Saginaw after three days stuck in equatorial calms. Wiping the sweat from their brows with handkerchiefs, below the freshly laid asphalt is odoriferous and the humidity is oppressive.

"This town stinks," Alvin's words are in earshot of gawkers. "I would rather be in East Lansing."

The aphorism is put in the write-up. The city's dwellers scourge and pillage Kelly for having the effrontery to disparage their fair home in letters to the editor. Emmerling reads the unkind press, knowing even bad publicity can be used for a positive purposes.

"You cannot buy the razzmatazz that those yahoos gifted us. We'll be able to charge triple when we come back."

An invitation to a social bash at the Explorer's Club is in Emmerling's mailbox. The next day, he rents a cheap tuxedo for Alvin and tells him to be ready when the chance materializes.

A bloc of the idle meet in the institution's quarters at West 76th Street. In their inner sanctum, prominent gentlemen with rank take part in their monthly "smokers." Their active days are far in the past, yet the "blood-thirsty" cannibals repelled continues to distend in number in the next retelling.

The privileged cabal lounge in plush chairs eagerly debating the veracity of the clues leading to riches. The codgers whisper of bejeweled ziggurats buried under the sand in imperial Persia, fabulous golden ruins lost in the Bolivian jungle, and treasure-laden barges sunk near Fiji. The fraternity gossips about a new member surveying Africa.

The sophisticated erudite shuffle to an inner sanctum toward an aromatic snifter of cognac. Lushly curated the club rooms boast taxidermy safari trophies, brush-stroked-masters, and brittle maps. A utility pocketknife from Teddy Roosevelt's 1913 Brazil exploration and other artifacts of glory lay in the complex's well dusted glass cases. The shelves are stuffed to the gills with tattered medieval crusader's diaries, embellished Mayan codexes, and translated fragments of the "Kitab al Kanuz" collected by anonymous executants. King-sized ivory tusks frame the mantle, taken so many years ago that the specifics of the hunt are hazy.

A fundraiser is being held to benefit Senator Hiram Bingham, the archaeologist credited with the rediscovery of Machu Picchu— refuge of the Inca high-born in the Peruvian Andes. The invited are academics, intellectuals, and a few scribes. Attendees will be treated to a speech as well as an indigenous and unconventional repast.

The chef has outdone himself; the lucullan menu consists of the most distinctive fare. An appetizer of roasted Patagonian rodent is followed by Mexican Caldo de Quimgombo. The main course is Senegalese hippo stew and rice. Alvin jostles the delicacies around with his utensils, refusing to taste the fare until a palate cleansing raspberry sorbet is plated. An after-dinner liqueur is poured as speechifying gets underway. He sips that.

Stories swirl around like a wake of buzzards picking at an opossum carcass on an Arkansas highway. Joseph introduces his companion for prospective admission to curmudgeons chatting in regard to major advances in scuba diving.

"As Voltaire once wrote, 'Life is a shipwreck, but we must remember to sing in the lifeboats.' This is Alvin Kelly of the *Titanic* disaster. He lifted a lantern on the bow until the boat went to the depths. Ignoring the penetrating squalls in the North Atlantic until nearly submerged, he leapt into the arctic seas. He dog-paddles to a dinghy, near demise from the cold. He now embodies the spirit of a modern frontiersman. I advance his ingress into this esteemed federation."

"Stuff and nonsense," mocks a geezer with prominent muttonchops. "He would have been drawn into the depths."

"No one can live in such hibernal," joined in another contrarian with a handlebar mustache.

"I can acclimate to any boisterous climates, and storm-tossed seas," pronounces Alvin firmly as a few others gather. "With the fortitude to persevere in the face of the harshest weather patterns, I proved my prowess. I have held fast during godawful gales from Mexico to Madagascar. Chased by a cargo cult on an atoll nearby the Chilean coast, I avoided the headhunter's pot. I had no relief, except dew I sipped from a leaf. If the mind is inclined, the world will be forced to submit."

"Gentlemen, I say put his bearing to the test. A club banner is waving above this building? Can he sojourn at the brink, say for the weekend? No breaks. No frills. Three days," continues Joseph. "In a hour, I can have the tools brought to prepare the flagpole."

Emmerling asserts he is flush enough to match any sum and puts forward the wager's simple terms. Once set in place, withstand 72 hours and win the bet.

The beam is yanked horizontal and a tire hub is welded on the ball. A vinyl stool from the Square Diner in Tribeca is secured to the rim before being raised perpendicular. A rope and a basket will remit provisions. Club members scrutinize his position in case of deception. The Augean task is the topic the community chitchats about. Alvin climbs the pole and sets himself.

Members politely clap as he poses, confident he will budge. The longest he has balanced thus far is one day. This will add a full 72 hours to his lore. When he does not acquiesce in 30 minutes, or the second hour, or the third, his watchers grow bored. A day ends and then drags toward another. Alvin waves at the few baffled observers who denied his stickability.

Mist at dusk rejuvenates the sentinel. He studies the reading material sent from his manager; "True Detective Mysteries" magazine. The inaccessible man partakes no solid fare except a few orange slices. When he has to relieve himself, the reclusive figure signals for an amphora. As time elapses, he is victorious and a sporadic gathering congratulates him at the base of the pole. The bettors square their obligations with a sanguine attitude. The dividend adds up to $300.

The club's director explains, "the application to join their membership is denied."

"Those snooty bastards are upset we took their money. A few more solid showings and we will be rich as Henry Ford. I have a real story to transcribe to run in the Sunday edition. How are you feeling?"

"Good! I could have extended the sit longer."

Entering the living room, Vivian is at the table—shuffling her tarot deck haphazardly, practicing forcing cards from the pack. Alvin passes her a $100 bill.

"You are like a bad penny—no sense," she says as he sits.

"Tell my future."

She has him cut the stack and deftly pulls three pieces from the bottom. The stiff cardboard is turned with a flourish—the Emperor, the Fool, and the Hermit are on the tablecloth.

"The cards portend your providence. The king of dunces stands. A charmed divination . . ." She pulls another rectangle—the Tower appears. "An engrossing incident at the precipice is more consequential than steadiness. Millions will hold a fondness for you."

She weaves some other wifty mumbo-jumbo and he gawps at her moon-eyed across the table as she gathers the pasteboard.

"Joseph has dates set in Flushing and the East Village."

"You sound like a halfwit town crier relaying that the British are coming, 20 years after Paul Revere." Vivian, wearing her "not impressed" countenance, is resolved to drive a wedge to widen the rift between the friends. "Grow a pair, 'Square John.' It is obvious, he's manipulating you."

Alvin's favorable outcome provides a temptation to other promoters to join in the sitting sweepstakes. Theatrical agent Jack Curley recruits himself a solid prospect—a bodybuilder, Alfredo Smith. He is nicknamed "The Italian Stallion," but during his first test, a sudden hailstorm swirls. A golfball-sized clump of ice knocks the 18-year-old senseless. He gravitates from 24 feet above to six-feet-under. Curley flees the state to avoid arrest.

Steeplejacks, hardhats, and other assorted trades are trying their mettle at Alvin's knack. Bearing colorful monikers, these interlopers barge into a territory not exploited by the innovator and erect an unsteady structure. "Shipwreck" despises these pretenders and worries their practice will dilute his freshness. Anticipating lawsuits, Joseph has his legal shingle devise him a form to send demanding an immediate cease and desist of their actions.

Alvin is reclining as a catspaw flurries in from the bay on March 11, 1925. From Red Hook, he can barely see Lady Liberty's lit torch. He savors this solitude in the starlight when the city quiets. Taking in a bird's-eye scan, he adds to his repute. When he dislodges from his spot, a few newsies surround him. He feels awkward during their inquisition.

"Those of you who are acrophobic, know that I skylark for the fun," he clarifies to the coterie. One of Joseph's colleagues asks the sitter his opinion of Al Smith.

"If he watches the right polls," posits Alvin. "Someday, he could become president. The office I work at is the highest in the land. I should have my mail forwarded there."

The commonwealth gives little notice to his onerous act, but the quip gets a little ink on page four. The flagpole sitter pastes the sliver of black type in his binder.

"Say, that's a nice approach. We will re-use that quote to gain some noise during election years." Joseph feels a little jealous he hadn't thought up the comment. As much as he considers himself smarter, he admits internally that Kelly has a spark of brilliance for promotion. While deliberating about forthcoming sessions, Alvin verbalizes another genius thought.

"We should establish a friends of 'Shipwreck' club."

Short sits rise and recede like tidewater without incident in the next months as the prospects of turning a profit starts becoming more plausible. On a muggy August day in midtown, Alvin is not feeling cool on his unreliable nestle. Usually he is caressed by gentle puffs that flow at his level but today not even enough blows to rustle a grass blade. Vivian and Joseph assist in his hydration, taking turns sending moist sponges and butterscotch candies to his job-site.

He monologues until his throat grows hoarse. He repeatedly talks about many issues; however, most of his jibber-jabber registers upon deaf ears.

Children are taken with the prophet, staring until being herded away by their guardians.The evening cool ensues. Tomorrow, he will descend, shake hands with a few fans, and then, partnering with Tsukuyomi-no-Mikoto, the Japanese moon god, retire for a deep slumber. This interlude is his longest domiciliation yet, and other work is on the agenda until the forecast turns too frigid.

Prior to the holidays, a Hollywood accountant inquires how much it would cost for Kelly to perform a problematic and dangerous stunt sequence.

"The total you want to pay is too low to consider," differs Joseph before he disconnects. "He'll call back. That cheapskate ran numbers for the mafia, but now he's pulling funds from the teats of the studio like it's a blue-ribbon winning Holstein at a State fair. He will give us what we want. He needs the shot . . . to finish some picture. We are going to the coast."

Chapter 12 –
At the Highest Vantage Possible

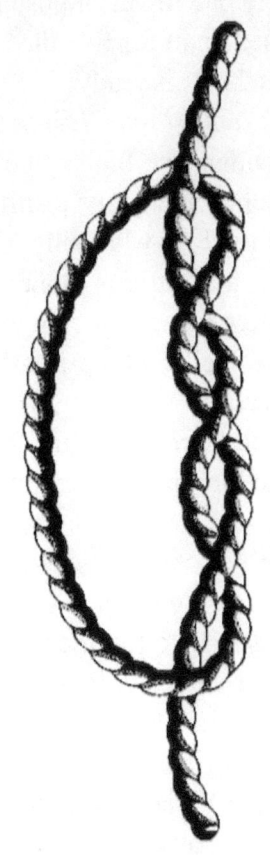

"Let me be the great nail holding a skyscraper
through blue nights into white stars."
— Carl Sandberg

Emmerling is induced to sell the concept of living higher than a skyscraper. He rawgabbits to merchants that Kelly's dauntlessness is on a burgeoning path and will draw a number to their shop. The year 1926 hatches, and a sit is scheduled at the Grand Union Market in the Vinegar Hill ward on St. Patrick's Day.

Alvin steps onto the Empire Theater outcropping in Port Richmond on April 12, 1926. He lowers a poster advertising the movie "The Devil's Circus" and settles in for five days of remoteness. If adversity should present itself, he is ready.

Joseph sends *The Staten Island Clarion* to his protégé. A blurb on page seven enrages the sitter—he fumes like sizzling lava solidifying in the tide. In Schenectady sits a similarly nautically-attired thin fellow with a shock of red hair who hails from the Bay Ridge area of Brooklyn. Fixed in place, that sitter is jubilant to be apart from his overbearing wife and his three kids. While he is irritated by his other rivals, Alvin despises Jim A. Kelly, who primarily bills himself as "The Irish Sailor," the most.

"The unmitigated gall," croaks Alvin. Others are trying his calling, but none exasperate him more. "Stealing my schtick is unforgivable."

Unbeknownst to Kelly, Joseph has met surreptitiously with the redheaded Brooklynite to embolden him as an antagonist. He makes arrangements with the local daily to run the report so Shipwreck will see it. A duel between bitter enemies will boost the trend to the forefront of the public's mind, he plans. If Alvin ever tumbles into terra-firma, he will have a plausible substitute to satisfy any prearranged bookings. Should Vivian ever attempt to bilk him, he thinks having a backup sitter in place is prudent.

"That goddamn nobody. Living off my fame."

Salty slang gushes out—disgusting terms exclusively fit for only the most tolerant ears. Emmerling's focus on advancing the opinion that his man is a rara avis is ready to bloom.

"I will not let some ass steal my image. I am going shoot that villain," the agitated stunter inveighs. "I don't care if I am ever released from prison."

Motoring north, his friends try to dissuade him from serious violence. He might be the monarch of resoluteness, but even he would not enjoy a prolonged spell in an oubliette. As they pull in to the township, his companions calm him sufficiently.

"You can bargain on the demoralized, and the desperate to try their hand at your expertise."

Alvin, however is full of haughtiness. He has aspirations.

"You are the champ," Vivian advises him softly as she clasps his hand. She gasps as she recognizes the sitter as an old confederate. "Hold yourself with the regal bearing, my prince."

His tranquil demeanor lasts a nanosecond. He harangues the false idol on the mandapam. He is indignant, yawping his foulest uttering at the wannabe.

"I was living in the sky far before you were in knee breeches."

"Leave me be, you pest," snips Jim. "I am trying to provide for my family."

The commotion does not dissipate. The doppelgänger glissades to confront his accuser. Bodies separate the enemies. Alvin pushes out of the clinch to avoid a glancing right. Cuffed and remanded for assault, he spends an eight-hour protraction in the penalty box. At court, the plaintiff involved in the brouhaha is nowhere in sight. The jurist counsels the defendant not to disturb the peace a second time in his jurisdiction. Without a complainant, Kelly is released.

On the domestic front, Vivian has found an irregular hobby that Alvin and Joseph both loath—mail fraud. The pair recoils at her skulduggery. She buys notices in the back section of sleazy pinup magazines that reap numerous responses from rubes. She implements the "sweetheart swindle," preying upon isolated rural farmers, forlorn widowers, and love-shunned schlemiels equally.

Communications flow into her many mailboxes. She posts handwritten letters packed with woo and, in some instances, a risqué image. She sobs about her loneliness and they respond in kindness. She is benumbed, and the abject wire her funds to buy a coat. When she propounds a holiday, her unrequited quarry—those lamentable men send rail tickets which she trades in for cash. She begs forgiveness, but her sick sister (or mother,) needs nursing. The clodhoppers send her checks to cover the medical bills. Alvin asks her to discontinue the ploy with disastrous results.

"You are going to be incarcerated in Sing-Sing, if you are not careful. Some sad sack is going to have a cousin who is a federal agent and blow the whistle on you."

"Keep your nose out of my affairs," she emotes coldly. She is irate, and he palpitates as her anger explodes like "Feu d'artifice" by Stravinsky. "I keep active while you loaf around. I am saving to buy our house."

Kelly's next commitment specifies three days on Max Schwarz's La Primadora Havana Cigar factory in Midtown. Alvin zealously rattles on to the wayfarers 15 feet away. He relates how much he enjoys the aroma of the stogie he is smoking.

Time crawls as slowly as an earthworm on concrete after a thunderplump. Emmerling ferries him trashy gazettes to read. On the precipice, Alvin thinks it is especially beautiful at dusk—a riot of twinkling permeates the canopy. Roistering on his purdah, he rests.

Wrapping his legs around the cable securing the sign, he gets into his catnap posture. Elbows rest on his knees with his pinkies in his mouth, he takes forty winks. Five minutes elapse before he marginally teeters, feels himself bite his finger and opens his eyelids. He re-balances, aware that a miscalculation will end his streak and maybe his aliveness. Recharging his internal batteries, he's saving energy for when he finishes his injudicious battle and the lingering ovations.

Under the stewardship of the Inuit moon god Anningan, he drifts to the time to come. He is being memorialized at a steel and concrete construct with an engraved bronze plaque placed in homage to his conquest of a western European menhir. Those stepping out, recognize him for the exclusive skew he has on the world. His expedition is uncomplicated, and he engenders others with a look at what a focused individual can perform. When the pessimistic surmise that his vocation is like herding cats, he will perform a miracle.

His woolgathering fades from sight like the three-card-monte dealer palming the ace. In the troposphere, the gargoyles affixed to the concrete leer vacantly and noiselessly at his lunacy. He conducts a one sided heart-to-heart with the stone grotesques to relieve the languor of his exile, sharing to no-one the complicated solutions to their inscrutable brainteasers.

He has achieved enough shuteye to continue his labor. A juice, cigarettes, and a muffin are shifted to his grasp with *The New York Daily News*. Page eight describes his evening in detail and he rips out the words to re-read later. While squaring his fee that afternoon on April 25, 1926, the boss gives Joseph a box of cheroots as a bonus.

Alvin's quotidian preparation entails a stretching and meditating regime. He eats sparsely as dieting is required on his catbird seat. No solid food is ingested two days prior to a stand and he sips chicken broth exclusively while aloof. Being unaccompanied is cooling to his inner being. Peace and quiet is his hermitage—alone in the hinterlands, dueling the savage, untamed universe. Kelly uses every second to good advantage, being unencumbered to cogitate leads to certain mania.

Just past May Day, the Henry Clay Hotel in Louisville has a setting deemed suitable for a stand. The bar is eased horizontally. Once the steel bolster is laid on the tar, an 18-inch tire rim is affixed, sufficient to subsist on after being pulled back to ninety degrees. Then with the scene set, Alvin crawls to his spot overlooking Kentucky. A traffic jam blocks the intersection at 3rd and Chestnut as a gathering stops to watch.

In June, Bess Coleman is in Jacksonville. Failing to cinch up her safety belt, her engine stalls and the Curtiss JN-4 lurches. "The Queen" is flung 2,000 feet, dead at age 34. The aviatrix had become an inspirational figure to her community who dare to strive for equality. Around 5,000 mourners pay respects at a hastily arranged memorial in Orlando, and afterward her casket is borne by rail for the funerary rite. An estimated 15,000 Chicagoans shed tears, shuffling past her final rites of sepulture.

After reading Joseph's take on Coleman's passage across the river Styx, Vivian becomes upset. His descriptions initiate a donnybrook as Alvin watches on in horror.

"He will splatter his head like a ripe casaba."

"He is putting his nose to the grindstone," rejoins Emmerling keeping his temper in check.

"The more tired he becomes, the more uncertainty there is."

"I agree it is problematic. As the pre-eminent name in his field, all during this summer, we will be raking it in."

"He is far too reckless," she complains. "A slip will make him a splattered blob. There wasn't enough of her to fill a 'Dixie Cup.' I will be a widow even before I have a chance to have a child."

Alvin considers interrupting but decides not to as she rages on.

"He can't buy insurance. He will always be poor with you taking the lion's share."

"He is well received. I guarantee that a ginormous cash-out is near. Others may try to replicate his province, but he is the spearhead who invented the game."

He directs his criticism to Kelly.

"Luck is volatile. I am the one that watches out for you in thick and thin times." Joseph has often expected Vivian's temper would boil over, and he has prepared. He swivels to jaw with Alvin's wife and tempt her greed with a carrot.

"I took you in as a favor—an addendum to my compact with Alvin. Neither of you lacks clothing, nourishment, or a pillow to put your head on. My duty is to aggrandize his endowments. In the morning, I will see my solicitor. He can craft a legal statement that Vivian will be your beneficiary with a lump sum for her 'contributions.' Say $2,000?"

"I will deposit that amount in a fund." Emmerling considers murder and adds, "But you won't be able to touch the money unless he dies . . . at his upright station."

"All-right, but if things become too iffy," lashes Vivian as she grabs a jacket and goes on the hoof out of the apartment. "He is earthbound in a jiffy . . . ."

Emmerling rephrases the original agreement. He rejigs the wording, retaining the right to pen Alvin's story. He adds an addendum that includes a clause in case of foul play. Each partner will also contribute 5% monthly to an emergency fund. As a minority participant in the corporation, they decide she will have no vote in their decisions.

The compact contains other protections such as relinquishing a per day penalty bonus upon termination to Alvin if Joseph severs their interrelatedness. If discontinuance occurs the other way, the agreement mandates he receives his portion, less her share. Joseph takes the document to his advocate to insure the legal wording is binding.

Vivian is not heard from for a few days. Where she disappears to, no one knows. Upon her return 72 hours later, she endorses the agreement. To celebrate the contract, Joseph transports them via the subway to the 7th Avenue station, to visit a bistro in the upper West side. The cafe, run by former Gibson Girl Evelyn Nesbit has added a discrete menu; certain teapots pour gin. The proprietress was involved 25 years ago, in what Hearst's *Evening Journal* referred to as the Trial of the Century. Emmerling returns to the narrative so both will know the hostess's tragic past.

"All of this came out in court, which is how I know the chain of events. Immigrating to the city in the early 1900s, she is a developing beauty and highly sought after as an artist's model. Her beautiful face adorns paintings, calendars, and advertising tins. Her alluring lineaments become iconic in the 'oughts."

As she walks by, Emmerling points out the matron. She is still stunning in her early forties.

"The ingénue acts in a small production. She meets Stanford White, a prominent exterior design consultant who is 40 years her senior. He becomes her benefactor supplying her living quarters and a maid while patiently grooming her affections. Reasoning he has impunity, induces her into a well-lubricated state with wine, and deflowers the underage model. He maintains the 15-year-old girl as his mistress until her guardian expedites her to a finishing school to separate her from 'unsuitable' admirers' like him."

"How do you know all about this?" Vivian asks.

"The details all came out during cross-examination at the first trial in 1907. I covered those proceedings for *The Washington Times.* Anyhow, while sheltered upstate in Westchester County, she is wooed by Harry Thaw, Jr., heir to a railroad tycoon's assets. He persuades his teenaged love interest to marry him in 1905, but, on their wedlock night, she is frigid. Refusing his affections, she laments her lack of virginity. Her husband is enraged at the sordidness she shares with him."

The waiter brings finger sandwiches. Joseph continues after he moves on to another table.

"I was mortified," the beauty explains to her mate. "I woke in an untied kimono, unsteady from a drugged cocktail . . . lying in my nakedness . . . humiliated and violated. The disgusting cad slumbers in the buff, clutching me. 'Had I a gun, I would have killed him and then turned the muzzle upon myself.' I felt so undignified."

The prospect of murder-suicide is appalling. Emmerling pauses while Nesbit approaches their table to exchange pleasantries. She has a charming demeanor and Joseph admires her poise. He inquires if she will consent to a "nostalgia" type-feature. The woman frowns at his boldness and excuses herself. He continues in hushed tones.

"The newlyweds run into White at a stage play. Thaw withdraws a .22 caliber automatic from a pocket and puts three lead projectiles into the architect's chest. After two court hearings, the jealous husband is determined by a psychiatrist to be 'unsound' and relinquished to the 'Matteawan Asylum for the Criminally Insane.' A bribe greases a palm and sends him out an unguarded gate. Thaw is suspected to be scot-free in Canada. But, she acts well, in spite of her horrible past," states Emmerling as he stares at Vivian. "It is possible to survive great anguish and remain conducive to polite society."

She wonders if he has researched her tarnished past but keeps her mouth shut.

Alvin domiciles a 48 hour tour of duty on a hardware store in Camden on April 13, 1926. Even though the Campbell's soup factory is a quarter-mile from his locale, he's been smelling the tomato aroma and pines for a bowl. He asks Joseph and the order is requisitioned in a thermos from the nearest diner.

"Ya know what part of Jersey I enjoy most? Leaving." Alvin quips while motoring across the Fort Lee span. Joseph will remind him to say that phrase during the next habitation in the Garden State.

The sufferance chicanery is catching on, but the finances are far from being in the green. Any gigs beyond "The Five Boroughs" are a financial boon. Alvin is treated like a king in some of the less populated cities in the tri-state area. The majority come out, messianic to pay a call on the "mad as a hatter" individual clad in the white livery. He waves from his whereabouts at the courthouse, school, or any other place with a pennant. Stardom will be won, even though naysayers and most others regard him a lunatic.

Brooklyn local Mae West is acting in her stage play 'Sex.' She arranges a box seat for Joseph. He gives her a favorable review to the scandalous dramatization she has authored. The two friends have a complicated bond. The acquaintances share an equal preference in both males and the written word. The actress teasingly refers to the rakish Emmerling as her "gigolo," and he chaperones "his gilded lily" around town. He brings her a huge bouquet after the final bow.

"Thanks, sugar. I just finished reading your novel's revisions, and I have some thoughts," drawls Mae. She notes a few adjustments and persuades him to talk to the newly created *Vanguard Press* in Los Angeles. "You wanna get marinated? I know a gin joint nearby."

Emmerling organizes some stunts for Alvin in California. Things do not turn out as planned with the manuscript. The vanity publishing house and press amalgamation offers to produce 2,000 copies of his novel to sell at 50¢ a copy. However, the fine print states Emmerling must purchase half the run in advance and flog them himself. He declines and tries to pitch his "Murder at the Carnival" story to the studios. Not one film producer options his treatment.

Vivian dines with her Los Angeles caucus who attempt to muster her to their side in a fruitful bait-and-switch scheme. She says no. Underworld partners, Milton "The Farmer" Page and Burt "The Barber" Busterno drift by their table to trying to hire her as concierge for their unlicensed casino tied to buoys, 12 miles out in international waters, but she declines.

"I am through with that," Vivian delineates her opinion in no uncertain terms. "I am pushing my chips all-in with the sitter."

Her friends doubt her resolve will continue to hold. Without a reason to relocate permanently to Los Angeles, the turbine bearing the three, chugs out of Union Station toward the Empire State.

The calendar becomes full as the yackety-yak that "carloads will be hypnotized by the odd sight," becomes an accurate prediction.

As a bonus, advertising banners are unfurled to flap underneath him. Alvin's need to be the "top-dog" is an irresistible motivation that impels him to loiter at loftier distances from the ground. His bauble is hidden in the bag around his neck, and he fingers the coin to reassure himself he is still on the right path.

The tour continues on to cities not visited before. Kelly is situated in the French Quarter of the Big Easy. Atop Loew's State Theater on July 26, 1926, he's promoting the film "Aloma of the South Seas." He has been sitting 27 hours and 30 minutes when a storm interrupts his thoughts. The refined ore in the canopy draws a bolt, melting the plastic alphabet. Firemen unfurl hoses to quench the blaze as Alvin packs his gear.

In New York City, Harry Houdini rests, immersed in a mortician-made mahogany box in the Shelton Hotel pool on August 5, 1926. After he releases himself from the tomb, the escapist briefs reporters. Emmerling is among those watching the subaqueous burial.

"I train on a combination of methods . . . controlled respiration and yoga," he leaks to Emmerling. He fails to blow the gaff about the hidden air recycler built into the lid. Joseph asks for a favor—let Kelly advertise the maestro's theater run. Houdini doesn't need the ticket sales, but Emmerling was a fervid exponent and agrees to the act of kindness.

Lolling on the National Theater at West 41st Street, mirroring Jesus preaching from the mount to the faithful, Kelly dispenses his philosophy, becoming erratic after several hours—running out of babble. He hypothesizes on a multitude of matters: a diatribe on the benefits of vitamins and his opinion on political scandals. As he natters, ground dwellers are enchanted by his animated presence. Depending on the quantity that gather to watch, he reacts to questions ferried to him by fishing creel. He's become a charming conversationalist, albeit one-sided.

"Today's sit is sponsored by Houdini. Tonight he is on this stage below me. He will unlatch any shackle and be unencumbered from its clutches. He will not say presto or abracadabra; he does not need magical catchphrases. He is better than that. Another question, please."

"Would you join me for a meal?" The utterance comes from out of nowhere. With a sudden poof of brimstone and the scent of cordite, the illusionist appears to materialize. "Shipwreck tells the truth. I shall escape as never before beheld."

The antiquated hoo-doo was prepared a few days earlier. Another smoke screen erupts as they duck into a casement and draw the blind painted to resemble a brick wall. It is as if the magician has dissipated into thin air. Riding an elevator to the street the two then come into sight in front of the venue.

"It is a shame Joseph has an another engagement," frowns Harry. "I appreciated his help when I was an unseasoned performer and enjoy his cynical sense of humor. After the jiggery-pokery, I am usually famished so we will see you and your wife at dinner. Now, if you will excuse me, I must pay attention to a few other pending business concerns."

The conjuring is mesmerizing, overflowing with dazzling illusion and escapes. The eatery is chosen for its elegant Old World cuisine. Crab-cake appetizers precede a Caesar salad. A jubilant menu is laid on the table . . . Wiener Schnitzel, asparagus, and potatoes. The owner personally brings an apéritif from his personal reserve with slices of *Schwarzwälderkirschtorte* for desert.

Cigars are lit. Harry flashes some covert hand-signs to his wife. Bess announces that she is going to "fix the shine on her nose" as Vivian rises from the table also. Houdini commiserates to Alvin on "being a slide viewed by a microscope."

"One day, you won't be able to dine without having some trick up your sleeve," he says as he puts his John Hancock on a menu for an admirer. "It is horrible when you begin to dread the adoration."

"You wafted playing cards to the balcony. I am acquainted with a Latvian who I think must know techniques to defy gravity. How might such a feat be accomplished?"

"I cannot say. Ancient texts say that Merlin used witchery to move rusticated stones across the English countryside to Stonehenge. Perhaps the Pharaoh's priests knew the solution to the paradox? The world would benefit if such knowledge were revealed. My art is a total bewilderment combined with scientific procedure. I am hoping my research will prove that the spirit continues on after we have shed this mortality."

While chatting in the salon, the women attune their rouge, eyeliner, and blush. Confidentialities that are imagined that ladies tell each other in the isolated convent that is the powder room are said sotto voce. Vivian tells Bess of her anxiety over Joseph and Alvin's quirky companionship.

"He is just a babe in the woods. My man leaves all monetary decisions to that rapscallion. He is streetwise and stalwart but still is a child. What he hankers for is what your husband has—fame. Is it taxing to be the mate of the world's most renowned personality?"

Houdini's wife produces cheap tin handcuffs from the recess of her handbag.

"Thin and worn from use," interposes Bess as she bequeathes the toy to Vivian. "These bonds symbolize everlasting commitment—manacles that the most masterful escapist cannot loosen."

The orchestra transitions into a Strauss waltz and both couples take a twirl before retiring. The theurgist says farewell at the curb before the parties separate. The women hug as Harry shakes Alvin's hand.

"Remember, my boy, the key that unlocks the heart's mysteries is patience."

In the boudoir, Vivian cavorts playing a torrid scene worthy of a bawdy novel. She ensnares Alvin in the magic restraints. She teases her inamorata with feathers, honey, ice, and other paraphernalia at her disposal. In total control, she prolongs her pleasure as he whimpers for mercy. Collapsing into each other's embrace, the two are spent after the lustful hubbub.

During the Summer months, Alvin travels to a few rewarding skylarking dates—Philadelphia, New Haven, and Virginia Beach are highlights. In each township, a small amount hold vigil, lest he take his final breath. A shutterbug takes a portrait of Kelly on his rig at the 'Mechanics and Farmers Building.' The sitter is galvanized when his picture runs in the *Raleigh City Gazette.* He tears the photograph out to save for he has never seen his likeness in print before.

On August 23, 1926, Alvin is exhibiting his expertise in Queens. Emmerling clumsily ascends a ladder to converse.

"Let us end this tomfoolery right now. With Valentino dying without warning, I am writing about the wake for *United Press International*. Mourners were hurt in the initial rush to lay eyes on the casket, and two women killed themselves right in the parlor! Anything else is of little consequence in comparison. This happening has captivated the fairer gender of the planet."

The "Great Lover" has crossed into the murk. The three roommates pay their respects at Frank E. Campbell's funeral parlor, observing the film idol's final starring role. As the actor lies in state, traffic in mid-town is gridlocked as an estimated 100,000 come to file by the casket. New York's finest keeps order as the devout dally, sweating in the humidity.

Alvin, who has a problem being in cramped, balmy areas, considers the experience agony. He perspires profusely while queuing in line behind actress Mary Philbin. His claustrophobia is at its height when he extends condolences to the deceased's former companion, Pola Negri.

The Polish actress becomes emotional and displays the swooning technique that has given her stardom. Alvin catches her mid-collapse. A doctor in her entourage revives her. Vivian whispers a few words to the physician, who looks astonished at what she says.

"He's no healer—that is a hoodwinker," she informs Alvin as they leave. "The man is an expert at masquerading as a foreign diplomat, but he's from Boise. Once he bilked an Arab prince out of a $5,000 fee by pretending to be the U.S. Counsel to Peru and promising a meeting where President Harding would take a bribe to do something nefarious. It was all bluster though and he disappeared as rapidly as the last stylish ladies hat at a milliner's clearance sale. He lived lavishly in Rio until Pinkerton detectives dragged him back to face trial. He's quite fortunate though. If the Sultan had gotten to him first, he'd have lost a hand, a much worse body part, or both. I thought he was still in Leavenworth."

"A considerable amount of spinsters came out. Still think you can boost me to be more well-known than him, Joseph?"

Emmerling ignores the question explaining he has to compose an article. Vivian leaves to call in some debts. Left to his own devices, Kelly heads to the wharf. He hates the over-packed subway and is hesitant when crossing the street. He feels jittery as the autos zip by, belching exhaust that is repulsive to someone who habituates in the arms of Zephuros, Greek god of the west wind. His mouth waters at the thought of bobbing on the foamy liquid and resists the urge to sidestroke to a tugboat as the first mate sounds the horn, preparing to leave the harbor.

Alvin galumphs to "Hubert's Museum" on West 42nd Street. He splurges a Mercury dime to shake hands with "Zip—the What Is It?" and goggle at other draws. "Heckler's Flea Emporium—300 Performing Insects," reads the painted banner pointing to the basement. He reaches into his pocket for five pennies to watch the old man make the chigoes jump under a magnifying glass.

Past the "Chock Full o' Nuts" store at Broadway and 43rd Street, he crosses into a den of iniquity that sells intoxicants. Kelly withdraws to a corner with a bottle. He drains a third of the liquid, and the inebriate reaches out to his ally by telephone. Joseph fetches his dollar-poorer pal. Opening the door into the cab, Alvin stumbles as he stoops to grab a lost token.

"Soon you won't have to worry about loose change," reassures Emmerling as he helps him up. *I will not ever bend the knee for discarded copper. That act is far beneath my station,* he affirms. *I prefer crisp bills.* "I speculate we'll be flush with money soon."

"An Indian head," Alvin bursts out with a drunken gleeful squeal. "I hardly luck into these old ones anymore."

"Could you draw out a gig longer than a week? This schtick would sell better if you can outdo seven days. Could you stretch to ten days?"

"That is not an impossible notion, even in Hoboken. Maybe even 14."

He smiles . . . *perhaps such a chore will bring me closer to god. Once I'm used to the regimen, spending more time should be easy.* When told, Vivian surmises that the longer time he spends in a stretch without sleep is more dangerous and voices her opinion.

"I have responsibilities . . . to my fans," states Alvin.

"To who?" Her verbalization raises to a shrill pitch. She is incredulous. "You know who gives a shit? Pickpockets and me. I love you, and, yet, you would abandon me to the wolves in the wilderness."

She recedes hastily to avoid more draconian words.

A month later, Gene Tunney wins the belt from Jack Dempsey in a hard fought match. Kelly muses, *should the athletic counterpuncher not regain the crown, how would he handle obscurity? The ring general would not retire but train endlessly to mount a comeback. I should aim at the same unbreakable tenet.* He pencils a conciliation to be transmitted.

YOU WILL BE CHAMP ONCE MORE. SHIPWRECK KELLY.

A skittish Western Union boy scurries up ladder rungs with a reply from "Gentleman Jack." Emmerling takes a photo and will milk this encounter like a Tibetan sherpa craving yak butter in his tea. When the employee brings the wire to the sitter at an altitude, the action lends credence to the conceptualization that Alvin resides on cloud nine. Joseph recalls delivering telegrams for his step-father in Berwyn and how a baksheesh of a thin dime made him feel like a rich maharaja. He tips the lad a veritable fortune—a shiny silver dollar.

German immigrant, Hugo Bihler, trumps Alvin by triumphing eight days in Philadelphia's sky. He mopes around the apartment in a sullen state. Even Vivian cannot alter his mood to 'cheery.' While not the reigning sovereign of loftiness, chances to work still flow in. Dates spike as merchants become tantalized by his power to tempt buyers to them.

Beating his own tenacity becomes a mania. He will wield the scepter as his sport's high monarch by any means necessary. In Kelly's judgment, no one is suited to hold the vaulted title except himself. He thrives on the 'being-on-the-edge' feeling. He is convinced that his renown will be eternal. He focuses on his special ambition to achieve. That act will incentivize those huddled far from his audacious platform to be better. His purpose to be victorious is ossified harder than any petrified bone in American Museum of Natural History at West 77th.

The tolerance game has become a healthy expression of the era. Alvin now considers all stoicism as a challenge to his purported mastery. If someone flew an airplane continuously or participated in a low-speed marathon rally, he had an inclination to eclipse their time.

"Can you arrange me a 14-day stint?" he asks Joseph.

Houdini dies from a ruptured spleen on Halloween. Joseph telegrams condolences to the performer's widow. Alvin and Vivian attend the services with him, at Machpelah Jewish Cemetery in Glendale. Emmerling pens an obituary so eloquent that 2,000 news outlets globally publish his tribute. He frames the column of print and finds a place on his wall despite having no byline.

Emmerling has gotten Kelly a task as an apprentice to a stone mason on Randolph Hearst's Warwick Hotel. His agility and balance plus his lack of anxiety at heights is a boon to his employability. A week in the trade disbursed pennies compared to the $500 fee Joseph is demanding as a minimum.

Alvin peeks down 6th Avenue toward the park through an unfinished brick wall. Snowflakes could descend at any day now. He is lost in thought for the wink of an eye. *I am anxious to take a break in the tropics and have a deep palaver with my mystical mentor.* He thinks upon a fragment of the very famous poem, "Kubla Khan."

In Florida, did Edward Leedskalnin, a stately pleasure-dome decree:

where South Dixie, the busy byway ran,

Through 1,100 tons, coral carvings perplexing to man

Down near a sun-filled sea.

So twice five acres of fertile ground

With walls and castle were girdled round;

And there were floras bright with tortuous rills,

Where sprouted many a flower-bearing tree;

And here were passions ancient as the hills,

Enfolding sunny spots of greenery.

Phillip S. Roberts

Colossal masses have been chiseled into nonconformist shapes. Exquisitely balanced, tonnage of the devotional project memorializing his lost love is implausible. Leedskalnin whittles and moves his giant sculptural creations absent of prying eyes at night. The artist, ensconced in his impenetrable fortress is forging ahead underneath a bare bulb. Any prowling nearby might hear the infinitesimal clanking of pickaxe and an imperceptible whirr.

When Kelly asks, 'How does he realize these mighty tasks?' the clarification is, "It's easy, if you know how." Alvin reflects on the quandary. *Is an unnatural force being harnessed? Do miracles exist? Is the Latvian's method science or practiced conjuring from a bygone age?*

The sculptor admits to plying a wood beam tripod topped with a copper box and a chain to heft the bulk. Alvin thinks the weight must be too heavy for his equipment to manage. He lags at the rear of the group as the owner conducts jaunts within his facility for the eager. Musing upon how the statuary was lifted, he reflects upon their abstract meaning. He scans Ed's monograph on perpetual motion. He buys a copy to re-read later.

Kelly and Vivian dine with Leedskalnin on the final night of their vacation.

"Love esst powerful. Mit eet, can move mountains vvithout a lever or fulcrum. Come 12-month to zee my vvonderful realm."

"When will your display be complete?"

"Agnes come, and eet finish," he recites with his broken patois. That visitation did seem doubtful.

"So, never."

After Vivian has gone to bed, Alvin cannot sleep. He goes and rings the bell at the hefty gate. The proprietor swings his eight ton revolving slab an inch, peers at his caller, and brings him in his ramshackle. Unscrewing a Mason jar, Ed pours healthy slugs of a potent flavored elixir. Kelly thinks it has quite a bite and a scant peppermint flavor. He lights a Pall Mall, but his host does not want one. He had once had the "consumption" so Edward does not enjoy tobacco. After an uncomfortable muteness, he breaks the silence.

"I giff my heart, but eet is not to be. I build zis for her."

"Yes, but . . . Do you use magnetism? Mysticism? Do you somehow . . . ."

"You know ze Egypt pyramids?" Ed replies while drawing a triangle in the air with his finger. "Dey vvere like elektric stations before vvriting. There iss vvone still active in ze deep vvaters near Bermuda . . . en Atlantis. I tap into ze power to move de rock."

A few more ounces of his bellywash flow from the carafe and the swabby is suddenly sloppy. *Clearly I am not solving the riddle of the ages this evening.* Alvin somehow stumbles back to the motel. He's in a stupor when he beds.

He visualizes Ed powering up an electronic gizmo on a panel. As a mad scientist might, his hands dart daintily across the dials, buttons, and levers. Out-of-this-world sounds resonate from the machine. Pulses and oscillating frequencies are emitted—a tonality that has the look of caressing the stone. The material is buoyed, enwrapped in an electrified field. The Latvian extemporaneously pontificates in an ancient tongue, chanting in an indiscernible vernacular as he revolves the object as if it were a soap bubble.

"Like a feather," says Ed. "Dis isst the fun part."

The floating rock is wondrous. Alvin gapes while a chisel chips an intricate design into the side. The artist emits a shrill whistle and the stone rotates ninety degrees. After working the chunk, Ed shuts off the panel. The din ends with a thud—gravity has returned to normal.

"No von utilizes this technique, nor vvill dey. Such power ist dangerous in untrained hands."

Alvin immediately wakes from his embrace with Nephthys, the Egyptian god of sleep. He has let his slumber in a pixilated haze run unchecked. The vision had felt so vivid. Vivian murmurs in the darkness.

"Imagine it. I'd never fall. We must find out his secret."

"Screw him yourself," she scolds as she rolls over.

Two flappers fervently gyrate; dancing the "Charleston" irresponsibly on the ledge of Chicago's Sherman Hotel on December 11, 1926. Their portrait runs on the front page in all 48 states and their romp is recorded onto celluloid by the Fox Movietone news. The surreal fringes of the "Jazz Age" has entered the mainstream.

Phillip S. Roberts

Chapter 13 –
A Proposal on a Tall Height

"Love is like quicksilver in the hand. Leave the fingers open and it stays. Clutch it and it darts away."
— Dorothy Parker

By 1927, many of Alvin's adversaries are attempting to trounce the undisputed "King of Longevity." Their actions trigger his ardor. The "idol of millions" can only watch as opposition crawls out of the woodwork to best him. A total of 20 regional sitters claim to be the bonafide thingamajig. Kelly crows any extended span will be overtaken in his quest to be an invincible champion. He gives his word to expound the very limits of continuance or die trying. Around-the-clock, he persists as those below reason that his motive is flumadiddle. When he comes near any newsie with a pad, Kelly becomes blatherskite if the talking point is any other flagpole sitter.

"That lemon is a second rate flub-dub with the smarts of a guinea pig."

Alvin is full of curiosity if historians will recognize his laborious feat. The town pulses as the population continue their pother. The man in the street is comforted by seeing him—a constant in a changing world. After three days, he feels solid when he trods his soles upon dirt.

Daly's 63rd Street Theater is raided by the N.Y.P.D. vice squad after 375 sold-out performances of Mae West's "Sex" on February 15, 1927. The District Attorney has been flooded with so many grievances of moral turpitude by local decency association members that it is as if Anthony Comstock was still alive. Obscenity charges are filed due to multiple ribald lines in the play. The actress is arrested and rings Joseph to bring her bail.

"Quick as you can. I've almost run out of conversation with these ladies of the evening and petty thieves with whom I'm jailed."

She uses her sojourn excellently questioning the incarcerated on the intricacies of being behind bars. The actress coos to a guard, bums a cigarette from him, and puffs while she reclines, patiently awaiting liberty. Judicial processes are put on the docket for April and Mae is released.

Shipwreck is unequaled in his diligence, nine stories above the pedestrians and cars on the West Gate Hotel in Kansas City on February 20, 1927. Sponsored by "Blony Chewing Gum," his total time aloof is 140 hours and 13 minutes. The ad-men praise his bulldog attitude and gift Alvin a case of the penny candy. He gives out the free samples to the fans at his meet and greet sessions. Scuttling in a coddiewomple gait in March, he takes possession of the Hilton Hotel in Dallas for a sennite. Texans halt their pursuits briefly to glimpse at the figure set in contrast to the skyline. While he lodges in one place, the world revolves as normals resume their business.

After an uncompromising month on the job, Emmerling deposits almost $2,000 in his bank account. Vivian aids her bone weary beau onto the sleeper car. Corrivals do not terminate their vantages while he snatches forty winks and is given the rundown on their developments upon awakening en route.

Vagrant "Blind" Elmer Emerson is testing his prowess on April 1, 1927. His choice of lodging is a Central Park bench and is firm that he'll leave on Armistice Day. The mounted patrol rousts the transient from his quest citing the anti-vagabondism statutes.

A few weeks later on April 19th, at the Jefferson Market Federal Building, Mae West's trial starts. The fifth estate has filled the courtroom. Emmerling is watching the proceedings as well.

Seated at the defendant's table, the Broadway actress clears her throat as the charges are read accusing her of "obscenity and behavior designed to corrupt the morals of youth." The gallery laughs and the judge addresses the defendant.

"Are you showing contempt for this court, Miss West?"

"On the contrary, I was doin' my best to conceal it," quips Mae as if her witticism had been prepared beforehand. It had. The retort costs her $20. She disregards the fine, mindful that the joke will reap dividends in the future. The actress pleads guilty to a lesser charge, and the magistrate metes out the penalty—ten days incarceration on Welfare Island. She rents a Rolls-Royce Phantom to take her to capitulate to trustees.

During her incarceration, she grants an exclusive jailhouse tête-à-tête to Joseph. She gives him sordid hearsay to print; candlelit dinners with Warden Schleth, the pinkness of the soft, silk lingerie she wears under her state-issued prison stripes, and the amoral guards who offer to trade privileges for favors. Emmerling is cut a nice check from the scandal quarterlies, enthusiastically bidding for the right to print his scoop. He uses his remuneration to settle her fine.

Kelly is relishing *The Farmingdale Post*, 12 feet in the air. On page three, Alvin considers the misfortune befalling WWI aces, Charles Nungesser and Francois Coli. It is suspected that their biplane evanesces into the Atlantic on April 8, 1927, while trying to win the Orteig prize by completing the transit from Paris to New York.

"Those poor 'Frenchies' will be forgotten as soon as someone else attempts that chancy test," he chirps while nesting on his aerie. "It would be a miracle if they were rescued. Those twists of fate don't happen that often."

As soon as his boots hit sidewalk, he exaggerates his importance to the *Long Island Journal*.

"I saw an automobile pileup last night," avows Kelly. "My vision is so sharp that, if I was asked to, I would be able to testify in a court of law."

The reporter continues his questioning until he decides he has wasted enough pencil lead. Emmerling pulls him aside, deposits a tenner in his hand, and lists a few points he would be grateful if he included. The manager is gratified with his stratagem.

"Every corner magazine stand I slink by hawks your nonsense," verbalizes Vivian. She has been more testy than usual lately. She's also been feeling a bit queasy. *I might be with child,* she internalizes. *If I am, that's even more leverage to move into our own place. Certainly that fag won't care to have an infant around.* "Alvin, you are the most stubborn peabrain I ever met, but I love you."

She airs her grievances on a regular basis to her mate. *Why don't we break away from Joseph? How come the count isn't equitable? What about that house you promised me?* Despite that, Alvin is obsessed with her. That intimate night is a fiery, gratifying experience. She whispers in his ear that the pair are perfect for each other. Afterwards, she bathes, and he decides not to be dissuaded from marriage any longer. In the morning, he confides in Joseph, despite knowing his companion is less than "hammer and tongs" about his intended. He envisages a sermon, but, instead, some bills are handed over with a beatific expression.

"Purchase her a ring. Create a special memory that she will cherish forever."

Alvin browses jewelry at a pawnshop and purchases a modest band set with an itty-bitty diamond. He takes Vivian to the newly opened Russian Tea Room in midtown to dine on borscht, savory beef stroganoff, and cheesecake; finishing the meal with thick Turkish kahveh. Afterward, they go to take in the sights from the Paramount Building at 501 Broadway. He fiddles with the gold circle in his pocket and trembles at the thought of a denial. She thinks his nervousness is due to being in the congested elevator.

Once in a high place, he is unflappable and in his familiar realm. He envisions himself as a Sapa Inca on his teocalli, surveying fertile lands. He pops on a knee and asks the question.

"I love you. Will you marry me?"

"I will, silly," she replies as he slips the hoop on her dainty digit. Sightseers clap and congratulate the lovebirds.

"I am the luckiest fool on earth."

When they return, Emmerling insists on footing the wedding bill. He waxes lyrical—popping the cork on a chilled 1904 Veuve Clicquot Ponsardin Brut Champagne he has been hoarding. Since the pair is besotted, Joseph arranges a civil ceremony with the honorable Kenton Stevenson during his midday break on April 10, 1927.

After an aphoristic reading of a dissertation praising love and a short liturgy, the justice performs the ceremony as Joseph witnesses.

Then they head off to the Biltmore Theater to take in the afternoon show of "The Barker." The melodrama features actress Claudette Colbert as a snake-charmer with a scandalous streak. Joseph is annoyed that the plot is vaguely familiar to his own work. Afterward, he takes the openly affectionate duo to a splendiferous banquet at "Ruben's On Broadway" at 58th Avenue. Alvin thanks his "best man" for the great evening. Vivian announces she is expecting.

"That is wonderful. I love you. I will work diligently to find us a place of our own soon," pledges Alvin. "For us and the baby."

"As a wedding present, I am taking care of the honeymoon," elicits Emmerling after the revelation. "I have arranged rooms with a view and a chartered boat ride at Niagara. We leave tomorrow."

"I am not being sealed in a barrel," protests Alvin. He can almost envision the gears interlocking in Joseph's cerebrum. His manager always has a plan to advance his recognition.

"You are too important to be wasted on that harebrained objective. We announce at a presser that you are in the planning stages of a plunge, but then Vivian announces she's pregnant. For the sake of the unborn, you give up your plans to brave the raging waters and instead announce a chockablock tour—10 cities in a month—several at our most expensive rates."

A little more than a month later, Joseph arranges for Kelly to have a photograph taken with Richard Byrd on May 14, 1927. The North Pole reconnoiterer is preparing to attempt the New York to Paris flight in the three-engine Fokker christened "America." During a test take-off, a strut deteriorates. The flying machine skids, lopsided—aluminum scrapes on the runway cement causing sparks. Byrd's mechanic has to request a number of delicate broken parts be fabricated. The interview with Emmerling is cancelled.

Capitalizing on Byrd's delay, Charles Lindbergh rushes airborne. On May 20, 1927, he unearths from Roosevelt Field in his monoplane, "The Spirit of St. Louis." Advancing steadily despite stinging winds and zero visibility over open ocean almost 34 hours, his plane's rubber tires bounce on the ground at Le Bourget Aerodrome.

"Lindy" is the pilot to who conquers the Trans-Atlantic crossing first. His aeronautic feat is the foremost reification of the modern age. Umpteen lives have already been lost in the watery grave he's just flown over. He wins the "Orteig Prize,"—$25,000 put up by a hotelier, awarded to the first completion of the "impossible" task. Droves of French break the barriers and rush the landing strip. Gendarmes encircle "The Spirit of St. Louis," to protect his now important, and soon to be venerated plane from rabid souvenir hunters.

His vanquishment of the sky is transmitted to America on May 21, 1927. His great accomplishment captivates the United States. He is hailed by both politicians and plebeians. Grandness comes instantly, and the proud nation hungers insatiably to hear news of even his most mundane activity. Newspapers go crazy over the spindly, brown-haired, blue-eyed hero.

"The Lindy Hop" dance craze is invented by frenzied-flappers who extend their arms like wings. Lindbergh is gifted a cabin on the Cunard Line and his plane is lashed to the deck. He is honored with a lavish ticker tape parade when he arrives from Europe. Alvin is matching the length of the pilot's sequestration in various municipalities as a tribute.

All of a sudden, the sitting compulsion has gone national. Three impetuous fellows embark upon a quest to wrest the atmospheric headlines from Kelly. On June 10, 1927, Rex Hinton faints, strapped 100 feet above Omaha's boulevards. The would-be conqueror is carried to the ground by firefighters after 36 hours.

Roy "The Spider" Haines has a goal to sit 120 hours in Denver's thin air. He retires his high spot, truncated by a day but announces stubbornly to reporters that he will try again.

"I admit, this pursuit is harder than you would think. I am used to climbing buildings by hand, but I will honestly tell you this. Flagpole sitting is the most dangerous sport in the world."

Former gambler Joe Powers is at a 637-foot elevation at Chicago's Morrison Hotel. "Hold-Em" is provided with "all the pampered comforts of home" by the catering department. Meals and reading material are sent to him by pail. The management connects a telephone so "well-wishers" can chat with him.

"I do it the old-fashioned way . . . ." Alvin mocks his carbon copies before he mounts his oblong at the Saint Frances Hotel in an effort to prove as he is as tough as a British climbing expedition on Everest. "With resolve and bulldog temperament, but little else, I shall ascend like those brave English fellows and their sherpa, to stand on the North Face Summit of the highest mountain in the world."

TIME – JUNE 15, 1927

ALMOST A MONTH AFTER THE UNITED STATES WOKE TO THE GLORY ACHIEVED BY COLONEL LINDBERGH AND HIS EMULATORS, IN NEWARK, ALVIN "SHIPWRECK" KELLY AFFIXED A STOOL TO THE 50 FOOT RISER AT THE ST. FRANCES HOTEL. THEN HE PROCEEDED TO SIT.

THE THEORY IS THAT IF HE LIVED IN MID-AIR MORE
THAN TEN DAYS HE WOULD REAP A MUNIFICENT REWARD. INDEED,
HE EKED OUT A LIVING BY UNFURLING AN ADVERT THAT READS:
"BABY PEGGY AT LOEWS" THEATRE."

MRS. KELLY, A PUGNACIOUS REDHEAD, TENDED TO HER
HUSBAND FROM THE BASE BY CORDS. AS HE DWELLED, HIS WIFE
SHUTTLED HIM CHICKEN BROTH AND GRAPE JUICE, — BUT NO
SOLID FARE. HE INHALES ALMOST FOUR PACKS OF CIGARETTES A
DAY. HE HAS DEDUCED HOW TO SLUMBER TEN MINUTES AN HOUR.
HIS THUMBS ARE THRUST INTO SLOTS BORED IN THE EIGHT INCH
DIAMETER WOODEN STOOL, THE PAIN WAKING HIM WHEN
HE TEETERS.

Vivian hands out a statement to reporters that her husband,
"Shipwreck" survived the *Titanic*, then joined the Navy. After the war,
he attempted to earn the milk and honey as a boxer, a longshoreman,
and a steeplejack, before choosing "Pole Sitter" as a career.

"I'd rather have a penny Kool-Aid than a nickel Coca-Cola,"
he calls out to bystanders. "After 48 hours of this, you don't care about
the height, but standing here sure is thirsty work."

THE JERSEY CITY NEWS — JUNE 18, 1927

HUNDREDS WINCH THEIR NECKS BACKWARD AT KELLY.
SOME ARGUE WHETHER OR NOT HE IS A HERO. SOME WENT AND
LOOKED FOR THE DEFINITION IN WEBSTER'S DICTIONARY: "A
PERSON OF DISTINGUISHED FORTITUDE IN SUFFERING."

IN ST. LOUIS, "SHIPWRECK" SURVIVED A PERIOD OF
SEVEN DAYS—MUCH OF THAT AMID CHILL, SLEET AND SNOW. THE
EXPERIENCE THUS GAINED CAUSED HIM TO MAKE ELABORATE
PREPARATIONS BEFOREHAND. THE FLAGPOLE SITTER RELIEVES
HIS BOREDOM WITH RHYMING GAMES, HISTORICAL FACTS, AND
READING SHERLOCK HOLMES STORIES.

Farmingham steeplejack Frank Holl mounts a townhouse after
accepting a dare. "The Sparrow" notes that having insomnia is better
than somnolence. Immature, yet hardy, oddsmakers figure he has a
chance to beat the champ.

The Boston Herald rings on June 21, 1927. Joseph stalls the reporter, promising a statement later. Not wanting an opposing sitter to grab attention from Alvin, Emmerling calls in a favor from a guy he knows at the New England Motoring Club.

Subsequently a bureaucrat swears that "numerous collisions" are being spawned by the unlicensed novelty. An injunction brings law and order to Holl's position with a bull-horn. He resists their demands temporarily before deciding to wave the white flag and is detained for disturbing the peace. At arraignment, the charge is dismissed.

TIME — JUNE 27, 1927

SHOULD YOU LOB A TENNIS BALL AND CATCH IT, THE ACTION WOULD BE NO UNUSUAL FEAT AND AROUSE NO INVESTIGATION. BUT SHOULD SOMEONE COMPLETE 100,000 TRIES SUCCESSFULLY, HE WOULD BECOME SOMEONE WHOM PATRONS WOULD LAY OUT DIMES TO SEE.

ALVIN KELLY HOPES SOON TO BE $1,000 RICHER PER WEEK PERFORMING IN VAUDEVILLE. NO SINGER OR COMEDIAN IS 'SHIPWRECK.' HE IS A SITTER. STIFF, SORE, AND WEAK FROM 12 DAYS UPRIGHT, HE RETREATED FROM THE STALAGMITE ON THE ST. FRANCES HOTEL.

"I deserve my payment," exclaims Alvin. Joseph is pleased at being able to arrange two mentions in the most circulated periodical in America, Time magazine. His residency at the St. Francis terminates after 288 hours. He bags $6,000 for the stretch.

"Do you think women would participate in your line of work?" asks a scribe from The Bayonne Times. "Could any withstand the same amount of time as you?"

"I think 'up' ain't no place for a broad," derides Kelly. "Frails would be too worried, that someone will be ogling their privates under their skirt."

Alvin is wrong. Simultaneously, as he is being grilled, the inaugural female sitter, Bobbie Mack, slews to the concrete streets in Los Angeles. The 21-year-old embraces her anxious fiancé, Thomas McNamara after a week in fresh air on June 27, 1927. The couple recite their wedding vows at the base of the pole and leave for a romantic week honeymoon on Catalina. The bride never mounts an erection of the steel kind again. She is inclined toward the stimulation of managing a family.

After Shipwreck is finished and down, the hotel's owner has a bright idea; he straps a mannequin to the pilum until the local bureaucracy force him to remove the dummy, citing it as a traffic hazard.

"Ah, this stirs memories of when I was barking," says Emmerling during Kelly's next appearance—pumping up the crowd at the Minnesota State Fair. "In an incredible stroke of felicity, you are witness to this astounding feat. Shipwreck will dangle, far from the comforts taken for granted. Imagine that risk . . . a mere scintilla in the bucket for a daredevil, sequestered on the world's tallest buildings. They never refer to him sagacious. He does this for the adrenaline rush. He has withstood numbing, tempestuous blizzards. He is extending the boundaries of scientific knowledge. He uses no net. The possibility of a crippling injury, that will not allow him to satisfy his wife, is ever-present."

A few of assembled fellows in the crowd shift uneasily at the mental image.

"A blunder or an out-of-the-blue bird could shepherd him to heaven—this flagpole sitter does not know the meaning of the word, 'Fear.' This decorated war veteran and *Titanic* rescuer has amused celebrities and world leaders by the hundreds."

Joseph takes a dramatic pause. He rams his ham hock of a hand with an extended finger skyward for emphasis. He is in the zone now —a trance-like state that snake oil salesmen achieve after untold renditions of the same gabble.

"Should the worst materialize, he will be interned by 'Hoffman's Mortuary.' Now, the 'stick-to-it-iveness' specialist will bring you a few words before he rises."

"I am flouting tolerance and extreme limits. As Lindbergh is triumphant, I parallel the jaunt he spent in the cockpit," recites the naval uniform-clad madman soon to be high in the sky. "A healthy mind can overcome any obstacle. Devour less meat and more grains. The supreme-being created these resilient tools to benefit you. Deny bathtub gin, and guzzle herbal tea instead. The natural brew's healing benefits far out weigh those of any other drink. I implore you, heed my advice as someone who has run rings around strife. The smartest medical practitioners say a man cannot continue to be lucid without sleep longer than four days. I will prove those quacks wrong. It is always darkest during the night."

To prove his resolve, he is set to reside at an astonishing loftiness. Resting his foot on the bottom of the windlass, he rides effortlessly to his engineered domicile 45 feet away. Kelly plans to spend three days and nights in the sky. Over 20,000 visitors come during the weekend, and Alvin is an undersung conversation there. He can hear, (or imagines,) audible laughing and barbs coming from the midway. While he is serious about his supremacy and his sport, he realizes many consider him a freak to be ridiculed.

"That flagpole sitter has backbone. I will give him that."

"He must be a cousin to a donkey."

"What a fool."

Kelly pours soup out from a thermos and settles in to pass the night. With the aid of binoculars, he watches a comedy being shown on a nearby livestock barn. He cherishes the cool relief from the days that are roasting and sticky. He wonders how his rival flagpole sitters are doing in their quest to unseat him as the "best in the game."

Joe Powers is chasing Alvin's record of sitting unaccompanied in perpetuation atop Chicago's Morrison Hotel on June 29, 1927. The steeplejack from Illinois, refuses to cease while a fierce thunderstorm saturates the "City of Big Shoulders," nor will he leave his spot when a summer windstorm blows through. He soon regrets his choice. A wild blast of wind propels him awry. He is shrieking as he slams face first into the unforgiving iron mast. His four front teeth are knocked out by the impact. While the tether bound around his middle saves his life, "Hold-Em" is never the same.

Roy "Spider" Haines (in his second attempt,) continues into hour 26 in Denver with no hankering to leave his position. Asked for comment by a newsman as he alights his summit, Kelly parries with a vicious witticism.

"That simpleton, if he fails, at least it will be while valiantly trying. That is the American way—to strive to be better. End quote."

After 15 days, Roy Haines proves the adage, "what goes up, must come down." His ledge held by two steel cables is lowered 367 feet and he timorously trods upon solid concrete. He's greeted with a warm reception by a few local dignitaries on July 15, 1927. He retires to an uninterrupted siesta. When he rises, a cortège of barbers, tailors, and masseurs are attending his temporary abode, cleaning him in time for a testimonial banquet. At the dais, he takes a swipe at Alvin.

"I hope Kelly takes as many movie roles as he can before Hollywood calls me," basks Haines. "I'm sure to be turning away contracts now that I have flown from my perch. I am much more handsome than that Shipwreck runt."

Kelly is set to try 16 days on a poker in mid-town on July 18, 1927. He takes a shufti at the Chrysler Building, salivating at the thought of working that height. The payday is $1,600. Joseph devises some perfunctory calculations. If the trend continues at the same pace, the consortium will clear $37,000 by year's end. Reporters are at the base of the jamb awaiting a statement.

"Hand them a bissel of sizzle and a smidgen of pizzazz," opines Emmerling. "But just a little so they'll come back when we gain a bigger reputation."

He relishes the popularity, but he tells the newsies what he truly hungers for is to have a hero sandwich named after him at "Katz's Deli." The next time he is there, Alvin orders a custom creation wishing the owner will put his invention on the menu.

"I will order 'The Shipwreck,' please." He lists the hoagie's ingredients. "That's pastrami, peppers, sweet pickles, sardines, onions, limburger cheese, and a slab of baloney between toasted slices of pumpernickel with spicy mustard."

"Why not throw in a few slices of ham, too?" the clerk asks, repulsed by the stacked combination.

"Please have some mints." Emmerling pinches his proboscis after Kelly takes a bite. "As I was saying, hopefully, we can be more selective. Fame is much more harder to achieve than we both counted on. Are you still with me, my champion?"

Phillip S. Roberts

"Absolutely," retaliates Alvin. "More know me now than ever."

"Vivian doesn't trust our strategy."

"She knows her onions. She yearns stability; to own a property with a white picket fence. I guess that is her main problem. On the move nine months out of the year, from burg-to-village—she feels a little like a vagrant. Do we have enough to put a deposit on a small house?"

"Maybe soon. Right now we can't sustain the extra expense."

Emmerling is working on multiple streams of income besides managing the sitter. He has proposed a sponsorship with the *Otis Elevator Company* and hopes Alvin will be their spokesman. Vivian shuffles in to the deli, very pregnant.

"Joseph thinks soon he might be able to arrange us our own place . . . for us two . . . and the baby. Would that please you?"

"That would be the bee's knees."

"It is not exactly financially possible yet, but let us figure what you need in a residence."

She leans in to kiss Alvin but retreats arms length.

"Jesus," she criticizes. "If you ever want another kiss, you'll gargle. You stink."

The Associated Press reports that the masked character who has been balanced on the "Theatre DeLuxe" on Wilshire Boulevard will cede his spot on August 4, 1927. That day, actor Jack Lipson removes his disguise for *The Los Angeles Times.* He tells reporters that his movie, "The Stunt Man," debuting in the hall that night contains "many hair-raising sequences."

Gladys Roy is planning to try a continuous flight to Rome that no-one has succeeded at. She autographs a few programs at the Watson Air Field. The 25-year-old pilot hops into a cockpit to take a photo shaking hands with an admirer. Exiting, she snags her dress sleeve on the control panel and steps from the fuselage into a now whirling propeller. Rushed to the nearest medical facility with a brain injury, she cannot be saved by physicians. Joseph submits a tribute to the stunt flyer's career for *The Detroit Jewish Chronicle.*

On August 28, 1927, Kelly is straddling an 18-inch ball, 20 stories above West 48th Street at the Bristol Hotel. He inks a few notes to well-wishers. After eight daylight hours, he trods away with $400. As the most well known personality of his sport, he does not have to constantly marathon. Simply posing at an insane height garners respect.

The next day, Kelly is on the Hudson Hotel. Nedick's sends him their signature orange fizzy and a donut to nibble on. The producer of "The Circus Princess" playing at the Winter Garden Theater gifts him vouchers to attend the show when his labor is done. An hour later, overcast skies, have him dashing from his prop due to flashes of close by lightning strikes.

At the start of September 1927, the Glenn Hotel at 928 Monmouth Street is the scene for a 100 hour shift. Alvin is being sponsored by the Brotherhood of Railway Clerks and Trainmen to foster interest in their annual carnival. A license to sit was denied in Cleveland, so a nearby town is chosen instead. Traffic snarls due to pileups caused by the sight. Emmerling prints out handbills advertising an autograph session at the Strand Theater, and 24 fans come to meet Kelly. With their gizmo in the trunk, the jalopy swerves toward the state of Maryland.

Babe Ruth slugs his season's 60th four-bagger on September 30, 1927. No other major leaguer has hit more home runs in a season than the Yankee. Kelly's doggedness of 23 days overlooking the Bronx is relegated to an inch in the Sports Section. He sends "The Bambino" a cable since he considers the outfielder his sporting contemporary.

WAY TO SOCK IT, CHAMP. YOU ALMOST HIT ME. SHIPWRECK.

A real estate concern in Wisconsin has contacted Emmerling regarding a sponsorship of the pole sitter to bring sales prospects to their sub-division. Joseph warns not to accept the task.

"It's not right to earn $100 a day for three weeks in late November and early December. If you complete the contract, the enterprise will gift you a choice plot to build on. However, you won't earn anything unless you last the whole time. The algid region will be hazardous. If our spring engagements hear the word on the street that you are cutting a discount, that would be bad for business overall."

"I agree."

A pregnant Vivian, has been listening. She becomes visibly upset, goes to the bedroom, and returns with a plain package that she hands to Alvin. He opens the brown paper wrapping, and out tumbles frilly emerald lingerie.

"If you are going to act a bitch, you might as well dress the part. I love you, but I think this idea is worth the risk. We could build a house on the lot. Or sell it for cash. Do it for me."

"Joseph thinks it's a bad idea. He is a good decision-maker. Without his acumen, I would be just another swabby slaving at the boatyard for low wages. I haven't the smarts to . . . ."

She repudiates the end of his articulation, fuming like a bull rushing at a matador's cape. He glowers at her.

"Do you comprehend we need our own space? We are going to have responsibilities."

Kelly takes the contract despite Emmerling's advice but decides on a mysterious stranger guise. He applies a fake beard and takes a bus to Green Bay on October 26, 1927. Co-sponsored by the Milwaukee Sentinel, Alvin is in full "mystery" mode. He wears a "Lone Ranger" mask, hires a helper to build a derisory box and affix it on the riser. Guywires steady the temporary structure. The plan is to reside in that cubicle despite minus zero temperatures, wind, and any other meteorological instance that might onset. He is installed 35 feet above a residential parish in Fond Du Lac.

He calculates his métier makes this job a cinch. *I will suffer in this shack to put my hands on a house and gain her respect. I am positive that I will endure the 21 days.* His aide fetches his requirements—hoisting snacks, blankets, and other items to Alvin.

The masked oddball's Fondale resting place is brightly lit during night. After seven days, a few hundred have swung by to gander at the model instillations. He plays catch with the community boys from his station, uses a phone on a lengthy cord to chat with radio stations in the region, and swills copious amounts of caffeine.

A strapping wind swooshes through on November 18, 1927. An arch topples, pulling the steel cable holding his spot tight. The spire bends like a catapult primed for a salvo on a walled citadel. The strand gives, and he is sent into the air as if he is a spitball set in motion toward a hated classmate. He is knocked out by his jarring collision with tundra. The night watchman phones the hospital and then rushes toward the prone figure whom he suspects is pushing up daisies, but Kelly is still alive. Doctors triage, transport, and treat the sitter for exposure to the extreme gelid. He has an inclination to re-mount the splintered spike, but is restrained from leaving the hospital by orderlies.

When Alvin is released two days later, he goes to survey the cleft shaft. It is unmountable, and he is forced to relinquish his task, hitherto payment. He gets shaved by a barber and takes a 15-hour bus ride to Manhattan.

"I've learned my lesson, Joseph," wheezes Alvin. "I will never take on another vacancy without your blessing."

Vivian is glad he is alive but nonplussed at the loss of a domicile.

"I'm sorry. I will keep saving for a house."

"It's okay. I figured out a sure-fire scheme to earn the dough. I will fill you in soon."

Chapter 14 –
The Fad in Full Swing

Wait a minute, wait a minute, you ain't heard nothin' yet! Wait a minute, I tell ya! You ain't heard nothin'!

—Al Jolson, The Jazz Singer

Kelly is plying his trade in Detroit on February 10, 1928. Frigidaire sales rep Alan Richards takes the chance to call upon a prospect that cannot avoid his iron-clad sales ploy. He uses a ladder to talk to the sitter and furnish his clincher.

"I will fill your new icebox with prime cuts. You are in air so frequently, you will never run out of cow."

The appliance dealer is content with a signature from the outlier, but Joseph explains the bill is not a valid sale since he handles all the financials. The salesman promises to sue for breach of contract.

Marianna Jaque and Albert Bonack outlast 28 other couples, prancing for 61 hours and 53 minutes to reign supreme in the "Steel City Long Distance Dance Finals." In the next day's edition, editors reply to a reader's question of why the paper has inflated coverage of hare-brained mischief like these marathons.

THE PITTSBURGH PRESS — MARCH 22, 1928

OUR MOSAIC OF HOOFERS, PHILOSOPHERS, AND PHILANTHROPISTS IS VARIED. WE RESERVE A WORD FOR ALL INCLUDING LUMINARIES CHARLES LINDBERGH, ALVIN KELLY, AND SARGENT YORK. WE HOLD VERACIOUS A RUMINATIVE OPINION TO FOSTER THOUGHT AS WELL AS CORRECTIVE ACTION. OUR WRITING EMPHASIZES THE BETTER SIDE AND IS YOUR CHOICE TO DRAW ON THAT KNOWLEDGE OR NOT. THAT IS WHY THESE BAFFLING ITEMS ARE CHRONICLED. TO SOME, WASTED SPACE, BUT OTHERS ARE ENGROSSED BY THE FIVE-LEGGED CALF.

Alvin is rendering advice to distant watchers in Ithaca on May, 17, 1928.

"Hey Kelly," shouts a pedestrian walking his dog. "Who will win the Kentucky Derby?"

"Place your bets on 'Mis-Step.' That filly's odds are a cinch to clinch," declares Alvin. "I know that one slip will end my days. Adversity compels one to be in the running. She will beat the odds-on favorite, 'Reigh Count.' In fact, I'll back that nag. I tell you, I know a sure thing."

He drops a $2 bill to the guy, but his pick runs second.

A few days after the "Run for the Roses," Vivian is rushed to the Sloane Hospital for Women on 168th Street. The pregnancy is laborious. Rather than pace a furrow in the floor with the other soon-to-be patriarchs in the "Stork Club," Alvin lolls in a tree al fresco near the entrance. He sits on a bough and solicits baby names from those trudging by.

Alvin Kelly Junior is eight pounds and three ounces at birth on May 21, 1928. Alvin leaps from the branch to be at his wife's bedside. The nurse lifts the boy so Shipwreck can wiggle his ears and generate funny-faces at his namesake behind the nursery glass.

I am incredibly lucky to have an heir. He is elated at his thoughts. *It's yet another miracle come to pass.* A crib is added in the room at Joseph's apartment where the pair reside. Emmerling chases the imperious papa to the nearby taverns, gifting cheap cigars to drunk patrons. A few weeks later, the two strand Vivian at home with the strawberry-blond-haired fledgling. As much as Alvin is gaining stature, other "attention-getters" across America are competing with him to grab headlines and have their day in the sun.

A cross-country race, advertising a carnival ends to abundant hurrahs on May 26, 1928, in the Madison Square Garden Arena. From the 200 runners who begin from Los Angeles, 55 finish the 84-day "Bunion Derby." Andrew Payne breaks the tape at the finish line to take home $2,500. While handing out the prizes, organizer Charles Pyle proclaims that the second annual "corn and callus" race will run the opposite way across the nation next year.

Pasadena's Clifford Hayes terminates 60 hours on May 31, 1928. At 45 feet above the street, he rodomontades that he is the "West Coast Champion." On the other coast, Alvin is seated at the Orient Photo Plays Cinema on 125th Street near 7th Avenue and Lenox. Joseph has arranged a sponsorship with Wrigley's Spearmint. Promoting "The Flavor that Lasts," he flings sticks of chewing gum to those out taking a morning constitutional.

Benny Fox has been lallygagging a week on Chicago's Masonic Temple. On June 8, 1928, he abandons his seat at 306 feet to meet the press on the pavement.

"We heard the cops served you for bigamy?" asks a reporter. "Is it true that you have two wives?"

"No. I'm happily married. My wife Nona is more than enough woman. I tell you this filthy rumor was started by Shipwreck Kelly. He is afraid that I will mature into a much more prominent star. I possess skill, artistry, and style. He just lazes around. That is the difference between us."

"Are you going to try to restart this sit once more?"

"I was performing this grueling task to grab some loot, but now I'm going to break Kelly's World Record out of spite. I will achieve that, even if it is my parting shot in this life."

A reporter telephones Joseph to ask if Fox's allegations are true.

"No. Alvin has never met or even heard of him. He's been perched in mid-town for 36 hours . . . Yes . . . Booked for stands in different cities all summer long . . . ."

Emmerling smirks, and hands $20 to Vivian.

"Here. You earned this. That was a master stroke, telling the cops that you were his secret wife. I made sure the press got a whiff so they were there when the server handed him a subpoena. That lummox is pissed and so is his spouse."

Robert Johns and his confrère Serena Bergandi are crowned as "Hardwood Dance Champions." Beating all others on the cedar floor by unwavering for a sole blistering 259 hours and 43 minutes, their outing dominates the front page of the *Chicago Evening Post* on June 30, 1928.

The same day, The New York Department of Health forces a halt to the "Winner Take All" marathon series at The Roseland Auditorium. After firing the blank pistol to set off the dancing 480 hours ago, promoter Milton Crandall is pelted with garbage when he announces the premature end to the contest. He also clarifies that the 18 couples still dancing will share in the $1,000 prize equally. He retreats to reconcile receipts with his partner Charles "Cash and Carry" Pyle. Each criticizes the other as responsible for the debacle. The allies turn on each other, come to blows, and their cooperative separates.

A few nights later, Alvin and Joseph are listening to the radio in the living room of the apartment. After strains of an orchestra fades, the studio announcer breaks in.

"This station's management encourages responsible townspeople to take part in the WABC electric soap-box. And now, an editorial from Dr. Clifton Levy, Ph.D."

In the studio, Levy is zealous and ostentatious, bloviating as a politician might rile up his ardent supporters on election night.

"Why are Americans so engrossed with these weird matches? Why should the masses want to eat hard-boiled eggs, quaff coffee, or jig perpetually, more than any other ever did before? The physiologist conjectures that they are moved by a quest for renown, to have their pictures published, and think this is an easy way to wealth. Promoters are the ones gaining riches; gathering any funds that can be liberated from the credulous."

Joseph snorts at the diatribe he is hearing over the radio. *This schmuck,* he thinks. *Why do the people believe his crap? Just because he has fancy letters after his name and sermonizes like evangelist Sister Aimee Semple McPherson through a radio microphone?*

"The restless lasciviousness of the jazz-loving, marijuana-smoking youth's lust to never to be unremembered is freakish. Second, in the effects upon those who take part. Science is interested in the indefatigability. If these trials were conducted with scientific technique, they might add to our knowledge of the sensorium to solve pain and lethargy. In my opinion, this is wasted effort. When Miss Bobby Mack sat seven days, she exposed herself to acute apprehensions. She was vulnerable to the ethos, even though protected, more or less. Mack must have exercised incredible self-control to be able to lodge that length, with the limited amount of slumber that was possible. When she came to the end, she was accorded with a loving cup and $500 whereupon she decided to escape her loneliness by an instant marriage. She did not suffer any ill effects from her stunt. I worry her fate is that physical problems may resort in some disorder after a lapse of years."

Emmerling pours a whiskey and takes a sip of the potent amber liquid for "medicinal purposes" while he listens to the man continue to spout gibberish.

"When Alvin 'Shipwreck' Kelly ate nothing solid during nine days in Kansas City, he was taking the chance of several pitfalls. He placed a humongous strain upon his internal system by the wakefulness necessary to complete the task, but he added to the fatigue by abstaining from life-giving nutrients. That he was weakened temporarily, and a physical examination by an expert after his stunt could have quantified the amount of harm incurred. No wonder that most say, all these contests are hogwash. And the pole itself, a phallic symbol that symbolizes unchecked, unrestrained copulation, and corruption of America's infected youth. This 'flagpole sitting' is an evil, reckless trend . . . ."

The opinion continues, bashing gluttony, physical rigidity, and drawing dire conclusions by citing an Italian study conducted with rats. Emmerling clicks the switch off and ridicules the shrink.

"What an ignoramus. He's just like that Comstock sap. Are you diminished, Alvin?"

"I feel . . . just swell, great in fact. That doctor was talking about ME! I'm famous."

"That guy is a quack. Maybe I should ask the station to provide equal time."

Joseph never does.

Across the nation, Seattle approves a statute banning dance marathons in its borders. The law is enacted after a participant dances 19 days and then is eliminated in fifth place. In a malaise, she slits her wrists in a bathtub. The tragedy becomes a front page story in *The Star.* Emmerling is apprehensive that future regulations could be proposed in other cities, hampering his ability to promote endurance.

Alvin is thriving au natural on St. Louis's Stratford Hotel. Under a harvest moon, the night is mild. He spies on the comings and goings in the hamlet. He has become a bit batty from the withdrawal, adding four days, nine hours, and 14 minutes to his total amount of isolation when he discontinues sitting on September 9, 1928.

Elinor Smith taxis her Waco 10 biplane out of the Roosevelt Field hanger on October 21, 1928. Her 11th grade classmates have dared her to carry out a "mind-boggling feat." She darts below the four east river bridges. Airport authorities suspend her pilot license ten days. Readers thrill over the 14-year-old's gumption. Joseph dubs her "The Flying Flapper of Freeport" in *The Gloucester Journal*, and her nickname sticks.

Vivian is perpetually beseeching Alvin for a domicile. The two bicker constantly. Finally, Joseph leases a bijou apartment in the Cobble Hill section that satisfies her, and she embarks on the process of buying furnishings. Alvin and the baby move in with her.

Emmerling is relieved to have her and the infant out from underfoot. He is happy to have a full night's sleep after months of being woken in the middle of the night by the crying in the next room. He continues to meet with Alvin daily about business when they are not earning. Internally, Joseph misses not having his friend nearby.

Vivian is running simultaneous petty dodges to earn extra money; one of her most recent is when she takes her dresses to the dry-cleaner, she lifts a receipt pad. She uses a carbon paper on her sales slip and sends copies out to extortionate restaurants. The notation explains that the staff had spilled soup on her, and she wants to recoup her cleaning bill. Owners do not want to deal with the nuisance, so most send a pittance of reimbursement with an apology. There are other tricks that gain her a small return, which she hides away in a breadbox. She is always asking Joseph and Alvin to provide grocery money. She skims a portion of every dollar to secret away.

Chapter 15 –
Different Kinds of Depression

"You know that redheaded fellow? Yes, well, get those flagpole sitters of yours to find him. Come on, boys. We'll soon get to the bottom of this."
— Groucho Marx, Animal Crackers

As the year turns to 1929, Wyatt Earp goes into the sod at the ripe old age of 80. Joseph rifles in his file cabinet and pulls out his hastily written shorthand penned after his chance meeting with the lawman. He pounds out a tribute to be published in *London's Daily Express* Sunday supplement and 287 other newspapers carry the article. He hopes he has told Tombstone's sheriff's legend correctly and will not be haunted by the shootist's phantom. The writing is framed and put on his wall of achievements.

America continues to be infatuated with staying-power. Occasions of pertinacity are being scrutinized as if the event had an earth shattering ramification, and Kelly is the reporter's go-to to obtain a quote. It seems as if the nation is glued to these goings-ons, even though, in reality, few care. The less well-heeled citizens have little to occupy their rare leisure time, except listen to radio drama.

In contrast, the affluent summon their friends to elegant functions with catered smorgasbords. Many of these ceilidh's hosts pay a fee to Joseph, considering it a hoot for a "man of the hour" like Kelly to join their party. Vivian is rarely invited since she has little self-control at social events. Her intake of intoxicants causes blackouts and unfortunate consequences. When alone with the one-year-old Alvin Kelly Junior at the Cobble Hill apartment, she doesn't drink, preferring to stay sharp. Working on the particulars of her stratagems, she role-plays out all the angles, and anticipates the possible outcomes in her mind. She uses an ancient gypsy code to write copious notes and plans for scams on the pages of a leather-bound journal with a lock.

Contestants in the inaugural "Rocking Chair Endurance Challenge" have been bobbing to and fro 14 days on the veranda of the Egyptian Inn. While the other 12 wobbling entrants are vying to win a $500 prize promised by promoter Phil Wolfe, participant Clara Wagner faints and is rushed to the hospital due to exhaustion. Her prognosis causes Belleville Mayor Rollie Hail to order the tournament halted on February 19, 1929.

"Renown was close, but government must curb this frivolous contamination that is sweeping across the continent for the safety of the citizens in this country," the politician adds. "Illinois must lead the way. I will enact regulations to outlaw such stunts in our city."

Herbert Hoover is sworn in as president on March 4, 1929. While this pageantry is going on in America, Vivian is enmeshed on a petty shoplifting charge at Bonwitt and Teller. A store dick nabs her in the act of pilfering a 10¢ lipstick tube. She lets loose crocodile tears, but the store's policy is to always file charges. Her five-finger discount garners her a $10 fine. Alvin pays and escorts her out of court. The pair argue all the way back to Brooklyn.

Around eight weeks later, promoter Milton Crandall hires Kelly to provide "play by play" from the rafters. On a bench, hanging above the floor at Madison Square Garden, he monitors the 66 mazurka marathoners competing at the "Second Invitational Shake-A-Leg Derby." Aspirants are eliminated from the torture on their soles, and the event finishes with a winning couple on May 7, 1929. Alvin receives $500, for spending the 480 hours above the dancers.

Powerful urges exert pressure on Alvin to an extended promontory at Carlin's Park in Baltimore. The community is accommodating; his many school age fans conduct meetings of the "Keep Kelly Awake" club after twilight in the "Million Dollar Playground." Those that can, linger to engage him with questions. A paltry mist onsets and his fans serenade him with the hit song from the film, the "Hollywood Revue of 1929" by "Ukulele Ike."

"What a glorious feeling. I'm happy again. We're dancing and singing in the rain . . . ."

Kids across the country are participating in the stationary pensiveness inspired by their idol, Shipwreck Kelly. Carbondale 6th-grader Avon Freeman asserts he is the "tree-sitting gold medalist" after eight hours on a bough. He would have stayed resolute; however, his mammy insists he "come in for supper, or git the strap." Emmerling types a letter congratulating him on his achievement and has Alvin sign a photo for him.

Earle Rogers, who is nine, reclines on an eight-foot tall fence but shuns his post after 11 hours when a warm cherry pie's aroma is too much to resist. Colgate teen William Rucker takes to an unused 18-

foot wooden picket in his front yard. Three days later, his streak finds
its culmination as the truant is hauled to school.

William Wentworth sits a week. "Wee Willie" is handed a
trophy by the *Maryland Leader* editor imprinted to the "Loftiest King
of Kid Sitters." Baltimore's mayor, William Broening issues a
proclamation that the 12-year-old's achievement is a "substantiation of
the pioneer spirit." Many of his constituents are not in agreement.
Cosmopolitan magazine states the hobby is "competitive imbecility."
Alvin abseils after 30 days and speaks where the rubber meets
the road.

"This town has 'pep.' I send thanks to my fans. Without their
encouragement, I could not have lasted a month," he imparts to *The
Baltimore Sun.*

"Why do you do this activity?" asks the reporter. "Your
frivolous display seems futile?"

"I am saving to buy a house, and since the missus knows where
I am, she doesn't think I'm chasing skirts when I'm out late . . . ."

Rio Rhonde's Bill Williams uses a bent paperclip fastened on
his nose to thrust a peanut, 18 miles to summit of Pike's Peak in
Colorado. The "screwball" crawls to the crest, while fending away
rodents attempting to pilfer his pods. The lanky Texan finishes his
onerous task on June 26, 1929, winning a $500 bet. A Georgia peanut
distribution conglomerate contributes an engraved silver loving cup to
his winnings. He shows reporters the remaining surplus husk from his
breast pocket—he is quite unhinged.

"Dang vermin. I had to replace 184 of these during my hike. It
was enough to drive a man to the brink of madness. I hate them darn
pesky squirrels. Varmints, always trying to chew on my nuts . . . Hey,
why you fellas laughing?"

Well known pilot Wilmer Lower Stultz takes two prepubescent
riders in his Waco "Taperwing" on July 1, 1929. The boys who have
"begged him to fly," get scared after he spins the plane at 4,000 feet.
Jamming their shoes under the steering bar, renders it inoperable. The
pioneering aviator who first established the mail route to Cuba and
flew Amelia Earhart her first time across the Atlantic can't budge his
guidance stick. The aircraft shatters upon impact, killing all three.

At the coroner's inquest, the rash flyboy's reputation is tarnished by an accusation that he had been soused before rising into the empyrean. The allegation of him being three sheets to the wind turns out to be fallacious, but the reputational scarring is done. Joseph writes an Op-ed praising the airman, tries to set the lies aside, and speak the truth—to no avail.

An eye-catching feat is being attempted by Point Loma sophomore "Porky" Jacobs. He is on a barrel tied to an Ocean Park trestle, 150 feet from shore. An employee of *The San Diego Union* rows out to him on August 16, 1929.

"What is this, um, whatever? What is this activity called?"

"I been "wave riding" almost 24 hours. Hey, did you bring any food? I'm starving."

It is wheels up from Santa Monica as 19 ladies fly in the inaugural All-Women's Air Race on August 18, 1929. Hearst syndicated columnist Will Rogers refers to the tournament as the "Powder Puff Derby" and the catchy phrase sticks. Amelia Earhart, Evelyn "Bobbi" Trout, Edith Foltz and other celebrity-aviatrix are trying to arrive to Cleveland in the best time. During the contest, carbon monoxide from a leaky hose fills Alaskan bush pilot Marvel Crosson's cockpit. The fumes cause her to lose consciousness. Her flying machine crashes on the second day of the race. She dies, burning in an Arizona cotton field.

Landing on the tarmac at Cleveland Municipal Airfield, 15 other ladies celebrate the end of the race. At the finish line reception, Joseph pours a champagne, handing the narrow flute to the third place finisher, Earhart. He asks her to give him a quote for the *Marietta Daily Times.*

"What would you say sets you apart from these other women, Miss Earhart?

"The way I squeeze, suck, blow, and bang in the cockpit," she titters as he squirms uncomfortably. "I understand those four things better than any of these ladies."

"What? . . . Excuse me?"

"I can baby a piston engine to get more power out of it. I understand how the four cycles make it work better. They just know how to fly. That is the difference between us, Mr. Emmerling." Despite others courting a cuckoo awareness, Alvin dominates the papers regarding toughness. He has the salt and sirgacity to persevere on as others fail. Joseph is charging an ample fee, both to be profitable and yet be affordable to merchants.

Harry "The Original Human Fly," Gardiner is climbing in Fredericksburg on September 30, 1929. He is attempting to advance to the top of the four-story Athens Hotel with just his physicality. He clenches and claws to the apex. When he does summit, cheers erupt; however, the contributions from the more than 3,000 observers totals a paltry $48. Joseph is observing for *The Free Lance-Star.* He tells the enraged climber that he was watching that fateful day at Grant's tomb.

"Cheapskates. A fellow spends his whole allotted span to beguile and . . . I ought to . . . ."

"You are not retiring Harry, are you?"

"Spoiled rotten kids. The youth have leisure time now. Movies . . . dancing marathons, flagpole sitters . . . radio. It is not the same as in the golden, olden days, when I was climbing for my own amusement and was the wildest game in town. I am taking great risks; to entertain the whippersnappers, and most don't care."

The stock market has been dipping constantly the last month. The floodgate bursts on October 29, 1929. Wall and Broad is deluged with sellers as the nation grasps for a handhold. "Black Tuesday" losses are calculated at $14,000,000 worth of value. The individual investor is socked in the jaw; feeling the pain from the hysteria. Hoover's administration releases statements to stem the worry, but the unruly do not trust the government. Their disquiet causes a run on financial institutions who shutter their teller windows without repaying their depositors.

The trinity have lost a hunk of their livelihoods to varying degrees. A depression is imminent, and its oppressiveness is breathing on the nape of their necks.

"So, anyone holding any money?" asks Joseph when the trio is assembled that night at the kitchen table.

Emmerling has a stash of cash in a safe hidden behind his bookshelf. The funds from the sale of his wire service should let him ride out a bleak downturn if he is careful.

Joseph worries, *I have lost a substantial amount of my wealth by selling short. I receive a monthly retainer to write about aircraft innovations, kooky scenarios, and other tidbits, but various assignments from United Press International will only take me so far. Maybe I can squeeze in a free-lance story for a reputable paper once in a while. I can wrangle jobs for Alvin. Vivian will have to buttress her own weight.* He opens the balance sheet and crunches numbers.

"I hid some dosh in the mattress, but a bulk of my liquidity is unretrievable," moans Vivian. She lies. *I have cash secreted away, but I prefer to plead poverty. I'll spend Joseph and Alvin's money. My secret slush fund is for MY graceful retirement one day.* "My investments are spread out. Much is in speculative efforts and a great portion of that will be thorny to recoup."

"I went to grab my moolah, but the bank was shut," posits Alvin. "I was in a line but they didn't open, so zilch. I was afraid the depositors would riot."

The loss of his savings account frightens the jack-tar. The house he feels impelled to provide now seems beyond his fingertips. He briefly considers selling his keepsake and contemplates divulging his heirloom to his spouse but thinks about Jacobi's counsel. Now is not the tick of the second-hand to yaw. Vivian joins his side, cooing while rocking Junior back to sleep.

"We will certainly be fine . . . ."

"We will have to vacate the Brooklyn apartment," notes Emmerling sourly. "Financially we cannot to keep the luxury when you are not there most of the time. There is no telling how long this trouble might last."

Alvin will do better than the majority of residentiary because he has the chance to earn a mountain of money, fast. During the preceding 12-month period, Emmerling estimates the gross is $27,000 before expenses. Even if bookings hold steady, it is doubtful they will clear the same amount in 1930.

"The common voters will be thirsting for insulation from today's decline," verbalizes Emmerling. "I'm sure there will be a plenteousness of tragic stories to tell."

"I've concocted a clever plan. Wanna hear?" interjects Vivian. "Bought Florida swampland—200 acres. I paid $1 each, and now I'm going to give them away."

"How is that going to help you accumulate you any wealth?" questions Joseph. "I'm not seeing your endgame."

"I'm paid when the dolts try to register the deed. My partner assists with that and encourages an assessment of the land for an additional small fee. We split the proceeds."

"Is that legal?" asks Alvin sounding a little alarmed.

"My hands are squeaky clean. No geetus from the foolish ever comes directly to me . . . and the paperwork to own the land is real. If no law is broken, is it an illegal act?"

"You are revolting," snipes Emmerling. "Playing with the aspirations of good flesh and blood. Claiming innocence on a technicality. Disgusting."

In fallow eras, Joseph feels civilization's tapestry becomes more intricate and enthralling. Each worry line on an indigent exposes a parable that could be catalogued. Emmerling's intellect and agility will increase their chance of survival. He mollifies Alvin's sense of unease with his own coolness.

"We will forge forward," ripostes Emmerling. "I will devote the next months to replacing any lost dates. I have a plan. We will drive to see Al Jolson for advice. He is one of the most clever minds I know." A few days later in Atlantic City, Alvin and Joseph shake hands with the entertainer.

"His inimitable knack could appeal to the bosses," cogitates the singer as he sips illicit Canadian Club. "My opinion is a grandiose proceeding is required to affix the perception that stagnation can be an art instead of being deemed as nonessential loafing."

The vocalist pauses to shake an admirer's hand who had approached to obtain an autograph. Now that the singer has achieved fame, he considers his followers rude and intrusive.

"Your fans recognize the navy suit you wear, even when are so far removed. Your brand is like the blackface I wear. The minstrel makeup enables me to be free onstage," muses Jolson. "Removing my greasepaint grants me the ability to be incognito; and go mostly unnoticed. You could set some kind of unbreakable star performance? Rivals will flock here; to be in the same league as him. The prize—an inaugural 'World Series' championship of a sort, to create lore of an emerging sport. Maybe wear a belt, like wrestlers win, ya know to show his mettle."

Emmerling is convinced this is a watershed moment. It is a great idea. He contacts the ownership council at Atlantic City. It takes the promise of a sizable bribe, but the aldermen approve the competition to take place the Summer of 1930. The trio must survive until then, and Alvin will become illustrious. There will unequivocally be funds when that happens.

Kelly feels a sense of gratification. *It will be all me. Succeed or fail, I will have no one else to blame. If any interloper dares to attempt at my title, I will simply accommodate longer. I am going to wangle superiority by creating a thing of beauty no one can ever eclipse.*

Alvin is on the B. F. Keith Theater Building in Union City on December 20, 1929. After sunset, thermometers dip toward zero, and he withdraws from his newel. Kelly adds 145 days and six hours in various cities to his grand total of remoteness. Between the double feature, he chats with patrons while peddling autographed photos.

"I am so glad you all came out. I know things have been thorny since the bottom dropped out. Trust me, the affairs of state will improve. I have the faith that things will turn out if each of us believes in the promise of America."

Alvin is motionless at Proctor's 125th Street Theater in April of 1930. He is glad the capacity to be in tranquility is ingrained in his psyche. Groundlings rubberneck at the perfervid figure silhouetted by the fluorescing neon. Some take an abridged break from their troubles to take in his grandeur. Emmerling prepares a schedule three months prior to their date with fate. Those in their springtime, for some reason, before you can say "Jack Robinson," decide sitting is fun. Kelly's success influences more kids to stretch out on a limb trying to shine.

Racine's Jimmy Clemons claims he owns the (unofficial) title of "Age Ten World Champ" after finishing 24 hours on June 13, 1930. In California, E. B. Landry proves two days on a tree bough is easy. He answers questions sent up by *The Oakland Tribune.*

"I am going to set a mark ain't no kid can topple," blurts out the teenager. "I hope that you tell Shipwreck Kelly."

Landry's age induces Alameda mayor John L. Davie to ban such episodes in his city limits. Joseph surmises that legislation will not hurt business in the east, if it becomes law in the west, but he touches base with a "fixer" anyway. Municipal commissioners vote to not enact a law about such practices.

In Muncie, 14-year-old Jack Evans has been in the branches three days and avows to be the "Midwest's Best Youth Sitter." In Oak Park, best friends Truman Kirkpatrick and Jack Owens are attempting to last longer from trees across the street from each other.

Withdrawn in his remote kingdom, Alvin grips onto the sides of the wood, jocose to be unhampered from the oppressive sunshine glaring upon him. The sustenance is half a roast beef sandwich and soda. Once in a while, he wrests out a vest-pocket bible and studies scripture. As an ex-sailor, he feels a kinship with Noah, imagining himself at Mount Ararat's peak surveying the dwindling blue. Emmerling keeps him current with the status of the youth sitters.

"Let's elevate those kids to honorary Vice-Presidents in the fan club," suggests Alvin when he hears about them.

Joseph has cut substantial price breaks to merchants so Kelly can keep sharp. The discount keeps appearances steady. The foursome trudges across the bridge to the Jersey shore where Alvin will spend an extended summer residence. Quarters are set aside to house his entourage.

"The Showplace of The Nation," built in 1896, advertises "15 acts. One 50¢ entrance fee." The slats built on the beach house a range of amusements from "Rex the Boxing Kangaroo" to minstrel singers. Patronage is drawn-in to see the hot jazz bands fronting "Banjo Eyes" Eddie Cantor, fan dancer Sally Rand, and other acts. The surrounding properties bring in blockbuster income as nearby township's residents come to bask on the shore like a shrewdness of apes to a waterhole in the savanna. Bootlegged hooch and unlicensed gambling is available to those in the know. Cars park on the roadside in any spare space around the Jersey shore in June of 1930.

Chapter 16 –
An Unbeatable Record

"No one ever made a difference by being like everyone else."

— *P.T. Barnum*

Alvin can see almost nine miles in the distance from his rod and hears the music emanating from the calliope on the carousel below. Occasionally the rapturous whoops from the out-of-towners enjoying the pier reach his ears. From three stories up, he imagines he can smell the aroma of roasted peanuts and frankfurters being doled out to vacationers.

Children below on the boardwalk hold balloons, lollipops, or ice cream. When he sees their heads tilt, he waves. Exercising his sore neck muscles, he muses, *I wish I had a frosty mug of beer. It is unfair that I cannot have one due to prohibition.* Despite that minor disappointment, on his flimsy board, he is in a stellar mood.

"Let them pick their pole and sit," halloos Kelly through a amplified microphone. "I will score a resounding victory no matter who tries."

Emmerling raises his hands for quiet. A steel worker walks to the stage and uses the public address system to talk to the crowd.

"I am Lee Rapport from Allentown. I am used to the height, so I think I can last awhile."

Also signing on the dotted line is an immigrant with an extravagantly waxed handlebar mustache.

"I ess Hugo Bihler from Munich. Europe's number von sitter, haffing survived weeks on sie Notre-Dame cathedral spire. I haff come a far vey, unt vill take zis dare."

The band whips into a fanfare as out of the hotel, the nation's second best-known sitter, Joe Powers struts out like a gunslinger. The ringer grins broadly—his four gold front teeth glinting in the sunshine. "Hold-Em" is guaranteed an opulent compensation after ten days.

"Illinois's favorite son is here to bring home the bacon. This Joe ain't got nowhere to be this next month, so let us git this contest of wills, a-going."

"Any other participants, please present yourselves."

Joseph checks his watch. As the promoter, he's encouraged Jim "The Irish Sailor" Kelly to be there, but he does not show. A few other foolhardy individuals put their name down to try their adroitness. Not serious threats to his title, they wriggle around on a greased column, scrambling a few feet before quitting to the mirth of the lookie-loos.

Phillip S. Roberts

Clad in his trademark white suit, Kelly is protected from the punishing rays by an umbrella. The shade also functions as balance. With a pop from a blank, the duel commences. Alvin takes out a telescope and sights his competitors two points abaft the beam on the starboard side.

Those guys will not be heavenward for enough time to acquire a sunburn, he says to himself. He is not wrong.

Rapport lasts 30 minutes. Joseph hands him $100.

"Thanks for helping out in a pinch, Lee. I heard from 'The Irish Sailor' this morning. The silly 'jackass' went on a binge last night. He asked me to arrange his bail. Exactly what took place is unclear, but I guess after a few snorts, Jim became turbulent. When the coppers tried to calm him, he punched one. He is in lockup in the Bronx at the 41st Precinct on a drunk and disorderly charge. He will not be around at least a month."

Bihler is second to touch the walkway, also lining his pocket with $100. The remaining two men in contention are locked in a duel of wills on poles opposite each other.

Three days after the aerial match begins, on July 24, 1930, chimney sweep William Penfield is quite comfortable in the thin air, 100 feet over Strawberry Point, Iowa. Kelly does not know about this combatant. "Treetop Bill" says he plans to stay at least 43 days.

"If a city slicker can sit, an ornery mid-westerner can do it better," he crows to a reporter from *The North Iowa Times*. "I will demolish any duration Kelly can set."

Powers lavishes ten days at his loft. He descends to the wood, and Joseph hands over his compensation of $2,000. "Hold-Em" heads back to Topeka to his employment as a steeplejack.

The sailor-suited figure set in the sky now reigns as victor. Emmerling and Vivian cater to their luminary from a storefront on the Boardwalk. Provisions shuttle to Alvin: a snack, a thermos, peppermints, Lucky Strike cigarettes, and detective novels. Anything less than a pristine feather in his cap would be a disappointing payday, so the squatter soldiers on valiantly, padding his time.

The concession is reaping more than financials. Alvin's exclusion is being chatted around water coolers nationally; daily question sessions are held early enough to allow for scribes to get their articles in before the evening deadline. Kelly responds to passerby's written questions sent him in the bucket. At ground level, Emmerling opens a returned query that points out the ever increasing amount of sitters and reads the reply.

"Kelly's response reads . . . I worry about my waist line more than I think about them. I've had to reduce my meals to twice a day. The hotel chef is so good here. Ask those guys who left—they'll admit they don't have half the sand as me."

ATLANTIC CITY PRESS — AUGUST 1, 1930

THE IRISHMAN HAS PROVEN HIS ACUMEN. CONSTANTLY, THE OUTLANDISH HUMAN PROVIDES MIRTHFULNESS. KELLY'S HOBBIES INCLUDE READING LOVE POETRY FROM HIS WIFE, HANDICAPPING THE RACING FORM, AND TRYING TO REMAIN COOL DURING THE SUMMER. WINCHED TO THE SAILOR, A TAILOR MEASURES HIM TO HAVE A CUSTOM VICTORY SUIT MADE. DAILY AT NOON, A MICROPHONE IS SENT SO THOSE BELOW CAN GLEAN KNOWLEDGE FROM THE CRUSADER WHO NEVER SEEMS AT A LOSS FOR WORDS. WHEN A HURRAH RISES FROM NUMEROUS VACATIONERS ON THE SLATS, HE BEAMS WITH A GAP-TOOTHED GRIN, AND LIGHTS A CIGARETTE. SUCH IS SHIPWRECK'S TENURE AFTER A MONTH.

Vivian puts her boondoggle into motion. She puts on her best clothes and hits the trendy spots with the two-year-old Junior in a stroller. Armed with numbered titles of her worthless swamp in Polk County, she holds a prospectus featuring drawings depicting mansions, an 18-hole golf course, and an opulent clubhouse. When a stylish, single gentleman orders at the bar, she edges closer to him and flirts.

"You are fun," drawls the fraudster. "You should be my next door neighbor."

She weaves the fairytale that her husband has traded her substantial real estate to not contest a divorce. She excavates a beautifully constructed deed from her handbag. Printed on expensive card stock and bearing fluid strands of calligraphy, the document has an intricately incised border. She then unfolds her glossy brochure and singles out her lot on the map. She gabs—we are building a state-of-the-art, re-vitalizing vacation community. Many rich families have already purchased lots. She lays the double-talk on thick, dishing rumors of plutocratic upper-class—5th Avenue society dynasties like the Vanderbilts, and the Rothschilds. She then, without any notice, signs the title and hands it to the schlub.

"We will have so much fun playing tennis," she insists, while pretending to be a little tipsy. "I prefer to surround myself with a certain type of intellect and bearing."

"Oh, I could not . . . ." the born-yesterday protests as she hands him an indenture.

He does not want to insult her, so the mark takes the document. Vivian points out the phone number to call so the plot can be registered so her planning can come to fruition. The telephone goes to an associate, not the actual state employee. Telling them, "mail $25 to file ownership on the acre," the voice at the other end additionally suggests that the sap have the land assessed.

Those that nibble the bait, usually take the rest clean from the fishhook. In reality, the chiseler doesn't even bother to complete the transaction. Her confederate uses a stolen "official government" rubber stamp on the deed and mails back the parchment with a dubious document proclaiming "their expert opinion of the Everglades land." Few ever venture south after hearing the acreage is worthless and unable to be constructed on. The beauty of her hornswoggle is in the fact that the patsies pay someone else. The bright conspiracy comes with little uncertainty and copious rewards.

Frequent naps keep Kelly from teetering off his stanchion. Elevated above the gaiety, he is resolute despite the relentless humidity. When showers williwaw, he pulls a tarp around his shoulders. Emmerling exaggerates to reporters that "the glare from the searchlight beams shining upon the sitter at night is visible in faraway Trenton."

Alvin hears a pennon flapping nearby. He is without anxiety, although he once had a gull come close to hitting him. The smell of the ocean salt rejuvenates his morale. Fans, mostly preteens send him letters, addressed to "Shipwreck—General Delivery."

Ropes groan as eight men lift a female barber. She hangs mid-air, tied by a strap to the bosun chair. Before she gives him a trim, a straight razor shave, and a manicure, she sprays a lemony smell on him to mask the stench of the unwashed, undisturbed lodger. He feels much more clean after she scrapes the stubble from his chin. He hands the beautician a fiver, telling her to keep the remainder as she returns to her salon.

"Soon, I will be amongst you," bellows Kelly. "I feel much more aerodynamic. Her steady hand is the one to seek out, if you want a nice shave or trim."

Alvin has created another highlight at "America's Summer Vacation Destination" on August 10, 1930. The country is gripped by sedulous acts despite the economic tumult and upheaval. Smug to be tops in his field, he is ready to relish in the fuss and be spoken of in the same cluster as his idols. Solid fare and a soft bed are among the comforts he will indulge in soon. Most importantly, he will be with family—the reason he gambles his subsistence.

Kelly does not feel friendless at the monumental elevation. He has many thoughts in his head. *I miss my wife and son who are in the hotel underneath me. I wish I could hug my loved ones right now; however, that would lessen the payday. My internal grit will allow me to pass the next few hours and benefit my clan. I am positive I could survive another month if it were needed. Joseph has told me that a guaranteed fortune awaits. Hopefully I can put a sizable payment on a homestead. Vivian so intensely wants that house. I need her to be content and happy. Maybe that will enable her to give up her life of crime and settle down.*

From his elevated spot, he surveys the beach resort where families have fled from the mugginess to the gentle froth blessed by Poseidon. Shifting an umbrella to shade his temporary habitat gives only minor relief. He will be leaving his nosebleed privacy as his unique sport's undisputed ruler.

His handler sends him a clean jersey embroidered with his name. He changes, plonking his sweat-stained shirt into the roof below. *Perhaps the Smithsonian will want to add those rags to their museum of American exceptionalism. I am creating a legacy—testing the limits of durability.* He twists the stem on his wristwatch. *It has completed 473,040,000 ticks from the day Joseph gave it to me at the beginning of the World War.*

Twitchy and on-edge from many percolations, he ingests as many as thirty cups a day of Monarch Coffee to combat the tug of Chuángshén, the Chinese deity of the bedchamber. His eyes are bloodshot. He takes note of another day with a hash mark on the wood seat. He is not getting enough sleep.

Today, is almost identical to the day before, sitting above the fluttering Stars and Stripes. The ensign is not waving much in the becalmed air today. This hour feels like the last and is possibly identical to the next. Was it a five or ten days ago when a fearless 14-year-old named Johnny was pulled up to shake hands with me? The time blurs as I chase fame and fortune.

He must stand until noon. Comfort at his locus is unattainable; his temporary residence is far too compact and sleeping is fraught with jeopardy. Kelly tires of sitting and now decides to rise, trying not to shift his weight too radically in any direction.

Wiggling his toes, he exercises his arches. He diverts himself with a yo-yo at a chancy 225 feet in the sky. Like a trained seal with a ball on its snout, he thrives on the adoration. Anything that breaks his tedium is a nice moment to be savored. He improvises mental activities while wasting the day; after reading the local paper, he finishes the crossword. He needs more cigs.

He yanks a cord that rings a tinkling bell in the booth, so his helpers will send a bucket. When the pail reaches him, he crumples the cigarette package inside, and, craving a juicy peach, he notes that on his pad before lowering the pail. Joseph or Vivian will send what he requires.

His wife uses a rope to hoist the tub. He taps a Chesterfield out, catches the tobacco with his trench lighter and takes a drag. His handlers have found him a tangerine. He peels the rind and sucks a juicy section while reading a few epistles from the youthful admirer's fixated by his quest.

He gropes in his pocket to locate a golf pencil; scribbling his name on postcards. Kelly whangs a few out, studying the cardboard twisting in mid-air. He sponges his brow and kneads his sore calves. The 35-year-old has become thinner due to the 49 days of sparse living on his 36" by 36" square of lumber affixed on the flagpole. It is not simply the physical demands of his performance but the mental aspects as well. Quarantine reshapes a mind, and he is zealous. He has been acclivous, without contiguity at the zenith.

No hothead has ever had such a session on a picket and he secures more prominence with the passing seconds. His competitors have ceded their views, so he is self-assured with the musk and glow that bursts forth from being victorious. Kelly has engendered an unrivaled existence but is not contented. Others are plying his trade thus, he must pad the session, so all competition will come up lacking.

What bravado hath transferred him to pursue his aberrant persuasion? His gluttonous desire is to be more recognized than any ballplayer, actor, or adventurer. The conception nurtures his steadfast ego. He has kept his eye on the prize industriously—to become "the" name that is on their lips when the world considers his distinctive dominion.

As the highest billed, both figuratively and metaphorically, he considers himself *the topmost inducement that is bringing in the customers.* He is, in his opinion, *is as popular as the Ferris Wheel, or any other mechanical ride at the seaside.* At the dome on "The Steel Pier," he is teetering on the fringe, wallowing in his tenancy.

Alvin is excited that today is to be his sublime day, sporting on his underprop. The Boardwalk is jovial with families taking in undemanding pleasures. Merrymakers meander past an arrow that has his name spelled out with lightbulbs and pointing to an animated billboard of a Spanish Galleon. Most do not equate the billboard to the individual on the flimsy square; many are having too much fun on the slats to notice him.

He feels well, albeit exhausted. Kelly suddenly feels an itch. Trying to disregard the tingle, he chews a fingernail, but the sensation grows unbearable. He sends a request; could a new "true crime" magazine be sent? While he waits for reading material so he can follow the exploits of "Pretty Boy" Floyd and gangsters of his ilk, he deliberates upon *if he were to drop a coin from this elevation, might it maim some hapless mortal? Those who inhabit the normal world below, must admire my chutzpah—for I am the only man who could complete such a rigorous mission.* He thinks, *"I am their great conquering hero."*

In a few minutes, he will be having a chat with WMCA-AM. Joseph has purchased a slot and has sent a list of sponsors to mention. That radio interview is going to reap premiums. He has been an animated topic inspiring kids to sit in trees, the focus of editorials and sought after for his off-kilter wisdom. A ringing telephone is heaved to him on a cord and he's on with the deejay Donald Famm.

"So, how is it up where nestlings dwell?" asks the announcer on the other end.

"Sweltering, even at 225 feet. Thanks to my benefactors at the Boardwalk. I will tell you, there's no panorama in the world like the one I see in Atlantic City, New Jersey."

"When did you conceive of living in the sky?"

"Many years ago. It is dodgy to be at a place over so many heads. I am feeling loopy in the thin oxygen." *For me,* he observes, *today is as unforgettable as that day in 1923.* "The most tremendous minute is almost here . . . when I finally walk among my fellow man after 49 days."

"I asked, when?"

"I began as an orphan and became a hero." he prattles into the receiver. Alvin's memory harkens to when the infatuation began. As the interview draws to an end, the announcer thanks him.

"Thanks Alvin. See Shipwreck Kelly come earthward at noon."

WORLD RECORD: SITTER KELLY ENDS 49-DAYS ON POLE.

The front page is emblazoned with bold type. After a month and half of duress, he is entitled to respect. What Emmerling and Alvin have worked so unyieldingly to achieve has been realized. This is the culmination that their organization has been steering to—a legacy his heir can be proud of. The patrons steadily grow larger as his shining moment draws near. The aerosphere is bright and breezy as almost 30,000 crane their necks to gain a better view at the anomaly.

"I am going to come down, more fit than when I began," growls Alvin. "In 60 seconds, I will meander among you after 1,177 hours. My hobby is stamina. This leisure pursuit is the greatest sport in modern times."

He sprays himself with rose-scented eau de cologne so as not to foul any delicate nostrils. He asks the crowd to count from ten, and, in unison, they comply. He salutes and slowly moves smoothly on a wire to meet his well-wishers and the nosey-parkers.

An elated Kelly is greeted by his wife and the public. There is pure pandemonium as his knees almost give out when his heels hit the solid wooden promenade. He takes a few wobbly fawn-like steps before regaining his land legs. Paparazzo expose film while an Irish band strums the "Flogging Reel" and he does a little jig. Has the entire Jersey shore has turned out to express admiration for his ascendancy? It seems so. The bustling attendance is a propitious omen, as word of mouth is an appreciable part to fabricating the ensuing legend that is Shipwreck Kelly.

The sit has been burdensome on his physiology. Emmerling directs his luminary between the sea of adoring well-wishers, basking in his shining star a little while. On the hotel veranda, he readies for a crush of reporters. The manager raises his hands for quiet. After the laudation abates, he wields a stack of telegrams.

"I clutch felicitations from a group of the prominent," sermonizes Joseph to the assembled. He is on the pulpit, channeling the Barnumesque talkers from his youth. He lies. No one famous has sent congratulations. "Lindbergh cables, 'Masterful effort, Shipwreck.' Charlie Chaplin sends, 'Well done, Alvin.' Robert Ripley, the 'Believe It or Not' cartoonist, guarantees to make him a featured drawing in a panel. Countless others send their regards. Let me praise this extraordinary giant."

He grasps and raises his protege's hand. The ovation from the witnesses to the history is loud.

"I submit to you, the incontrovertible World Aerial Champion, flagpole sitter, Shipwreck Kelly."

"Let 'em have a taste of excitement, Champ," utters Joseph as Alvin clears his throat.

Phillip S. Roberts

"I tell you, I feel dandy, beating the hotel out of 50 days of rent." The concentration chuckles. "I double-dog-dare any who think they have the moral fiber. I would be ready to go another month again, right now, if need be. Thanks to my wife, our son, and my associate Joseph. I am in debt to the aldermen who brought me to fascinate you with my specific expertness. I could not have succeeded without your prayers. Thank you all."

He pauses to take a sip of apple juice. He is feeling the effects of gravity and its sugary sweetness gives him energy.

"I accredit my unwavering vigor to a healthy diet. You too can be sharp with clarity and vitality, if you heed the advice from a Hell's Kitchen native. I am THE Shipwreck Kelly. God bless America."

He salutes and takes a bow as the whoops subside.

"Come on, give us a statement," the press pesters the gob. "While interest is at a fever-pitch."

"The cosmos shimmered in the night sky. My pole careened more than a hophead hunting for a fix in Singapore."

"How are you feeling?" asks a reporter from *The Paterson Evening News*. Alvin is a bit indisposed but doesn't let on.

"I have plenty of energy left. I could grin and bear it another few days or so, but I'm looking forward to a nice hibernation in a soft bed. I am humbled to have originated a meaningful instant that will be never be consigned to oblivion. If prohibition wasn't the law of the land, I'd toast you with champagne."

"Did you ever worry you might slip and take a dive?" asked another one.

"Look, I'm ambitious and don't mind taking a risk, but my thorough preparation keeps me from suffering a devastating consequence of pride like Icarus."

"Did you miss human contact during the 49 days?"

"I was never really companionless. All the vacationers beneath treated me with gusto. I took comfort in the bible and sang sea shanties. I am blessed with how many opportunities America furnishes. Where else could a stray rise to become a celebrity?" says Kelly as he stifles a sneeze. "I kept sharp by reciting mathematical tables, figuring crossword puzzles, writing my family, and other pursuits. I got to catch up with some good reading this summer. I quite enjoyed 'The Maltese Falcon,' and that magazine with the Burroughs story about Mars. Thanks to my boosters. Their cards and letters were greatly appreciated."

"Are you hungry? What will you order for your first meal?"

"A lamb chop plus a baked potato piled with butter, chives, and sour cream. Perhaps a slice of cherry pie."

"What is in the works Shipwreck?"

Joseph intercedes.

"Hold on to your bench boys. Our plans are going to be a wow, and that's no phonos-balonus. This comes directly from the feedbag. After being "dead in the water" almost two months, Kelly will greet his fans at the 'Forum Theater' this Saturday afternoon as he receives an engraved loving cup. We will announce what cities we visit on tour."

Applause lifts as if plebeians are rooting for their chosen gladiator in ancient Rome. These cheers are his *raison d'être.* He has become prominent. Alvin raises a thumb and feels his legs give out. Bellhops assist him into the vestibule, hoist him into the elevator, and lift him to the bed.

"This means easy money, and better times," he assures Vivian before he snoozes. "That grand home you want to build is almost in our grasp."

The somnambulist saws logs, oblivious that Penfield is even now still sitting. Joseph goes to settle the finances.

"Perhaps we could hold an annual competition, Enoch?" Emmerling probes as he hands a thick envelope to the alderman. "The pier was pretty lively."

"Don't call us pally," comes the gruff riposte from "Nucky" Johnson as he riffles the crisp treasury notes. "Receipts from our little beachside resort are roughly identical. You have gotten exactly what you wanted from this deal—real publicity. We earned our share because 'WE' did that for you. If we want more cabbage, we'll let you know. Savvy? Now scoot."

Alvin snores as if he was a hibernating bear in a wintery den. He drifts into dreamscape, secure with the protection of the Aztec goddess of the moon, Mētztli. After he bestirs, he counts his blessings —his missus, the health of his son, and the associate who steered him to prominence. He might live happily ever after, after all.

In a few days, normality reigns. Alvin reads his mail. Vivian finishes the chat with her confederate in Polk County and is tickled pink. Of her deeds, 151 were registered and 80% of those were "surveyed." Her 50% from the deceitful campaign comes to almost $3,200. Joseph finishes the Kelly manuscript as he now has an ultimate coda to conclude on. It adds a degree of verisimilitude to the project. Typists are duplicating copies and he has plans to visit all the publishing houses over the next weeks.

"The third estate will want to read your story. With sharp promotion, we can have a bestseller. We will do sits and autograph signings. You are a big-wheel now."

"How much did Alvin earn from this 49 day stand?" Vivian inquires. "Is it enough for an installment on a property?"

"No. I actually had to pay for this razzle-dazzle," Emmerling sheepishly admits. "He benefits from the noteworthiness and we can charge . . . ."

"Bupkis? Nothing? That is not what I want to hear out of your mouth."

Emmerling clams up after realizing she is not paying attention. Alvin is horrified. He is at the grandest nub—then in a trice, life veers like the arm of a monkey grabbing a child's piece of fruit through the bars at the zoo.

"You reap dividends, so why doesn't he?" she continues ranting. "Alvin promised me a house, but I am stuck in this pocket-sized, cheap dump. What good are your pledges, you charlatan? You ARE a bad man."

She lets fly a dainty fist as Alvin hops in between the two. Her hand connects, solidly. Her husband hits the floor smarting from the impact. She grabs the child.

"This discussion is not closed," She rages on the way out of the apartment as Alvin's shiner purples like a blueberry. Joseph grabs a bag of frozen peas from the freezer as she screams and slams the door. "I'm going to hire a legal practitioner to handle my interests."

"Our terms were always 'I take care of financials and in exchange, I helm your life story.' That's what you agreed to in 1912 and 1918. The revised entente we signed says she earns a share in case of an unfortunate incident in concise verbiage. My attorney verified that clause is 100% iron clad. If you break our agreement, I promise to publish my creation, without your input even if I have to pay myself. She will not have a leg to pirouette on in court even if she hires a hundred 'trumpeters' to play her song. That woman will never have a penny of my money. She is like Lorelei, drawing sailors to her deadly rock on the Rhine. If you choose her, those schemes of hers will end with you deprived of liberty and I'll be no worse off. Unless she keeps her schnozz out of our affairs and expresses regret, you will leave with nothing but memories."

Vivian returns five days later. The first thing she says is "Why didn't you pay the ransom to the kidnappers sooner? I had to convince them not to send you a toe." Alvin can smell the liquor on her breath, and does not ask any details, but lets it be known "how things are going to be" in no uncertain terms to his wife. He insists she apologize to Joseph. She complies and tranquility reigns until they are due to return to the tour. As they travel to flagpole sitting jobs, she persists with the tot in Manhattan and buys more Okefenokee swamp-land to traffic now that she has the diddle on how well the scam works.

Betty Fox is setting her station up on August 28, 1930. She claims the title of the "Women's Sitting Champion" is hers, even though there is not really such a thing. She clambers 52 feet higher than the Fort Pitt Hotel and plans a stretch of 100 hours. The 20-year-old, wearing a skintight swimsuit enunciates she is in "the most phenomenal shape."

"I am ready to wipe out the conventions of normality," states the platinum blonde to the *Pittsburgh Post-Gazette* reporter. "My brother, Benny will assist me from the rooftop during my isolation."

Betty hides a truth to engage single gentlemen to her cause. The blonde is not his sister as billed but his wife, Nona. As she heads to the tenth-story, many are watching from Penn Avenue. A cramped, fiesta-street-fair has germinated with vendors peddling binoculars, hamburgers, and other impulses. Benny sells cheesecake shots of

Betty; enlargements of her wearing a skimpy dress. A dedicated
telephone number is available so homeowners of the hamlet can ring
her during her formidable feat and ask questions while she trifles
with uncertainty.

The long distance operator connects Alvin. He congratulates
her on being the best known female sitter.

"I got a communiqué from Benny Fox," shrieks the platinum
blonde. "My husband says you are a giant ass. He promises to slug you
in the nose when he sees you."

Joseph reads an editorial from *The Salinas Index-Journal*. The
editor is lobbying lawmakers to ban these "high-risk" activities. The
position piece did not mince words; entrenching these "witless
concerns" could cause maladies to the indigene, inducing brain
seizures and malignant tumors. "Frivolous, ill-advised, inane, useless,
without merit, promoting sloth," are the double-barreled phrases
wielded. His essay culminates, "Why the elected, in any town, would
sanction this type of foolishness is outside the range of our
comprehension." Emmerling pens a rebuttal to their arguments but
decides not to send it.

Penfield ends his span in the heartland on September 12, 1930.
An estimated 3,000 clap politely when he has had enough. Extending
the current record by two days, he has resided in the air now for
51 days and 20 hours.

When Alvin is informed he was beat by the Iowan, he is angry
that he did not pause a longer time on his throne. He is determined that
his pursuit will be unassailable and that any statistic set will abide.
However the climate is souring on the east coast.

"We have contracts; a few well-paid short appearances before
the frost," notes Joseph. "To have a seemingly endless sit, we'd have
to cancel all the little ones. We'd lose money, and you know, we need
cash right now. There is a depression going on after all."

"Next summer, when I defend my title, we should stay 90 days
at Atlantic City."

"Their entertainment committee will probably not have us,
Mein sitzfleisch," Emmerling winces as Alvin bristles at the German
verbiage. "You've become of unexcelled import. That Hawkeye

managed a teeny foothold in the midwest. We simply ignore his feat, and he wanes from the mind."

The sin of avarice is ever-present in his imitators. His competition asserts they are better than him. Kelly feels he has to keep bulldozing forward . . . longer, higher to solidly advance his physical doggedness as dominant. He badgers to be scheduled for even steeper and extended obstacles.

"Let me be brusque Alvin. We are done with multi-week sits. They are not consistent enough to be cost-effective. During a two-month spell, we lose out on numerous abbreviated sojourns. We would sacrifice the cash; it is a rare habitué that can nourish us for an extended term."

"Others are forging a good living doing what I perfected," mopes Alvin. Joseph perceives his amigo is frustrated. "What about these blood sucking leeches? Why don't we sue?"

"Impersonators are actually good. There is a delicate balance that keeps the focus on us. We have an implied trademark. What can we gain from expensive litigation? Taking these others to court would negate any judgements we could take in. And, we'd lose jobs. Even if these gnats had the means to pay, the pettifoggers have to skim their juice off the top."

"Without you, I would be behind the eight-ball, I guess. I shall pray to 'Saint Brigid of Kildare' for you to get the book published."

"Thank you. We have some fruitful sits ripening, champ," placates Joseph. His soft filibuster is a bromide. "Things will be fine."

The manuscript of Alvin's life continues to garner bad reviews. "Repetitive" and "Lacking thrills," are prominent criticisms in the responses. Emmerling is distressed that his boisterous memoir may never be in a reader's hand. He continues to revise, endlessly.

On September 15, 1930, Kelly is practicing his trade on 6th Avenue near West 44th Street. He is on a corner pillar topped by a globe with electric bulbs and can be seen from almost any vantage. Vivian pops by, blows a kiss, and asks Joseph to provide some funding. He antipathetically hands her a $20. She melts into the multitude that are taking a glance at her husband ply his trade, lifts a billfold from a wet behind the ears onlooker, and absconds with the wad of ducats. If the citizens can take comfort in his diligence, perhaps they will survive this recession.

Alvin's stockpiled prestige has him being invited to swanky parties as an oddity. Explaining to Vivian, he's "working and cannot bring guests," does not go over well with his wife. When she argues with him, he reflects, *I'm glad to have an excuse why she cannot come. She always drinks far too much when she wrangles an invite. That can be embarrassing. And unprofessional. How can I be certain that she won't cause a scene? What if Vivian lifts a purse or pulls a paring knife on an unsuspecting guest? It's better not to tempt fate and have the cops called. I'll just tell her she cannot come.*

He takes advantage of the complimentary fodder, pretending not to notice the other guest's mocking and cruel comments behind his back. Vivian continues squeezing him toward a "normal-nine-to-five" that would qualify for insurance.

"What would happen to me and your son if you had a tragic accident?"

Merchants become hesitant to hire his act. More than a few cancel their dates. Joseph spends hours on the telephone, trying to save bookings. He assures the owners will not be held responsible for any bizarro injury. Finances are scant as the economy continues to plateau. Alvin is acquainted with hobos who have surrendered, resorting to living in a grimy, hardscrabble shantytown by the east river. Vivian has secured a supporting role at Coney Island as the fill-in performer of the "Tanagra the Mermaid" act.

"See the live fee-jee mermaid," busks Vivian from behind the glass of the water tank illusion. "A real miracle. Just 5¢."

Emmerling is unable to interest any shopkeepers in weekly stands, so he schedules a string of 13 hour unpaid publicity sits through November outside of the Five Points and anywhere in the five boroughs. He arranges daily appearances for Kelly at the grocery or a car mechanic's garage; anywhere between Mulberry Street and West 95th Street's Symphony Theater, unfurling banners for businesses that will trade Joseph publicity for goods and services.

"He is stealing from you," she rebukes when Alvin returns from one sit, his arms full of groceries. "With his devil-may-care commerce. If we take what he owes us and flee to Europe, I hear we could live well; rubbing shoulders with expatriates in Paris and Prague. Think of all the money we could make there. They've never seen you do your stuff."

Kelly explains he'd return to the breakers, if he wasn't considered a 'Jonas.' Any normal job would not reap nearly as much. His mate does agree. Nearly 10% of America is without work, thus he is happy to keep striving at what he loves.

Catherine Hartwell's goal is to spend 1,000 hours on the roof of "Patriotic Bird," a barbecue stand near the nation's capital. Upset after gaining 20 pounds from the free grub, the well proportioned maid ditches the roof of the Washington D.C. shack after 14 days on September 30, 1930.

Alvin straps himself in for a 30 minute flight on October 26, 1930. On a 10-foot steel rod, a western saddle is strapped on the fuselage. He perambulates and throws a leg over the trembling shaft. Seated, conspicuous abstractions stimulate his brain as he locks his feet in the stirrups.

What if we hit an albatross? Can I breathe in the thin, cold air? Will I survive if a mechanical malfunction happens? Am I strapped in tightly enough?

He clings to the pommel in fright. Carter Buton nosedives the field, while Joseph uses a Kodak as Kelly soars. With the gusts nipping his ears, the reckless passenger pisses himself. His reward is a singular spot in antiquity; sitting on a pole on a flying plane at 3,000 feet.

Joseph is congratulating him as he saunters the tarmac. After such a feather in his cap, Alvin was expecting a squadron of reporters. He is cross—none are at the airfield to interview him.

"I told 'em . . ." sneers Joseph sarcastically. "But something apocalyptic must have happened in this burg. Maybe a car had a wreck, or a nag got loose. Perhaps even both."

"Do not tell Vivian. She would murder me. I hate to admit it, but, she was right. Flying is for the birds."

Joseph and Alvin traverse the eastern region as sits are set in Hartford, Philadelphia, Boston, and Scranton. He has added an unfamiliar twist to his gimmick; stilts. By welding two tire rims to the ball on the pole, he inserts the extensions in each hole. An additional five feet is achieved during the stand. Vivian tends to the little nipper at the apartment and schemes on how to steal enough money so she can be rich enough to purchase her own house on 5th Avenue.

Kelly is the vertex of the 19th floor on the Paramount Hotel at 46th Street West near Broadway on December 10, 1930. Hell's Kitchen is contentious with rioting below his seat. When he withdraws from his pylon due to the subzero climate, Joseph councils Alvin to "Knock off the commie stuff. It's not a good look." Alvin still tells the reporter from *The Daily Worker* that his renouncement of his seat is in support of the "working class."

"I saw pure bedlam from my locale. The fat-cats are firing the proletarian to improve the bottom line and their bonus. I resolve not to labor, in fraternity with my fellow man. My hardship mirrors their rage —inimical to injustice for an adequate wage. The cold was unbearable, but that is incomparable to the icy-hearts of these rich tycoons. These oligarch's decision is not only barbaric, but it's right before the holiday. Shame on them. Oh, and Merry Christmas . . . ."

Chapter 17 –
The Phantom International Tour

"Brother, can you spare a dime . . ."
— *Yip Harburg*

Phillip S. Roberts

New Yorker magazine contributor Lois Long's debut column entitled "Bed of Neuroses" runs in the January 10, 1931 edition. The 29-year-old describes in her opening paragraph the distain for the frequent social gatherings she's invited to.

> I WON'T GO OUT ANYMORE TO PARTIES. NO DEAR, I'M AWFULLY SORRY, BUT I HAVE A PREVIOUS ENGAGEMENT WITH A GOOD BOOK. I DON'T WANT TO MEET 'SHIPWRECK' KELLY. I WANT TO SIT AT HOME AND THINK IDLE THOUGHTS AT MYSELF.

Joseph hands Alvin the disquisition. He does not appreciate the irony.

"Perhaps we have been at too many dinners. I guess. Still, it is nice to be thought of."

"She did not give you a polite mention."

"I still think it's great."

He beams as he adds the text into his compendium. Alvin is anticipating a temperate Spring. Joseph estimates bookings overall will be fewer due to depression but steady once the weather changes. Vivian is nurturing Junior and advancing her petty hoodwinks.

The "Star Spangled Banner" is enshrined by congress as the National Anthem on March 3, 1931. Emmerling purchases a portable 'Serenader' Victrola to play the acetate disc to signal the beginning and end of another day. Alvin thinks the music is a marvelous addition to the pageantry. Coin of the realm is not easy to come by, yet Joseph keeps a trickle dripping in. If not for the unconventional blurbs he pumps out, meals would be scarcer.

The Empire State Building is completed at 1,250 feet on May 1, 1931. The world's tallest erection is a symbol of the nation's supremacy. President Hoover presses a button in Washington that illuminates all 102-stories at once. The Art Deco skyscraper is a rousing sight, a voltaic torch glowing in the night sky. Emmerling sends a proposition to the edifice's management advocating their forte, knowing full well that his protégée will never be allowed to spend a day on a spike that thrusts that far into god's abode. Alvin is angry that he cannot be part of the grandest construction in the city's history.

William Hill shoots the rapids and tests Niagara Falls in a padded steel barrel on May 30, 1931. As 25,000 watch, he is stuck in a whirlpool. When he cannot coax his container from the writhing undertow, the stunter becomes confuddled and dizzy. Paddling into the swirling rapids, his eldest boy Bill Jr. secures a line to the drum. A score of non-participants assist in tying the rope to a tree and effectuate the rescue. In the morning, the sore and dauntless elder Hill remounts his unique tank and continues floating to Lake Erie.

June is mapped out as a junket, with short stops scheduled in wens from Boston to Bangor. Alvin is tickled pink to be indefatigable. He's brought "The Murder at the Vicarage" by Agatha Christie to his locale to pass time with. His work is more desirable than selling apples like the legions of unemployed who are manning street-corner-stands across the city.

Wiley Post attempts to transit the globe quicker than the German-built Zeppelin that covers the distance in 21 days. The daring pilot in his Vega dubbed the "Winnie Mae," culminates the odyssey in eight days, 15 hours, and 51 minutes on July 2, 1931.

A mob swarms Roosevelt Field to lift the one-eyed airman on their shoulders. Motorcycle cops surround the taxiing plane in a protective outer halo, keeping the advancing well-wishers at bay. The enthusiasm of the assembled engulfs the security detail, who swing batons to control the rumpus. The exhausted flyer and his navigator are taken to meet the president. Alvin extends his sit at the Hartford Union Station by 39 hours and 51 minutes to match their feat.

"Any awakeness anyone can manage, I'll equal," exaggerates Kelly. Those in the queue, waiting on their train, do not appear to care how tirelessly he has been sitting. The populace worry that the depression is deepening. "Post and his navigator, Gatty set a time not easily beaten, but, above all, I am patient man."

On July 10, 1931, Alvin is onstage after two days at the Eckel Theater in Syracuse. He has been promising a surprise and tells the audience that "as of now, films cost a quarter instead of 35¢ and those in the theater are due a refund." The venue is at capacity and cheerful as a hockey fanatic after his team lofts the Stanley Cup. Owner Gus

Lampe is shaking a bag of dimes. Ticket-takers and ushers tithe the silver slivers to patrons before the cartoon like John D. Rockefeller.

"Well done, Shipwreck," the shrewd operator beams. "We handed out $8, but we will earn more in concessions and repeat business once the word gets out."

Alvin joins his missus as the opening credits finish and brutish actor James Cagney is on screen.

"They gave me the dime too." Vivian purrs in glee before she turns to the black and white images flickering on the screen. Alvin is already dosing. She wakes him as the end credits roll.

Mounted at Toronto's Sunnyside Amusement Park, Kelly waggles to the fun-seekers in the roller coaster car rumbling by. August 17, 1931 is a stifling day in the province, and Shipwreck pleads they fetch an "Oland & Sons" Canadian lager. Joseph refuses due to the fact his aerial storefront is not licensed for consumption. If taken into custody, he will forfeit his visa and be deported.

Asked to clarify, Mounties affirm 4.4% pilsner must be swilled in a private residence, not in public. Unless ordered though, the division would not interfere if he chose to wet his whistle in the sky. An amber bottle is lifted to the thirsty attitudinizer who guzzles. A hobbyist captures the second with his 35mm camera and *The Montreal Gazette* runs the resulting picture.

The next day, a statement comes from Canada's Beverage Control Board's senior member, Sir Henry Drayton attending to the controversy. He instructs the authorities to inform the kickshaw that "if he thirsts, the law restricts consumption to non-alcoholic types" in a community setting.

Alvin is atop, although he's a day more sober. Browsing the sports section, he becomes enraged that his nemesis, Jim "The Irish Sailor" Kelly is working a pole in Long Branch.

"The nerve that imposter has," he pettily complains to himself. "That double is probably wearing a dress-white uniform too."

He demands to confront the masquerader. After a bumpy 10 hour drive, Alvin shows his face at the town on Shrewsbury river. He makes such a fuss that the sheriff is mustered. The other sitter comes down halfway to fathom what is causing the commotion, hoots in delight, and lugs himself back to his secluded setting.

"That ginger punk is stealing my identity," exhorts Alvin with all the volume his lungs can muster. His holler sounds like the mating call of a flamboyance of flamingos. He is waving an envelope. "This is a statutory order forbidding the underhanded portrayal of my image. I am THE Shipwreck Kelly. I grossed $50,000 doing this in 1930. My legal right is to sue this imitation for felonious infringement of my trademark."

"Your writ ain't worth the ink. You can't copy-write a birth name, halfwit," came the speech from far away from the foaming at the mouth accuser. "Perhaps you are the forgery. Well, say hi to your pretty wife for me . . . ."

Alvin's indignation rages and he becomes exacerbated. He insists on settling the dispute in a "loser quit the profession forever" match. He invokes the most wicked of Irish curses.

"Jim Kelly, for your foul atrocities perpetrated on me, I cast an evil eye on ye' traitor. Back-stabber. I hope you will fade into nothingness, as the seed of your loin will be too embarrassed to admit your linage. May you scuttle and drown, eternally mewling in immortality as a baby does for his mother's nipple. I contemplate the day when your skin will putrefy and wither from your bones in the most painful manner. I wish you die with no cleric nearby to confer the rites and the devil consume your body. I hope soon you are cast into the bottomless pit of hell without an ale to quench your thirst. Bad cess to you."

"I am not taking that from you, pipsqueak," hollers the man in the chair above but he doesn't come down.

The gathered townsfolk are amused at the ridiculous, flustered figure. Alvin rams a finger into the mayor's chest. The elected functionary has had enough of the tomfoolery and orders the malefactor run out of town on a rail. The chief of police chaperones the handcuffed, scruffy accuser to the train depot. Emmerling takes the auto back across the bridge and idles the motor across from Grand Central Station until Kelly arrives. He's still angry.

THE ARGUS — SEPTEMBER 4, 1931

WHEN SHIPWRECK ARRIVES IN LONDON, A WELL-KNOWN STORE WISHES TO ENGAGE HIM SAYS THE DAILY MAIL. AT SEVEN, HE BEGAN HIS SCAMPERING ONTO A TELEGRAPH POLE TO ESCAPE AN IRATE GENTLEMAN HE WAS TAUNTING. AFTER THOSE YOUTHFUL DAYS, HE TRIED VARIOUS CAREERS SUCH AS A HARDHAT, PAINTER, AND BOXER. ALTHOUGH HE WON THREE AMATEUR BOUTS, HE WAS KO-ED IN HIS 13 PROFESSIONAL DUST-UPS. HENCE, THE PUGILISTIC FANS WOULD CHANT "THE SAILOR'S BEEN SHIPWRECKED AGAIN."

HIS TASTE OF PREEMINENCE CAME IN 1924, ATOP A THEATER IN LOS ANGELES. SINCE THEN, HE HAS SAT NEARLY 5,000 HOURS. HE HAS BECOME THE "GUY OF THE SKY." HIS ADROITNESS HAS MERITED HIM $100 A DAY, AND, ONCE, 312 HOURS NETTED HIM $1,200.

Joseph seeds the bogus article in a few scandal sheets to shroud Kelly's absence from the scene. There are major gaps between his engagements. He defers Alvin's ache for an international foray with a rejoinder that is a variation of "Your fans are mostly Americans, not Europeans. Without something to counterpoise our losses, an extended voyage is not viable."

"Your pal tempts you with the carrot, but you get the stick . . . to sit on. Mark my words, unless we break away, your life will end in sorrow," invokes Vivian. "You will never understand, will you, you dumb donkey."

She is right. She holds dudgeon taking care of 3-year-old Alvin Junior while her husband galavants, trying to earn. He has not put a retainer on a house of their own. The realities of the depression has forced the duo to return to living with Joseph in his brownstone and that infuriates his wife of four years. She is still pursuing her career of knavery as a sideline when the men are out and about. Having a home she can launder her stolen proceeds through, appeals to her.

Occasionally Emmerling has to play referee during their dust-ups—convincing the couple to retreat to neutral corners. He continues revising his finished chapters even though publishing companies have shown no interest in the Shipwreck Kelly narrative.

America is saddened when Thomas Alva Edison dies on October 18, 1931. Joseph's necrology, brands the prolific inventor as an "Exceptional American" ubiquitously. He also retells the joke that Tesla told him in 1893. The obituary is run in 1,317 news-outlets worldwide. Proud, he frames the column of print and adds it to his wall despite having no byline.

The George Washington Bridge spanning the Hudson river is opened on October 24, 1931. Metropolis is now connected with Fort Lee and the city skyline is forever recast by its addition. A total of 30,000 come to the ribbon cutting ceremony including Governor Franklin Delano Roosevelt. The happening is festive with speeches and fireworks. Two elementary school students roller-skate on the bridge before being opened to foot traffic and cars.

North in Maine, a few hundred gather to watch the five-foot, 185-pound, Timmy White attempt to conquer the Raulf Hotel on November 2, 1931. Portage City locals never watch the rotund chap mount the building as "Baby Fly" is arrested in the lobby, nabbed by the F.B.I. as a suspect in a bank robbery in nearby Lewiston.

Alvin next job is at 6th Avenue and West 27th Street across from an animated billboard advertising "Taystee" brand bread. He has signed to complete a three-day residency, even though November's temperature is usually cold. He can see a Cessna with a defective engine is trying to land in Central Park. Passenger Robert Bailie, a lion tamer by trade, parachutes safely from the light plane. The vehicle crumbles nose-first into the 5th floor of the Y.M.C.A. The body of pilot Charles Reid is removed from the mangled cockpit by the Metropolitan Fire Department.

Alvin is tirelessness. The temperature dips to 20-degrees. He only has a thin tarp to keep warm, and the night air feels more frigid than a dogsled on the Siberian tundra. Chilled to the bone, he starts coughing unrestrainedly and departs the job when his manager arrives at dawn. Joseph's doctor instructs him to stay motionless in bed a week at minimum.

Metro-Goldwyn-Mayer has bought the rights to the hit Broadway musical "Flying High" starring comedian Bert Lahr. The studio has plans to send out a bevy of attractive ladies to stoke interest in the movie after the spring thaw. Kelly will instruct the women in his unique art and be paid as a technical advisor. The studio will also remunerate his labor with a screen test and a month of lodging. The decade of courageousness and perseverance flagpole sitting has paid off with a real run at stardom.

Joseph wakes Alvin and Vivian to tell of the good news. A west coast excursion might be exactly what his ornery and sullen associate requires. She will be happy to see her friends. Emmerling relishes the chance to meet with executives over a pastrami on rye at Canter's Delicatessen. The studio sends the details by messenger. He countersigns the contract and hands the papers back to the courier to return.

Chapter 18 – Everyone is Having a Hoot Except for Lindy

"All I know is just what I read in the papers, and that's an alibi for my ignorance."

— Will Rogers

Vivian's oddly-named associates file by the Los Angeles Biltmore Hotel to pother over the baby. Junior has her melancholic, distant blue pupils, and sandy red hair, they say out loud while speculating taciturnly if she will join in their shifty cajolery. She responds by saying "she is roping steer" with a collection of bamboozlers in New York. Alvin does not care for her devious felons and their influence on his wife. She tells him not to worry, refusing to become entwined in their smoke and mirrors games.

The film test materializes at the Movie-tone Studios. Alvin is balancing on his portable equipment. His froggy-timbre, gravelly, and anxious voice simplify the intricacies to the lens and the models.

With the Hollywoodland sign far away in the hills as a background setting, he chats with a blonde, a redhead, and then a brunette on his portable rig on the roof. The shoot is slow going, filming Alvin with various angles and focusing tight lenses on him during many activities—shaving, telephoning, and performing acrobatics. The director urges Emmerling to introduce Alvin. Editors will insert his scene into the production. Surrounded by eight chorus girls, the chubby manager is vocalizing his overweening ballyhoo, gleefully rattling out the superlatives that are his apostle's trademarks.

"It is my pleasure to bring you *The Guy of the Sky*. He's known as *The King upon High, The Toast of the Post, The Undisputed in-the-Air Endurance Record Holder, and World Champion Flagpole Sitter— Hero of the Titanic Rescue*—Shipwreck Kelly."

The women part as Alvin steps from behind and shakes hands with his publicist.

"Hi champ," elucidates Emmerling. "Ready to demonstrate to these damsels how to have an enchanting evening?"

"Sure. Which of you budding starlets would enjoy mounting my massive shaft?"

The ladies all raise their hands. The director vociferates for a cut. He explains the reason that Kelly cannot say the suggestive phrase; the double entendre will not pass the rigid production codes. The producer orders reshooting the scene with other wording, but none satisfy the censor on set—finally settling on the following: "Who will come to assist me?"

The studio is like the cat that has licked the cream. A month zips by, and Joseph extends the vacation. He feels no urgency to return to the bleak wintry east when Los Angeles is sunny and 68 degrees. Emmerling dines at the Formosa Cafe, pumping studio flunkies and aspiring actresses for fodder to transmit to the *United Press International* news service.

Mae West is in town and wrangles the triangle an invite to a cocktail reception hosted by Lieutenant Roscoe Turner and his wife Carline. The stouthearted airman is well connected in the film industry. His soiree attracts Tinseltown up-and-comers Barbara Stanwyck, Dashiell Hammett, and Rudy Vallee. Joseph hopes the handlebar mustached host can introduce him to producers. Vivian grows more smashed before dinner and is feeling bibulous. She feeds appetizers under the table to Turner's pet lion cub, Gilmore.

Alvin chronicles his experience soaring where the Cormorant glide. The party guffaws at his insanity except for his wife, who is hearing the tale for the first time. She becomes irate that he ignored his "warning not to fly." Gliding across the parquet floor, she sneaks like a panther in the underbrush in her sleek black satin cocktail ensemble to coldly empty the contents of her glass at him. She grabs a steak-knife from the table. After a brief tussle, Vivian takes one on the chin. As she sleeps in an upstairs bedroom, Kelly is apologetic to the hosts. After a slumber, the blackout lush's slate is blank and her jaw sore. She does not ask what happened.

M.G.M. is not interested in the Shipwreck Kelly biography script Joseph's been pitching, nor is any other film studio. Word comes that his movie debut will be inserted in a "Behind the Scenes" one-reeler. He would be in cinema but just a week. Joseph arranges a screening so Alvin can watch himself frolic on screen. At the end of February, the company treks back east on the transcontinental train.

Charles Augustus Lindbergh, Jr., is kidnapped from his nursery on March 1, 1932. The nanny, Betty Gow, detects the absence and yells so cacophonously she wakes the adjacent neighbors house 440 yards away.

The baby of the most estimable person on the planet is 20 months old. Troopers locate a $50,000 ransom request. The Federal

Bureau of Investigations is activated. Colonel Lindbergh receives a second solicitation and then a third. After an op-ed is printed in The Bronx Journal, several promising leads materialize, but to turn out false. The general public is riveted to the drama.

Kelly is to play a carnival in Nutley on March 17, 1932. Joseph has the roustabouts build steps that rise to a few feet in proximity to the iron pancake upon he sits. Spending a few pennies, the brave will climb to hear the simpleton vend his 2¢ logic.

The concession's owner realizes he is not bringing in enough to warrant the lolling. He incubates a nefarious plan to null and void the agreement: Force his feet touch grass before the week is done. He hires Alvin's adversary, "The Irish Sailor" to cross the bridge and hound him, just out of reach. Jim Kelly is ready to take his revenge on the solitary figure. Unable to tolerate each other, his tormentor spoons out a heaping bowlful—goading, pestering, and ranting at the sitter. Fair-goers egg the two nemeses on, hoping to see a brouhaha.

"You shrimp," browbeats the taller man. "I'll thrash you within an inch o' yer' life, you stinkin' mick. I'm gonna' sock you so brutally you'll starve . . . before you finish rolling."

Alvin accepts the challenge to brawl. He is boiling, ready to scrap, but his tormentor squirts away into an idling car. Joseph and the carnival boss, drawn by the ruckus arrive on the scene, finding Kelly off the paling. He's fired.

"I'm sorry I let my temper get the best of me. . . ."

"I understand that you are upset, but being hired to sit is our bread and butter."

In a few weeks, Alvin is gratified to be in the "Iron City." On March 27, 1932, he consents to an interview at ten stories. A few construction workers pulley Jack Turcott, contributor to *The Pitt Weekly* on a rope to his location. The questioner extends a shaky hand as the cats-paws jostles him.

"I gotta say you are brave to come up. I'm piteous sometimes; being with just my thoughts. Some say I am a dunderhead, but I do love this greatest of sport."

"You consider 'flagpole sitting' similar to baseball?" inquires his guest feeling moderately queasy. "Or tennis?"

"Yes. This avocation cherishes the very sedateness which schoolteachers try to instill to in our youth. In my opinion, as a country, attitudes have become far too lax. Whether diets or monetary policy, we should shake things up. F.D.R. is the candidate to vote in. Roosevelt will get prohibition repealed. This nation would all feel better if we could have an intermittent mug of beer."

The pressman adds to his pad. Alvin leaps in to ardent postulation with a 180 degree tangent.

"I am addicted to these heart-pumping nanoseconds. You know, at this height you aren't bothered by flies. Bugs never rise to this horizontal since most crap is on the street."

The correspondent doodles as Kelly continues verbalizing his nonconformist beliefs. He takes a survey of the gathering on the street. He is shaky in the harness, hanging in mid-air. He feels a fraction of the anxiety that the sitter must feel during countless jiffs. A sudden gust lifts the visitor's fedora. Having secured enough details, the writer is feeling dyspeptic.

"Would you want to enlighten our readers with some sage advice?"

"To Mr. Lindbergh, we pray you will be reunited with your son. If a bad outcome came to my baby boy, I would go ape. I was once in shackles in Barbados, but, when I told the buccaneers that I did not know anyone who could pay ransom, they cast me ashore."

Kelly gives the prearranged hand gesture. Like a raindrop streaking on a glass pane, his visitor returns to his life on the ground. *I am glad to be back amongst normal people, where I belong, pounding my beat on the street,* thinks the journalist. *That job is far too fraught with menace. I hope he's paid well. No wonder he's a bit daffy.*

When Alvin comes back from his travels, Vivian pops quicker than a balloon in a cage of porcupines. She is infuriated from having no housekeeping help while her husband is away. She has been fooling around with others, leaving the waif unsupervised. After a war of words, dishes break, and she pummels her partner. The juvenile cowers under the kitchen table, away from the rumpus.

Phillip S. Roberts

When Kelly raises a fist to defend himself, the little nipper dashes out and boots him in the shin. It hurts.

"Don't you hurt my mommy," the recalcitrant boy cries out as he darts away. Alvin gives chase.

"You asshole," shrieks his better half. "Oh, what a bastard you are to hurt a child."

He catches Junior and begins to dole out a spanking. The kiddie is screaming after one smack of the belt strap. Kelly halts. Vivian snatches her son and rushes out without another word.

Joseph surveys the aftermath. He produces a silver flask from his desk and hands the bottle to his partner. Alvin's face is discoloring like the aftermath of an explosion in a soup factory. After a swig, they converse on how to operate their coalition.

"It would be prudent to prune back the quartet. Our roaming life is plainly no place for the toddler."

"I love her, but she is becoming unstable. At least she did not pull out a shiv this time."

"You should concentrate on the decision without agitation."

During his next Augean task on May 15, 1932, Kelly mulls what is the best way forward while mounted on the bronco sculpture at "Kauffman Riding Goods" on East 24th Street. He is asking advice from those that traipse past his static mount. Out of nowhere, newsboys materialize, loudly oo-oo-ing and ah-ah-ing like a troop of screeching baboons—skeletal remains have been positively identified as the Lindbergh baby. Alvin is heartbroken at the resolution. The news spurs him to decide he needs to patch up the problems with his wife for the sake of his son. He alights, relinquishing the reins as Joseph walks up.

"Lindy's unhappy ending has convinced me. I cannot send her packing. Junior would be unable to stomach me. He is all I really have in life."

Emmerling cannot argue with that logic. After a while she returns cheery and as normal as any other day. She waves a grocery bill. Joseph's opinion of her is the same, yet he hands her a $20 bill and adds the outlay to his ledger. She goes shopping and brings home a stylist dress to hang in her closet.

In Boston, footsloggers pause to glance at the nonconformist on the Scollay Square Theater's twelfth floor. The radio drama, "Little Orphan Annie" is playing on the local station while he is settling in. Deputies send up a note in a pail on a string. Alvin is ordered to vacate his place by the Honorable Elijah Adlow. He complies and is brought before the judge to be energetically castigated from the bench.

"You are complicit in depriving taxpayers of their billfolds while loafing," declares the arbiter. "I have had more than a few complaints. As the unflagging workers chew over why you are on that towering prong, a torpedo dips their suit and fingers their money-clip. Motorists collide while looking up and you give no care to anyone but yourself. You are a most contumacious individualist."

"I can attest that the defendant is not involved with any felonious schemes," objects Emmerling. "He certainly is not in league with any criminals like the 'Mad Dog' Underhill gang or the Capone organization."

The jurist is not convinced and assesses a $50 fine. He orders him not to be a nuisance in the hamlet again or the penalty will be much harsher. If Kelly must prove his tenaciousness, the Boston Common will be acceptable 'if' he procures authorization. Joseph peels bills out from his diminishing supply. He hustles Alvin out before he can be found in contempt.

Kelly is isolating in Queens on May 19, 1932. He announces to the writers who assemble that he is taking up residence until "real beer" is legalized. A few hours later, a constable uses a ladder to hand court documents to John "Flagpole" Keely, but when the process server approaches Alvin he realizes he has called on the wrong individual and retreats down the rungs.

His hands tingle like he is being scourged with a horde of nanoscopic needles, but he does not ease his grip on his wobbly accommodation. At 37, he's feeling some residual effects of duress. When the sun arises, he decides to he'd rather not languish. Joseph sends him to a clinic, but the diagnosis is inconclusive. Later, the two men consult a divorce specialist and put him on retainer.

"She's lawyered up, so I think you should have one too."

Kelly is not ready to set the wheels in motion on the dissolution. He dreads how a parting of the ways might affect the sentiments of the impressionable youth. He fetches his mitt and goes to play catch in a vacant lot with Junior. A few kids walk by and suddenly sides are being chosen for a pickup game.

Vivian zips by in a Chevrolet sedan and honks the horn. She took possession of the car because the tipsy dupable was too engaged ogling at her tits to see her swapping out crooked dice during a craps game. She plans on selling the wheels before the fella can kvetch to cops. Junior hops in the back seat and she flips the bird to her good-for-nothing hubby as she drives away.

Amelia Earhart gambles on crossing the Atlantic this time unchaperoned. In her Lockeed Vega, she departs from Canada. The lone traveler flies 15 hours to reach safety in a pasture in Ireland on May 21, 1932. No one since Lindbergh can claim to have achieved the coup. A "Distinguished Flying Cross" is conferred to her by Congress. French President Albert Lebrun pins medals on the hero's breast, and she is awarded a large monetary prize from the board of the *National Geographic Society.*

Kelly hears of Earhart's feat while he is balanced on the "Nut Club" in Greenwich Village. The owner of the social hotspot (who favors screwy entertainment including cockroach races and other such odd enticements,) thinks the in-left-field promotion fits in. Joseph pootles into the dim bar to order a "Ward 8" cocktail. He eavesdrops on two men who are in hushed conference at the rail.

"Her opinion is that fellow will not be any richer than he is right now."

"Ya don't say? He is outside, up there, bringing in dough. How did she ever snare the sap?"

"Met him when she was a kid. Being domestic appealed to her and popped out a bundle o' joy. Now, she gots the hots fer ice and furs, but he won't give 'em to her."

"She is going to leave him as if he was a deviled-egg sitting on the counter after 48 hours in the August sun. She'd like to score a stack from the boss, but he is ignorant to her sorcery."

"Even the worst fisherman knows ya gotta have the right bait."

Joseph is across his desk from Vivian a week later. As she sidles nose to nose to give voice to her clincher, he feels slightly ill. She intends to rotate the screw a full turn to pressure him for a healthy sum.

"I am bringing you in on a cinch. I know a chum who burgled an estate upstate in Westchester County. He is on the run, so he needs a sprightly score. For two grand I take possession of four sacks containing $20 'Double Eagle' gold coins. The bullion is 100% untraceable. My plan is to deposit small amounts in different banks— so there will be no chance of being noticed. I'll withdraw the clean funds the next day, pay you back first and then split the profit equally. But, I need the stake now."

The aroma of her perfume revolts him. The smell reminds him of the cheap French whore that gave him a handjob at the Columbian Exposition back in 1893.

"You want $2,000? Even if I did have the wherewithal, I do not want to hear your slimy perplexities or become involved in your slippery conduct. You larcenous kleptomaniac, aiding and abetting a heist is serious stuff. However, I will let you earn your talent of silver, Vivian Francis Steele."

She becomes interested, unnerved and then scared. She comprehends he must have looked into her past. A spittle of drool comes out of the corner of his mouth as he continues in the most sadistic tone he can muster.

"Divulge your descent into the Tartarean hell in the deep, shadowy recesses of that dark jungle. I want to hear every terrible, filthy, sordid detail of that carnal ecstasy. Confess every lurid, erotic feeling. Make me feel like 'Big Bertha' snaring a rabbi in her net. Tell me how much you loved that taboo and how you itch to experience the feelings of that forbidden fruit again."

"You degenerate, perverse . . . I will never . . . ." The screaming meemie is so unsettled she can hardly vocalize the phrases to express her distaste. "You are a ghoulish, filthy, lavender fruit. You disgusting uncouth . . . pig. How dare you."

Her fury rises until he can almost see the animus smoldering in her irises. He does not flinch nor tremble. She tries changing tactics.

"I need this score to buy a place with a yard . . . for Junior. We will not be underfoot and you can have Alvin. Come on, I know you have oodles stashed. This is a monumental chance to triple your pile. If you front me the boodle, I will add a sweetener. I will not oppose a divorce and you will see me like the raven, nevermore."

He is not sold. He giggles, for she does not understand Poe's poem. She moves on to her alternate plan. It is callous. It is blackmail.

"If you won't front me, I will squeal to the law that you raped me. I have a confession typed on your own typewriter and signed in your 'hand.' If Alvin does not bash your head in, cops will lock you away on Welfare Island. I know, you have five times what I need in your vault."

He has been expecting rancor from her at some point. This was one of the scenarios he'd had role-played many times in his mind. He has even pre-composed a speech.

"A safe?"

"Move those fake books."

"Oh, this one. It would be empty if you figured out the combination. You would never have guessed." He twirls the dial. "It is the date I first met Alvin. 04 — 15 — 12. You want to know what is in this strongbox? Okay. I'll show you . . . the vile, venal, and evil woman you are, Vivian. You are a horrible, untrustworthy harridan to cheat on your virtuous, sweet husband who loves you. From the day I was introduced to you, I could tell that you were dirty and corrupt. This thick file contains evidence of your numerous infractions of the law and decency. I've kept a record of your efforts; from the time this chain letter was delivered. This is a notation of every shady meeting, risky dodge, fraudulent scheme, and petty bunco I've witnessed that you have been involved with. You are a habitual thief and a confidence woman, clamping onto us like a leech . . . sucking on the teat of our industriousness. What, to whom, and how you did your crimes, it is all here, unequivocally. A dictionaries's worth of stolen words. Perhaps, I will write your wretched life story. That would be ironic indeed: to profit from your mistakes. However, your tale of woe lacks an ending, something I'm occasionally told about my own work. I expect that day is coming, you cheap daughter of Xanthippe. You have a shitload of enemies. I will not have to cool my heels long before I get to write 'The End' on your chapter."

He flips through the crammed folder and lists her many odious transgressions.

"I bought this deed from your swampland swindle. That fellow was delirious to get his $50 back. This receipt pad I stole, is part of your dry cleaning scam. These 'Lonely Hearts' magazine notices I clipped are ones you used to commit mail fraud. This envelope contains a counterfeit $20 that you handed me one night. Recognize your friends in these morgue photos? You should. Look closely; you are directly responsible for the bloody deaths of your gang including 'Soapy,' 'Yuk-Yuk,' and 'Shuffles.' Must I continue, you manipulative, disgusting grifter? I am not playing your duplicitous game, sister. Tread lightly, you venomous asp, because in case of accident, my counsel sends a copy of this dossier to the cops. I also know a rich, vindictive gangster in California who will be most interested in your current whereabouts . . ."

Frustrated, she pulls out a butterfly-blade. He yanks out a Remington Derringer, cocks the pistol, and aims between her eyes. Joseph laughs.

"Seriously? You brought a knife to a gunfight? Oh, honey! That is so cute! I shall inform your husband that you will be residing in other lodging from now on. If he severs the ardent entanglement, I will not shed a tear. He is smart enough to separate himself far from your depravity. You are shit out of luck. With your meal ticket gone and on the lam with that brat you'll be hoisted on your own petard. You are nothing but a washed up, middle-aged lush. Your best days are behind you, I do not even need to read tarot cards to prognosticate your bleak doom, you dime-store prostitute. That's the door. Get the fuck out. Or did you want to wait a minute to hear the dirty limerick I composed about you? It's a doozy."

She promises she will have her retribution. He sniggers as she hastily retreats. Joseph opens his desk drawer and returns the tiny two shot gun to its case. He retrieves an envelope from the cavity, opens it and reads the handwritten poetry verse aloud.

Phillip S. Roberts

There once was a woman named Vivian.
Whose life could be called quite bohemian.
She met her a sailor.
Who strove to impale 'er.
And left her facing oblivion.

"You can continue living here, if you want," says Emmerling later as he brings Alvin up to speed. "I know you did not have any involvement in her shifty machination. Due to her attempted extortion, she is not ever welcome in these lodgings."

Kelly rents her chambers nearby at 964 Amsterdam Street. The lease depletes most of his monthly allowance, but he feels he must take care of his son in spite of his wife's shortcomings. He informs her he prefers to continue working with Emmerling.

"Fine. Stay with that aging queen."

Weeks later, stage actor Joseph Späh grandstands on the Chanin Building on June 21, 1932. The veteran stage trooper is billed as "Ben Dova." With thousands watching and the newsreels rolling, he performs his comic routine. Near the ledge, 680 feet from the street, the vaudevillian in tailcoat pantomimes being "inebriated." Watchers gasp as he bumbles on the ledge and pantomimes sparking a cigarette from a prop gaslight.

With the Rocky Mountains in the distance, Kelly finishes six days, four hours, and 23 minutes at a height of 110 feet on the Hotel Denver. As he dismounts on July 1, 1932, he is glowing in quintessence. His manager Joseph is glad to have any payday during this bleak summer.

A few weeks later, *The Associated Press* insists Ernst Heisch is the European "sitting" titlist finishing 60 days on Hamburg's skyline. If verified, the span would be nine days longer than his mark. Kelly communicates a challenge by telegram to the man he considers a "Filthy Hun" but there is no response.

On December 23, 1932, Betty and Benny Fox enact a hairy performance, gyrating on a horizontal platform five-stories up in San Diego. The performers most adrenaline inducing move involves him bending her backwards to pick up a handkerchief with her teeth. After two hours of tango, samba, and other assorted steps, they pronounce themselves "The Royal Family of Air Dancing." The partners pose as paparazzi expose negatives with the sparkling Pacific in the distance.

"Photograph my good side." warbles Betty as she flaunts her pearly whites.

"You think that no-talent putz, Shipwreck Kelly can pull off an amazing feat like we've just done? Betty and I got both skill and grace," Benny comments to the reporter from the *Imperial Beach Star-News*. "Please print my quote exactly. I want that jerk to know exactly how educated and classy people feel about him."

Across the nation, Emmerling is gifted tickets to the inaugural charity opening at the Radio City Music Hall featuring the debut of "The Rockettes" chorus line.

"A first-rate end to a crummy 12 months," squawks Alvin to his companion.

"There are quite a few dates on the calendar," replies Emmerling. "I think 1933 will be much better regarding our finances."

Chapter 19 –
A Parting of the Ways

"You're a rose; you're Inferno's Dante.
You're the nose on the great Durante
I'm a lazy lout, who is just about to stop,
But if baby I'm the bottom, you're the top."
   — Cole Porter, You're the Top

On February 1, 1933, Kelly is atop the Lenox Sports Shop on Flatbush Avenue advocating their clearance sale on radios. Pounding his beat, Seamus O'Malley observes nearly 50 people loitering around. Among the gathering, an unaccompanied five-year-old is wearing a kid-sized Navy uniform. He asks the boy his name.

"Alvin, sir. But my parents call me Junior."

"Are you all by yourself, Junior?" inquires the policeman. "Where is your father?"

He points to the sky.

"Him? Shipwreck Kelly is your dad?" He nods in assent. "And, your mom, Sonny?"

"Mama told me if anyone asked, to say that 'she is getting that jerk to pay the grocery bill.' Don't worry. She leaves me all by myself plenty times."

The cop is disturbed. Vivian is raucously insulting her husband from an uppermost rung of a tall ladder. Her blue vernacular is loud enough to wilt a daisy as a blowtorch would.

"I think I'll wait until your mother returns so I can have a chat with her. Would you like an ice cream cone?"

"Vanilla please," reflects the boy. "Two scoops. Their fights usually last a while."

Alvin is languishing lackadaisically on the Stanley Theater three months later. The cut-rate cinema is playing the Buster Keaton and Jimmy Durante comedy "What No Beer?"

"Hey, Shipwreck, which pony will win the Belmont Stakes?" asks a stroller who is taking his dog for an early walk.

"The only sure bet is that most of this year's field will end up as some mutt's grub or at the glue factory," predicts Alvin as he scans the racing form. "I ain't picked a lot of winners lately but put a Jefferson on 'Hurryoff,' would ya?"

Kelly drops him a $2 bill. When the gelding wins, he is slightly surprised that the man does not return with his winnings. A depression is going on, after all.

"The Century of Progress Exposition" opens on May 27, 1933. Joseph is hired by the *Chicago Daily Tribune* to pen an evocative recollection of the jamboree. He questions organizers to see if Alvin, as the doyen of his unique sport, could lend his presence. The promoters decline, having already engaged a 31-year-old sitter, Richard "Dixie" Blandy.

The "Queen of the Charleston," Bee Jackson, is fronting a "Roaring Twenties" stage revue when the flapper collapses. She is rushed to surgery; doctors perform an emergency appendectomy, but the role model who epitomized the jazz era dies on the operating table at the age of 26.

Alvin is set to 'bang a drum' at America's ultramodern draw, the drive-in movie. The Park-In Theater in Camden charges 25¢ a car plus 10¢ a head. On July 9, 1933, Kelly, reclining on a ledge to the side of the screen delights in the films as well as all the soda, hot dogs, and popcorn he can consume. The venue is deliriously cost effective with families and teenagers whose finances are tight. Over the next few months, similar screens open across the nation.

Wiley Post effectuates an around the globe flight by himself in the "Winnie Mae." He has invented an auto-direction device and is now able to fly without a steersman's aid. When the eyepatch wearing pilot touches the field at Floyd Bennett airport on July 21, 1933, the Oklahoman has surmounted 15,400 miles in the upper hemisphere. Factoring in refueling pauses, his total time to fly around the world is seven days, 18 hours, and 50 minutes.

Alvin has spent much of that week in jail in Bloomington. Arrested for chucking a brick through the storefront window of a dry cleaner who cancelled a job at the last minute, Kelly admits to the judge he is unrepentant and obstinate. He is sentenced to five days in the pokey to think about the error of his ways. He replies, he feels falsely imprisoned without justification like Edmond Dantès, "The Count of Monte Cristo," and two days are added to his incarceration for his insolence. Emmerling visits the surly and sullen prisoner. He slips him a few bills through the bars for a train ticket and tells him where to meet after his time in the pokey is up. His handler is writing a series on the Century of Progress International Exposition in Chicago and is not going to miss out on even a second of the fun.

The inmate telephones Vivian. She drives to meet him as he leaves confinement and they tool along to the 'Windy City.' Sipping ice cream sodas, the whole family enjoys a nice outing. After riding the Cyclone and other scream-inducing rides, they peruse the scientific demonstrations. The family poses at an old-west photography booth. Alvin wears a fake mustache and a Sheriff's badge while Junior twirls a toy six-shooter for the novelty "wanted" poster.

"I care deeply," says Vivian while posing in a dancehall girl outfit. "But, I wish you would settle down. We should have a safe place so our child can grow up in a real home—a house you come to after work and ask how his day at school was."

"It's not so easy right now. You have heard that America is in a depression, right? Joseph says . . ."

"I am not interested in what that flaming Uranian thinks," she interrupts. Alvin is exasperated by her attitude. He implores her to apologize to Emmerling. She refuses, making an ultimatum. "You can choose him or us. I am watching out for our son's best interests."

Vivian takes the schoolboy back to New York. The sitter and his manager rendezvous and journey to their next scheduled emergence. The two seriously delve into the marriage during the many miles drive, and Alvin is finally ready to start the paperwork to sue for a separation.

"If I am working in the sky, she does not want to be with me."

"Sounds inevitable," says Joseph. "Let me call the lawyer so we can mitigate any settlement."

Kedron Coats and his Spitz "Renny" have been nesting on a low tree branch for 12 hours. On August 3, 1933, he evacuates their spot after receiving a stern warning from his mom.

"I was gonna set a record fer setting. Shipwreck Kelly don't git told to come in for supper or git a whipping," the moppet moans to *The Baltimore News*. "At least my pooch is now the champ. He sits better and longer than any dog in the world."

The August 16, 1933 edition of the *Los Angeles Examiner* reports that Paramount Pictures wishes to engage Kelly to instruct a bevy of chorus girls in his "peculiar art." The concept is part of their think-tank's publicity for the Ginger Rogers film, "Sitting Pretty." Replies come in from 129 applicants, desperate to sub for the real victor ludorum. Joseph finds out the article is puffery with no real vacancy being offered.

A body matching Harry Gardiner's general description is found beaten to death at the base of the Eiffel Tower on August 17, 1933. Gendarmes consider the crime a botched robbery as no identification is found. According to *The Paris-Soir,* "The Original Human Fly" had been scouting locations in Europe, but an instance of his climbing buildings never is printed again.

Alvin is prattling on insanely in Arkansas on his roost. The weather is inclement on August 21, 1933. His spar is creaking, but remains unsplintered. He clings to his resting place as it wavers to and fro. A stringer from *The Fayetteville News-Express* poses a question to the sitter 12-feet-up who cannot hear him due to the howling wind. He has decided he wants to be separated.

He is using a loophole in the state law that states "any husband who is estranged more than 90 days can break a wedlock with no fault." Habituated 20 dog days, he wants to last 70 more so he can truthfully swear that he has not been with his wife. With a decision in his favor, he has a better chance at custody.

A day later, a lovely brunette who says she wants his autograph is lugged up on a boatswain plank, he signs a paper, and she hands him a legal document. He is being sued for emotional sabotage and general marital disparagement. Alvin is in disbelief by the order but admires the process server's guts. He dismounts and pontificates to a small gaggle of reporters.

"I think highly of a frail that will rise to such an apogee. It takes a lot of sand to deliver the bench's writs in thin air. Maybe I should have asked if she was single, as I will be soon. I don't begrudge my wife's filing. I wile away time, so it is natural she wants a proper disassociation," explains Alvin honestly. "I was going to ask her to divorce me."

The hearing is set at the federal building. Joseph has purchased Kelly a coat and tie to wear. Vivian is attired in simple blue gingham dress. Their mouthpiece voices his case, and her shingle Daniel Bosh elegantly states his opinion on whom would be better at raising Junior.

The adjudicator takes heed patiently, glancing at the usual questions he asks litigants. They won't fit.

"I detest when a family is to be torn apart, but I must decide. This complicated epoch has so much sadness going on. In your charge, you contend that his chosen field is the equivalence of abandonment?" prods the mediator during Vivian's testimony at the hearing. "Please explain."

"I hardly see him except unless I'm looking through a telescope."

"You knew what your husband's line of work was when you married him?"

"Yes, but I assumed he would become tired of it and quit."

Watchers simper at the statement. The bailiff is directed to quiet the cheap seats.

"So, you know how he spends his nights? That must be a comfort to know he's not running around with other women."

"He wouldn't dare do that. My friends tell me, 'Your husband is pissing in the wind again.' It is disgraceful and embarrassing."

The people watching think this dialogue is funny as well. A gavel silences them.

"What was different after your marriage?"

"He became obsessed being the best. Sometimes, he is gone a whole month in pursuit of glory. He only came to this court because he was compelled by a summons. Even the lady who served him the papers said, 'He STUNK.' Honestly."

The judge turns his questioning to Alvin.

"How are you feeling, Mr. Kelly?"

"Generally conditions could be better. I understand there is a depression going on. I embosom a potent love for her and our boy," he states contritely. "I spend countless hours trying to provide. Just four years ago, I was saving to buy a house, but I lost my nest-egg. Our love is like Sisyphus pushing a boulder up that hill; challenging and frustrating. As much as I try to please her, I have to labor again every morning. Anyhow, I have toiled like an ant to win significance with my diligence. At the end of the day, my knack is 'flagpole sitter.'

Society glares at me like a misfit. I am sorry if Mrs. Kelly feels I am not doing all I can. I want my wife and son to be happy."

His heart-felt speech has hushed the chancery who were surprised by such candor. The judge weighs his statement. Taking the boy into his chambers, he probes Alvin Junior's feelings. After exiting his inner sanctum, Vivian is designated custodian. Kelly is ordered to provide some support monthly. He promises he will pay the rent on the apartment. Upset, he is escorted out before he can raise a fuss and held in contempt. He wants to wrest guardianship, but Joseph reminds him that barnstorming is not a stable environment.

"We can file a motion with a more virtuous tribunal," states Emmerling, although he knows no other court will take up their case. "Until then, let us hit the road. We have a fortune to earn, my champion."

The former Mrs. Kelly is cohabitating with her ambulance-chaser. Daniel "Posh" Bosh specializes in cases where the defendants are not honorable and upstanding citizens. He defends dippers, racketeers, and shakedown tricksters. The well-attired, ginger haired lawyer asks Vivian to marry him, but she declines so that Alvin will be inclined to keep paying rent on the residence.

The men head across state lines, but Alvin is restless in the motel. He tosses and turns until Joseph hands him a pill he has obtained from a chemist. The tranquilizer, puts him in a supine state.

"Joseph?" moans Alvin groggily. He has an epiphany . . . one all-encompassing purpose.

"What?" bewails the promoter.

"I want . . . real fame."

"Unless you were to join Bonnie and Clyde's gang, I do not think you'll be any more of a luminary," comes the return volley from his handler who lights an 'Old Gold' cigarette in the darkness. "When another tries to imitate your ingenuity, most watching assume it is you up there. Are you certain you are ready for more? When dining, would you want to be interrupted by some crazy fanatic? Will you shoo your supporter away or ask him to join the table to monopolize your late afternoon with banal praise?"

Alvin comprehends the questions, but he has no response. His friend continues.

"Will you be satisfied with a nameless normality? Could you savor the last of your days as a janitor, having once experienced near-deification? Mae West must have a wry, suggestive quip always at the ready. Al Jolson is loath to provide the demands upon his allotted span. The two of them know the day will come when their stars will fade. I am preparing too, setting aside 10¢ from every dollar earned for retirement."

Kelly does not say anything. He has finally entered into in a lucid state, aided by the Norse goddess of dreams, Njörun. He dreams of sailing through a sea of glittering gold and silver coins.

The flagpole sitter sets up his rig at the Iowa State Fair in Des Moines. Organizers have introduced nighttime horse racing under galvanic lights and the activity brings the crowd like the faithful to the Zerzura oasis in the Sahara. Hawkeyes come to observe the butter cow sculpted in the refrigerated agriculture hall. Others come to eat deep fried foods, see the prize-winning livestock, and ride the Tilt-A-Whirl, but few take heed of he who indulges in none of those activities from his bollard.

On August 30, 1933, Kelly is on his twig. Sightseers are enlightened with the ascetic's short and sweet street-smarts. Joseph sends cinema magalogues and other reading material to his banneret reclining in the angel's abode. He also repeats what his spies have gleaned regarding Vivian's felonious activities. As the grounds get deserted closer to closing, Alvin spots a few ill-raised delinquents sighting their raised quarry with slingshots. Their pebbles fail to broach his 25-foot outlook.

"Hey, boys! Come nearer! I want to show you something special," he razzes. When the children approach, he unzips, takes aim, and lets gravity take effect. "Run home and cry to your mommies, ya stinking brats."

While showcasing in the heartland, Alvin informs the scribbler from the *Iowa State Journal* that the sure way to tell him from frauds is the tattooed crucifix on his arm. Even though profiles keep being written and the work is still semi-frequent, he feels his luster is fading like the ink cross on his left shoulder.

By October, Alvin's current gimmick is drawing scrutiny in the Big Easy. On a Canal Street theater vertex, Kelly is wearing a gorilla suit. He's advertising "Son of Kong." He bellyaches to Joseph—the humidity is brutal and the costume has a musty stench. He browbeats his boss, pounding his chest, and pledging to never, ever play the monkey again.

"The press will come soon, so don't swoon. Don't forget kiddo, you told me to get you any paid work that was available. 'No matter the discomfort,' you insisted. So clench your teeth and soldier on."

Joseph arranges other busy work for Alvin until the winter comes. When he's not sitting, he's washing casements on skyscrapers in Manhattan. The task, while not prestigious, keeps him accustomed to heights.

Prohibition is repealed on December 5, 1933. Alvin and Joseph start on a bender like the many Americans having a legal drink that day. The friends end up in a slug-driven, demented, gathering drunkenly singing Christmas carols to a beat cop on the street at 4 a.m.

Working at the Roseland Dime-A-Dance Palace, Alvin is wearing tails and a "John Bull" hat. He is grossing $10 a shift plus tips. Valentine's Day, 1934, has been unpleasant. After too many dowagers step on his toes, he leaves and orders a vodka martini at the nearest bar. He orders another. After the third nightcap, he rings his ex-wife, exhorting her to forgive him.

"You are drunk. I've told you, we are through. I am sure you will be very happy cuddling up with your boyfriend."

"You know it is not that way," he pleads. "I am going to the George Washington Bridge and leap the rail."

He hangs up. A brusque call is placed by Vivian to protect her meal ticket.

Emmerling notifies the Port Authority that Kelly is unhinged and might try to pull a "Steve Brodie." The toll booth notifies security who apprehend him after an abbreviated struggle, before can leap from the span. The distraught and disheveled tuxedo-wearing fashion plate is manhandled to Bellevue's psychiatric observation ward. After a 48 hour stint, the staff determines him to be in possession of his faculties and release him. A stringer wants a statement, but Joseph declines with a simple "No Comment."

Scottish Doctor Robert Wilson develops a grainy image of a behemoth that he claims is the "Loch Ness Monster." The blurry exposure printed globally on April 21, 1934, dominates chatter locally.

Vivian rings up her ex-husband. After some conjecture about the mystery, (her opinion is that it is a hoax,) she asks Alvin meet her in Chinatown for lunch at a chop-suey joint.

He is hesitant to oblige. "I don't want any part of your ploys. Joseph told me . . ."

She curtly silences him. "That poof is infallibly nattering dreadfully about me. I had designs on discussing a reconciliation with you, but it is obvious you are not ready."

She ends the call before he can say another word.

"Shoot the Works" is released three days before the Hollywood production code takes effect on June 29, 1934. The studio rush releases the film to skirt the censor's regulations. Otherwise scandalous scenes in the Jackie Oakie film would have to be re-shot. Joseph and Alvin catch a matinee. A subplot involves the glib talker promoting a performer on a pikestaff.

"I don't understand why the studio did not cast you after how well you did in that screen test," moans Joseph. "But it is probably better they didn't. I can't see this flop doing much in ticket sales."

Kelly is interregnum in Columbus on July 22, 1934. He is tuned in to a mystery radio program. The local station breaks into the broadcast with a news bulletin.

"America's most wanted by the F.B.I.—Public Enemy # 1, bank robber John Dillinger, has been cornered and shot. The gangster is reported dead at Chicago's Biograph Theater," announces the studio. "The weed of crime bears bitter fruit. Now we continue with 'The Shadow' brought to you by *Detective Story Magazine* . . . ."

Alvin suddenly feels lonely. When he is sure no one is watching in the darkness, he sneaks furtively to the payphone booth on the corner, even though it would terminate his contract if anyone saw him. He asks the operator to connect him with Vivian.

His ex-wife is livid at being woken up at three in the morning and clearly reminds him she has no interest in rekindling their marriage. She uses some coarse verbiage.

"You've become 'a voice of the past' whispering with all the others in my head. I have powerful friends," she jabbers. "You had better watch your step."

"Always," mumbles Alvin as he hears the dial tone. He remounts before anyone notices. "I watch everything. Especially where I walk because cars are so dangerous."

It is a sultry Summer night in 1934. The Globe Theater facade announces "Bathing Beauties Compete in Ice Sitting." A fraction of the city streams in to escape into the air conditioned hall as the idiosyncratic clash begins in mid-town. Camera buffs photograph the six swimsuit clad models incubating frozen blocks. The pageant continues slightly more than three hours until the fifth shivering participant leaps from her oversized cube. The extant maiden is crowned "The Ice Queen." Babette Gordon wins $200 and a rhinestone tiara from the organizer. Teeth chattering, the brunette leaps to immerse herself in a cozy bubble bath. Promoters do not run the contest again.

A few days later, the hook and ladder brigade are called to wrest a trespasser from the Capitol Theater's peak in Union City. Unwilling to leave his resting place, John Keely is brought earthward by force. He is handed a divorce decree that accuses him of neglect. "Flagpole" promises to sue as police take him to lockup.

"Serves the layabout right," Alvin reiterates to the reporters who ask him to comment. "He's an odious individual. He smells bad too—like old cheese and circus-folk."

While Kelly is entrenched at Buffalo's Jubilee Theater, Vivian is detained shoplifting at Gimbel's perfume counter on September 22, 1934. The management presses charges, and she uses her free phone call to contact Alvin. Emmerling's switchboard operator passes on the urgent request. His manager briefs his friend.

"What are you thinking, champ?"

Alvin reluctantly scrambles to his "Indian" motorbike, revs the motor, and rides from upstate. He is in a lather that his six-year-old son is unattended while his ex cools her heels in lockup. After springing her, she thanks him with a cheap smooch on the cheek. She does not let him into the apartment after he walks her to the building's entrance.

"If it wasn't for the boy, I'd leave this town far behind. You are so infuriating. I'm certainly not in love with you anymore, you loser."

She slams the door in Alvin's face. He buys a sardine sandwich and listens to the leaves crunch under his feet as he dejectedly dawdles to the Central Park Zoo. He's tickled at the sea lion herd's antics—four females and a bull called "Joe." His cacophonous wooing echos so much that the classy occupants of 5th Avenue constantly complain. The beleaguered park employees respond to so many nuisance calls that they consider relocating the animals to the zoo being built in Prospect Park.

"Keep your chin up," yelps Alvin while pitching an oily fish to the barking mammal. "My trouble is with one woman. I cannot imagine how you can juggle a foursome."

He heads to Joseph's building at East 89th Street. He doesn't see Vivian again until Christmas Eve when he gifts a wire-haired fox terrier to Junior. The minor adores the mongrel.

"I love him. Thank you, Daddy."

"He is the same breed as Nick and Nora's dog, 'Asta' in the movies. I was lucky to get him."

"I will call him 'P-asta' because he's got spaghetti legs," yaps the boy as he plays with the animal.

Vivian is absolutely not thrilled to have a puppy in the apartment. She flips her lid and demands Alvin fork out more towards its upkeep.

After the new year on January 11, 1935, Amelia Earhart pulls aloft from the runway at Wheeler Air Field in Honolulu. Her intent is to fly to the west coast unaided. Many have perished trying the transpacific crossing. The pioneering aviatrix lands after 18 tension-filled hours. After completing the 2,408 mile pilgrimage, she adds $10,000 in prize money to her net worth. Her companionless traversal allows her to say she's conquered both oceans, a feat even Lindy hasn't accomplished. Alvin sends her a congratulatory telegram. There is no response from the adventurer he considers a like-minded peer.

Eight weeks later, Kelly finds himself situated on the Fidelo Beer billboard, four stories up on the George Washington Hotel on 23rd Avenue. It is March 7, 1935, and he feels blessed to have a unique calling. The nation's unemployment rate is hovering around 20% and the economy is getting increasingly worse. He is paid $460 after completing a week conducting his off-beat profession.

Nabbed during a sting gone bad, Vivian is left holding a valise of fraudulent $20 bills. The con-woman is caught in a pickle between two G-men who have been sweating her unceasingly under a powerful light in their interrogation room. The agents imply she will face incarceration in a federal facility unless she squeals on the false greenback's source.

"Sister, we don't want little fish like you," catechizes the undercover cop with conked hair and a wide hand-painted tie bearing a Dalmatian. "We usually throw 'em back. We want the engraver who makes the phony-baloney.

"You are what, forty-ish?" inquires his square-jawed partner. "We are in receipt of the solid goods on you. Even the number one legal beagle won't be able to wriggle you out from this tight rap. I'd guess you'll be out of circulation for a stretch of 20 to 35 years in Alderson Federal Reformatory . . . unless you cooperate."

"You want to be wrinkled and grey when you are released? The math does not add up. Come on lady. Do yourself a solid, and spill the beans. Tell us where the fake Jack is from."

Knowing the jig is up, she turns informer on her oldest, shadiest accomplice, Victor Lustig. To save her skin, she decides to betray him and testify for the government.

"Okay, gimme a phone. Operator? Can you ring the Rialto Bar and Grill? Medallion 3-5338. Lemme jaw with Victor. Yeah, thanks," she says nonchalantly as the bartender fetches him. "Vic? Viv . . . . Your bills definitely cut the mustard, so I need to borrow another $25,000 worth to finish off a boorish oaf I am playing. 10% rental fee? Okay. Half now and half after? Grand Central Station information booth? Three? Sure, see you then."

"The Count" meets her to retrieve the bogus bills he has stashed. After he produces the key and opens the locker, Federal

226

Treasury agents swarm and clamp the steel bracelets on him. He struggles like Houdini to no effect.

"Jezebel. I vow I shall have my revenge," screams Lustig at Vivian. "I will make sure the word gets out on you. No wise-guy in any of these 48-states will ever work any game with you again. Enjoy your two-bit swindles, you shrew."

"Ah, you're all wet, Victor," she says superciliously as he is dragged to a holding cell at the Rikers Island House of Men's Detention. "I will mail you a carton of smokes, so you can bribe the screws." They release Vivian with the proviso that she "not leave town."

He is not laboring on June 27, 1935, so Kelly takes Junior to a Yankees game. At the "House that Ruth Built," the home team drubs the Washington Senators by ten runs. His former wife denigrates Alvin when he brings the boy home afterward. She complains about pretty much everything.

"This place too undersized. That dog pees everywhere, and your reliance on that fairy Joseph is, well disgusting. You must like taking a pole up the ass. A lot."

"No. I have told you many times before. Joseph and I are simply business partners . . ."

"That poof has corrupted you so much that you think he's helped you. But the truth is that he has ruined your chance of ever being normal."

"Like you know anything about that . . . ."

A month later, Kelly is affixed on the Greenwich Bank Building. He plans a week of staunchness, collecting an $800 fee. His sit is interrupted four days in on July 10th. Vivian is inculpated, swiping the purse of a salesclerk containing $15. She sends a pleading note to Alvin. He posts her bail, rides her uptown, and informs his ex-wife he cannot continue to save her.

"This is the final straw. I cannot continue to help you out of these sticky jams you seem to get yourself into."

Junior is at school; so, she invites him in for "coffee."

I know he will always do what I want. He is still in hopelessly love with me. I've got him twisted around my little finger, she thinks.

Phillip S. Roberts

I don't love him anymore, but I certainly may need a favor in the future. I guess I can throw him a bone to keep him on a string a tiny bit longer.

Vivian steps out of her garms with indifference. She lays naked on the bed and blandly encourages him to undress. She belittles him in the most bored tone she can muster.

"Yes, sailor . . . More. Ooh. Just like that . . . That's right . . . Give it to me, you stud . . . Oh . . . . You are done? Is that all? Really? You call yourself the king of endurance? Oh, please."

"I love you," pants Alvin.

"Sure. Okay. Now, get the hell out."

He leaves fully unsatisfied and extremely melancholic. He grabs a pint of whiskey on the way home, and wonders how he'll tell Joseph he broke another contract.

At 871 Knickerbocker Avenue in Bushwick, John Keely is settling in at a four-story locale on September 12, 1935. He possesses a promissory note for $600, payable after seven days. A writ charging he is "a menace and a hindrance to student lessons in a nearby school" is delivered.

An attempt by police to cajole him to the ground fails. His refusal to obey has the law flummoxed. "Flagpole" warns that he will "slather the staff with butter from his watercress sandwich," should anyone try to dislodge him. The cops produce an axe, and Keely surrenders. After a garrulous disquisition, he is sanctioned $100.

The same day, across town, in the Bronx, the genuine Shipwreck Kelly's appearance is being underwritten by the University Heights Businessman's Association. He stands above Tremont Avenue promising to best his own longevity, but the boys in blue gather at the base of his sit, waving a citation and he is remanded into custody. He is brought before a magistrate who hastily metes out a $50 fine.

"They did not give me a chance to . . . ."

"He was discharging his obligation," propounds Emmerling. "Our sponsors forgot the permit. Some other sitter was fined twice as much as we did for doing the same thing. You realize the nation is still in a bad economic state, right? It is opportune you and I do not to have to rely on breadlines or soup kitchens."

With Junior loaded in the rear of the car, the boys are ready to globetrot south for a few weeks near the end of November 1935. Vivian is predominantly unpleasant as the car starts, ready to leave. She has not seen Joseph since being evicted out of the apartment after her unsuccessful subterfuge.

"You're taking the boy," she harangues Alvin. "But you are leaving me to take care of that mangey mongrel . . . ."

"The motel in the panhandle doesn't accept pets. I told you that a while ago," reminds Alvin.

"Give me something to soothe my inconvenience then, you fruity tight-wad." Joseph rolls down the glass and passes a $10 bill through the open car window.

"You cheap polecat. That is not even enough to hire a child to be a dog walker."

"You will probably just take him yourself so you can save the money, you soused-tart." Joseph yells brusquely. "Buy some cheap firewater, ya pie-eyed drunkard. Have a Merry Christmas, you repugnant fishwife."

She is expelling obscenities like water from an open fire hydrant as the car speeds away. Kelly broods until the auto pulls into a North Carolina Texaco.

"I am sorry. What she said was dreadful," Alvin recoils at having to talk about Vivian's astonishingly unladylike tirade. "After all you've done . . . ."

"I have heard much worse before. Frankly, I am flabbergasted the insufferable witch did not say more."

Joseph thinks a conference with the Latvian will perk up his familiar's attitude. After checking in at the motel, Kelly proceeds to the Rock Gate. A board is nailed to the limestone wall. "Homestead location opens after Christmas." Leedskalnin has loaded his entire citadel unassisted into a flatbed, moving the load five miles from Florida City with the help of a single driver. Alvin and Junior take a taxicab to see the artist. Edward is delighted to have visitors.

As the sculptor takes the rug rat to inspect his art, Kelly skims Ed's current thesis. "Mineral, Vegetable, and Animal Life." The tract provides little insight into unraveling the paradox of how to defy gravity. *The carefully constructed passages must contain clues,* he reasons. *I however comprehend very little of what he has written in the pamphlet.*

Back in Manhattan, the city is covered with fresh snow from a storm. Vivian has been drinking. "P-asta" is scratching at the door and barking to be let out. Cursing, she finally grabs a coat and escorts the dog outside; heading toward a bodega that is open late to buy another bottle of gin.

The neighborhood seems quiet as she crosses against the traffic light. Out of nowhere, tires squeal and she is mowed down in the crosswalk, flung by a sedan's speedy impact. The car stops, shifts gears into reverse, squashing her beneath the wheels as the slush around her body steadily becomes more claret-colored. The canine escapes into the night as the vehicle flees.

When Alvin, Joseph, and Junior return from the Panhandle, a card is tacked on her door with a note to ring the nearby precinct. She does not have a private telephone line, so they return to Joseph's apartment to call from his. Thinking his ex-wife is in lockup due to some petty infraction, Alvin becomes somber when a detective fills him in on the macabre details.

"Yes, I was away . . . with our son, on vacation, in Florida . . . Hit and run? No witnesses. Are you sure it's Vivian? Oh, her pocketbook . . . I see . . . Yes. Tragic . . . I will break it to him gently . . . Yes, I will come and speak to you tomorrow. Thank you. Yes. Have a good night, officer."

He chokes up as he replaces the receiver on the phone's cradle. Alvin's thoughts are crushed like fresh mint in a mojito cocktail. *Was her death a senseless drunk driving accident, or something more sinister? Could this have been payback for something heinous she did? She has conned many people out of their money. Is it possible a victim or a disenchanted confederate put out a hit on her? Was it God's will or just a fluke? Either way, the tragedy confirms my fear of inebriated automobile operators.* He feels a knot in the pit of his stomach larger than a "Turk's Head" and tighter than a "Four Strand Square Sinnet." *I struggle on the best way to tell my offspring about his mother.* He sits next to him on the couch and speaks softly.

"Junior? Let's have a talk, okay? You will be staying here, a while, I guess . . ."

The seven-year-old stares blankly at his father, unwavering, showing no hint of emotion; stone faced and resolute like the Sphinx bleaching in the sun on the Giza Plateau. *This man was mostly not there when I needed something, and when he was around, the two were always arguing. Mom did everything for me. She was always telling me he was a bad man.* Kelly speaks haltingly as he attempts to give some comfort.

"First off, you should know I love your mother very much. There was a time when she cared for me more than anything. And, because of that love, we made you, who I love. You are probably feeling just terrible. I want you to know, nothing you did, caused this. You are not a jinx. It was just her time. Nor is there anything you can change about it. Death is just a fact of existence. Your mom . . . has passed on . . . and is, um, maybe sitting . . . on god's right side . . . as one of his favorites . . . in heaven. She is not coming back, ever, but we'll see her again when we become angels."

"I don't wanna' be an angel," bawls Alvin Junior contrarily. He does not weep. When Alvin tries to explain further, Junior insists he is wrong with one word answers.

"Things won't be the same without your mom," Alvin wipes a tear away from his cheek. "I am sad, but I think it is okay for us to be happy when we think about the good times we spent with Vivian. Remember when we rode the bumper-cars, ate burgers, and then took that cowboy photograph at the fair? That was a fun day, huh?"

Alvin's voice trails off as he realizes the terrier is gone. *This conversation has already been a disaster,* he thinks. *How can I tell him his dog ran away?* He trembles as he speaks.

"Um . . . we think your mom took 'P-asta' . . . to a nice farm upstate, but we don't know which . . . If you want . . ."

"I don't wanna' another." The thought of his pet in an idyllic setting upsets him as his father's words ring false. He suddenly wails. Junior starts hitting and kicking his father, devastated about loss.

"I wish you were dead instead . . . ."

"What?" Alvin is staggered by his son's words.

Phillip S. Roberts

"Just leave me be," Junior lashes out. "I hate you. Mom usta say . . ."

"I am certain she said plenty of things. We can talk about all that later, but I want you to know, I'm the last family you have and I would walk on hot coals, broken glass, anything, to make you happy. You must have some questions to ask, but those can wait. Now, try to sleep. It's been a very emotional day."

"I think you handled the situation well," consoles Joseph later when Junior is snoring under the covers in the spare bedroom. "He is grieving right now, but sooner or later, he will realize you care. That is not an easy conversation to have. You probably never had to hear a version of the "talk." You were orphaned at an early age. Most people don't have to have a heart to heart like that frequently. I can cast my mind back to how shocked I was when my parents were killed in a train accident. Of course, I was much older than he is and able to process the grief better."

In the morning, Vivian's attorney, Daniel Bosh, clarifies she left no will. Alvin is now solely responsible for the boy's well being. Searching her rooms, he and Joseph stumble upon $2,000 stuffed in the mattress. A total of $200 is hidden in a flour tin and another $800 is stashed in a hatbox. The two miss the bulk of her ill-gotten-gains, concealed in an envelope taped under a dresser drawer. Emmerling takes the notepad containing details of how she conducts her petty house of games. Kelly burns her fake credentials, dubious land certificates, and other incriminating evidence in a wastebasket. The furniture reseller takes most of the apartment's contents, and the second hand clothing shop buys her dresses. Joseph thinks there is enough to pre-pay a few years tuition at a boarding school in Cornwall on the Hudson.

Junior recoils when he is informed that he will be enrolled in the New York Military Academy. During the drive to the campus, the men explain that it is what is "best for him." Feelings of desertion and disgust return to the forefront. Alvin reminds him he will be welcome during school breaks and vacations. He says, "he doesn't want to." His father attempts to hug him before leaving, but is pushed away.

"You make me sick. Just go. I don't want to see your face."

Chapter 20 –
The Fair, Mae West

"If a little is great, and a lot is better, then way too much is just about right!"

— Mae West

As 1936 dawns, the country is trying to claw out of sluggishness. A loaf of bread costs 8¢, gasoline has risen to 10¢ a gallon, and rent at a modest abode hovers near $24 a month. With the added outlay toward Junior's room and board at the New York Military Academy, Joseph is trying to keep up with the bills. Even with President Roosevelt's reforms, economic conditions worsen as whistling twisters strip fertile topsoil away from Arkansas to Nebraska; former verdant farms are useless dust bowl and a significant amount of the Midwest migrates toward California.

On February 11, 1936, Kelly is involved in a "loser-leave-town" duel with Jack Allen in the French Quarter of New Orleans. Diner cashier Olivia Paulos asks to take pictures with the sitter on the Mercier Building. The curvaceous 19-year-old brunette joins him, and cuddles with Alvin on the crosspiece until Emmerling demands she descend due to insurance concerns. "Tap-Dancing" Allen soldiers on until sunset, then cedes his spot onto Canal Street. Alvin is mounted in resilience on "The Pickwick Turret" until morning to guarantee his $300 premium.

Junior spends his Spring Break in Manhattan. The eight-year-old is not taking to the military school. He complains he is always being bullied by upperclassmen. Alvin, educated by his own austere immaturity, offers superfluous advice to his son.

"Times were much harder when I was your age," he lectures. "In the orphanage, I had to fight for table scraps so much, I ran away to sea. Many days, I wished I had a father . . . ."

"Not me, pop. I would be glad if you conked out and was six-feet-under," ripostes the brat. "I am ashamed to be related to you. Maybe a judge will let me change my name."

Alvin scowls at his hurtful phrases and ships him back to boarding school. Then he is thankfully occupied with jaunts to Schenectady, Nashua, and Worcester that consume the Spring. He draws a few hundred in each burgh, country cousins drifting in from surrounding counties to see the square peg fit in a round hole.

The sitter takes a drag from his Marlboro, blowing the smoke into Sunset Park's morning air. With his feet in saddle stirrups, Alvin is copiously re-reading Leedskalnin's pamphlet while relaxing on a tall piling at the 44th Street Hotel on 6th Avenue. The cover reads, "A Book in Every Home—Ed's Sweet Sixteen, Domestic, and Political Views." If hints are contained between the covers exposing his perplexing method to lift the bulky poundage, Kelly cannot discern the explanation to the problem. He folds the handout to fit into his pocket.

How he does the work is mystifying. Is it a ruse or real magic? I believe miracles can happen once in a great while. He racks his brain for the clarity that must be right there before his eyes. *I wish I could figure it out, but, I'm not any smarter now that I've read his words.*

The Texas Centennial begins on June 6, 1936. Alvin wants to sit through the end of November—177 days. *None could ever excel that number*, he broods. *I need that feeling of being the champion again.* Notwithstanding Kelly's desires, Joseph is scarcely able to secure a week's compensation. He arranges appearances in other cities after that week to keep the income coming in. He'll have to give Alvin a good reason to withdraw from his baluster prematurely.

Natives come from every part of the South to ride the "Lone Star" Ferris Wheel, scrutinize the 4-H raised animals, or catcall at ineffable ladies in the State beauty pageant. Kelly is in the sprawling midway above an amalgamation of booths. The semi-permanent structures contain the usual carnival games and concessions. Other diversions range from country square dancing to a Bavarian town built to house 100 beer-swilling, little-folk wearing lederhosen. Music fills the air as bandleaders Kay Kyser, Tommy Dorsey, and Woody Herman are piped through the tinny sound system. Singing cowboys Gene Autry, Spade Cooley, and Montana Slim, all take a turn at the main stage.

A paddle-driven riverboat sails on a fabricated lake, while salesmen push their innovative wares from air conditioned kiosks. Street cars shuttle visitors in and out from sweltering mornings to battery lit vespertine evenings. A giant-sized register clangs as patrons pass through the turnstiles—reaching 117,000 by the opening day's conclusion.

President Roosevelt addresses the fair on the third day. Kelly cups his hand around his ear to better hear his speech. The heat flirts with 100-degrees, and Joseph keeps sending him wet sponges. Parched by the sun, he relishes the Coca-Cola being ferried up so he can hydrate. Alvin is reading a paperback of James Cain's "Double Indemnity," wishing there was some breeze.

Among the profusion on day seven is Mae West. Her presence is not mere chance. The cosmopolitan comedienne is on a junket to promote her film, "Go West, Young Man." Joseph had read that she was arriving in Dallas. He purchases enough bluebonnets and roses to fill the hallway to her room. After a few magnums of brut champagne, he asks her to add an appearance to her schedule. She agrees to do her "fancy" a good turn. The actress sketches out a script to perform with Alvin.

"Hey Mae, why don't you come up and see me sometime?" replies Kelly into his microphone.

"I must admit I prefer my dates more grounded. I am typically partial to being the one on top," the platinum-tressed actress cleverly replies in her sultry contralto intonation. She continues to pepper Alvin with her ribald assertions. "Ahoy there! My friends, I've been acquainted with this halfwit sailor many years, and there is nothing deficient about him. Folks, did you know they based 'Popeye the Sailor' on this muscular soul? Take it from me ladies, he's a real man. He's strong to the finish, and I ain't talking about spinach. I seen many long, stiff things in Hollywood casting rooms, but none compare to his mighty pole."

A few conservative busy-bodies blush at their routine of improvised repartee.

"I am thrilled you came. You are prettier now than when you were in that 'Klondike Annie' movie," booms his voice. "This is my element. I invented this sport, and I am acknowledged as the best. I am a thoroughbred you can ride all night. As they say, it is not the size of the waves, it's the motion of the ocean. Resoluteness is my game. Through sleet and snow, women call me *The Mailman* 'cuz without fail, I deliver."

"Oh swabbie, I swoon when I hear your sugary words. You naughty tease. Come here so I can give you a big smooch."

He hears nervous chatter from below as he performs a little dance at 52 feet up.

"To kiss those lips, I will be right there. Lemme tell you how wonderful the huge Texas hospitality y'all have shown me is."

The hurrahs lift to his ears.

"This is truly the grandest fair in the land."

Alvin has the impeccable excuse to decamp from his vantage. His muscles hurt and he chalks the pain up to maturity, noting he is not as spry as once was. He slides down quickly like a fireman to cuddle with the blonde-tressed sex-symbol.

"Once they go West, they never go back," the movie star quips and squeezes him gently while locking lips. He has not had a kiss since Vivian went to the happy hunting ground and this one is a humdinger. Her fragrant perfume is so aromatic he becomes aroused from the contact.

"Ooh seaman," snickers the buxom actress as she grasps his bulge. "Is that a mast in your pocket? Or . . . Oh, sailor! You ARE happy to see me!"

Back on the eastern seaboard, near the Williamsburg Bridge, Alvin settles into a stool. This time, instead of showcasing his endurance in the air, he plans on getting snookered at the former speakeasy, hidden in a kosher delicatessen near Delancey Street. "The Back at Radners," is secreted behind a revolving shelf holding salami and pepperoni. He is on his third gin fizz. It tastes tart. He winks at a woman who reminds him of Vivian. She ignores him, lights her cigarette and sets her veil on fire. Kelly bounds to save her, snatching a bottle from behind the bar and spraying seltzer to extinguish the flames. Angry and sopping wet, she wallops him as if he is Curley from "The Three Stooges."

"Ouch. Come on lady, that smarts . . . ."

Harold Parrot, *Brooklyn Daily Eagle* columnist writes up the incident. Alvin adds the item in his loose leaf folder. He points out the column to Joseph.

"See, some people still consider me a hero."

"Had you told me before him . . . " Joseph says acerbically. "I would have played it up, commodiously."

"I did not tell him . . . I guess he was there; watching, or drinking, or something."

Jesse Owens wins four Olympic medals at the 1936 Summer Games in Berlin. Germany's Chancellor is in a worked-up-state when his Aryan "super-men" cannot dominate the Americans. Alvin is thrilled to read of the Nazi's bewilder while he is working the sign of the Arcade Theater at Broadway and 64th Street. He still holds animus toward any *Deutschlander.*

On the Drovers Hotel, Kelly suffers a nervous breakdown after 12 days. Irate at being woken by his screams, the guests underneath protest to the night clerk who rings for medical assistance. Alvin slides to safety, collapses, and is transported to the emergency room. Diagnosed with "mental distress," the physician-on-call insinuates his next stoic feat should be spent horizontal for a span of two weeks. When the beat reporter from *The Kansas City Star* visits his bedside, Alvin refers to himself in the third person like Oofty-Goofty. He has gone bonkers.

"Shipwreck Kelly ain't got a fiber that ain't already been rattled. When it comes to Shipwreck Kelly's line, the man must be in tip-top condition; at his peak physical fitness. To give less than 100% to the audience who relies on Shipwreck Kelly to entertain, is irresponsible. Shipwreck Kelly's death-or-glory attitude will allow the hero to enter the gleaming halls of Valhalla at his end. This doctor ordered 'week of bed rest' will give Shipwreck Kelly a chance to respond to Shipwreck Kelly's many bags of fan mail. Kids love Shipwreck Kelly—almost as much as they love Santa . . . ."

Chapter 21 –
A Small Amount of Sea Change

"I suppose that's one of the ironies of life, doing the wrong thing at the right moment."
— *Charlie Chaplin*

Phillip S. Roberts

The Golden Gate Bridge in San Francisco is finished on April 19, 1937. Alvin asks if he can sit on the span in May during the grand opening. To Joseph the intriguing possibility is a long shot, but nonetheless sends a cable to the town's supervisors. Mayor Angelo Rossi does not reply.

Kelly is booked to be a guest on the radio program "Strange America with Robert Ripley." The cartoonist has another in-studio visitor, Philip Ostler. The German-American is a former railway engineer who saved a train by amputating his own foot to prevent a boiler detonation. The hostiles are having a ding-dong—yelling as loud as their lungs can project.

"Schweinhund. Even with ein gutes bein, I can kick your ass. How dare you refer to me as a heinie, you pipsqueak . . . ."

"Listen fritzie, if you weren't an ancient goose-stepping cripple . . . Never-mind. Come outside to the alley and I'll unleash a real beating—like I did to the Kaiser in the war . . . ."

"You jerk. Vot das you verk at? Oh ja, nichts, dummkopf. You zit around, loafing. You oafish, lazy Amerikaner . . . ."

The grizzled railway worker raises his fist. The announcer takes an unscheduled commercial break and both are hustled out. Few hear the disturbance, as most are tuned to comedian Jack Benny, or a program featuring Ed Jerome, the ex-court jester to Spanish King Alfonso.

Joseph shakes Alvin awake early on May 6, 1937.

"C'mon, we are driving up to Lakehurst to interview some society gadflies coming in from Europe."

Arriving at the airfield in the afternoon, Emmerling finds meteorological conditions have delayed the landing. At the Naval Air Station, film units are at the ready as the dirigible does a flyby. Joseph schmoozes with a radioman from Chicago. WLS announcer Herbert Morrison is standing near a box that is similar a turntable. He holds a bulky microphone.

"We can record audio—on the 'Presto-6D.' This portable box saves sound to acetate."

"That's an interesting machine."

"The plan is that I will talk to a few Hindenburg passengers to play back during my studio newscast. Charlie, let's run a test."

His engineer sticks the stylus on the disc. The airship is approaching at a leisurely pace. Morrison enunciates, setting the scene as sturdy cables fall from the blimp and are grabbed to stabilize the craft.

"It's starting to rain again—the rain has slacked up a little bit. The back motors of the ship are just holding it, just enough to keep it from . . . ."

Alvin is close enough to hear the radio announcer and thinks, *I would love to be drifting on that. It is probably as near to my dream of buoyancy as I will ever get.*

"It burst into flames! Out of the way, please!"

Epic catastrophe materializes; a brobdingnagian scale of carnage unfolds. Emmerling feels the rush of heated air flutter as if a 575 degree oven door had just been opened. He falls backwards, stunned by the deafening outburst. Alvin closes his eyes— he can still see the explosion in his eyelids as if a gazillion phosphorus candles were lit at once. The zeppelin lists as hydrogen gas ignites. Germany's pomposity burns expeditiously. Fire, cloth, and molten ore; debris rains onto the field as the cataclysm unfolds.

Alvin can barely hear the radioman's continuing narrative above the carnage. The cloth skin stretched taut on the dirigible is scorching. Choked by smoke, the ground-crew underneath is stampeding away like bison thundering across the plains as the ignited craft falls.

Morrison's narrative continues. "Not quite to the mooring mast . . . Oh, the humanity! And all the passengers screaming around here . . . "

Joseph is back on feet. He shakes Alvin who has been frozen in place—stunned like a trout hit with an oar as the devastation continues to unfold.

"For god's sake, man. Save someone."

Emmerling's voice cuts through the dissonance of the sirens. Kelly cannot hear him clearly over the cacophony.

Phillip S. Roberts

"Put you in the headlines again! You will . . . be famous again . . . celebrated. Don't you want to be known as the greatest of all time?"

The duralumin superstructure continues to smolder, pulverized as if a mammoth fist had slammed it into the silt. Diesel gasoline seethes on the concrete. Alvin bolts in the direction of the remnants. He rests, hands on knees, wheezing heavily in the parching air. A fortunate few are herded to well-being. Kelly reposes, exhausted on the warm asphalt. He limps to his companion's side—coughing and huffing.

"I am sorry Joseph . . . I could not get any closer . . . The heat was . . . I . . . ."

"I hoped to turn you into an even greater hero, but you are just a pathetic goat."

Joseph heads to a booth to phone in his report, but the news desk already has the information. He stews in silence during the ride across the bridge. Radio with its immediacy is crowned king, delegating the written word to squire.

Almost two months later, while trying to be the first female to circumnavigate the world, Amelia Earhart vanishes into the Pacific on July 2, 1937. The President orders the Navy to conduct an exhaustive grid-search. Joseph is drafting a remembrance in case she is not found. He reads his ode to Alvin.

"A shame. At least, she was lucky to be doing what she loved," acknowledges Kelly. "You have to pay attention or end up like Vivian. She never saw that drunk driver coming. To die in bed surrounded by loved ones is a gift afforded to the normal and we are not them. We have balanced on the razor's edge so long it is unbelievable that our feet are not sliced to ribbons."

"Say, that is pretty good. I can use that." His ode is eventfully published in more than 3,000 news outlets worldwide.

Fresh from a sit at the Brooklyn Trust Company building, Alvin is scheduled to benefit the "National War Veterans Association's Orphan's Fund." The Lexington Council Ballroom is thick with Rotarians, Elks, and Masons on July 13, 1937. Kelly has memorized a pithy speech that Emmerling has written. He signs the brochures that include a picture of him sitting while flying on the plane. When he is seated, the organizers explain the dinner is a "good-natured-roast."

"That's easy, she says. Lay the pole on the ground, measure it, and put it back upright," jokes the master of ceremonies, Milton Berle. "So Shipwreck says, 'What a dumb blonde, I need to know the height, not the length.' And now, please put your hands together and welcome to the stage, Alvin's best friend, another Brooklyn boy, Jim 'The Irish Sailor' Kelly."

"What an outstanding charity function benefiting orphans summer camp and roasting an iconoclast, this is. The inventor of the flagpole sitting game. A fellow who has sat during pouring showers, icy gales, and scalding temperatures at idiotic heights. A danger-seeker and champion to millions. Me. I am the one you should be applauding; not this fake, runt who stole my eye-catching innovation. I should have sued the imposture. Is his red-headed son even his? Because, let me tell you about the time, me and his hustler of a wife . . . ."

Alvin leaps at his enemy. The donnybrook culminates with the antagonists being separated by a scrum of older men wearing fezzes. Each threatens to sue each other, but no charges are filed.

Joseph proposes to write a feature article on Alvin to his contact at *Collier's*. The proposal is green-lit and Emmerling hires a professional photographer to profile the sitter. He turns in his feature that is scheduled to run in the October 13, 1937 installment. He deposits the check they send. When the monthly comes out, sure enough, the cover teases an article on Shipwreck Kelly. However upon perusing the magazine, elation turns to disappointment.

The pages contain a spread on former Kentucky Wildcat and current National Football League halfback, John Simms "Shipwreck" Kelly. The photo-feature showcases the sport star's 18-room mansion as he poses with his African safari trophies. Other pictures portray the society playboy entertaining his celebrity friends Bob Hope, Bing Crosby, Marlene Dietrich, and Noel Coward at the ritzy Manhattan hotspot "El Morocco." Joseph telephones his contact at the magazine.

"I handed your article to our features editor. I thought the writing was real good," replies his uncomfortable associate. "I'm sorry, pal.

"What happened?"

"The boss said, 'No one cares to read about that guy anymore,' and replaced the spread with photographs. You can keep the check.''

Johnny Betts, a 22-year-old bantamweight from Hoboken announces he's giving up boxing on January 25, 1938. Atop a street lamp on Platt Street, he tells *The Tampa Morning Tribune* of being taken to the esplanade during Kelly's 1930 record setting run in New Jersey. Pulled to shake hands with his hero, the experience left an influence on the hobbledehoy and now he wants to follow in Alvin's footsteps. The sports columnist speculates he is ducking his next opponent when Johnny's girlfriend drives by in her car. He jumps in and skips town in a hurry. He does not box, nor sit on poles again.

Alvin is lodging on a three-story storefront at 8th Avenue and Cathedral Parkway for the "Moe Levy and Son" tailor shop on Friday May 13, 1938. He wears a placard announcing a half price sale, seen by riders in the elevated car as it rumbles by his upright spot.

He has purchased a cartoon magazine to read during his 9 to 5 tenancy. "Action Comics #1" featuring a red, white, and blue clad hero named "Superman." Upon finishing his shift, he shows the cover illustration with the caped "Man of Steel" lifting an automobile to Joseph. Alvin has had a thought durning his many working hours.

"Maybe the authors can draw me in. He could leap by, and I alert him to criminals below . . . ."

"You think you are the thinker now? Who arranges to have those articles about you written?" Emmerling uses his Zippo to set the pulp ablaze. He consigns the 10¢ comic to a trash can. "Far better to not to be associated this joke that only kids read. That crap will never be popular with the grown-ups who patronize the merchants that hire us."

"Aw. I was gonna' send that to Junior . . . ."

The fissure in their interrelation widens further as he is berated. Alvin agrees their ship is not on an even keel. The opulent days are done, yet revenue is leaking in as if through a hole in a pail. *If a buck is to be had, I need it. There are so many without so much as a dime in their pocket. I wish Vivian had prepared a bit better. She left me with a lot of responsibility regarding Junior. I'm glad we can send him to a fine school so he can have a better life than me. Hopefully he can get past the loss of his mother. Captain Jacobi had an Oedipus-like thing for his mom that lasted his whole life.*

Emmerling apportions a percentage to fund Junior's schooling. The student in his boarding school bemoans his calamities. Alvin sends him what pocket money he can spare.

Kelly keeps obsessing on the subject of his legacy. As a "megastar" of 1920s, he does not accept the assessment that his time has receded. *I doubt we will turn a profit; invitations to work are so sparse now-a-days.* He is spending his mornings at the marina, pumping up his expertise to a few skippers, but boat owners defer to hire more vigorous hands than the wizened 43-year-old.

An infrequent height is summited. May though June is scheduled with limited agenda: a three day sit in Trenton, a 48 hour stretch in Charleston and a Friday night spent above Charlotte. Yet, even when he's at his best, Alvin feels glum. Tears streak his cheeks when he pictures a dead Vivian, and he has often thought about committing suicide.

"Chin up, Al. I found us an easy month-long gig in St. Augustine. Then we will head to Miami. We will luxuriate a month or two in Sarasota with the carney people and you can converse with that Latvian. Doesn't that sound nice?"

"What kind of work?" *He admits the mental picture does sound like fun.*

"The aquarium thinks that if you stand on a tank full of monstrosities; man-eating sharks," teases Emmerling. "That would bring a crowd . . . ."

"Wha . . ?" Alvin becomes unhinged. He has not had these trepidations recently. He is unstable and shrieking. "Soulless beasts! Devil fish! Man eaters! If I could stop . . . !"

Emmerling dulcifies his buddy, assuring that he was jesting and would never allow Kelly to be in danger. A few weeks later, the two reach the park a day before the venue is ready to open. Alvin stands on a post with the dolphins splashing below as he rehearses the patter.

"Elevate one," comes the disembodied verbalization. The Bottlenose leaps to seize the silver bait.

"Chum, you herring me?"

"Loud and clear."

"This job stinks."

On June 23, 1938, 30,000 clog the motorway, animated to wallow in the park. Sweating in the Florida sun, the crowd flocks to stands selling cheap hot dogs, lemonade, and pink cotton candy. Gallivanting clowns give children complementary helium balloons. Tropical fish swirl in the tanks and shallow tide pools. Emmerling's phraseology blares from loudspeakers. He is reveling in the fermenting hustle and bustle.

"Welcome to Marine Studios, an aquatic kingdom. Greet the seals, pet the dolphins, and gaze at an innumerable variety of saltwater schools. Kelly will squat on the rigging until dark, friendly feeding the creatures that once saved his life in the South China Seas. Becalmed five weeks in the trackless Atlantic, fishing with twine and nail, he struck up a close friendship with their kind." Emmerling continues with earnestness as the man whistles a nautical tune. "Facing certain dismemberment or suffocation should he tumble, aft or port, the pod kept him awake with their laughs, by splashing water on the sailor, and performing tricks for his enjoyment. Have you heard the parable of Jonah and the Whale? My 'World Champion' could be swallowed whole, yet Shipwreck Kelly will stand here all day."

His navy whites are more tight-fitting than in earlier days. Alvin toots a bosun whistle as he lifts up a silver smelt and the mammals leap for their meal. A few days later, he is replaced by a twelfth-grader on summer break who earns $8 a week.

Howard Hughes escapes Floyd Bennett Field in a Lockheed Electra on July 10, 1938. He stamps his passport in Paris, Moscow, Siberia, Fairbanks, and Minneapolis. The industrialist halves the best time around the world and enjoys a ticker tape parade thrown for the conquering hero. A week later, Douglas Corrigan rushes skyward. His objective is California, but he ends up in Ireland. He is the first to cross the Atlantic solo since Earhart. His pilot's license put in abeyance, the screw-up rides a cruise ship from Europe with his plane stowed in the bowels. "Wrong Way" is lauded in a celebratory cavalcade equal to the hysteria of any previous honoree.

Alvin is at the promontory of the McAlpin Hotel at West 33rd Avenue and Broadway. Joseph urges him to renounce his post on September 19, 1938, as a hurricane turns, battering the east coast with a flurry estimated at 120 m.p.h. He does not work a pole the remainder of the year.

Maryland's Pimlico track holds the "Race of the Century" on November 1, 1938. Triple Crown titlist "The Mighty Atom," War Admiral will test Seabiscuit in a confrontation that intrigues America. Alvin lays money on the older horse. Four lengths separate the two at the finish line as the younger Seabiscuit streaks ahead to win the "All-or-Nothing" stakes contest.

"I had a 50/50 chance," sighs Kelly while ripping up his receipt. "I cannot even guess that right."

Harvard student, Lothrop Withington, Jr. swallows a goldfish to win a $10 bet on March 3, 1939. A far-fetched mania is born as college undergraduates are releasing the wiggling fish into the stomach. At the mania's peak, MIT freshman Albert Hayes, Jr. ingests 42 in the same amount of minutes. College administrators, worried that students will contract some disease, put strict penalties in place effectively banning the practice.

John Keely bestrides a wooden bulwark in Prairie Du Chien on April 22, 1939. He plans to reside 60 days. "Flagpole" quits after 48 hours due to tepid interest from the local community, yet claims he is the world champion upon alighting. No one bothers to correct him.

Joseph attends a preview reception of the New York's World Fair on March 15, 1939. While Kelly rushes to check out the Westinghouse pavilion. Emmerling sidles up to the fair director Grover Whalen.

"May I convey interest in trouncing Shipwreck Kelly's most stupendous achievement at some tall place on the fairgrounds? Would you consider as adding him as a crowd-pleaser?"

"I'll be frank. I have had to refuse ludicrous larks by the score, lodged by far-fetched advertising agencies wanting to promote this festival. Front and center at this gathering will be 'The World of Tomorrow.' I will be patiently waiting for that day to come."

While Joseph does not mention it, Tesla's phrase he helped popularize grates at him internally.

"Our collective path should include the transmission of moving pictures via electric means, telephones compact enough to carried in your pocket, spaceships blasting far beyond the planetary system, complex machines that can calculate faster than brains, and medical breakthroughs that will save millions. One day, the our species will see ALL war, famine, and suffering—end. Certainly many innovations are coming that you and I could not think up if we lived a billion years. What we thought was impossible last year, is possible today. This expo is to be a harbinger of the time to come. We know one thing that is certain. The centuries that lie ahead will no doubt be wonderful and exhilarating."

Joseph understands the coming times will bring drastic evolution. *I've witnessed the horse-drawn carriage metamorphose into gas propelled vehicles and I've relished the augmentation. Alvin's power to draw eyeballs is outdated like a dodo's fossilized bones, a fee-jee mermaid, a captured cannibal on exhibit from Borneo's trackless jungle, a hoax about creatures living on the moon, or an Algerian torch singer billed as the world's ugliest woman.* His train of thought is derailed as Kelly barges in.

"Wow. I just came from seeing 'Elektro' the Westinghouse robot. That metal brain figures out math equations and even owns a mechanical dog," blurts Alvin. "Like something from Flash Gordon."

"Alvin, now is not . . . ."

"Junior will want to see these modern marvels. This is the world he's going to inherit."

Willow Woods is performing her human fly act blindfolded on August 12, 1939. Awed Philadelphians numbering 7,000 watch slack-jawed as the silver overalls-wearing, lanky woman tackles the 10-story Colonial Trust Building in Penn Square. "Tall-tree" Woods poses triumphantly with her husband on the ledge, holding her four-year-old daughter on her shoulders.

It is a month later, when vacationing Spokane rancher Faye Hubbard bets Alvin $250 that he cannot reside rent-free seven days on the 16-story Hotel Clairidge. Kelly accepts without asking Joseph.

After a while, he is persuaded to abstain by police. He does not have enough on hand to resolve the bet.

"I am not a freeloader," he embarrassingly pleads with Hubbard. "If you give me your address, I will guarantee you get your payment."

"Ah hell, forget it," says the cattleman. "I was jus' pulling yer leg."

November 5, 1939 is National Donut Day. Alvin feels a little clammy, but that discomfort is not enough to deter him from assuming a lofty cityscape. On the Chanin Building's 56th floor, basks Shipwreck in his glory. Seven years prior on the same edifice, Joseph Späh had staged his "convivial inebriate" act. Today, as many necks overextended, to gaze at the man on high rise standing on a plank over the side facing toward East 42nd Street.

Emmerling has arranged for Adolph Levitt, the owner of a bakery to pay a modest fee. Alvin will be locked in place in another metropolis soon and this promotion will drum up some interest. Zephyrs whistle past Kelly's ears as the cinematographers see that he is ready. The Fox-Movie-tone camera whirrs, saving the episode for posterity.

Alvin raises his voice. "I state the truth. This deep-fried treat is fit for a king."

Multitudes fix their gaze on him but do not hear his words because of the traffic's clangor. He has been jibber-jabbering endlessly with the cameramen. A few viewers, coerced to bear witness, receive a glazed pastry. The Salvation Army band plays while several of Emmerling's former co-workers drift by. None bother to take notes as his manager pours him a cup of black liquid and hands him a donut.

"Now, a handstand while dunking. I, Alvin Shipwreck Kelly, am the unequivocal flagpole sitting champion—the aerial endurance world record holder. My oomph comes from Folgers and Mayflower Donuts." He has memorized the bakery's slogan to recite.

"As you ramble through travel, brother, whatever be your goal, keep your eye upon the doughnut and not upon the hole."

Phillip S. Roberts

He raises himself into an upside-down position on the plank facing Lexington Avenue. Bulbs flash with an electric "Tzzzt" as he dunks the pastry in his porcelain cup and nibbles.

"That is first class to the last plunk. That is the way to eat 'em correctly."

Joseph calls in his eyewitness report and is informed by his editor not to write any more of those "damn flagpole stories." The *United Press International* boss informs him unless a fluke calamity arises, the wire service will not waste any resources on the bygone mania. Back at the apartment, a telegram has been delivered, informing Emmerling that the sit in Boston is cancelled.

Kelly's niche is now so inglorious that hordes do not thirst for his exploits, yet Joseph inexplicably does not send him packing and their arrangement continues. Maybe his confidante cannot live without him or perhaps he is sorry for the predicament he has gotten him into. His agent quotes lower figures, yet, no clients are interested—he is obsolete. Joseph procures Alvin a few days a week as a window washer, designed more to keep him out of the apartment than the revenue his paycheck provides.

Alvin is inconsolable and retreats to the corner bar. He has stood in any place the patrons were from and flips in his treasury to show them. He complains "how things were better then" while nursing a cold alcoholic beverage.

Junior is on Christmas vacation from Military school. The 11-year-old starts an altercation, sucker-punches Alvin and runs away. He is picked up in Yonkers and returned to the campus. The school's commandant mails Kelly a bill to cover the extra two weeks of room and board.

Just before January of 1939, Joseph is on a peregrination to Louisiana for a freelance writing gig. Alvin, left to his own devices, ambles into a barbershop on St. Charles Street. He is welcomed into a chair where he has had his locks styled in his more youthful days. The barber snips three gray strands and holds a mirror.

"Not much to cut. No charge." The 44-year-old feels more weathered than a shed that constantly faces the sun.

"Boys, can you figure out a spot overviewing the Sugar Bowl?" Alvin says loud enough to hear despite the clipper's buzz. "I would like to watch the game, but I ain't got a ticket."

One grizzled frequenter inquires, "How's the racket?"

"It's been difficult," Alvin says cheerily. "But, my kid is in a good school. I seen him at Christmas. Say, anyone holding a flask? I sure would use a slug."

Chapter 22 –
The War Years

"The greatest lesson in life is to know that even fools are right sometimes."

— *Winston S. Churchill*

Joseph hosts a 60th birthday gala for himself on February 5, 1940. The fete is well attended by his journalism cronies. One well-wisher, an ancient handicapper from *The Daily Racing Form* whose vocabulary becomes cruder as he drinks, corrals Kelly in the corner.

"I never saw a worse brawler in all my days. You are the luckiest idiot on god's green Earth. I was in the cheap seats when you was mauled you like the bum you are and ended your boxing days. Joseph would never tell you, but you know that he loves you."

The elder checks to see that Emmerling is absorbed elsewhere.

"Your cornerman; he saved you. That hoodlum was ordered to knock you into extinction because the mob lost a pile on you. He gassed you with chloroform so you fainted before the boxer had a chance to croak you. Scrammed you both out of town in case a gangster decided to snuff you. You are a trustworthy fellow. As superb as he has treated you, I am sure you will be a good companion to him in his gray-bearded days."

"A toast!" shouts Joseph over the merrymaking. "Raise your glasses to the undisputed King of the Skyline, Alvin Shipwreck Kelly! A man o'er them all!"

The boozer cheers in a spontaneous acclamation and more than a few line up to buy Alvin a drink. After the night's merriment has subsided, the friends cling to each other, bracing themselves, scuffling up the stairs leading to the brownstone. After unlocking the door, the pals stumble a bit in the hallway, while singing an inebriated, off-key, dirty little blues ditty as they clunk up the stairs.

Hold me in your lovin' arms.
Squeeze me till my clock alarms.
You've got to keep your tongue on it.
Use all your lovin' charms.
Rock me! Roll me! Tease me a bit.
I love the way you don't give a shit.
Keep me satisfied.
Yes, make me satisfied.

Phillip S. Roberts

Old aunt Jane had too much brew.

Oh, the things she made Jim do.

You've got to keep your tongue on it.

They stop on the landing. "I ain't bringing in a lot. Are we going to be okay?

"Yes. Thanks to my miserly ways, we have some capital. When the country's economic climate improves, I hope I can find you some worthwhile paydays. Until then, we'll survive if we are careful. We have enough to keep Alvin Junior in the New York Military Academy for another few semesters."

"You saved me. You used knockout stuff so that brute did not murder me in the ring."

"I couldn't let the racketeers bump you, kiddo," he slurred, a little relieved that the truth was out. "I was the one that involved you in that crooked game, and I will honor our deal to the end . . . I owe you that . . . debt."

"I could hire on with the merchant marine so you could relax a bit. There is a lot of money in supplying Europe. I could fight Germans again."

"Alvin, you are a little old to be involved in that mischief again. Maybe I can find a way your talent can benefit some charity."

Stumbling clumsily and saying goodnight, they go to their respective bedrooms. The shared peril experienced as a pair during their 38 years has forged the chains of their friendship stronger than any marriage.

A few days later on February 9, 1940, Universal Pictures releases the W. C. Fields and Mae West comedy "My Little Chickadee." She has not acted in a film lately and the comedic romp does well. Joseph pens a glowing critique describing the combination's chemistry as "unwilted and ebullient." Mae calls him from Hollywood to thank him and they end up conversing on the phone for almost an hour.

Junior visits in March coming the 60 miles from Cornwall to the city. Alvin is amazed his son has grown equal to his five-foot-six-inch frame. They are on friendly terms until he takes the pre-teen to Walt Disney's "Pinocchio." They have an unpleasant taxi ride back to the apartment as Junior complains about the "kiddie pictures."

"That movie was for babies. I am thirteen. I do not want to watch cartoons."

"What kind of films would you want to see?"

"War stuff. And ones with naked ladies. One boy at school sold me a nudie magazine his dad gave him. Why can't you send me those instead of socks?"

"You are not old enough to read that filth."

Alvin Kelly Junior gets even more upset at his father's disapproving response.

"I'm almost fourteen and as tall as you. Most of the guys at school are joining the Army. Will you sign a waiver so I can enlist?"

"No. You are far too young. I saw combat in the 'Great War' and I tell you it was no picnic—it was hell. A 'Kelly' should be in the Navy anyway," pronounces Alvin. "To join the infantry wastes your pedigree. I will not allow it."

"Allow it? You told me, 'you'd do anything to make me happy,' when my mother died, but you lied. You never let me do anything I want. I hate being related to you. Mom was right about you. You are a pathetic failure. You don't even know how to act like a man."

Alvin slaps him. Junior hits him back harder. More uncurbed scuffles continue between the two. Kelly realizes what he's doing and stops—unsettled.

"I'm sorry. Son? Can you ever forgive . . ."

"Save your breath, you gasbag. Am I even your child? I don't even look like you. If you were my real dad, you'd want me to be happy. I want to join up. I will, with or without your consent, to get far away from you."

A partial solar eclipse will be visible on April 7, 1940. The chance to take in the astronomical rarity in the Empire State has not been seen for years. Kelly desires to practice his skill during the peculiar environmental conditions, but Joseph does not purchase a permit.

Alvin is going to reign over a holiday weekend in Toledo. It is May 30, 1940, and he is settled in the Kroger Master all-night market's rafters. He is promoting the slogan "Roaring prices from the twenties." He has labored so infrequently, he is adrenalized to be on display. The franchisee provides a walkie-talkie so patrons can chat with him and hear the items on sale. The owner is gladdened by the many shoppers on Decoration Day and pays $500. Joseph does not have another job scheduled on the calendar.

America is still not involved in the war in Europe. Charles Lindbergh gives the keynote speech at the America First Committee rally on April 24, 1941. The Manhattan Center roars as the aviator articulates his anti-semitic and isolationist screeds. Alvin has despised the Germans from the time a U-boat sunk the ship he was aboard during the first World War. Joseph is repulsed by the Fascist rhetoric, pens a choleric Op-Ed and transmits it by telegraph to all the Metropolitan papers. His aggressively worded prose is printed in one paper with a small circulation, *The Westchester Jewish Weekly.*

Alvin tries to volunteer to join the Navy but is spurned. He ends up three sheets to the wind in a sleazy taproom by the boatyard pleading to be shanghaied. None will allow the rummy to put his mark on their articles. The Axis battleship *Bismarck* scuttles the H.M.S. *Hood* in the North Atlantic on May 24, 1941. Alvin efforts to sail again but is sent home due to his age.

When "Joltin' Joe" DiMaggio's 56 game hitting streak ends in Cleveland on July 17, 1941, Kelly uses Emmerling's account to send a congratulatory message to the center fielder.

I KNOW HOW TOUGH IT IS TO KEEP IT UP. SHIPWRECK.

Joseph admonishes him; telegrams are not gratis anymore. No reply comes from "The Yankee Clipper." Alvin assumes the response went to the other "Shipwreck." Professional football star, John Simms "Shipwreck" Kelly is in every Manhattan society column again, having recently married "The Millionaire Debutante," Brenda Frazier.

"I guess this country has enough room fer two people to share a nickname," harrumphs Kelly whenever the former Kentucky University player comes up in conversation. "As long as he ain't climbing flagpoles, we won't have no rhubarb."

August has Alvin at an opulent gathering; the gangster and gun moll-themed partygoers have a hoot rubbing elbows with a genuine fossil from the "Rip-roaring Twenties." The social function is not his usual bailiwick, but as the only luminary invited, he amuses the guests with his agility. His parlor trick, standing atop stacked chairs, earns him $30 from the host.

As the festivities conclude, he notices that his ride has left. He points at a car and asks the valet to bring him keys. He twists the radio dial, tuning to Jimmy Dorsey's Orchestra and floors the pedal. The grey Chevrolet skids onto pavement near Cherry Hill and hits 80-m.p.h. on the straightaway. A siren spews out from a police motorcycle, and, after a laconic chase, he pulls to the side. Without a license or title to the borrowed car, he's taken prisoner and spends the night behind bars. His call to Joseph turns tense, but his comrade agrees to come up to Bridgeport and spring him.

The magistrate parses the law. Due to the fact no damage befell the car, the owner does not press charges. He pleas out for a reduced sentence: 14 days for drunkenly operating a vehicle without a license. Alvin is remanded into Joseph's custody with the proviso he return weekly to satisfy the mandated punishment.

TIME — AUGUST 25, 1941

KELLY, THE PREMIER POLE SITTER OF THE TRIVIAL 1920S, IS UNAVAILABLE DURING HIS SUNDAYS, COOLING HIS HEELS IN A CELL. THE PLEA ARRANGEMENT FOR DRUNK DRIVING KEEPS HIM TOILING AS A STEEPLEJACK DURING THE WEEK.

He pastes the item on a leaf in his dusty binder of memories. It will be awhile until he adds another. In spite of current events, Joseph still honors his arrangement with Kelly despite the fact that gas rationing has curtailed any unnecessary movement. Flagpole sitting is out of the question. He is able to arrange a few high altitude chores like window washing for the former sailor. Alvin is a mess; constantly brooding because of the loss of Vivian and his repute.

After the raid on Pearl Harbor, Kelly tries to volunteer again for the Navy. The salt is jettisoned as too advanced in age and classified as 4-A. His ambition to fight the Kriegsmarine is denied like a panhandler asking an industrialist for a bite of his Monte Cristo sandwich. The 46-year-old veteran is not considered as an asset to the Armed Services. He is distressed by his inability to serve his country.

Junior attempts to volunteer with the infantry. He is not accepted due to being 14 and is classified 1-H. He sneaks into the back of a trailer belonging to the Adams-Floto Animal Show and rides all the way to Burlington before being being discovered. The owner turns the teen in to the Vermont county sheriff. The runaway has no choice but to call Emmerling's number. His elder borrows Joseph's clunker to pick up and hasten him back to the military institution. Alvin's son flips him the middle finger as he steers away.

Emmerling arranges for Kelly join a tour that is selling government bonds. Alvin is eager to entertain. He succors a group of C-list actors, introducing their skits from his elevated lectern; employing a net to allay the disquiet that the 47-year-old might injure himself while impressionable children watch. Shipwreck feels a spasmodic tightness in his hands as he fabricates monkey-paws, sheep-shanks, and other twisted ship knots out of twine as part of his act. After taking a bow at the conclusion, the sailor suited chap hands the intricate constructions from the proscenium to the kids sitting in the front row.

A few days later, while setting up his equipment at Palisades Park, Kelly hurtles from the ladder to the stage and injures five ribs. The ensemble presses on without him as he heals. Someone tells Leonard Lyons who runs the mishap in his syndicated newspaper column. Alvin does not return to the tour.

Nikola Tesla dies in his suite at the Hotel New Yorker, January 7, 1943, at the age of 86. Emmerling, pens his obituary for the *United Press International's* over 5000 subscribing newsrooms worldwide, writing, "Ironic that the great intelligence that lit the world, will soon be buried in the darkness." His words are translated into most of the

world's languages and read by a record number of people. He frames
the article and finds a place for it on his crowded wall.

The next day, Junior enlists with the Army by changing his age
on his birth certificate. After boot camp, he ships out to Italy. The 15-
year-old sends a spiteful message before he leaves, but his father is too
late to terminate his entry in the army. Alvin is so riled up that Joseph
takes him to converse with the recruiter upstate who signed his son up.

"But he forged his application. He is not 17 yet."

"Sorry, Mr. Kelly. Once he has graduated basic training, he is a
United States serviceman. His Uncle Sam will tell him when to sleep,
where to march, and who to shoot. You should be appreciative that
your fine young soldier wants to serve his nation in wartime. His
bravery shows you gave him a good upbringing."

"Sure, but he is not even 16. He does not know the world,"
contradicts Alvin. He is frantic and tacks to a different concept. "You
have a flagpole in front. What if I stand on your storefront all weekend
and draw in recruits? Will that prove I am fit enough to serve? Can you
waive the physical and let me sail with the Navy? Could you at least
tell me what unit my son is in?"

"Please, Mr. Kelly," grimaced the Sargent in charge. "I've
already explained to you several times, I have regulations to follow.
Even if I had that information, military secrecy . . . ."

Alvin is upset during the ride back to the island of Manhattan.

"You were a youngster when you struck out on your own,"
says Emmerling in a mellifluous tone. "The world, has become much
more complex."

"I have suffered through harsh times, but a father hopes his
descendants will have a better life. Maybe I should have talked to a
Major or at least a Captain."

"I don't know how you'd find him. There are probably ten
thousand 'Kellys' involved in the armed forces."

On June 1, 1943, Joe Powers is filmed by British film company
Pathé during an eight-hour sit in Miami's lower environs. He does all
his tricks including balancing on one leg. "Hold-Em" explains to the
cameras that few care about his sport now for the reason that "real
heroes are dying on the battlefield everyday."

Alvin is hanging around the Brooklyn anchorage trying to work freight. On June 6, 1944, the Allied invasion commences on Normandy. When news of the assault hits the radio, Alvin goes to St. Patrick's Cathedral in midtown to spark a prayer candle for Junior. He assumes he is attempting to liberate occupied France. The Army dogface is not there. The private is skinning a brace of pack mules in the Italian Alps as part of the Quartermaster corps.

Joseph subcontracts Alvin to paint the Irvington Town Hall. Kelly works in a larghetto rhythm. He is being paid by the hour so he daubs white paint slowly until his joints are sore, putting a finishing coat on the steeple. When he comes home, Joseph asks his opinion on a piece he's roughing out. Death notices are the only oeuvre he is still being compensated for. Most of the proposals the 64-year-old sends out are repudiated or ignored. Radio reports that band leader Glenn Miller has exited stage right while crossing the English Channel in a transport plane.

"The trombonist's music echoes in the celestial as he conducts a band of angels in Zion."

"That sounds like a million other things you've poorly written."

Joseph just stares at him.

"I am sorry," Alvin realizes he has been cruel. "I am worried about Junior."

"Why? He does not care about you. Not one iota."

The best friends seem to quibble as if they are an old married couple a little bit more lately. Ultimately, things return to their normal calmness.

Victory in Europe is announced by Truman as "a solemn but glorious hour" on May 7, 1945. Times Square floods with celebrators like a skulk of foxes converging on an unguarded coop of Golden-Laced chickens as soon the news is broadcast. Alvin wistfully wishes he was watching the revelry from above. Instead, he tries to squeeze himself into his old sailor ensemble and hops a subway to 42nd Street. Fortunately the car is not too crowded, but when he gets off, Times Square is. As the precipitating shredded reams fall like snowflakes, he corrals Staff Sgt. Arthur Moore into a bar and buys him a cocktail.

Kelly retreats, frustrated when he's not bought a libation in return. In the packed street, he sees a midshipman joyfully smooching with a nurse. He clutches a nearby lady, too, but she slaps him in the face.

"Fresh," shrieks the matron in abhorrence. "I oughta' call a cop to teach you manners."

"Gee, I'm sorry, lady. I was sure we met before."

Marshall Jacobs who claims to hold the title of "America's Best Steeplejack," is set to reside on a pole starting June 17, 1945. "Maddog" plans to summer on the Muskingum riverbank in a packing crate suspended 106 feet in the air.

His fiancée, Lonnie Cosmar, is heaved up as he meets her in the middle to steal a kiss. In midair, he puts his engagement ring on her finger and announces he will marry her in 10 days. *The Associated Press* transmits a photograph of the sweethearts kissing while in the atmosphere. The article ends up on page four.

"It's a revival," squawks Alvin. The 50-year-old is visibly jaunty at the prospect as he waves the newspaper. "Let's arrange a tour —one that could continue on until Kingdom Come. I bet the curious would come in droves to see the original Shipwreck strut his stuff."

Emmerling contacts a few businesses but secures no positive reaction. Alvin is optimistic, and tells his chum to be patient.

"Once the globe is ready to conduct itself normally, the world will beat a path to our door."

Joseph is 65 in 1945 and distracted by his own aches. Panegyrics are not raking in much profit, and he feels his studious labor should have yielded a gracious retirement by now. He is frustrated by his inability to become published despite producing reams. He has written an epistolary novel based on Vivian's dossier, notebook, and her cruel house of games during the last decade since she died. He chooses the title, "A Tragic Ending for the Queen of Cons."

It is his most coruscating and witty effort, yet no one important will give the 316 pages a read. He does not talk to Alvin about it since the novel is based on his former wife. *I've emptied my file cabinet of ideas into this tome—double checked every word, punctuation, and paragraph. I've quizzed detectives and hoodlums alike; offered restitution to her victims to gain insight on her methods, and researched her tragic past in newspapers from 1904. I've turned over every stone and pulled every weed in search of a nugget of truth. I've left nothing out, even though I know this tale of woe would be extremely painful for Alvin to read.* Rejection letters about the novel based on Vivian's crookedness give him no pleasure as he watches the paper catch ablaze in the hearth. The light flickers, dancing upon the roadmap of furrows on his brow.

Emmerling sells his property but negotiates a reduced rent for his lifetime. *I can no longer afford my sidekick and I feel abysmal that I am in this position of choosing. The two of us have been joined at the hip for 30 years.* Yet he cannot mute his thoughts and speaks frankly.

"I cannot continue to subsidize you notwithstanding how much I care. Haven't I told you how cumbersome things are? It is humiliating to say, but I'm almost broke. I had to sell the building."

Alvin internally panics. *I feel as if my stomach is tied tighter than a Carrick Bend knot. How can my best friend abandon me? I don't know how to survive without my manager's help.* He feels the pressure of having no bookings in months. Joseph continues to talk. As usual, he has a plan.

"A producer was in a jam when he was an usher, and I helped him from being in the poorhouse. He is rich now, and I arranged a consultation. We'll lay out a grand exhortation—a '20s revue. You will preside as the emcee prior to your retirement. I hope to score you a nice, juicy fee."

"What? Retire?"

Joseph dismisses his response and continues.

"Honestly, this praxis is done. Our unique spellbinding has exhausted its magic. These decades have been a grand run. You and I have squeezed this stone with all our might; little is left but grains of sand. Without your pièce de résistance to utilize, you are a heavy burden sinking me to the river bottom. I have to disband our affiliation."

The prospect frightens Kelly to his core.

"I am too tired to go on tour again," groans Joseph. "So, don't screw this up."

On the appointed day, the pair reclines in Willie Hammerstein's outer lobby. The producer is late. Alvin, who is used to endless inactivity, has to keep himself from prattling lest he be interpreted as infirm. Joseph is internally mesmerized, rehearsing his soliloquy. Welcomed in to the producer's inner sanctum, Emmerling is gleefully greeted by his bygone friend.

"Joseph, my boy! I haven't run into you since we shipped that skinny she-devil Polaire back to Gay-Paree. Remember that day on the docks when I handed her the ticket and luggage?" He cackles hysterically and cruelly. "She started bawling so much her mascara was streaming down her face like Victoria Falls in the rainy season."

Joseph and Willie hug with the fondness of lost siblings. Alvin is introduced to the Broadway magnate who shakes his hand. The cigars he hands out are the finest; rolled from the best Cuban tobacco. After pleasantries, Hammerstein pours 40-year-old cognac and clinks glasses as the huckster glibly depicts the scenario.

"I have a gilded opportunity." He feels happy, dusting-off his feathery sales vernacular. "We screen classics at the theater during the day and present a follies at night. We cast the musical with the era's icons. Jolson and West are my friends. The former headliners both owe me a favor. I will write some funny boy-meets-girl sketches. We will interweave a few familiar standards as a chorus line performs 'The Lindy Hop' and the 'Charleston.' That'll add some razzamatazz. Alvin will sit on the marquee for weeks leading to his retirement. His final stand—a curiosity like 'Custer at Little Bighorn.' By now, I figure pre-war nostalgia should be the rage. If a hit, you know the receipts we would reap would be gangbuster."

Their host did not consider this as the boffo opportunity. "Passé," is the kindest word he uses in his assessment. Even if best-known stars signed on, tastes are different.

"Well, champ?" quietly intoned Joseph.

Kelly thanks the financier and reminds him about 1930, when almost 100,000 watching in Atlantic City hung on his every move. He begs to kickback his fee and then offers to do the job for no charge. He grovels; falling on his knees and sheds real tears to no avail. Willie buzzes his chauffeur to give them a lift home.

Phillip S. Roberts

"I'm sorry, Joseph," says Alvin in the backseat of the Mercedes-Benz 230 Cabriolet B roadster. "You are my best friend. You have treated me better than anyone. I'll move out as soon as possible."

"You don't have to leave. I was being selfish. He wasn't ever going to back that show. He's too good of a businessman. I'm sorry. I set you up to fail. Just, well, you know how bad things are . . . Please, just don't waste money."

Kelly gets guttered on Friday, July 13, 1945. With other soused patrons of the Skid Row Bar and Grill Restaurant egging him on, he climbs the storefront of the Alabama Hotel at 217 Bowery; pulling himself upwards by grasping a drain pipe. He is pulled into an open window on the third floor balcony, is tackled by a cop, and tossed in a cell with the other drunks. He has to spend the weekend in jail. Monday, after a tongue lashing, the magistrate proscribes a $25 fine. Alvin assures Joseph he will not ever waver again.

"Thank god the prosecutor did not cite the 'Human Fly' law," Emmerling admonishes his associate. "I would have left you to rot."

Chapter 23 –
The Voluminous Decline

"We learn the rope of life by untying its knots."
— Jean Toomer

The world does not have the appetite for such an antiquated notion as flagpole sitting in 1946. Emmerling wrangles what sustenance writing he can such as death announcements, oddities, and historical profiles. The lack of renown is driving Alvin nuts, but he works an occasional shift at the docks. The heights and the solitude that pacifies Kelly in a congested milieu has dissipated. They both pray that 1947 will be better, yet, in their hearts, they doubt a savior is coming.

"Mike the Headless Chicken," has become the greatest draw on the freak show circuit. On March 17, 1947, Emmerling is typing out an obit for the venerable poultry. During the precursory 18 months, the Wyandotte breed is selected as the Sunday night meal. Fruita resident Lloyd Olsen deftly swings his sharply honed cleaver. Unbelievably, the fowl cheats execution, obliviously preening its feathers with the stump and blindly scratching for worms. The Colorado resident brings the bird to scholars in Salt Lake City. Medical professors theorize that, as a result of the brain stem and one ear being still in tact, the rooster lives on. Rumors of the miraculous fluke spreads far and wide as purveyors visit the farm bidding to own his rarity. Farmer Olsen accepts $10,000, and the outlier goes on the wing making impressions with memorable vibrancy in major cities on the two coasts and then in less populous hamlets.

"Miracle Mike" is insured for $100,000. Not since "Jack Pershing" had any chicken been so well known. That Iowa chanticleer, named after the General was re-sold and re-donated during WWI, raising $40,000 to benefit the Red Cross Nursing Corps. Upon his demise, the brown plumage is sent to a taxidermist and is currently in a glass case at the State Historical Building in Des Moines.

Joseph pauses his penmanship to reflect. The two had gone to glimpse the phenomenon passerine when it was shown in New York. After paying 50¢, both chat in the procession amidst the other intrigued, all ardent to take in the queer rarity. They look upon the unaffected quirk and the amputated head preserved in formaldehyde.

"Maybe Houdini was right, and there is a hereafter," exclaimed Alvin while leaving the viewing.

"No. That freak accident is not proof of an afterlife," his running mate countered. "And what would be 'chicken heaven' anyway? A world without ovens or frying pans?"

Emmerling writes that the "clucker was an abnormal corollary." It had finally died, a year and a half after the stroke of the axe failed to kill it. In an Arizona motel, Mike's handler had gotten stinking drunk. Unable to find the sugar water he uses to nourish the fowl, he dropped a corn kernel from a can into the gullet and the nestling chokes. The torso as well as the bottle containing the head are discarded in a waste bin, but the myth persists. Joseph postulates decapitated hens will become a fixture at "pickled punk" museums and medicine shows.

"I envision the hue and cry boys will have a field day. 'See the grouse that defied the Dark Angel,' is what will be repeated ad nauseam. Agriculturalists are testing different hatchet strokes, hankering to duplicate the supernatural marvel. This story will play big anywhere fowl is raised. Even while finally roosting in the 'Beyond,' that dead bird will continue to generate coin. That is the very definition of a bread-ed winner."

"Are you implying that when I'm not on flagpoles that I am less valuable than a fried chicken dinner?"

"That was not my intent. You are a good egg."

"That obituary is eloquent," Alvin mimics a sardonic British articulation. "You are sure to earn a certificate to nail up on your wall, mister reporter. It is high-brow writing."

"How dare you mock me. Do you know who spread the terms 'Thrill-seeker,' 'Dare Devil,' and 'Stunt Man' to the masses? Me. I coined the marginal phrases 'Escapist,' 'Human Fly,' and even 'Flagpole Sitter.' I am society's metronome, writing the first draft of history. A chronicler who has been instrumental in forming the English lexicon. I have contributed to the muniments through three wars, ceaselessly. Who popularized the phrase 'The World of Tomorrow?' Me. I have met the notable, including *The Greatest Showman, Barnum* and *The Man who Invented the 20th Century, Tesla.* I rubbed shoulders with the exceptional individuals that have shaped these explosive times—Thomas Edison, The Wright brothers, Annie Oakley, Charles

Lindbergh, Enrico Caruso, Amelia Earhart, Harry Houdini, Wyatt
Earp, Mae West, and many others who will be reminisced about long
after you are dust. You are privileged that I even be considered you as
a candidate to be boosted as an abstruse off-ramp on the highway
of life."

"I am sorry," Alvin realizes he has been cruel.

"When you die, I will profess that 'You were the greatest of all
time.' Even Saint Peter will be pleased with my honest assessment."

"Um, thanks. Say, I need $100."

Joseph can feel the hairs on the back of his neck bristle in
anger. He clenches his teeth as his blood boils. *I've told him before
how poor we are. Has he not been listening? His acolyte has not
always been a millstone around his neck, but now I wish that the
fellowship would have dissolved.* He is furious.

"What? If not for these necrologies, we'd be in the poorhouse.
We cannot count on your once flourishing faculty. That means of
support is gone like dinosaurs. You have not done one sit lately. Why
do you need a c-note?"

"I had a sure-thing, but the horse ran fifth." Kelly winced. "I'm
no welsher. I, kinda, borrowed from some ruffians. I gotta' pay, or I'll
end up with a busted leg. I'd be unable to work while I recover."

"How could you? You know how things are financially."
Joseph calms himself with surprising aplomb. "Anyhow, the well
is dry."

"Don't we have any of the 'rainy day fund' left?"

"Your outlay far outstrips our intake." Emmerling is incensed
but measured in his response. He snaps his fingers for emphasis and
the discussion turns into an acrimonious argument like battleships
sighting each other in the Adriatic. "We spent a bunch on room and
board for your brat as well as other such nonsense. My spine is sore
from carrying you."

"You told me I would have stardom and the luxury that comes
with it. You saved me from something that I would not have been
involved with, if not for you. I am in worse straits than Oofty-Goofty."

"I tried to elevate you in every way, but as it turns out, you
ARE a jinx."

Alvin has always feared this thought. *Perhaps I was born a Jonas or simply star-crossed? Every ship I've been on is on the bottom of the ocean. Anyone I ever got close to, is dead or hates me. Do I deserve this pain for the bad things I've done? Is it retribution? Were things always going to end up this way? Is a man's destiny set in stone? Was Captain Jacobi wrong?*

"I could have qualified for government benefits without your silky, glorified, niminy-piminy talk of fame. I wish I'd never met you."

"You didn't even hold a cent then," Emmerling reprimands him. "You still pick pennies up from the gutter, you fatherless mick."

"You think I'm dumb, but I'm not. I didn't graduate from a college, but I'm still smarter than you. I've read lots of books. I think that no one published your novels because you are a crummy writer. You pick too many flowery words, you pansy."

"The opus was first-rate. The subject wasn't, you egomaniac. You are stupid to boot—thinking that immigrant misfit could float giant rocks. I saw Houdini perform the Indian Rope Trick when I was nine. Many years later, when I interviewed him, he explained the illusion, and I never believed in miracles again."

"You are wrong. Miracles exist. I'm proof. I should have been dead a thousand times. Vivian was right. She always said you were a 'bad' man." His internal dialog is running rampant with questions. *What did Joseph originally want from me? Was he attracted to me in some kind of depraved sexual way? Did he plan to maroon me like Ben Gunn in "Treasure Island" once he'd fulfilled his dreams and achieved his own fame? Was this ever about me or always about him?* "She begged me to take what I was owed and leave before your perversion engulfed me like the pull of a sinking ocean liner."

"I try not to speak ill of the departed, but she was an uncouth criminal. Her gang of thugs were watching us from the moment we embarked on the train to Los Angeles in 1912. Her associates knew we were running from the mob, so they thought we were easy pickings. Then it turned out she knew you and that changed their plans. She has been trying to pilfer my bankroll and you have been a tool toward that end. I doubt she was ever really in love with you. I am glad I licked a stamp on the letter to that vindictive oilman in California she swindled.

You can count your lucky stars he, or one of her victims caught up to her before the law clanked the jail bars shut. She would have turned on you as soon as things got dicey. To save her skin, she'd betray anyone in an instant like rats affrighted from a house on fire."

"That is not true." *Deep down, Alvin knows his friend has no reason to lie. I would have eventually reconciled with her if she had not been killed.* "Vivian loved me."

"She loved having a cash cow to milk for a monthly check. The woman enjoyed not having to spread her legs more than twice a year. Who is to say that rotten kid is even from your seed? Ask yourself this, 'When she disappeared, who did she turn to for comfort in her more emotional times? Her ginger mob lawyer? That 'redheaded Irish sailor,' Jim Kelly from Brooklyn? Some rich jew she was screwing over?' I have taken care of your needs for 30 years; from a roof over your head, to your wedding, through your son's birth, and until her final resting place. She left when you would not buy her a mansion to launder her felonious revenue through. You know all those hidden twenties we found at her apartment? She stole those, from you and me. We'd have been flush if you'd never met her."

"Well, I have squat now, so what's the difference? You told me in 1912, we would always be friends."

"I was never going to be your daddy no matter how much you needed guidance from a strong man. I own you, lock, stock, and barrel. I paid out plenty toward that end. I thought I could boost you into a celebrity and enrich myself in the process. By creating a book about you—after you became famous, I would have become the best-selling author I envisioned. I have failed. I clearly chose the wrong man at the docks to talk to."

"I'll fight you," spits out a dour Alvin. *He is frustrated. He is older and bigger than I am, but I am quicker.* "If you win, I'll leave. If I win, you compensate me for every day I was aloof."

"Fists then? On the rooftop? We will not be disturbed there. I will clobber you," intones Emmerling. *I have no doubt I will school my fosterling in the sweet science. I might come away with some bruises, but I'll be rid of him. I should have done this years ago.* "I will give you the hundred if I lose, but that's all. Our partnership is concluded either way. Good luck to you, sir."

After conquering the stairs, the truth is evident that neither is fit enough for a protracted skirmish. Both pause on the rooftop, catching their breath with their hands resting on their knees. They glare at each other, swearing.

Alvin's initial bop just misses Joseph's dimpled chin. The younger man's flailing fists have little effect but this time, at least he does not faint at the thought of fisticuffs. His older opponent's untrammeled paw hits its mark, sending the 52-year-old reeling. The men dust-it-up, stop, and then resume with the invective. Ruffled, they scratch at each other with a primitive ferocity like combatants at a cock fight in Manila. The friends who once viewed themselves as close as siblings, grapple like schoolboys. Emmerling knocks his erstwhile wingman so mightily he collapses, spent. The hostilities are quickly finished. Kelly moans, prone on the tar, unable to rise to continue. His compatriot turns to leave. The partnership has come to an end in short order.

"The sailor's been shipwrecked again . . . ."

He extends his hand toward the doorknob leading to the stairwell but doesn't grasp it. Joseph T. Emmerling collapses; the 66-year-old is stone cold from a massive coronary.

Alvin is bloody and battered. He howls like a band of prairie coyote during mating season. The "Frick" to his "Frack" over the last 34 years has infiltrated the abyss. The Japanese have a word meaning being beyond hope—*shimensoka*. Kelly does not know it yet, but he is there—between the devil and the deep blue sea.

The police come to the expiration scene and ask the morose, lugubrious fellow to tell a detailed version of the fracas. He is not arrested, but told not to leave town. Alvin arranges for his benefactor to be buried in the plot adjacent to Vivian's final resting place. He is convinced that *both would hate lying next to the other for eternity, especially if the next world exists.* When the coroner rules the death was due to a heart attack brought on by stress, Kelly is not charged with manslaughter.

Phillip S. Roberts

A lawyer informs him the rent is paid until the next month and Emmerling has left him the estate. He locates the lockbox behind the books in the Joseph's office, but does not know the combination. He hires a locksmith who forces the iron open. The safe is empty . . . except for the folder holding notes about Vivian's criminal past and the voluminous typed manuscript about her. *Joseph must have spent years composing this masterpiece in secret,* he estimates. *The story must not be any good if he could not get published.* Joseph was right—the truth hurts and he's angry about that. Kelly weeps like a newborn while reading the beautifully crafted pages as he burns the numerous leafs in the basement furnace. Gone is Alvin's frenetic *joie de vivre.*

He feels guilty selling Emmerling's possessions but smartly uses the proceeds to prepay for a long-term residence at nearby lodgings. He shifts the equipment he needs to practice his unique discipline to his no-frills accommodation at the "Rooming House for Wayward Seamen" on West 51st Street.

In his despondency, he guesses Junior might be stationed in West Germany, so he writes to the Army requesting aid in finding his son. If his desperate appeal is promulgated, his alienated offspring does not respond. The unopened, returned envelopes are stamped "Delivery Refused."

Alvin pleads to all the stores and movie houses he has ever worked, hoping to revive his past crowd-pulling antics. He sends communications to the Shriners, the Masons, the Odd Fellows and other fraternal lodges proposing his services at a bargain rate. He tries any contacts he can put a name to, pleading for a referral. Aside from his measley veteran's monthly allotment check, his mailbox continues to be devoid of responses.

Time is a blur without a guiding mind to direct his predilection. He hires an emissary, Dr. E. T. McDonald, Esquire. The ne'er-do-well does not have the acumen to aggrandize the act. "The Professor" convinces the Carlton Theatre in Pleasantville, N.J. to test if the archaic device still has legs. The bow-tie wearing, sharp absconds with the deposit while Alvin is situated. Kelly never sees the scoundrel again.

At the Tennessee State Fair in Memphis, Richard Blandy is pedaling a bicycle welded to a bar on July 5, 1947. He has been going four days straight, and, as he contrives vertically to exert himself into a handstand on the handlebar, the metal disintegrates. He slams 12 feet onto the sod.

"Landed right on his mush," a witness tells the orderly loading him on the gurney. "I was sure he was gonna be dead as a doornail."

The unconscious bloke is raced to the hospital. His prognosis is determined as "satisfactory." Doctors examine him a few days before releasing him. He convalesces in Baton Rouge. While he heals, the flagpole sitter nicknamed "Dixie" spends time tending bar and inflating tall tales to his patrons.

Kelly contemplates selling his golden doubloon. His military pension is not enough to be a tower of strength to him. He has never revealed the rarity to anyone. The shylock at the Stuyvesant Curiosity Shop on 3rd Avenue salivates at the coin he's been brought, and somehow contains his avarice. With a staleness, the pawn broker inspects it, performs a purity test, and reproachfully estimates a low value based on the metal's weight. Alvin is sure that the appraisal cannot be right.

"It has to be worth more. I was told the item is priceless . . . worth a king's ransom . . . from a buccaneer's hoard . . . a scarcity. That was 40 years ago . . . ."

"I buy plenty old gold, and this one is simply worth its weight. I don't see anything special about it." The usurer lays money on the counter behind his metal grate as he talks. "If you were to use your coin as collateral for a loan I could offer $200. If you were to sell, I could manage a bit more, maybe $300."

Kelly urgently needs the currency laid out before him.

"Which is it to be? Or perhaps you would want to take something in trade?"

"Sell, I guess. But would you throw in that bike?" The moneylender behind the counter knows he's looking at his once-in-a-lifetime chance to own a real rarity and nods. He can hardly stop himself from drooling. "That, plus the cash please."

Phillip S. Roberts

The owner takes the two-wheeler from the rafters. Jacobi had warned Alvin to steer clear of pawn brokers, but he is in a tizzy. Earlier he got a reply to one of his many letters, proposing a paid job to flagpole sit. His hastily pulled together to-do list contains purchase a bus fare, obtain supplies, and prep the gimcrack stunt. His uniform barely fits, but he packs it in his tattered portmanteau anyway. He requires this promotion to be well attended and takes a bus south.

The 400 Supper Club's grand opening night on South Tamiami Trail is sold out. Sarasota is anticipating Kelly's unhackneyed sitting variation. His whereabouts will be the Schwinn bicycle welded, atop the nightclub. The 52-year-old pledges to ride, despite any meteorological conditions. The owners agree to pay the suspended cycling enthusiast $1 per mile.

Well-wishers fill tables to meet the curio before he kicks off his Bellerophonian feat. A florist brings out an elaborate arrangement of asters shaped like a horseshoe with silver letters spelling out, "Good Luck, Shipwreck." The disposition is festive as patrons dine. Some twirl to the band's musical stylings. The customers become restless when the sitter does not appear. The bar owner sends a few staff members to scour the town. Checking the hospital as well as the jail, a parking valet finally locates Alvin in his hotel room— worse for wear after slipping in the bathroom. The manager announces Kelly's appearance is rescheduled until the following week and the patrons are all invited back.

A week later, on December 8, 1947, Kelly is feeling healthy enough to mount the bike. He has a recurring pleurisy that interferes with exerting himself, but he will not give up his chance to fulfill his contract. He returns to the club's roof, ties himself to the bike frame, and rides 40 feet in the air.

He pedals almost constantly nine days, 16 hours, and seven minutes until he cannot continue further. When he stops, the speedometer is fetched from the handlebars. Kelly suspects a cold. He leaves with an intermittent cough, but is in fantabulous mood.

"Well done, Shipwreck," beams the owner. "You certainly deserve your payment; $1,747. You brought us plenty of recognition with your mighty task."

"Thank you very much. Can I please ask for a favor? Would you mind cashing the check? I don't have a savings account. Banks—Am I right? I haven't trusted those institutions since I lost everything in the crash of 1929."

At an Amusement Park in Long Beach, California, George "Ozzie" Osborne is above the wooden "Cyclone Racer" rollercoaster. The ex-funambulist and annual "Five-and-Dime" store Santa poses sedentary at the "Pike" on July 18, 1948. Wearing a purple robe and a rococo crown, the "King of the Stratosphere" brandishes a gaudy scepter. He is poised upon the piling that doubles as his throne.

In San Francisco, 22-year-old Milton Van Noland vows to linger in the air longer that "nitwit harlequin in Southern California" and settles into a stiff cowboy pillion. He is 50 feet up fronting the "Horsetrader Ed's Kar Korral" at 790 Van Ness Avenue. During his tenure, the lot is mired in controversy; the city claims the proper permits were not acquired, the draft board asserts Van Noland did not sign up for selective service, and there are also weekly squabbles with the auto dealership's owner, Ed.

The rivals grouse concerning each other to any one in earshot. Osborne, after 52 days, 13 hours, and 53 minutes, hops a helicopter to earth on September 8, 1948. Van Noland out-lasts his arch-enemy; 71 days, 23 hours, and 30 minutes. He is vainglorious to wear the laurels and hold a 3-foot, $1,500 cardboard check.

Kelly is convinced that a resurgence is coming but cannot arrange a bower that pays enough to attempt a sit in 1948.

Baseball fanatic Charley Lupica is squatting atop a pole in Cleveland to root his Indians to victory on May 31, 1949. With "The Tribe" dwelling in the American League cellar, the grocer swears "scout's honor" to not vacate the temporary shack constructed on his two-story store until his team holds first place in the division. *The Cleveland Plain Dealer* devotes a daily square in the sports section to his mission. To keep contact with the real world, the pillarist relies upon phone calls to the WJW-AM play-by-play duo Jack Dudley and Jack Graney. Lupica holds up the score while pedestrians amble by his stationary position. He misses his second child's birth while in the temporary construct.

Phillip S. Roberts

In August, The Indians are behind the Yankees by a few games, and their diehard zealot announces he will settle above the tree line until the season is finished. By September, however, the baseball squad has tumbled to fourth place in the division. Club owner Bill Veeck convinces the super-aficionado to move his birdhouse by flatbed truck to Municipal Stadium. Lupica surveys the remaining games from his personal box in centerfield, and the public address system announces a $100 bounty will be paid to any player who can homer into his temporary residence.

After 117 days on September 25, 1949, Charlie timidly relinquishes to outfield grass to watch the game versus the Tigers from the owner's box. He rounds the bases and is rewarded for his loyalty. Among the prizes the chamber of commerce donates are an Oldsmobile station wagon, a puppy, a bathtub, and a brand new fifty-foot flagpole.

While Lupica has been stagnant, a few others have tried engaging in the same practice to uneven results. Alvin is unable to revive his glory days. He proposes to duplicate the feat for all three Major League Baseball teams in the city. He rings the Yankees management from a payphone, but Casey Stengel doesn't come on the line. He puts another dime in the slot and dials the number for the Brooklyn Dodgers' headquarters.

"Can you connect me with Leo Duroucher please? Yes? Um, I sent him a . . . . Yes, I'm a personal friend. I know 'The Lip' is busy. Can leave a . . . . Yes, Shipwreck Kelly . . . . No. Not him . . . . Oh, I don't have a number. I guess I'll try back . . . . Okay, thanks."

It is October 1, 1949, when 357 pound, five-foot-two Percy Coplon vows to complete a 100 day commitment at 30 feet. He plans to live in a compact six-foot square shed with a commanding perspective on Birmingham, Alabama.

"I am tolerating this grueling torture for the advancement of science," says the rotund, former miniature auto racer. "Believe that I can be cured by abstaining from unhealthy food. I am going to shed a pound per day."

With a telephone receiver strung up to his haven, "Cannonball" Coplon consults his dietary specialist. He imbibes chicken broth. He grouches—being stung by wasps and a stiffness in his knees but perseveres. On day 60, he weighs 257 pounds. His medical advisor orders him to end his diet and his solitude. He complies, but neighbors find him unresponsive on his bathroom floor the next day. *The Birmingham News* reports he is buried in a double-wide Mahogany box, the largest standard size available.

Phillip S. Roberts

Chapter 24 –
Fifty Years into the Century

"Fame is a vapor, popularity is an accident, riches take wings, those who cheer today may curse tomorrow and only one thing endures - character."
— Harry S Truman

Alvin's savings are gone. His modest annuity subsidizes the room he leases, but, even with his penny-pinching, he cannot splurge on luxuries. Work is rough to obtain for the 55-year-old. Selling plasma as well as performing odd jobs and errands is the only way he has any extra funds. He writes to General Eisenhower, pleading for his help in locating Junior.

In May of 1950, platinum blonde bombshell Erma Leach reposes at Horsetrader Ed's secondhand car lot in San Francisco. On August 1, 1950, she finishes three months in the headlines and drawing thousands to the dealership. The former burlesque showgirl's compact stipulates a $7,500 payout.

"The bank teller would not honor this huge cardboard check," testifies the peroxide blonde to KGO-TV. "I was also promised a mink coat and a pink Cadillac Eldorado. I guess I'll have to sue for what I am due."

She files a breach of contract lawsuit for $20,000 against used car salesman and owner Ed Shapiro. The pitchman is infamous from his commercials that run endlessly on radio and television in the Bay Area. He is indelible; galloping onscreen on a white charger while hollering his slogan and firing his 6-shooters—"You Want 'Em? I've Got 'Em!" The dealer is too busy selling jalopies to give testimony. Among the witnesses Leach's ambulance-chaser will subpoena is Milton Van Noland. Her attorney's private investigator has located the sitter who had spent 71 days working for the dealership to share his insights. The litigation is settled before trial.

On December 7, 1951, Juvenile delinquents hunting for Edward Leedskalnin's savings, break into the sculptor's shack at the Coral Castle. The teenagers batter him barbarously, but he says nothing and there is no treasure to find. The next day, he sends Alvin a cryptic note, which reads, "Please come and see me. I must tell someone. I know you will keep my secrets safe." In a tremendous pain, Ed takes a bus to Jackson Memorial Hospital and is admitted for observation. He suffers a stroke, and succumbs from pyelonephritis at the age 64. If he knows the scientific method to levitate heavy blocks as the pyramid builders did, his secret is consigned to oblivion.

Alvin opens his mailbox containing the letter from Ed. After reading the page, he buys a ticket he can barely spare the price of and heads to Miami on December 15, 1951. He taxis to the colossal walled facility. The Coral Castle is a beautiful, serene place at dusk as the diminishing light casts faint shadows on the perplexing architecture. While marveling at the epic effigies, he reflects upon where things have gone amiss. *Times are bad. Vivian died, and Junior hates me. Then things took a nosedive when Joseph passed. He would have told me what to do. I miss my pal.* He softly recites a prayer for the mystic sculptor. He stays around until the caretaker closes up. He boards the "Scenic Cruiser" at the Greyhound depot. Past Savannah, assisted by Iškar Zaqīqu, the Babylonian god of sleep, a happy dream comes where he defies gravity, effortlessly floating amongst lighter than air boulders.

A few days before Christmas 1951, Richard Blandly is 50-feet above a mall in Memphis. Appareled as Santa, his resting place is a "La-Z-Boy" recliner locked onto place. The cold dips below zero and he is suddenly afraid. "Dixie" cannot feel his toes and fears frostbite. He yells to gain the security guard's attention, urging him to summon the paramedics.

As 1952 begins, Kelly's sole enjoyment is re-hashing his younger, daring, and more scintillating times. The other rooming house inhabitants, having grown bored with his stories, huddle close to the television set's glow. The set is tuned to the "Texaco Star Theater with Milton Berle."

"I know that emcee," Alvin is giddy at seeing someone he knows on the flickering black and white screen. "He was the roast-master when I was the honoree at a dinner in 1937 . . . ."

"Shut up, loser," scolds a tenant brusquely. "We are trying to watch."

Disappointed, Alvin goes to his bare-bones room and retrieves his thick folder of clippings so he can brag about his fanciful crusades with a glass of whiskey. Walking home from the bar, he becomes waterlogged in a deluge and his cough worsens. A week later, he sees a doctor at the free clinic.

"Your liver is diseased owing to the fact that you knock 'em back like a fish. Both your lungs are bad; you smoke too much. You have a heart defect. I would definitely admit you."

The patient manages a silly grin, straightens his hat, and tie. Alvin moseys to a nearby tavern. He buys a round for some patrons and, for once, does not brag about being "THE Shipwreck Kelly."

He becomes louder and more verbose after the alcohol loosens him up. His phrases, become more animated and precise in descriptions while rambling stories to the other amiables in the tavern. His wisdom about the past is like King Solomon as he thumbs through his anthology. The pickled patron on the barstool next to him buys Alvin a shot glass full of rye.

"Thank you. Where are you from? Cuz I am 'a guy that knows a guy from' almost everywhere. I used to have a lot of friends. It's harder for them to see me nowadays. Let me tell you, I have experienced this world from an ambitious vertical . . . splendid vistas that extend far into the vast reaches. I've experienced the most sparkling shades of blue having sailed on endless white caps and seen the promised land. Mind my words. Take the time to think deeply . . . aloof, and I tell you, above all, hold your family in the highest esteem."

The alcohol warms his insides. Intoxicated, Kelly buys another round for the bar.

"I was wrong to think that I could juggle celebrity and family. If I'd gotten my wife that farmhouse, I wouldn't be so far gone. I never met my father. You lose yourself without that teaching and interaction. I had a few that tried to guide me, but that is not the same thing. My son, Junior, would be been better off if I had tried harder to spend time with him while he was growing up. I might have his respect. Instead he is embarrassed by me. It must be irksome to be confronted with the fact his dad is a washed-up bum. He doesn't even think he's my son and I don't even know if he really is. Is he?"

"Well, buddy, at least you have your health."

Kelly laughs. He now understands irony. In front of this audience, he is the most interesting, gracious fellow on the planet. Skimming the folio, he regales the grizzled dipsomaniacs at the watering hole with his audacity. At closing time, he is blubbering, facedown on the bar. Someone assists him to his room.

In the morning, he rides the Staten Island Ferry to gaze upon the Hudson River surf hitting the shore. He decides not to hop the rail and drown himself. *My attempt at suicide would probably fail anyway, and the thought alone is a mortal sin not easily absolved by my priest at confessional*, he deems bitterly to himself on the windswept deck. *I have put up with so much misery.* He does not need to create a will for there are no goods to bequeath. Alvin has not heard from his successor in many moons. His son would now be 24.

He returns to his room, lays on the firm mattress, and sleep comes easily. When he is finished conversing with Somnus, father of Morpheus, the Roman god of the dream world, he finds an envelope under his door that has been left for him with the landlady. Another of his pleading requests to let his handiwork shine has been accepted. Alvin craves being in the limelight again.

Kelly takes a Trail-ways bus to Orange, Texas on October 4, 1952. He has convinced the Lion's Club to let him promote their "Harvest Biennale." He ploddingly mounts an abandoned Southwest Bell telephone pole. Alvin perceives a rapid beating in his chest while clinging onto the foothold. He struggles getting to the top, so he takes a crisp break halfway, and luxuriates in the view, his feet dangling from the piling. He feels another sharp pain in his chest. His left arm goes numb. He wonders, *Is this the end? Am I dying? Now?* He waits a bit to calm his nerves and dismounts. His soles contact the sand, refuses treatment, and heads home. Two days later, he is back in his room, slumbering deeply under the influence of Untamo, the Finnish god of sleep. In a reverie, he is calculating when an alignment of certain star patterns will unlock the Latvian's lost technique to render great weight buoyant.

Alvin Kelly wakes up feverish. Someone would have cared 30 years ago. Today, he is just one of several far past their prime tenants at the rooming house. In his bare-bones accommodations, he is desolate. He tears a page from the "One-A-Day" 1952 calendar, and scratches the word 'hospital' on October 12.

He is muzzy. When he regains enough presence, he clutches his treasury of clippings. In the frayed folio, lies his validation. Without the book, he'd just be another anonymous person in skid row.

He collapses on the bottom step, panting. The landlady hails a taxi while a burly, unshaven Bulgarian assists the frail tenant to the backseat and the hack is handed a buck to ferry him to the Polyclinic.

Alvin wishes that his legacy will not be erased like chalk on a blackboard by a teacher's star pupil. His ambition is to be perpetually reveled as the "best ever," yet he has come to the realization that he has failed. He has two major regrets: the alienation of his son and not being able to fathom the secret to levitation. Either procurement would have made all the difference. He gasps.

"Tell them your fare was 'The Luckiest Fool on Earth' . . . ."

The cabbie doesn't hear him due to the vrooming issued from the Dodge Meadowbrook's six-cylinder engine and the exultation from the Redwings hockey game on the radio. The cab skids to the curb, and the chauffeur pounds impatiently on his horn. He can find other riders, perhaps ones that will tip. When he opens the door, a feverish Kelly thinking he sees his golden ducat, bends down, trips, and falls head-first onto the pavement.

Alvin is near the end and does not hear the ululation of a siren echoing through the mostly deserted avenues. His overstuffed compilation loosens from his clench and, as it bounces, bursts its binding. Aging newsprint, grainy photographs, and autographs once carefully glued to pages, scatter on West 50th Street, destined to be swept away by the cities sanitation division. His compendium of newspaper clippings is now just litter on 5th Avenue. The abundant documentation of his incredible times would have been fascinating reading had it stayed intact.

His body feels how a catcher's mitt must after 100,000 fastballs, worn and supple. A doctor exits the hospital, kneels to triage him, and motions the orderlies to bring a stretcher. A freelancer uses a bulb to capture the scene. An inquisitive few edge nearer in ghoulish fascination. The beat cop intercedes, ordering those milling around to move along. He asks the restless taxi driver where his rider had originated from and releases him to prowl the streets.

Phillip S. Roberts

As he is being hefted on a plank, Sacred Heart priest Francis Cambell comes upon the scene, recognizes his parishioner, and apportions the obsequies. Alvin manages to grin and is gone. The tattered shell, who compared himself with luminaries such as Charles Lindbergh, Amelia Earhart, and Admiral Richard Byrd, is at quietus.

He had cogitated himself as the foremost in his field—the original "aerial athlete." With his eternal rest, the final peal sounds on his unwonted domain. His memories, an unbridled zeitgeist of a tumultuous era, are lost in perpetuity. His anomalous allure had enraptured despite innumerable distractions. The focus is on more crucial substance since the world has ceased to be amused by avant-garde madcaps. The next generation has moved on, idolizing personages from the spheres of war, film, and science.

His quasi-acclaim had not emerged instantaneously; he had strained to achieve cognizance. To become fixed in the mind throughout "The Roaring Twenties," Alvin lived incautiously. It became his best option for survival. In a sensational era, whims enchanted, and his notability endured longer than any might have imagined. His fame rocketed him to the stars and then, fuel spent, ploddingly fell back to earth. Such is the rigor of ascending the mountaintop of household names. The challenge for those who quest celebrity is to create an ingrained influence or dissipate.

As the flagpole sitter is placed in the facility's basement, a detective emerges at his former billet. The squalid suite is opened by his landlady, Mrs. Frank Davis. She is unprepared for the clutter she sees. His tools: ropes, blowtorches, and wrenches hanging on the walls have patinated from disuse, waiting in vain for a revival that never came. The room has been ransacked by others lodgers, hoping to find his supposed riches—amongst the tangled mess of cobwebbed belongings. Despite having pried up all the floorboards, the treasure hunters locate nothing of value.

Ultimately, Shipwreck is buried unheralded in the Farmingdale National cemetery. In an unmarked barrow, he desiccated silently. He was not eternally so quiet; the cloistered recluse doled out wisdom to any that cared to watch his assiduity. The general populace once congregated to the false prophet set upon an absurd battle withstanding the elements. His statistical numbers are mind boggling. The swab spent 20,613 hours where vexillum flutter. The nearly 1,000 days of resplendence included 210 in a pouring torrent, 47 in sub-zero environments, and the balance in sweltering Summer heat. The rabble pining for an interruption from their dour realities had once tilted their gaze upward and felt a sense of security that he would still be remaining when they looked up once again. His perseverance is assurance that as much as things evolve, they also stay the same. The masses admired him for his daring and foolhardiness equally with a mild dose of *schadenfreude*.

Who is this demented codger? Why is he doing this? No rational reason could be divined from entrenching unchaperoned, protected from the ills of the world. Surveyors of the human condition wonder what might impel someone to live that way. Most everyone enjoys the antics of a daredevil and a zany. He conducted both roles with deftness. His virtuosity was rare because his imitators became droves. The media manipulation he honed set an archetype for the "obscure for being in limelight" subset that is sought after today.

From his humble birth in 1893, he held an quiddity unlike any other being on the planet. Alvin Kelly helmed a dissimilar heading than other unexceptional blokes, encouraging him to take in picturesque views.

Chapter 25 –
Epilogue

"Imitation is always insult — not flattery."
— Frank Lloyd Wright

Alvin Kelly's demise on October 12, 1952, rates a minuscule salute in The New York Times, above the port arrivals and departures. The bold typeface headline reads "Shipwreck Kelly, World Champion Pole Sitter dies on NY Street." He would have been ecstatic to receive that much praise. *United Press International* sends out the factoid to their subscribers. Even though the originator of the flagpole sitting vogue has passed into the void, others continued to try to revive the whim in the ensuing years.

Salesman Jim Martin is luxuriating in a 'penthouse' 21 feet above Miami on February 23, 1953. His structure is equipped with a heater and a television. Subsidized $75 a day by his boss, he raises funds for "Jerry's Kids." In those three weeks, he garnered almost $3,000 in pledges to benefit the Muscular Dystrophy Foundation.

Jim Kelly suffers from heat stroke 25 feet above Tucson. In 112-degree heat, the senior vacated his stave after 58 minutes and is admitted to the hospital. After being released, "The Irish Sailor" is nabbed by police while passing a forged check and put into lockup. Alvin Kelly's most virulent foe suffered a massive stroke in an Arizona jail cell and died on July 30, 1954.

Milwaukee resident Bill Sherwood, who considered himself the Braves's greatest enthusiast, is living in a temporary structure on Hadley street. On June 5, 1955, he commits to not quit until they win seven straight games or season's end. In September, he's despondent when the team finished 13 and a half games out. A few days after the season concludes, he commits suicide.

On June 4, 1956, William Howard hunkered down above John Ascuaga's Golden Nugget in Reno. To soothe "Happy" from his detachment from others, a phone is strung so casino patrons can ask his advice on which numbers to play. During his residence, he provides eyewitness traffic reports. A dentist is ferried to him so a bad tooth can be drilled and filled. Bill beckons the Sparks Fire Department when school-age hooligans try to set his wood stake aflame. A quarter of the year after going up, Bill clings to a rope ladder sent by a helicopter and is conveyed to turf. His compensation is $6,800 and a sterling silver belt buckle. He cannot capitalize on his plaudits and does not work the contrivance again.

Phillip S. Roberts

Marcel Proulx has a temper tantrum while elevated 71 feet in a spot commanding a view of Ottawa's skyline on September 4, 1957. His knees are swollen from hanging off the edge of the radio antenna he's held a vigil on for 13 days. Informed that the Lions Club has withdrawn their support, he pushes his mattress off the structure in anger. Mounties urge the sparse watchers to a safer perimeter. A deluge of items pulled by gravity follow: a radio, a telephone, trash, food, clothes, and baggage. When he has no more items to offload, he still refuses to vacate the tower. He dares authorities to shear the tensile lines. The stand-off is deadlocked while troopers match his sufferance. A few hours later, he walks (haltingly) again on soil—demoralized, yet uncharged.

Paul Hatfield scampers up to a 65-feet vantage, projecting a 60 day postponement from normality in the rust bucket mounted over DeFoe Motors. 'Sky-High' is salaried to rivet buyers and announce sales on a low power radio broadcast on the lot. Three weeks in, a severe gale pounds his locality, and he demands hazard pay—$500. The dealership refuses, and he leaves his job after three weeks on August 20, 1958.

Mauri Rose Kirby finished her 70-foot domicile in Indianapolis on March 14, 1959. She allows a physical and Dr. Charles Roller attests that the 221-day seclusion has not harmed her physically. She claims two records, beating the women's mark of 169 days as well as eclipsing the longest term.

In Oklahoma City, a 50 m.p.h. gust breaks Richard Blandy's wooden structure. "Dixie" caterwauls as he tumbles 30 feet on August 21, 1960. The plucky Cajun survives yet another fall.

"As soon as I am well, I will be in outer space," he sings his own praises to his tipsy friends at a 'welcome back' gathering. "I am usually so far out I should apply to be an astronaut."

After establishing his 1930 moment in the sun in Iowa, William 'Treetop Bill' Penfield ended his sitting at dizzying heights to farm corn and soybeans. The 84-year-old expires in 1961 peacefully, surrounded by family.

On the Claiborne Towers in the Crescent City, Betty and Benny Fox concluded their time as a duo. He tangos with the third woman to

take the "Betty" persona on an elevated terrace 123 feet up, with
Pontchartrain Beach as their backdrop on May 11, 1961. Benny
remained perennially active in show business until the 1970s. He never
did break Alvin's penchant for flagpole endurance.

The Atlantic City town council hires an investigation firm to
locate Alvin Kelly, Junior. The plan is to celebrate his father's
achievement and present him with a trophy commemorating the 49-
day sit during a live television celebration being broadcast from the
Steel Pier on its 66th anniversary. The gumshoe the promoters hired
cannot track his whereabouts. The son distances himself from his
legacy while dawdling across America with a traveling circus under a
fake name.

Instead promoters hired 60-year-old Richard Blandy to beat
Alvin's pole-sitting run from 34 years earlier. On day 50, "Dixie" is
interviewed by Johnny Carson, live via the NBC satellite on "The
Tonight Show." He ends his seclusion on August 10, 1964. He died a
decade later, tumbling 30 feet from a flagpole and cracking his skull
wide open in Harvey, Illinois.

John Keely is threatening neighbors with a Smith and Wesson
35mm in Tujunga on June 17, 1972. Police are called and set a cordon
around his property while pleading with him to capitulate. Television
converges on the scene and interrupts programming to broadcast live.
His lack of proximity to others lasts four tense hours before yielding to
the authorities after discharging his firearm through his roof. Police lift
the agitated 72-year-old in wheelchair into the paddy-wagon and take
him to be arraigned.

"Flagpole" is charged with use of a deadly weapon, community
endangerment, and attempted murder. His sister remits his bond, and
the crotchety senior is arrogant to television camera crews waiting by
the jail exit. He claims he could have "outlasted his own greatness—
six months and four days, had he not run out of Coors." He dies before
his trial date.

Alvin Kelly Junior had been working with the "Clyde Beatty-
Cole Brothers" circus caravan as an animal wrangler. He has taken
inordinate pains to steer clear of any comparisons to his patriarch. The
troupe plays a matinee in Tenafly, New York on June 3, 1973. Caught

day-drinking rye and docked pay, the 45-year-old is unrepentant. After the matinee, the surly employee is directing "Beatrice," a two-ton female elephant to water. He smacks the beast with a cane and it spooks, trumpeting loudly.

The berserk animal grabs her handler with her trunk and thwacks him into the dirt. Bleating as the hapless person is brutally trampled, the irate creature continues to maul the offspring of Alvin and Vivian Kelly until trainers converge to shoot the mad pachyderm dead.

Junior meeting his maker does not end the fad instigated by his progenitor. The strength of will game his senior started suffered a brisk collapse, yet every few years some imprudent personality will attempt Alvin Kelly's game with some twist.

The painstaking lack of shelter that Shipwreck tolerated is echoed by David Blaine's 2002 "Vertigo" stunt. The performance artist is lifted by crane 100 feet to an obelisk in Bryant Park. Ironically, the whereabouts chosen by the magician is mere footsteps from Kelly's demise. His contemporary version is timed at 35 hours, far shorter then the 1930 Atlantic City sit.

The major contribution of Alvin Kelly seems to be the notion that a foolish individual pursuing approbation need only scale a nearby cumbersome structure. Masses will gather to watch, even in today's era of short-attention spans. Many have felt isolated due to pandemics, loneliness, and other reasons in our modern world. Living in the twenty-first-century, many crave social kudos, but that spotlight can come with a heavy cost. Others may have isolated longer and completed more stunning shenanigans, however it is the flagpole sitter's unique story that survives. As light-hearted as his stunts may have been, he could not escape the more grounded problems of his life. The man has become a quirky, occasional footnote in the American pantheon of the Twentieth Century. His bearing to popular culture might be summed up as a hint to a crossword puzzle solution—an eight letter word describing "Shipwreck Kelly's perch." Alvin would have pasted that clue in his vade mecum and been extremely glowing over the proof he was someone famous. He was, after all, "The Luckiest Fool on Earth.

The End.

Phillip S. Roberts currently lives in Arizona with his wife and dog. He holds a Bachelor of the Arts in Radio and Television Communication Arts from San Francisco State University. A long-time radio personality in Honolulu, his love of the tropics drove him to create an homage to Waikiki and the many Tiki that inhabit island of Oahu. He enjoys history, and quirky truths from the dark side of the tracks. "The Luckiest Fool on Earth" is his debut novel.

Visit https://zazelpublishing.com/
Feel free to email Phillip for interview requests at zazelpublishing@gmail.com

The other book by Phillip S. Roberts —
Waikiki Tiki: Art, History, and Photographs
2010 Bess Press Hawaii.
https://besspress.com/